RAWN

Well-Behaved
Indian Women

Well-Behaved Indian Women

Saumya Dave

BERKLEY

NEW YORK

BERKLEY
An imprint of Penguin Random House LLC
penguinrandomhouse.com

Copyright © 2020 by Saumya Dave
Readers Guide copyright © 2020 by Saumya Dave
Penguin Random House supports copyright. Copyright fuels creativity, encourages diverse
voices, promotes free speech, and creates a vibrant culture. Thank you for buying an authorized
edition of this book and for complying with copyright laws by not reproducing, scanning,
or distributing any part of it in any form without permission. You are supporting writers
and allowing Penguin Random House to continue to publish books for every reader.

BERKLEY and the BERKLEY & B colophon are registered trademarks of
Penguin Random House LLC.

LIBRARY OF CONGRESS CATALOGING-IN-PUBLICATION DATA

Names: Dave, Saumya, author.
Title: Well-behaved Indian women / Saumya Dave.
Description: First edition. | New York: Berkley, 2020.
Identifiers: LCCN 2019059243 (print) | LCCN 2019059244 (ebook) |
ISBN 9781984806154 (trade paperback) | ISBN 9781984806161 (ebook)
Subjects: LCSH: Mothers and daughters—Fiction. | Indian women—Fiction.
Classification: LCC PS3604.A9424 W45 2020 (print) | LCC PS3604.A9424 (ebook) |
DDC 813/.6—dc23
LC record available at https://lccn.loc.gov/2019059243
LC ebook record available at https://lccn.loc.gov/2019059244

First Edition: July 2020

Printed in the United States of America
1   3   5   7   9   10   8   6   4   2

Cover art and design by Farjana Yasmin
Book design by Nancy Resnick

To Samir, for making every day an adventure and
giving me the space, inspiration, and encouragement to write.

Prologue

Nandini
1989

N andini, please think before you speak. Please. We need things to go well today. This is our only chance." Mami fastens another row of safety pins into Nandini's sari. Even one slip of fabric could mean disaster.

Nandini nods. "I know."

She does know. She knows her family's reputation depends on how she behaves today. She knows this is her only chance to fix everything she did last year, everything they've tried to forget.

"They'll be here any minute. I'm going to make sure the chai is ready." Mami puts the extra safety pins onto the wooden dressing table, next to a bottle of Pond's talcum powder.

Ever since the incident, Mami was frantic when people came over to their house. Her energy was contagious. Their maid, Kavita, peeled ginger and cut mint leaves at record speed. The man who delivered vegetables scurried in and out of the house with trays of okra and bell peppers. Even the monkeys that roamed the trees outside their bungalow jumped from branch to branch as though they were in a rush.

Mami knocks on the bedroom door. "They're here. Come out when I call you."

"I will." Nandini ignores the warm, tight dread that's looming over her chest. She can't let her thoughts race today. She won't.

Nandini takes one last look into her mother's chipped dressing-table mirror. Her hair is smoothed down with coconut oil and tied into a low bun. A silk peach sari is draped around her thin frame. Her large, almond-shaped eyes are lined with kohl. Three gold bangles are on each of her wrists. She looks like the type of woman who has nothing to hide.

Beads of sweat erupt on her forehead. Nandini dabs them with a tissue and turns on the ceiling fan. She takes deep breaths, the way her therapist—her therapist nobody except Mami knows about—taught her.

She pictures taking her past, putting it into a box, and shoving it under the bed. Just like that, and it would be out of sight. Gone. But time has shown her that this isn't possible, that the past isn't like an old journal she can hide. No, the past has blades and will rip her to shreds if she doesn't handle it properly.

Nandini sneaks into the kitchen. From here, she can make out her parents' voices.

"Nandini loves music," she hears Papa saying.

"That's nice. And Ranjit wants a doctor, so that's good," Ranjit's mother says, as if her son isn't sitting right next to her. "But does she cook?"

Nandini presses her bare feet against the smooth, cool stone in the kitchen. Everywhere she looks, there's food. The counter is covered with tiny steels bowls of roasted peanuts, onions, and cilantro. Biscuits that Papa dips into his tea are arranged on a silver platter. An assortment of chutneys is on the small, wooden side table.

"And has your daughter, uh, learned from everything before?" Ranjit's dad asks.

They know about what happened, Nandini thinks.

Of course they do. Everyone in this part of India heard about what Nandini did. There were people who made sure of it. Shame coats her in waves, a shame she'd tried hiding from but couldn't. It lodged itself into her organs and never went away. It became part of her DNA.

"She is ready to move on," Papa says.

He's been getting short of breath just by speaking now. His ankles are always swollen, and every time he walks, there seems to be a weight across his shoulders.

"Nandini!" Mami yells.

Nandini takes a deep breath. She is supposed to walk in slowly, with her head down, her facial expression neutral.

Everyone is quiet as Nandini comes into the living room. Black-and-white photos of her grandparents are hanging on the walls, with garlands around them.

"Hi, *beta*," Ranjit's mother says.

Nandini nods. She catches Mami giving her a look of approval. She sits between her parents and gives one-word answers to all the questions from Ranjit's parents. Yes, she likes cooking. Yes, she would like to have children. No, she has no concerns about moving to America. Of course she will be able to take care of her in-laws.

It takes everything she has to be docile and demure. An hour passes this way.

Just when she thinks that the guests are getting ready to leave, Ranjit clears his throat and speaks for the first time. "Do you think we could sit outside together? Alone?"

Nandini raises her eyebrows in surprise. Is this allowed? She turns toward Mami and Papa.

Mami speaks before Papa can. "I think that's fine."

Nandini guides Ranjit to the wooden swing on her parents' veranda. They sit down, and she's hyperaware of everything. The small distance between them. His thick mustache. The way the warm breeze spreads his scent of Pears brand soap and talcum powder. His clean feet, with trimmed toenails and a smattering of hair on his big toe.

It has been so long since she's been this close to a man. The last time, she found herself overcome with a consuming self-hatred. *Never again*, she told herself then. *Never again will I let myself be put through this.*

"You're not like other women I've met," Ranjit finally says.

Nandini faces him. "That's probably true. Listen, I know you're looking to get married to someone more tradit—"

"What are you trying to say?"

She looked him deep in the eyes. "I'm difficult. You won't be able to handle it."

He chuckles. "I like that you're difficult."

Nandini soaks in the lines around his eyes, the kindness of his smile. Is this man accepting her? Why? She isn't sure about any of that, but she is sure about one thing: there's something comforting about him, something safe.

An hour later, they go back to the living room and join their parents. There will be no diamond ring like the American movies they've watched, no requests for a private date. There are just their parents, enjoying cups of chai. But that is enough. The message is clear. And by moving to America, by uprooting her life and letting go of everything that is familiar to her, she will make sure things will be different for her children. They can have the types of romantic relationships that are based on a true connection, not a need to survive. She pictures her future self hearing about their first dates, and later, their happy, easy marriages. All of that makes this worth it.

Mami and Ranjit's mom hug while the fathers shake hands. They all walk out of the house together, discussing plans for a small, religious wedding ceremony.

Ranjit turns to smile at her when he's helping his mom get into a rickshaw.

Maybe the past could be put away after all.

Simran
2018

The first thing Simran hears is *NSYNC blasting through the speakers.

"What have you gotten us into now?" Kunal laughs; first at her, then at everything around them.

Roosevelt High School is transformed for their five-year reunion. The entire space is the perfect mixture of nostalgic and ridiculous. Banners reading, WELCOME, GRADUATES and REUNION in shimmering red and blue letters are hanging from the tiled ceilings. Teal lockers are covered with stickers of their mascot, Tim the Tiger. The posters haven't changed. Some are inspirational quotes with pictures of eagles or waterfalls; others warn against the dangers of drug use. The air smells the same: a mixture of sharpened pencils, Elmer's glue, and sweat.

"You'll have fun. I promise." Simran rubs the sides of her forehead. She shouldn't have had that extra glass of red wine last night. Luckily, the thump of "Bye, Bye, Bye" is helping her forget about her headache. Boy bands would always have the power to distract her.

"I believe you," Kunal says, raising his voice over Justin Timberlake's. "And you were right before. It's nice to get away."

It's clear. Her boyfriend needs a break. The first year of medical school has been even more grueling than he thought it'd be. His days are filled with a steady stream of worry and work. Work and worry.

"I just want you to relax. You deserve it," Simran says.

She's going to talk to him tonight about all of it, her growing worry about his lack of sleep, his preoccupation with his student loans, how he barely has time for himself, let alone them. She still doesn't know how he'll receive her concern. Kunal is, among many things, proud. It's one of her favorite things about him, his certainty in himself, in his future, in everything. But it also means that he doesn't always know when to make a change.

Kunal leans toward her and kisses her forehead. "You always make sure I do. I really don't know what I'd do without you."

Simran and Kunal's classmates are in clusters around them, taking selfies for social media and exchanging blurbs of their lives. Some of them gained weight. The popular girls have started getting their first Botox injections. Others exchange pictures of their babies. Simran can't believe there are people she graduated with who are real parents.

Josh, one of their classmates who is now an Instagram influencer, approaches them.

"You two! Still so cute together," he says. "The real-life Cory and Topanga from *Boy Meets World*. You make the rest of us—especially the ones stuck in online dating Hell—sick."

Kunal smiles, giving a sudden softness to his usual serious disposition. "We'll take that."

Josh pauses to take an impromptu selfie. "Are you both planning to stay in New York for the long term?"

Simran nods. She gives Josh an update about Kunal's first year at NYU Med and her master's in psychology program at Columbia. A wave of gratitude washes over her for this being her life, her choices. She and Kunal are on the cusp of real adulthood. Together.

If anyone had asked Simran at sixteen what she thought her life would be like now, she saw herself traveling and creating and jumping from place to place. Even when they were at NYU, while she floated in and out of classes, devouring novels and articles, Kunal went to the library on campus every night to study. He had a plan. He always did. Simran preferred to live in the moment and not worry so much about what was ahead. She would have never believed that all these years later, her favorite moments would still be when she wore pajamas and ate pizza with her boyfriend, when she felt simple and still and at ease.

Once Josh walks away, Kunal points to a glass display that's filled with trophies, medals, and photos from school events. "Look, it's us."

Simran follows his gaze to a professional photograph of younger versions of them from senior prom. They're wearing big, glittering crowns to match their big, glittering smiles. Ku-

nal's expression in the photo is a mixture of pride and amusement. He hated wearing a tux, much less a crown and sash that
read PROM KING in bright blue letters.

"Look how young we look." Simran takes note of their acned
cheeks. "We've been together so long."

"I know. It goes by so fast. This picture is unreal," Kunal says.
"Remember how I picked you up at your house and we were so
nervous about your parents?"

"God, dating behind their backs was so scary," Simran says.
"I'm glad that part of our lives is over. But then again, sneaking
around was kinda fun. It made me feel like some sort of rebellious Bollywood heroine. You know, taking a stand, living on her
own terms."

"You *would* say that." Kunal shakes his head in amusement.
He glances at the picture again and scans Simran in her gold,
shiny dress. For weeks, she had begged Mom to buy it from the
sales rack at Macy's. Mom didn't see the point of prom—or
any school dance, for that matter. School dances didn't exist in
India. *School is for studying,* she'd said. *Not thinking about boys.*

"You're so beautiful." Kunal wraps his arms across Simran's
waist and then sneakily grabs her butt.

At first, the picture seems to cheer Kunal up. But then he slips
back into himself for the rest of the day. He's quiet while Simran
and the other graduates cheer during the pep rally that's in the
gym, with its basketball hoops, shiny floors, and hooks on the
ceiling where Simran used to climb the dreadful rope. She notices he doesn't laugh during the presentation of everyone's old
yearbook photos. (Simran's photos seemed to be about hair or the
lack of it: the frizzy locks on her head, thick eyelashes, her
threaded eyebrows.)

She tells herself that he's stressed because of school, that they're in the midst of an adjustment period. They've gotten through plenty of them before and will now.

"Let's get back to the city before dinner," Simran says. "I'm sure you have a lot of studying to do."

"Yeah . . . that sounds good," Kunal says.

"Are you okay?"

Kunal gazes at her. "I'm fine."

This was always his response. *I'm fine.* Kunal was never good at naming or talking about his feelings.

"Are you sure? You seem preoccupied."

Kunal sighs. "I've got a lot on my mind."

"I can tell. Let's just head back. Get out of here."

Kunal nods. "Okay. But before we go, can we walk through the main hallway again?"

They pass through crowds of their old classmates. Kunal gives them polite nods while Simran asks them about what she's seen from their lives on Facebook. The speakers are now playing a series of Usher songs.

Kunal stops once they're at their old lockers. "They still look the same."

"They do. Just as beaten up as ever." Simran glances at them. They have the white residue of peeled-off stickers.

But on a second glance, she notices there's a sticker with their names on it. "Hey, wait, our names are still on here."

"They are?"

"Yeah . . . how is that possible? We haven't been here in five years."

"I don't know," Kunal says. "Do you think these are still being used?"

"They must be," Simran says. "I wonder if they're actually locked."

She fiddles with the black combination lock. "It's open."

"I wonder if there's anything inside." Kunal stays behind her.

As the door swings open, it takes Simran a second to register the velvet, maroon ring box in the back corner of the locker.

"Look, there's a—" Before Simran can finish her sentence, Kunal reaches over her to grab the ring box.

When she turns to face him, he's bending down on one knee.

"Wait, what are you . . ." Her voice fades as she slowly registers what is happening. Is her mind playing tricks on her? Her boyfriend is on one knee? It can't be real.

But it *is* real.

This is it, a voice in her head says. *This is what you've always dreamed of.*

"Simran, ever since you stopped me on the lacrosse field, I haven't been the same. You're the reason I've been able to accomplish anything. You inspire me every day, and I feel lucky to even be in your life. I know I've been acting weird lately, but it's because I wanted—needed—this to go well. . . ."

He continues to say more, but Simran can't process any of it. A mixture of adrenaline and excitement run through her. Is this really happening? To her?

The moment becomes a blur of colors. The white of Kunal's Nike sneakers. The chipped teal of her old locker. The deep maroon of the ring box. The red and blue of the school's decorations.

The past few months run through her mind. No wonder Kunal seemed to be miles away. He must have been thinking about this the entire day, the entire *month*. When did he tell her parents about this? How long had he been thinking of it?

"*Yes!*" Simran blurts even though Kunal is still talking. "*Yes,* I'll marry you."

Kunal laughs. "I love that you didn't even need me to ask."

Simran extends her shaking left hand. She loves that Kunal fumbles as he tries to slip the one-carat, princess-cut diamond ring on her finger.

Kunal kisses her hand. "I love you."

"I love you, too, honey." Simran turns to lean against him.

They stare at each other in silence, processing it all. She had been thinking of this moment years ago, when they started dating. But the reality was even better than what she had pictured. She now understood why so many movies and books revolved around this. Because when it was happening with the right person, it was surprising and thrilling but also peaceful and stabilizing. It gave her a sense of freedom and belonging. It was all of the right contradictions at once.

"Are you happy?" Kunal asks.

"I am *so* happy. So, so happy," Simran says, unable to stop hugging her fiancé. Her *fiancé*! *He wants to be with me forever*, she thinks. *We are in this together. Forever.*

They stand that way for what feels like hours, not knowing how much things would soon change.

One

Simran
Present Day

To her left, Simran can see her mother, Nandini, adjusting the folds of her bloodred sari and pretending to be proud of her.

"Try to forget about what you told me and just focus on everyone here. You don't want them to have a bad impression of you." Nandini motions toward the room, which is stuffed with an array of first-generation Indians, most of them in arranged marriages similar to her own. Women in salwar kameezes and saris, men in dress pants and button-down shirts.

"I'm going to take a wild guess and say that I'm not in danger of that at all," Simran says, taking a dainty sip of blushed champagne.

"Simran! I'm saying this for your own good."

"That's what you always say. That somehow, everything is for my good. As if every time you criticize me, you're doing me some sort of favor."

"Look, you're young and . . ." Her mother's face falls, and for a second, Simran considers telling her that she's sorry and understands.

But then Nandini's features twist back into a scowl. "Don't

you understand that I'm your mother and that means I know what's best for y—"

Her lecture halts as Simran's father approaches them, wearing a suit and striped crimson tie—a dramatic change from the goofy, smiley-faced ones he wears when he sees patients. With graying sideburns and a confident posture, his physical traits echo louder than his transient accent, giving him a gentleness ideal for any pediatric surgeon.

"I'm proud of you, cupcake," he says, pulling his daughter into a hug.

Like the Princess Jasmine snow globe on Simran's dresser, their interactions tend to remain frozen with childhood tenderness, despite how fervently the world around it is shaken.

"At least someone is," Simran offers.

"Ranjit, don't push it," Nandini says. "We are celebrating this one time, but after it's done, it's time for her to move on."

Simran opens her mouth at the same time that Ranjit motions to her with a finger to his lips: *Keep the peace for now.*

While the three of them make towers of her books on empty tables, Simran wonders if it was a terrible idea to tell her mother about the argument with Kunal. Indian women, especially the ones in their family, take pride in suffering quietly, in knowing when to stop lamenting and start serving cups of chai. Even her feisty mother manages to conceal her naked emotions within the ridges of her heart, where they are protected under her white lab coat.

But Simran and Kunal *have* suffered enough already. The first three years of their relationship were "forbidden." Most Indian parents are appalled by the idea of high school dating, so their interactions were forced to be strategically planned. She likes to think it's similar to Romeo and Juliet's union, minus the whimsical balcony scene and tragic ending.

She glances at her mother now, double-checking the final gift baskets and making sure to ask Ranjit his opinion. "I let him think he's the boss even though I'm really the boss," Nandini always says.

Simran drifts to the transatlantic words she and Kunal exchanged just one hour before the official start of her book party. This time they couldn't stop fighting about which type of food to serve for their wedding lunch. His mom wants a traditional Gujarati lunch—with lentil flour cakes; eggplant, green pea, and potato curry; and puffy, fried bread—while Nandini and Ranjit envision something fusion. Phone arguments are always the worst, just one step ahead of online ones; not only do they feel impersonal, but making up is even more difficult without the physical comfort of the person.

Not that they made up, anyway.

Kunal started yelling and instead of taking the high road, Simran yelled back and hung up the phone. It was a childish move; a mini quiz to see if he would call back.

In any case, tonight Kunal is left with the power, because the one who can care less is the one calling the shots. The one who can be hung up on and continue saving malnourished African children. A surge of pride runs through her as she pictures all six feet and two inches of him, head to toe in teal scrubs, scribbling symptoms onto a notepad and handing out iodine pills.

Of course, she shouldn't be upset with him in the first place. Their recent distance—both physical and emotional—is due to the fact that, even with a taxing medical student schedule, he's doing something that most people only get around to in theory: making the world a better place.

The yellow light dances off the clear diamond on her left hand as a winking reminder that she's picked. She's lucky. She's exhausted.

This is how independent women behave, she tells herself. *They whittle down their lives into distinct compartments, so they aren't reliant on just one for fulfillment.*

She forces herself to focus on more important things about Kunal, like the way he finds her sexy in mismatched sweats. Or how he wakes up in the middle of the night to stack extra blankets on her feet because they always get cold. And how, despite his private personality, he always leans down and kisses her shoulder when they're out together.

From their parents' arranged marriages, they both knew that nobody was perfect and relationships required hard work, work that they were both willing to put in. Work that caused their bond to become more resilient throughout the years. Work that made daily, banal activities, like flossing before bed or putting in contacts in the morning, more enjoyable simply because they were shared.

As if on cue, Simran's phone rings with an out-of-country number. She darts from the room and finds a spot in the lobby. The buzz of Indian aunties gossiping vibrates through the walls.

"I'm sorry," she says without waiting for either of them to say hi.

"Me too. This is dumb. Can we move past it?"

Hearing Kunal's deep voice instantly gives her a sense of peace. He's always known how to calm her down.

"Yes," she says. "It *was* a pretty dumb argument."

"You know, we're going to have so many decisions to make over the next year."

"And we can't let those decisions cause arguments. We won't. This is just the start. And we'll get through it all. We're just adjusting to this."

"Yeah. I agree." He sighs. "I really do wish I was there with you. I'm so proud of your book release."

"I wish you were here, too," she says. She refrains from telling him that it isn't the same without him. It'll only make him feel worse. Besides, she wants him to be able to take advantages of the opportunities he gets in med school. She gives herself a mental reminder that everything is going to be fine, that part of being a med student's partner is dealing with an unpredictable, grueling schedule.

On Kunal's end, Simran hears people singing in Swahili.

"How's it going?" he asks. "What were you doing when I called?"

"I was just talking to my parents. The decorations look good and everyone se—"

"Sorry, honey, can I call you right back?" Kunal says. "Something came up. I'll call you back in one minute."

"Sure," she says as he hangs up.

After ten minutes of mindless Instagram scrolling, Simran decides to go back inside. She approaches her mother as her father attends to his sister and three brothers, who have just arrived.

Nandini squints at her. "Where were you?"

"Just on the phone with Kunal. We're fine."

When she doesn't say anything, Simran whispers, "You knew I was having a bad enough day even though this is supposed to be an exciting time for me. Did you really have to remind Dad and me how much you didn't want to throw this party?"

"First of all, calm down. Second, we didn't throw this party just because Nani insisted," she says, referring to Simran's grand-mother, the only person in her family who has supported her writing. "Even though I'm sure you'll tell her *all* this when she's here for your engagement party."

Simran nods. "If the pipes didn't burst in her house, she *would* be here now, and she'd see for herself how unfair you're being. I wouldn't have to tell her anything."

Nandini's eyes narrow. "I'm not trying to be unfair. I just want you to remember the importance of being practical. Right now, you're just a student. Writing isn't something you can sustain once you're a full-time psychologist."

"This project is important to me. Being a psychologist isn't the only thing in my life."

Nandini shakes her head. "You'll see how hard it is once you're working. And not to mention, you don't want your future husband and in-laws to think you're some flighty girl they can't take seriously."

Simran rolls her eyes and scans the restaurant. At the entrance, there is a bronze statue of Ganesha, the Hindu god of good fortune and new beginnings. Every table has signed scarlet bookplates and a mountain of red velvet cupcakes. Nani suggested that red be the primary color since it's auspicious for Hindus. The scent of grilled paneer and fried samosas permeates the room in the way only heavy Indian food can.

Luckily, they're interrupted by her newly married brother, Ronak, and his wife, Namita. They are what Simran likes to call a "modern-day arranged marriage": introduced by each other's parents but still allowed to date and make the final decision on whether to marry.

She checks her phone again. Nothing.

Something about her brother arriving forces perspective. So what if her mother isn't excited for her? So what if Kunal's not here? She reapplies lip gloss and puts on her I-am-fine face, an essential for being surrounded by type A people.

Ronak rustles her hair and whistles after he soaks in the room. "Whoever thought my baby sister would be such a rock star?" He kisses the top of her forehead and places a Tiffany & Co. bag on the gift table.

"Don't worry," Simran says, handing him and Namita glasses of champagne. "According to Mom, I'm still not good enough."

He places a finger over his lips, similar to her father from earlier. "Don't go there. At least, not tonight."

"Fine, but don't worry. You're still the golden child."

"Golden child, my ass. You should have seen him all day." Namita laughs. "He cancelled three of his patients, but two of them still showed up . . . and he was cursing like crazy when the train was late. We thought we'd never make it out of Boston."

People who have physician parents either crave or abhor the idea of becoming doctors themselves. Ronak went the former route; Simran, the latter.

They briefly catch her up on how relieved they are to be done with wedding planning.

"Thank God we went straight from the wedding to that villa in Bali. We literally spoke to zero people for days. It's the only way to recover from an Indian wedding . . . complete isolation from society," she says as she twists her gold Cartier wedding band. Namita rarely wears her engagement ring since she's always washing her hands at work.

"That sounds exactly right." Simran glimpses around the room at the clusters of aunties definitely passing judgment on what everyone is wearing, who is dating whom, and anything else that's none of their business. She can only imagine how much material they'll have at her wedding.

"You're next. And it'll be perfect," Namita says with the smile and self-assuredness of someone who has never screwed up in her life.

Simran's uncle Rajan Kaka, an electrical engineer by day and self-proclaimed astrologer by night, appears and immediately wraps a plush arm around her, remarking, "I *knew* you'd be the first writer in the family. It was in your destiny."

Although many Indians refer to horoscopes for auspicious occasions, her uncle uses them for everything, even claims that they predicted Brad and Angelina hooking up.

A few minutes later, Sheila and Vishal, Simran's two closest friends and the only people who have read every draft of her book, arrive with some other friends from NYU. They all talk in a large circle as more guests come in.

She weaves through her extended family and parents' friends—adults who have known her for decades. They sprinkle in mentions about their children's MDs and JDs and PhDs, and investment banking jobs.

"Thank you so much for coming," she tells one cluster.

"Of course, *beta*," they chime in, one after another.

Charu Foi, her dad's sister, grabs the last samosa from the appetizer table. "Simran, when is your wedding happening? We've all been waiting for so long!"

All of the women around her nod in agreement, as though she's been depriving them of oxygen. Indian weddings pretty much guarantee that a stampede of overbearing, opinionated aunties will be poised and ready to trample everyone with their unsolicited advice on everything.

Payal Auntie, one of their closest family friends, smiles at her. "I can't believe we're talking about *you* getting *married*. You still look like a baby with those chubby cheeks!"

She beams, as if this is the highest possible compliment she could've given. Simran watches her tighten her fingers in preparation for a pinch. She leans back just in time to dodge her.

"So does that mean we can plan for an uncle and auntie dance sometime soon?"

Whether it's the dance party after a reception or various group dances, an Indian wedding isn't complete without dancing. Her parents' circle seems to have an endless list of adults who want to do a dance for the next wedding. Since they've all become empty nesters, they've divided into two groups: those who need to choreograph and be in the middle of every dance and those who prefer the background.

It's easy to pinpoint the Indian aunties who need to be in the center. They tend to stand taller, wear brighter colors.

Payal Auntie is stretching her neck and staring into the distance, likely picturing herself bowing to applause to the latest Bollywood medley. "When can we start preparing for this dance?"

"Actually, we just set a wedding date," Simran says. "June 20."

"Really?" Charu Foi's eyes widen so much Simran thinks they may bulge out of her head. "Next year?"

She nods. "Next year."

Charu Foi frowns. "But that's so far away."

"Oh, it's fine, Charu. You just want another occasion to eat and drink and socialize. You can do that in your own home, so what's the rush?" Payal Auntie shakes her head as if she's any different. "Simran, where are you having the wedding?"

"We only just started planning, since Ronak and Namita's wedding was just last month, so most of the details aren't finalized," she says, finding the interstitial area between what they want to hear and the truth. "Anyway, please let me know what you think of my book and if y—"

Charu Foi leans into her. "We are all so happy that things are finally working out for you. Your psychology schoolwork, wedding . . . I always told everyone they didn't have to worry about you. I *knew* you would settle down and get your priorities figured out. You wouldn't be our little misfit forever. I mean, there was *no* way Ranjit and Nandini's daughter could stay a mess! It might have taken forev—"

"Thank you, Charu Foi," Simran interrupts. "Thank you so much."

The rest of the conversations are similar. Nobody seems to be concerned about the book, and everyone seems to be concerned about Kunal, who still hasn't called back. She gives rehearsed answers and shakes off the heavy isolation, the type that can only come when you're surrounded by people who care about you. Sheila confiscates Simran's phone after she catches her checking it for the tenth time.

While she's talking to her cousins, Simran notices an unfamiliar guy saunter into the room, more than fashionably late, the fashionably part being apt, considering his light gray buttondown and navy blue blazer over dark jeans.

That guy can dress, she thinks as he grins at everyone he passes, a grin that reaches all the way up to his square glasses and reflects back twice as strongly. He seems to be in his late thirties.

His build is slender but not puny, reminding her of Leonardo DiCaprio in *Titanic*—the kind of guy who is splashed with just the right balance of passionate aggression and sensitive romantic.

At first, Simran assumes the guy is just friends with one of the many guests her parents invited, since their network includes every Indian on the East Coast. She focuses on the carpet, ashamed that her eyes hang on him. He isn't conventionally handsome but still falls into the attractive category. (Not that she prefers conventional looks anyway; she may be the only woman who doesn't find Brad Pitt hot.)

As she scans the room, she notices a lot of people are facing his direction.

But then she takes another look, and his face registers. She knows him. She's read about him multiple times. How is he *here*?

"Holy crap. Do you know who that is?" Simran leans toward Vishal and catches a whiff of his minty Armani Code.

Vishal shrugs. "No. Why, do you?"

Simran takes a deep breath. "That's Neil. *The* Neil. Neil Desai."

Vishal responds with a blank, wide-eyed stare. Simran can see that the only thing this means to him is that this guy's parents gave him a name that automatically pardoned him from the cringe-worthy discomfort many Indian kids experienced whenever a teacher called roll.

"Neil Desai, Neil Desai," Simran repeats. "*New York Times* Neil Desai? Ring a bell?"

"No." Vishal almost chokes. "It can't be."

But of course it is.

The *Neil freaking Desai!*

Neil Desai is a contributing writer for the Opinion section of the *New York Times*, which has also been part of her breakfast for the past two years. He generally writes satirical pieces about economics and politics, until last year, when he compiled his pieces into a bestselling book. Neil rarely interviews and prefers to keep a low profile, even refusing to have a public Facebook page.

Simran's learned everything about him through her mastery of Google: he graduated from Princeton summa cum laude, almost followed the Indian path of becoming a doctor but decided to pursue journalism, is happily single, has two siblings, and is a die-hard fan of Duke basketball. Every time she acquired a new fact about him, she shared it with Kunal, who would roll his eyes, as though she was divulging trashy celebrity gossip from *Star* magazine. The truth is, she *does* swoon over accomplished writers the way other people gawk over movie stars or musicians (and Kunal couldn't care less about either).

"Shut up," she whispers in awe, digging her nails into Vishal's arm. "No way. There. Is. No. Way."

"I guess there is a way," Vishal says.

"What the heck is he doing *here*?!"

"He must have been invited through someone. It was an open Facebook event, and your parents told everyone to bring their friends."

"Wow, he doesn't look how I thought he would," Simran says, before realizing that judging someone by their writing is probably just as unreliable as judging them by their voice on the phone.

"*Very* different from his picture," she adds, referring to the faded headshot that was on his first Google hit, which eventually became his website. "I mean, that looked like some awkward yearbook picture."

Not that she has any right to talk; every yearbook picture of hers is unflattering, off-center, or both.

But before they can continue to dissect Neil's appearance, he approaches the table, gripping a copy of *her* thin collection of essays. She becomes giddy, embarrassingly giddy, the way she was when she was five years old and met Cinderella at Disney World and thought she was actually the cartoon from the screen.

"Am I too late for an autograph?" he asks, skipping an introduction and flashing her a flawless smile. Her mother says she always studies teeth because she's so conscious about her own, but she thinks anyone would notice his.

She puts down her champagne glass on the table. "Only if I can get yours."

He raises his eyebrows, sincerely surprised that she knows who he is. She takes the book from him and tries to keep her hands steady enough to turn to the title page.

"You know, I wouldn't have thought you were the type of guy who read essay collections about being an Indian adolescent girl. I should have known that whole economics thing was a facade," she blurts, surprised at how naturally the remark flows out of her, as though she's teasing a friend, not a writer she's admired for years.

"Okay, well, I haven't read your work," he admits. "Or heard of you before tonight. But I'm supposed to keep up with new Indian writers since I joined the South Asian Writers Association as a mentor. They told me about your event."

"Of course," Simran says. How could she assume someone like him would seek out anything of hers?

"But if it counts for anything, my niece did read your essays."

"She did?"

He nods. "She did. And she *loved* it. Said I had to bring her a signed copy."

"That's so nice to hear," she says.

"I'll attempt to read it and decide for myself. No promises, of course." He gives her a quick wink.

Her heart rate palpably increases as she imagines him in his frameless glasses, sitting in front of his silver laptop (he strikes her as an Apple user), scrolling through her words.

"Thanks, I appreciate that," she mumbles. "I'm, uh, a huge fan of your work. I actually just read your piece on the US healthcare system this morning."

"Oh yeah?" He laughs, a dimple chiseling his right cheek. "Well, it's nice that somebody actually reads my stuff. Even my parents get bored of it."

"Oh, I know what you mean by that!" she exclaims. "Definitely know what you mean," she repeats in a softer voice. "My parents don't really read my stuff, either."

He nods. "I'm glad I'm not the only one. How'd you get into this project, anyway?"

She refrains from giving him her rehearsed speech. "To go *all* the way from the beginning, in high school, I thought about pursuing journalism because I liked the idea of educating others about what was going on in the world. Then, I double majored in psychology and journalism at NYU. I was working on an article about Indians raised in America for one of my journalism classes. And I realized that there were so many issues that affected Indian girls during adolescence and nobody had depicted those. So then I thought maybe I could be the one who educated others on what that experience was like. I started writing down my friends' stories and kept finding all these common themes, and then this data to back that up, which resulted in this essay collection. Of course, then I went all the way with my psychology major, and the journalism part sort of faded away. . . ."

"And why Indian girls and why adolescence?" Neil asks.

Nobody at the party has asked that (or anything else about the book) yet.

"Adolescence is hard enough, but when you're Indian, you deal with different hurdles, like your mom not letting you shave your legs or your parents saying you can't like boys because you have to do well in school."

"I see," he says. "That's very insightful of you."

Simran shrugs.

"It is," he says. "To make something that educates a lot of people and then gives solace to those who went through it."

"I've never thought of it that way before," she says, mentally repeating his words. Her family and fiancé never thought of the project as a source of solace.

"It's true," he says.

Her phone buzzes with a group text from Sheila and Vishal.

Vishal: You're still talking to him?!

Next to his question, there's an emoji of a face with hearts for eyes. She turns her phone around.

It doesn't take long for Neil to pull up a chair to continue their conversation. They sit in the same positions long after the cupcakes are eaten and the champagne is drained. She asks him about Princeton, how he felt about letting go of a career as a physician, and tells him about her master's in psychology. Somewhere between her latest research study and his refusal to take the MCAT, she realizes that she's no longer missing Kunal or even worried about the guests glancing at them, whispering to one another.

When Neil scoots his chair closer to hers, she reaches under the table and slips off her engagement ring. There is a split second when she asks herself what the heck she's doing, but she decides to ignore that voice. Sometimes it's nice to leap out of character. Not discuss wedding planning for once.

Thirty minutes later, her mom comes to their table.

"Simran," Nandini says in her ear. "It doesn't look good to ignore everyone and just sit with one person, one *boy*, in the middle of your book party."

"Oh, so now it's my *book* party?"

Nandini places a firm hand on Simran's shoulder. No daughter of *hers* will behave inappropriately. "Remember what I told you before. People are leaving and expect you to say bye to them."

Simran stands at the door to hug people goodbye but keeps glancing around the room to make eye contact with Neil. After her parents are gone and only her friends are left, she motions for Neil to join her at the table again. They discuss the trials that accompany being a writer: crappy first drafts, tedious revisions, countless rejection letters, self-doubt, and the tortured-artist complex that they both don't have.

If someone were to gaze through the glass double doors, they would see a pair of what seemed like long-lost friends, chatting effortlessly and cheerily, catching up on the years they've missed. The last people clear out, and the only sound is the clunk of cabs speeding over potholes.

It already occurred to her that Neil talks to all sorts of people at all sorts of times, is probably just being nice, and will more than likely forget about her. But for the rest of the night, she will not think of her life. Not when she and Neil are confined in the walls of her party, not when he places his hand on the small of her back as they cross Fifth Avenue to her favorite twenty-four-hour diner, and not on her cab ride home, when the streets are cluttered with cheap pizza and discarded beer bottles.

Nandini

"She just doesn't understand. She doesn't even think. If she just took *one* second to reflect on why I say the things I do, then she'd realize that I'm right," Nandini says.

"WHAT? I CAN'T HEAR YOU!" Mami yells into the phone.

"Mami, you don't need to yell the way you had to when I used to call India. You're not holding the phone up properly."

Nandini hears her mother mutter something in Gujarati, followed by the sounds of her adjusting her sari.

"Okay, I can hear you," Mami says, as if they don't go through this during every phone call.

Nandini repeats her earlier statement.

"You're doing what you're supposed to do," Mami says. "It's your job to set boundaries and show her right from wrong."

"Yes, but she just doesn't get it," Nandini says. "We don't . . . understand each other."

"Well, *are* you proud of her?"

"What?" Nandini asks, as though she didn't hear the question, when in fact her mother's words were clear.

"Are you proud of Simran? For her writing? For who she is in general?"

"What kind of a question is that? Of course I'm proud!"

"Of *what*? You have to say it." Mami commands her like an elementary school teacher telling someone to recite the alphabet.

Nandini clears her throat. "I think it's impressive that she put together an essay collection. A book! It doesn't even sound real when I say the words out loud. My daughter wrote a book. I know that couldn't have been easy. And the way she depicted what girls go through during their teenage years. . . . It was thoughtful . . . and empathetic."

"It was," Mami agrees. "And what about her? Are you proud of her?"

"I am. . . ." Nandini's voice trails off.

"But what?"

"But nothing," Nandini says, and then adds, "I think there's a lot that Simran still needs to realize, to learn. She's getting married soon. And you and I both know that's an entirely different game. To be spending time with another person—a boy—just sets her off on the wrong foot."

"I know what you're saying, but that's not what I asked you about," Mami says. "Simran has said you never tell her you're proud of her. That you just point out what she's not doing right."

"That's not true!" Nandini says. "I try to tell her, but she doesn't hear it. When I say something—anything—she's already waiting to take it the wrong way."

"That's not true," Mami says.

"It is true. She never really hears what I'm trying to tell her."

"She's coming from a different place than you. What do you expect?"

Nandini bites her bottom lip. What does she expect? "I don't know. I guess I hoped she and I could talk the way you and her talk."

"Our relationship is different."

"Yes, I know," Nandini says, not bothering to mask the irritation in her voice.

"Is it possible that maybe you, you know . . ." Mami's voice trails off.

"What? Is what possible? Just say it."

Mami scoffs. "Is it possible that you're being a little harsh with her?"

Of course her mother would go there. It doesn't matter that Nandini has built a life in America, become a physician, and raised a family. Mami could always find a way to ask a question that poked a hole through all the self-confidence she spent years building.

"Me? Harsh with *her*? And this is coming from *you*?"

"I'm only ask—"

"You took pride in being harsh with me when I was younger! You said that kids in my generation were too sensitive. And now, you get to be all soft with your granddaughter? How convenient! How things change! No wonder Simran talks to you more than she talks to me. You are completely different with her than you ever were with me."

Nandini sits in the recliner. She takes deep, heavy breaths. There was no point in going through this with her mother. It wouldn't get them anywhere. It never did. She would never admit (not out loud, at least) that a part of her takes pride in Mami's tenderness with Simran and Ronak. It was as if a new part of her came to life when she became a grandmother.

"Never mind all of this," Nandini says with a sigh. "How is the pipe repair?"

"It's fine. Just fine."

"At least something's fine." Nandini forces herself to get out of the recliner. She's so tired that if she lets herself sit for too long, she'll fall asleep. She walks toward the foyer. There's an antique silver mirror by the front door, a gift from Ranjit's sister, Charu.

Nandini studies her reflection. Mami's stubborn, strong DNA ensured that both Nandini and Simran inherited her slim, straight nose; her large, almond-shaped eyes; and her delicate chin. Nandini's face is covered with products she only started using in America: Bobbi Brown blush and Elizabeth Arden lipstick. She still uses Pond's talcum powder under her arms. It's one of the few ways she's managed to hold on to home. To Mami.

"*Everything* is fine, Nandini," Mami says in the same cheerful tone she uses with customer service representatives over the phone. Mami has that ability, to make people feel better just by talking to them and make them want to confide in her. Simran once overheard a Bloomingdale's employee tell Mami about his wife's affair and then offer her a free makeover.

"Really? Fine? You can seriously say that?"

To her surprise, Mami laughs. *Laughs.* As if Nandini is a little girl saying her first word.

Something is going on with her mother. She's been more detached lately. More relaxed. One year ago, her pipes bursting would have meant daily phone calls, maybe even a request for a visit to Baroda. But now, she doesn't even seem to be rattled by the fact that the skeleton of her bungalow, the one Nandini grew up in, is slowly breaking.

Should she be concerned about early dementia? Maybe she needs to get Mami's thyroid checked. Nandini sees the changes that come with aging through her clinic patients every day. But it is entirely different when it is happening to Mami. She wonders if things would have been different if Papa was still alive.

"Nandini, it's going to be okay," Mami says, her voice softening. "It always is. It was with you, right?"

Nandini feels something inside of her crumple. "It was very *not* okay before it was."

"I know, *beta*."

Mami sighs, then clears her throat. "And speaking of . . . have you thought of telling Simran about . . ."

"About what? That?"

"Yes. That." Again with the laugh.

"What are you even saying? You think I should tell Simran about *that*? Now? Or ever?"

"Maybe it would help. Dr. Phil had an entire episode on the importance of not keeping secrets."

"Well, if Dr. Phil says it, then it must be true." Nandini covers her eyes and shakes her head. Why did she ever get her mother access to every television channel in the world?

"I happen to agree with him," Mami says with defiance, as if Nandini insulted a relative. "If you talk to Simran, she might understand you better."

"Understand me better? That would ruin her. Ruin everything! I can't believe you would even think to bring that up as a possibility."

Nandini treated her past the way she treated the Atlantic Ocean. She visited often, even dipped her feet in at times, but always refused to be submerged.

She couldn't tell Simran about what happened all those years ago in India. Somehow, there are more things she's kept from her daughter than she ever wanted. Simran doesn't know about Nandini's postpartum depression after Ronak's birth. That entire time was a blur of fluids: Ronak's urine, his tears, her tears. She remembers the endless mornings she spent carrying his stroller down the uneven brick steps and clutching him close to her.

There were so many times she wondered if after everything she had been through and worked for, this was all it amounted to. Exhaustion, loneliness, and a gnawing sense of inadequacy.

In India, after a woman gave birth, she usually had a tribe of women in her family waiting to help her. In America, everything had to be managed alone. When Nandini told her family in India about her crying spells, fleeting thoughts of jumping off a balcony, and the weight on her chest, they told her to "stay quiet and get over it because it's all in your head." Mami was the only one who covertly offered to give her money for a therapist.

But omitting that part of her life from her daughter was nothing compared to what Mami was referring to. How could her mother possibly think Simran could handle that?

"Okay," Mami says now, her voice still gentle. "Forget I said anything."

"It's my job to protect Simran," Nandini says. "And make sure she doesn't make mistakes that cost her everything."

There's silence on the other end, but she knows what Mami's thinking. *Make sure she doesn't make mistakes like you did.*

"Maybe this is what I should have expected from settling in America. This culture promotes kids to think for themselves, act on emotion. I just . . . don't want her to get hurt."

As she keeps talking, she hears her biggest fear crystallize. She came to America to escape what had happened in India, but what if, despite everything she's done, she somehow screws things up for her daughter?

"She won't get hurt," Mami says. "She'll be fine."

"Okay . . . she won't." Nandini repeats her mother's words again and again, hoping that with enough time, she'll believe them.

Two

Simran

It only takes five days for Simran to see Neil again. Five. Days. He ended his nice-to-meet-you e-mail with an invitation to his favorite dessert place. She still can't understand how this is actually happening to her, how in a matter of one week, her world is larger.

She pictures her mother's face during the party, insisting that she think of the guests. That's what she's done her entire life: think of the guests. Even after she left for college, if there was a family party, she always took the PATH train home to help. Evenings before a family party were spent frying pooris, a crispy fried Indian bread, and taking out the folding chairs from the basement. Evenings of a family party were spent making sure the men were dining while the women prepared gulab jamun, sweet donuts, for dessert.

Today, the East Village is bursting with its usual characters: post-college guys in colorful socks and even more colorful glasses, girls with pink hair and multiple piercings, women gripping a bottle of water in one hand and a tightly wound yoga mat in another.

As Simran makes her way downtown, Beyoncé's voice blasts

through her headphones and encourages her to be a powerful woman. New York is settling into spring, with its pungent cherry blossoms and Lululemon-clad joggers. Food trucks spread the whiff of fried treats. A group of break dancers collects tips in a giant white bucket. Next to them, a homeless man naps on a frayed slab of cardboard. He has a sign propped up behind him: VETERAN WHO SERVED HIS COUNTRY AND HAS NO FOOD OR MONEY.

After months of winter, the warm weather seems to infuse new life into the city. Everyone's in a good mood. Even the homeless man has woken up and started bobbing to the break dancers' music. He somehow still manages to flick off random pedestrians for not dropping money into his box.

She passes Fourteenth Street and Second Avenue, where she once saw John Krasinski, her celebrity crush, and Emily Blunt walking their dog. They all locked eyes as she was in the middle of biting a massive cinnamon roll. She likes to tell herself that under different circumstances, they surely would have become instant friends.

Her heart starts pounding when she's two blocks away from Neil. In a matter of moments, Milk Bar isn't just going to be a place where she, Sheila, and Vishal ate cake pops to avoid studying for finals. Now, it's about to be a place where she'll see a role model. A fleeting opportunity to be around someone doing grand things.

She runs her fingers through her hair. If only she had a mirror. She shifts her lackadaisical walk into a strut, because that's what Beyoncé would do.

Neil is already standing outside the restaurant. He's reading something on his phone and grinning, the dimple marking his cheek like a tiny crescent moon.

Her eyes take time to adjust to him, the way they take time to adjust to darkness when the lights are suddenly switched off. He's GQ casual in a fitted, white crewneck shirt and slim-fit jeans. She envisions this to be the type of outfit he wore while he sauntered through Princeton's plush campus, contemplating his next writing topic.

"Hey, you!" Neil says when he sees her crossing the sidewalk. "It's good to see you again."

He puts down his camel messenger bag and reaches forward for a full hug at the same second that she stretches for a handshake. She somehow ends up giving him a ginger pat on his back. *Very smooth, Simran. Very smooth.*

"Good to see you, too," Simran says, her breath slowing down but her fingers still tingling.

"You look . . . elegant," he says.

"Thanks." A rush of warmth spreads from her cheeks to her neck. She's wearing a white dress and pink pumps from Zara. An outfit that's flattering and understated, she hopes. Nani always tells her that her eyes are her strongest feature, so she spent extra time making sure her eyeliner was even. One day, she'll be effortlessly chic, like those women who always have fresh manicures and blowouts. One day.

"Shall we?" Neil asks, motioning to the restaurant.

Milk Bar doesn't have any chairs but instead has one C-shaped wooden table where people are standing and sharing desserts. The piping is exposed, and silver lamps are spaced across the ceiling in an "industrial chic" look.

Once they're inside, Neil asks her if she's thought of writing another essay or article.

"I'm not sure," she says. Nobody else has asked this. But Neil's sincere curiosity makes her *want* to have creative ideas and not dismiss that part of herself.

"There are so many topics I'd like to learn more about so I can spread that information to others. But therapy is more about focusing on the individual patient and working with them over a period of time. So even though I've had some ideas, it's been hard to focus on them with school."

"What are some of your ideas?"

She glances at his even, clean fingernails. "I thought of doing a piece about how in our culture, boys are treated differently from girls, whether that's in Indian villages or even here. Then I considered researching how a girl's ambition changes from elementary school to adulthood based on messages she's received from people around her."

"Those sound like great topics," Neil says. "And ones you could do a lot with."

"And I really think that people need to know about them. Think about them. Discuss them," she says. "There's some data that was recently published about rates of depression in Asian American girls, so if I touched on that, I could combine my journalism and psychology background. You know, I thought journalism and psychology were so similar. And they are, to an extent, but there are certain differences that I haven't appreciated until I started school."

"Such as?"

"It's funny, I've been thinking about this for a while but haven't been able to talk about it with anyone," she says, hoping Neil can understand how much this means to her. "Well, I knew therapy was obviously about working with people and their issues privately, but there's something to be said about being able to pass that information along to others. Make sense of it on a bigger scale, you know? I didn't think of that in college, or really, until my master's program."

"Yes, I can see what you're saying," he says with the same patience and understanding she imagines he has with people he interviews for his own articles.

"It's so nice to be able to actually talk about this with you." She holds herself back from saying that he's made her feel more encouraged in a few minutes than everyone else has in a few months.

"Always important to find your people." Neil gives another Crest-commercial-worthy grin. "Have you by any chance heard of Laura Martinez?"

"I only have several of her articles printed and taped to my wall!" Simran says. "And I *might* have preordered her next book the first second possible."

Laura Martinez writes monthly psychology articles for *The New Yorker*. She has a book about sociopaths coming out in two months.

Neil laughs. "She's a friend."

"Really? A *friend*?" Simran asks. She shouldn't be surprised.

"Really. She's probably going to have an event for her next book at the Strand."

"Ah, the Strand." Simran pictures the tall rows of books and book-related accessories. "Easily my favorite place in the city."

"Not surprised to hear that. I think you could do something similar to her, if you wanted, considering your background, as you said."

"I don't know. I mean, the psychology coursework is taking over my life right now, and there's still a lot I want to learn about before I even consider writing anything."

"So learn," he says, as if she just told him she wants an iced coffee. "Ask people questions. Research. And maybe your work doesn't have to be in the form of a book. Have you considered submitting articles to different publications? That might be more feasible for you right now, to do shorter pieces that are more spread out instead of something more time-consuming."

"I did write some rough drafts of articles during college," she tells him. "Maybe I could go back through those."

Neil nods. "Sounds good."

"Not that any of that matters right now," she says. "Nobody took my book seriously."

"Hey, my niece did! And I'm halfway through it myself . . ."

Her legs start to shake. "You *are*?"

"I am. And I think it's wonderful, to say the least."

Wonderful?! Neil Desai called something she did *wonderful*?

Before she can respond, Neil asks, "What about your family? I'm sure they think the world of your work."

"I'm not sure. I know my parents threw a party, but really, they've always considered it an innocuous side thing. A safe hobby. I worked on the essays throughout college and then submitted the collection to a bunch of small presses that didn't require an agent. An editor accepted it, and within a year, I had a book. Even though I saw it as a onetime project, it was exciting for me, but to my family—to everyone—if something isn't financially stable or in some scientific field, it isn't worth any time. Nobody gets the point.

"Except my grandmother, my mom's mom," she adds. "I grew

up with her telling me stories about the Indian goddesses, and she always encouraged me to write about them. But she's in India and doesn't like coming here, losing her independence. So, that's that. . . ."

She trails off, unsure of why she divulges all these details so willingly.

"You know, everyone thinks it's so fun and easy to write articles. People *still* ask me when I'm going to get a real job," Neil says.

"I know, right? Nobody thinks you're actually working when you're writing."

Neil thoughtfully stares at the blackboard menu and asks the girl behind the cash register how she's doing. She grins, a soft blush forming on her cheeks. He and Simran decide to share three cookies, a bottle of cereal milk—the kind that has the sweet, post-cereal taste to it—and a few truffles, which Neil insists she take home. He pays before she even has the chance to offer her wallet.

"So, you sure know the menu well," she says.

She sticks two straws in the bottle and then removes hers. It makes it look like two high school kids sharing a milk shake. She wrings her hands together, not knowing what else to do with them.

"I know. I know." Neil chuckles and splits a compost cookie into two uneven sections and hands Simran the larger piece. "I've been here way too many times. It's ridiculous how much money I spend on food. And by ridiculous, I mean terrible."

She smiles and looks down. Neil Desai is the type of guy to grab dessert on a whim. He's probably the type to do many things on a whim—make out in an alleyway, splurge on a wallet, book a vacation. Kunal has everything planned days, sometimes years, in advance.

Neil sighs and pats his flat stomach. "I'm such a glutton. Or, I'm so gluttonous. Which do you prefer?"

Simran strokes her chin and pretends to contemplate an answer. "Gluttonous. I always prefer a nice adjective over a noun."

"Same here." Neil breaks out into a large grin.

"You know," he says, "I don't think I ever actually finished a book in high school. Like those required readings. *Never* did them."

"What?" she asks, half suspicious, half surprised. "Yeah *right*. Mr. Princeton couldn't get through *Catcher in the Rye*?"

"Maybe I read that one." Neil smirks, as though he's actually a high school dropout. "But seriously, I was kind of a slacker when it came to school. I applied to Princeton early decision and turned in the application on the deadline day. You know how Indian parents compete with their kids' academic achievements? Well, my dad tried to teach me that 'B stands for bad' in middle school after some auntie told him her son was going to take college math—or something ridiculous like that—because everything else was too easy for him."

"There's nothing more annoying than an Indian auntie who won't stop bragging about her kids." She straightens her posture and raises one eyebrow at him. "Are you one of those smart people who acts like he doesn't do anything, when he secretly studies for ten hours a day? I can't stand those."

"No, *no*," Neil says, his smile becoming wider. "That's honestly why I knew I couldn't go to med school. I could never handle all that studying."

She pictures the way Kunal looks in the library, wearing a

sweat shirt and jeans, curled over his books with a thermos of green tea as his only company. She heard that medical school serves as a type of academic shock for people because after years of being at the top of their class in college, they join an entire group of students who were also overachievers and suddenly feel average. That never happened with Kunal. He's the king of the type A workaholics. He's the one who everyone follows around the anatomy lab before the practical. He's the one who doesn't need to abuse Adderall, like so many of his classmates, because of his sheer discipline.

"Yeah, I don't know how they do it," she agrees. "My fiancé's actually finishing his first year . . . at NYU Med."

At the word "fiancé," Neil's eyes dart to her now-adorned ring finger, and he almost seems to lose composure for a swift second before getting it back.

She moves her left hand to her lap. "Yeah, I really don't know how he does it. He's the most hardworking person I know."

"I bet." Neil whistles, running his fingers through his slightly parted hair. With the ends slightly curled out to the sides, it moves too much for him to use a lot of product. "So, tell me more. How long have you guys been together? How did he propose?"

She takes a deep breath, and her sentences emerge in nonsensical fragments. "It happened a few months ago. He hid the ring in my high school locker and told me there was a surprise in there when we went back for our five-year reunion. . . . We've been together since high school . . . for seven years."

Neil's eyes widen behind his glasses. "*Seven* years?! Holy shit. So when's the wedding?"

She laughs at this standard reaction to her relationship length.

"Next summer, so we have over a year to plan. Honestly, neither of us is really in a rush since we've both got a long way to go with our educations. But planning just started, so that means everyone is getting involved."

She still doesn't understand why she omitted that tiny detail about being engaged until now.

Neil laughs. "And the floodgates of expectations and demands have just opened."

"Exactly."

"Well, I guess if you two have been together that long," Neil says, "you're pretty much married."

Simran shrugs and nods, thinking that their union does often feel as though it contains the reliable comfort of a marriage. Or at least what she *thinks* a marriage would have, since she can't use their parents' arranged marriages as a measuring stick. She and Kunal often joke that their relationship is like an "arranged dating" situation: both of them embraced the commitment from their parents' arranged marriages and applied it to their own.

"Are you in a relationship?" she asks, regretting the words as soon as they leave her mouth.

Neil shifts in his chair. "Not really."

"Not really?"

"It's, uh, complicated. Long story."

"Sure, I get it," she says.

She doesn't get it at all.

While Simran and Neil eat, they learn that both of them come from doctor parents, have older brothers (Neil also has a younger sister), and love watching the Food Network. They also learn that they both had slob roommates during the first two years of college. The entire conversation passes quickly, and although

Simran can't remember if she's ever had this much fun with someone she barely knows, she imagines that Neil has this type of effortless, lighthearted time with many people.

She glances out the window and notices an Indian woman walking with her son across the street. She's wearing a blue, cotton salwar kameez, the type of outfit that Simran's mom only wears when she visits India.

"That's strange," she says. "That actually looks like my fiancé's mom."

"Really?" Neil asks, stretching his neck to get a closer look. "Do you want to step out and say hi?"

Kunal's mother, Meghna Auntie, and Simran have spoken several times since he's left for Africa. She pictures Meghna Auntie's face if she saw her here with Neil. No, thank you.

"No, no." She shakes her head. "I doubt that it's her. She never comes into the city. Usually stays at home."

Meghna Auntie thrives off domesticity; the kind of woman who gets excited about a sale at the grocery store so that she can cook more for her three sons, an ideal candidate for a wife during Simran's parents' generation. It's a matter of time before Simran will be expected to call her "Mom," something that still seems forced but yet is another part of her heritage.

She hears her own mother's voice: *The relationship with the man's mother is very important.*

Once an Indian woman is married, she's expected to embrace her husband's family as her new one. Her mother-in-law becomes a dominant force, and pleasing her might even hold more importance than pleasing her husband.

While Meghna Auntie sometimes seems like the opposite of her mom, Simran can't help but think that her future mother-in-law also finds Simran's ways inadequate, her preference of books over boiling vegetables, candor over compliance, a dramatic contrast from what she would have picked for her son if they lived in India, where parents have a heavier hand in their children's choices.

"You know," Neil says, "you and your fiancé should go to this place called Marta. It's mainly pizza, but they have *good* dessert, including a cannoli cheesecake."

She makes a mental note of the place—to pass on to Sheila, Vishal, or her family—but refrains from telling Neil that she and Kunal probably won't go there. Besides Kunal's general apathy toward trying new restaurants, his busy schedule and financial constraints don't allow him to truly take advantage of New York.

They saunter outside, and Neil makes a comment about the pleasant weather.

"Yeah. Ice-cream weather," she says, thinking of the way her father used to make her feel better about the weather by equating it with something she liked. *Hot chocolate weather. Good book weather. Long nap weather.*

She gazes at the now-closed street carts, the empty bus stop, and the stacked black trash bags on the sidewalk. Certain corners of New York pacify around this time, while the sky balances day and night. Her favorite element of this hour is the apartment lights turning on, each one its own wink of comfort. People share sparkling cocktails at outdoor tables.

While they stand at the corner of Thirteenth Street and Second Avenue, she rummages through her tote for her phone, which is somewhere in the abyss of her massive handbag. There's a text on their family group chat from her mom: *Simran, we need*

to run through the list of potential wedding photographers tonight. They
get booked very fast and if we don't do this soon, we may have to get one
of those terrible ones that makes every picture sepia-toned.

Of course, the text goes on with more anxious concerns, but
she stops reading and tells Neil she'll take a cab home. He walks
to the corner and raises his arm. She forgot how lean his body
was. It's fit, with a defined collarbone and flat stomach, but not
nearly as full as Kunal's.

As a van cab slows down, she gives Neil a full hug (no handshake) and thanks him. He shakes his head and smiles before
sliding the passenger door open for her. They linger against the
cab. She wishes she had more days like this with people like Neil.

When she sits inside, he leans in and softly kisses her cheek.

"I had so much fun," he says.

"I did, too," she says, wishing she could brush her finger
against his cheek. Instead, she finds herself stretching out of the
cab and into another hug, this one tighter than the last.

"I'll see you soon, hopefully," she says with a sigh, wishing she
didn't have to go home. She presses her cheek against his for a
split second.

From the corner of her eye, she notices someone standing outside the restaurant, facing her and Neil. She stretches her neck to
get a better look. Her breath freezes.

Meghna Auntie.

She's standing with Kunal's brother, Mehul, with an expression on her face that anyone else might call serious but that Simran knows is angry. Livid.

Shit.

Simran steps out of the cab with one foot, considers saying hi first. But Meghna Auntie shifts her weight onto her heels and turns in the other direction, as though Simran was someone she didn't even recognize.

Simran stands at the corner with Neil, not knowing where to go. Guilt isn't always in the form of an upset stomach or elevated pulse. Sometimes it's the smooth texture of a truffle or as light as a drained bottle of cereal milk.

Nandini

"*You're* the doctor?" Sarah, a twenty-year-old new patient who came in for her annual physical, squints her eyes at Nandini.

"I am." Nandini extends her hand. "Dr. Mehta."

Sarah offers a weak laugh, as if to give away her own embarrassment. "Oh. Nice to meet you, too. I thought you were just the nurse."

"No, you were with our nurse five minutes ago. Our very hardworking, smart nurse," Nandini says to make sure Sarah knows "just the nurse" is an unacceptable phrase. "And I'm the doctor. *Your* doctor. Nice to meet you."

Though her words are poised and polite, there's a palpable firmness underneath them.

"I see." Sarah shakes her head. "I'm sorry about my, er, confusion."

Nandini nods. After all the years Nandini's spent studying, all the patients she's tested and embraced and saved, she is still questioned about being a doctor on a daily basis. Never mind that medical school classes now have more women than men. Never mind that she got the highest board scores in her class.

She'll never forget the words from her first attending in residency, a chubby Russian man whose thin strip of hair provided a feeble attempt to cover his bald spot: "You have a lot going against you. First, you're short. Second, you're Indian. Third, you're an immigrant. And last, you're a woman." He held up four sausage-like fingers to indicate how many traits she had to work against. Four, as if he was simply making a grocery list and not breaking down her identity.

Her phone rings as she listens to Sarah's heart and lungs. It rings again as she tests her knee jerk reflex with the smooth, silver hammer. When she reaches into the bottom right pocket of her white coat to silence it, she sees five missed calls.

Meghna Ben has called her five times.

What could be so urgent? She almost apologizes to Sarah but notices that Sarah's too absorbed in her own iPhone to even notice Nandini's distraction.

Nandini steps into the cramped hallway that always smells like a mixture of antiseptic, pus, and the metallic tang of medical instruments. Her next patient, Melissa, is already checked in. She's in her standard outfit of a short skirt and crop top. She's also over three hundred pounds. Professionally, Nandini knows she's supposed to counsel Melissa on the importance of routine exercise and a healthy diet. Personally, Nandini is in awe of Melissa's self-confidence in the midst of a world that promotes women hating their bodies.

She waves to Melissa. "I'll be with you in a couple of minutes."

Melissa waves back and displays a fresh acrylic manicure. Nandini steps into the storage room that's filled with forever-needing-to-be-shredded patient files and broken office chairs.

If she doesn't finish Sarah's appointment soon, she'll be behind for the rest of her day. Her clinic books the doctors in fifteen-minute appointment slots. Nandini's supposed to make every patient feel comfortable, cared for, and examined without even having time to review their medical records, let alone ask them about their lives. She never has time to eat breakfast or lunch. Often, when she's struggling to write notes at the end of the day, she remembers labs she forgot to order, doctors she didn't have the chance to consult with.

Nandini still doesn't know how the other four family medicine doctors do it. Their boss, the medical director of the clinic, meets with them monthly and pushes them to be "more efficient" and "a better team player," all phrases that are code for "make the clinic more money." When Nandini was hired, she asked why the female doctors made less than the male ones. He responded by asking her if she was going to go part time "the way all the female doctors do."

Nandini clutches her stomach. She always has a pit of dread when her alarm goes off and she pictures the exhausting day unraveling in front of her. Every morning, she tells herself to stop feeling sorry for herself and start accepting reality. This is what her days look like. This is her life. There is no use dwelling on its difficulties.

It's just that . . . she didn't see her career turning out this way. In residency, she enjoyed making study guides for her co-residents and explaining complicated protocols to the interns. People told her she had a talent for teaching. She always saw herself as her own boss, splitting time between guiding residents and managing a private practice where she could spend quality time with each patient.

But after Ranjit set up his own private practice to see his sur-

gery patients, there was no way for Nandini to establish a space
of her own. Every day, a family member or friend needed her to
look at their sprained ankle or recommend cholesterol medications or ask her what to take for a sore throat. She tried to discuss
the situation with her husband, but his silence was enough. It was
expected for her to take care of other people before cultivating
her own ambition. Working for a larger clinic close to their house
ensured she would have stable, predictable hours and be available
whenever anyone needed her.

Over time, Nandini understood the difference between how
people saw her husband's career and how they saw her own. He
was allowed to be consumed by his job. If he made it to Ronak's
baseball game, people lauded his devotion to his children. If she
did the same, they accused her of not being focused enough on
her career.

She stares at her phone again. What could this possibly be
about? Did something happen to Meghna? To Kunal? Are they
upset about the venue that was picked? Do they hate the photographers?

Nandini ignores the twisting in her stomach. *Stop catastroph-
izing.* While she was being treated for the postpartum depression
only Mami knew about, Nandini started having panic attacks.
First, they happened only in the hospital, but after a few months,
they would catch her off guard throughout the day. She felt herself falling into an abyss, losing touch with her surroundings as
her breathing shortened, her legs gave out, and she was con-
vinced she'd die.

Her therapist taught her about how to control her thoughts
when they spiraled out of control. Look at rational evidence. Focus on her breathing. Try to stay in the present.

Since then, a dormant panic continued to linger inside of her, intertwined with her spine or hooked below her sternum. She pictures it now, a collection of energy anchoring and growing roots. A threat.

She finishes seeing her last patients of the day and walks to the front desk to fill out billing forms.

One of the clinic nurses, Lila, stops her in the hallway. "I'm sorry, Dr. Mehta, but two people showed up, and they said they have to see you."

"Me?" Nandini asks. "Are you sure?"

"I am. They're asking to see you as soon as possible." Lila gives her an apologetic smile. "Hopefully it won't take too long."

Nandini always appreciated the way Lila gave difficult news. She wasn't sure if it was her purple-and-pink-flowered scrubs or big, Julia Roberts–style smile, but Lila could always say things in a way that made people feel comforted.

Her phone rings. Meghna *again*.

Nandini peeks into the waiting room and sees Ranjit's brother Rajan. He's sitting with a man Nandini doesn't recognize.

"Hi," he says when she walks toward him. "This is Arjun, my classmate from India. He's visiting us for the week and wanted to talk to a doctor."

Of course, she thinks. *Of course you feel you can show up to my place of work and have my time the second you want it.*

Just say no, a voice inside of her urges.

But she knows she won't. As much as she thinks of herself as a woman who speaks up, she knows that at the end of the day, she gives into guilt, into what's expected of her. And there's no way she can do anything that would look bad when her daughter is getting married next year.

She makes a mental promise to finish the appointment as quickly as possible, call Meghna back, and go home.

Nandini clenches her fists and makes sure she's still smiling. "Of course. Let me take you back to one of the rooms."

As she predicted, Arjun wants to discuss his parents' medical history and asks if Nandini has medications she can give him to take back to India.

After Rajan and Arjun leave, Nandini goes into her office. She brightens her phone screen. Her finger lingers over the name. *Meghna Patel.* A well-behaved name for a well-behaved woman. If they were both attending a Bollywood soap opera casting, Meghna's heavier build and conservative salwar kameez would make her a shoo-in for the part of "nurturing housewife who makes twenty rotlis a day," while Nandini's white coat and under-eye circles would land her the role of "bitchy mother who chose to work full-time."

Meghna picks up before the phone even rings.

"Meghna Ben, how ar—"

"Nandini Ben, I just saw your daughter."

Meghna's voice has a combative undertone. What happened to the quiet, docile woman Nandini saw just weeks ago?

"Oh, I see. Were you in the ci—"

"She was with someone. And I mean, WITH SOMEONE."

Nandini tries to keep her voice down. "Could you clarify what you me—"

"YOUR DAUGHTER WAS HUGGING AND KISSING AN-OTHER BOY IN THE MIDDLE OF THE STREET!"

Nandini presses her chapped hands against one of the broken chairs. This has to be a mistake. "Meghna Ben, you need to calm down. *Now.*"

Silence.

"Are you sure you saw Simran?"

"OF COURSE I'M SURE!"

A surge of anger, humiliation, and sadness starts to build in Nandini. But she squashes it. "Okay, Meghna, I'm sure there's some sort of explanation. I strongly suggest that you take a couple of seconds to collect yourself."

She hears Meghna take a deep breath, then another.

"Now," Nandini says. "What exactly did you see?"

Meghna describes Simran, wearing the dress that's Mami's favorite, and the other boy.

As Meghna speaks, layers of panic mesh together until they form a weight Nandini can no longer ignore. She collapses onto the broken chair. It's the boy from the party. She doesn't even need any more description. It's him. She's sure of it. What is Simran doing? Why would she be so self-destructive? And at a time like this?!

The tingling in her fingertips returns as Meghna says, "If these are the values your daughter was raised with, then I don't know if Kunal will be able to handle it."

That's it. This woman needs to be put in her place. "Excuse me, are you suggesting that Ranjit and I raised Simran to do this? That is completely inappropriate."

Ranjit would tell her to calm down. The bride's side is never supposed to create conflict with the groom's. Even though the bride's family is paying for everything, the groom's side still holds the power and needs to be deferred to.

"All I'm saying is that children learn how to behave from their parents."

"I think it's best that I hang up the phone now, Meghna."

"Hopefully, you'll call your daughter."

Nandini raises her voice. "I know how to be with my daughter, thank you."

She hangs up the phone.

Years ago, in a part of India she'll never visit again, a man made her feel small. Insignificant. After that, she learned all the ways a man could try to take her power. There was the senior resident who grabbed her butt every morning (when she tried to report him, she was told "that's just the way things have always been"). There was the boss of the first medical practice she applied to who told her that to be accepted, she had to socialize with them at strip clubs. There were the countless men at national conferences who freely commented on her appearance as if she existed solely for that.

But this was different. Different from all those men and even the women who had gossiped about her over the years. This was a fellow mother doubting her. Doubting her daughter. And she wouldn't let that continue.

She just had to figure out what the heck was going on with Simran.

Three

Simran

"What were you thinking?!" Nandini barks to Simran just one hour later.

One hour. Meghna Auntie probably called her house before even boarding the damn PATH train.

"I wasn't thinking *anything*, Mom. I was hanging out with my friend."

Friend. That's what she can almost call him. He's no longer someone she just read about in the paper.

Despite her tone, Simran's heart is still racing as she occupies a corner of a park bench. What exactly had Meghna Auntie seen? More importantly, had there been anything *to* see?

Her phone beeps with a text message.

Neil: It was really nice seeing you today.
Keep me updated about your work!

A *text* from *Neil*? How is this happening? She ignores the excitement sprouting in her chest. She and Neil are now texting.

She drowns out Mom's yelling and debates what to text back. She can't hesitate in the text box because then he'll see those bubbles pop up and know she's self-editing. Hmm, what does one type to their role model?

After a few seconds of agonizing, she types, It was really nice seeing you, too. And I'll definitely stay in touch. Thank you for everything.

"Why are you hanging out with him that closely?!" Mom asks after Simran tells her it was Neil. "I know you might not think this is a big deal, Simran, but you know how important a girl's reputation is. Once it's ruined, it's very difficult to change it back, especially with your future in-laws. Is this really how you want to start your life with them?"

"Ruined? How the heck could anything be ruined for being in *public* with a *friend*?"

Nandini ignores the question. "There's always something with you, Simran, isn't there? There just has to be."

"Seriously, Mom? You think this is fun for me?"

Neil: Thank YOU. I mean what I said.

Oh my god . . .

Okay, so maybe seeing Neil was fun. But still, she's never understood how her family could believe that she does these things on purpose. It was like in seventh grade, when Kyle Wilkins asked her if it was fun to wear huge glasses. *Yes, Kyle, yes, I love these hot pink frames that take over my face. Thank you so much for asking.*

She texts Neil back: I mean what I said, too.

And then, without thinking, she inserts a heart-eyed emoji. It's only after she hits SEND that she realizes her message looks flirty.

She's about to send a clarification when Neil sends a winking-face emoji. Time to stop texting.

"Don't give me your sob story about being misunderstood," her mom says.

Simran hears her mutter something to her dad, and she says, "Look, Mom. You know me. You know I have guy friends."

"I do," Mom confirms. "But Kunal's family sees things a little differently. At least, his mom does. She made it a point to imply that Dad and I must have raised you to think certain inappropriate things are okay."

"That's ridiculous," Simran scoffs.

How dare Meghna Auntie imply anything about the way her parents brought them up? Simran knew Meghna Auntie had dropped passive-aggressive comments before about how Mom's busy career (and the nannies who were always around) had to impede her homemaking duties, but those seemed more sympathetic and understanding. Nothing like this.

"I'm not going to change anything with anyone because of her. That's just *ridiculous*."

"*Beta*, you don't have much of a choice. She . . . she called me back to suggest that the wedding be called off."

"Are you kidding me? She can't say that."

But despite Simran's defiant tone, she's scared shitless. Call off the wedding? It was never supposed to come *close* to that. This isn't the way she wanted to start her relationship as a daughter-in-law to Meghna Auntie. Everyone's supposed to be happy right now.

"Well, that's what she said. And I'm not going to have my daughter paraded around as immoral or raised with questionable values. If she thinks we need to prove to her that you come from a good household, we'll do it," Mom says. Simran can tell that as much as Mom's pissed off at her, she's even more upset at Kunal's mom for saying these things in the first place. She just has to be careful now that she's at home with Dad. He'd want her to please Kunal's family.

"Is that what you did?" Simran asks. "Accommodate whatever your mother-in-law wanted when you were marrying Dad?"

Mom sighs. "My situation was different. But yes, that is what I did."

"How was your situation different?"

"That's not relevant right now."

"Every time I ask you some specific detail about your engagement, you say it isn't relevant. It *is* relevant right now."

"At this point, our concern is you. *Your* engagement."

"So that means I can't even ask my own mom about her life?"

"Look, *beta*, things are always hard at first. There's this . . . loneliness . . . that comes with being a woman and starting something new where all these expectations are placed on you," she reminds Simran, her voice softening as she dodges her question. "Whether it's with a husband, mother-in-law, new job, anything. Just have patience, and it'll eventually get better."

Classic immigrant mentality: take pride in putting up with difficulty.

"You know Nani passed her stubborn streak to both of us," she continues. "But even with that, when I was growing up, Nani told me to do anything I had to in order to be accepted. That's just how things are. There's no need to make things so difficult. Believe me, it's only going to hurt you in the end."

"Well, unlike what you suspect, I hate making you upset. Or worried. This is supposed to be a happy time," Simran says.

When there's no response, she adds, "Mom, I'm not like you. I'm not all dutiful or selfless or able to become someone different on a whim. I don't know when to hold myself back, even if it's the appropriate thing to do."

In elementary school, when their family met a renowned Hindu priest who refused to speak to girls, Simran threw a fit (a screaming fit, to be exact) at the sexism. She couldn't shut the hell up and let him be. The same thing happened again when she learned Hindu women aren't supposed to enter a temple or kitchen when they're menstruating because they're considered impure. Now she still can't do what she's supposed to.

"I know you'd never intend to be hurtful, *beta*. And all of these other things, they'll fall into place, with time," Mom says. "Trust me, if Nani was here, she'd tell you I wasn't always this way."

"Actually, I was going to ask if you've heard from Nani. We spoke last week for a few minutes and she said that the pipes were being fixed. But I've called her twice this week and there was no response. Do you think she's busy with the girls at school?"

"I'm not sure. She hasn't called me back, either," Mom says. "We need to confirm her flight information for your engagement party."

"Do you think something's wrong? I haven't checked her Facebook page lately."

Nani's latest obsession (outside of Dr. Phil and any thriller with the word "girl" in the title) is social media. She shares inspirational quotes on her profile every day and is now attempting to use emojis. Unfortunately, she hasn't figured out that the emoji is supposed to correlate with the message, so her latest upbeat, optimistic quotes have been accompanied with red angry faces.

Simran tells Mom to hold on while she checks Nani's Facebook profile. Nothing posted for five days. The last time they didn't hear from Nani was when she fell, broke a hip, and didn't tell them for one month. They found out from her neighbor. Ever since Nana passed away, she has what Mom calls "pathological independence."

"No, I'm, uh, sure everything's okay," Mom says. "At least, let's hope it is. I'll call her again today."

Kunal's reaction isn't any better.

"What the hell is going on?"

"I'm so sorry, honey. I promise I can explain," she says. Hearing Kunal's voice snaps Simran back to reality. The past couple of days with Neil haven't been her real life. Kunal is her real life. Their future marriage is her real life.

"Then please do, because it was so shitty for me to hear all this stuff from my mom about you and some other guy!" he yells, his voice barely audible over the shaky connection. "What were you even doing? And who were you with? Vishal?"

"No." She pauses. What *was* she even doing? And why would she ever be with anybody in a way that looked inappropriate? That's not who she is. "I was hanging out with someone I met at my book party. It was Neil Desai, that Indian writer from the *New York Times*."

There's silence on the other end, and for a second, she's worried Kunal has lost service.

But then she hears his voice, heavy with a mixture of confusion and sadness. "What? You were hanging out with that guy you've been following? The one you're a fan of? How did this even happen?"

She sits down at her desk, her hands shaking as she explains that she met Neil at her party and the conversations they've had since.

"I'm sorry," she says. "I don't want you to think that you can't trust me. I promise I was going to tell you about Neil and that it's nothing for you to worry about. You and I just haven't had time to talk and I . . . I thought you'd be excited. He's actually a good— no, great—person to be in touch with. He wants to help me with some ideas I have for articles."

"Well that's just *fantastic*," Kunal scoffs.

"Fantastic? Really?"

There's only the sound of Kunal's breathing.

"*Hello?*" she says.

"So that's it? Nothing happened? He's just some mentor you're fangirling over?"

"Nothing happened," she says.

"You know," he says, his voice softer than before, "it's been hard for both of us since I've been in Africa. I haven't been able to talk to you as much, and when we do talk, we're fighting more. I know you think I take you for granted, but I don't mean to. I really don't. And yes, it's been challenging for me to accept that there are some interests of yours I simply don't share. Or understand. But hearing from my mom that you were with some dude came out of nowhere. Kind of knocked the wind out of me, to tell you the truth."

"I'm so sorry," she whispers, remembering that one of the first things she loved about Kunal was his tenderness. Being on the receiving end of it made her feel more special, simply because it only emerged with select people at select times.

"I realized, maybe for the first time ever, how you must have felt about Rekha and me," he says.

Rekha and Kunal became friends on the first day of medical school orientation after they both signed up for the neurosurgery interest group. Thanks to some Facebook stalking, Simran quickly learned that Rekha was single and attractive (of course—and in that athletic, outdoorsy way that makes you want to work out . . . or stuff your face with Oreos). She depends on Kunal for emotional support with her erratic love life, high blood pressure, and family problems. Simran's jealousy waned after she spent more time with Rekha, but every once in a while, she pictures them in the dark library, delirious from sleep deprivation and their inevitable isolation from the rest of society. . . .

"Kunal, I'm glad you have people in your life who understand and share your interests. And I want you to be happy when I have that, too. I'm sorry everything with Neil started this way."

"But why? Why were you with him in a way that looked inappropriate?"

She pauses. Why *was* she with Neil that way? What the hell is wrong with her? Kunal's syllables anchor her back to the present.

But then another thought emerges. What if Kunal is all she knows? What if their comfort is just that—a comfort—and that's why excitement with Neil had a chance to break through? She forces herself to stop thinking that way. No, she simply let herself get carried away. Kunal's her future husband. Her home.

"I'm sorry. I can't say that enough. And I promise you nothing happened and that we were just meeting to discuss some ideas. Look, I love you," she says. "I love you so much. Please don't be upset. I'm really sorry."

It's the truth. She tends to miss Kunal the most when they fight, after the fire of the argument is extinguished, leaving only embers of intense longing behind. That's what happens after you're together for a long time: you learn how to fight with rhythm, and you learn when it needs to end.

"Let's just talk later," he suggests. "I think I need some space."

Her actions come into focus as reality settles in. Her fiancé shouldn't be worried or angry or upset. He doesn't deserve that. Maybe she *is* at fault. A part of her wishes she hadn't met Neil, that this whole thing had never been triggered in the first place.

That Saturday, Simran's sprawled across an old blanket at the southeastern corner of Central Park. Solitude has become more of a need than a want since she's been engaged. She doesn't indulge in any of the behaviors she thought she would: staring at her ring incessantly, binging on trashy wedding shows on TLC, or looking up bridal diet plans. Instead, she craves space to reflect on everything from her career to wedding planning.

God, wedding planning. There's something about an Indian wedding that transforms an entire family. Every detail becomes a point of anxiety. Mom texts her with important concerns: How will they prevent her dad's older brother from drinking too much and breaking out in dance moves from *Saturday Night Fever*? Will Kunal's endearing but creepy cousin, Dev, try to hit on her picky but desperate cousin, Aarti? What if they run out of hotel rooms—or worse, food?

"Hindu weddings are supposed to be a time for the community to reunite," Mom tried explaining when Simran asked why they had to invite so many people. "A poorly done one reflects poorly on the *parents* of the bride and groom."

Simran doubts that the three-day occasion will be classified as "poor" by anyone. As of yesterday, six hundred guests are on the

potential invitation list. There are even people who are still inviting *themselves*, which can be common with Indian weddings. For
some reason, people have no shame against casually mentioning
their invitation "never made it" or "may not have been mailed
yet." One auntie even had the audacity to pencil in her grandchildren's names and a smiley face on the card.

Simran puts on her Chanel sunglasses and people watches.
Every New Yorker seems to flock here when the thermometer
crosses seventy degrees. A line of girls sunbathe on striped beach
towels while a frail, elderly woman skims through a novel with
a shirtless man and woman on the cover.

From the corner of her eye, Simran notices a group of teenage
boys playing lacrosse. She still wonders if she fell for Kunal during one of his lacrosse games, when his aggression and testoster-
one surge helped him win (the way they still do). Her mind drifts
to the most significant game she attended, when they became a
couple.

Kunal never directly asked her to be his girlfriend; like many
relationships where both people are friends first, things fell into
place in an unplanned way. There was no first date or "will you
go out with me" routine. To her parents, the adolescent years
were purely for academics, to earn that "My Child Is an Honor
Student" bumper sticker. All Indian parents saw relationships as
taboo (and all Indian children eventually learned how to sneak
around). Romance was an inappropriate distraction, something
she only had through books or television.

Not that she had a chance at romance, anyway. She spent
many middle school dances in the dark corners while her fellow
classmates swayed to songs by Savage Garden and *NSYNC.
(Side note: her parents forbade her from attending said dances

once they learned there was slow dancing. According to them, only married people were allowed to slow dance. She had to tell them slow dancing was "out of style" in order for them to allow her to attend prom.)

Luckily, by high school, she learned that:

1. Bringing rotli and chickpea curry for lunch is not the way to make friends at school.
2. Large, thick glasses don't pair well with low self-esteem.
3. A bowl cut is never excusable on an adolescent girl trying to leave the dork days.

Starting at the beginning of freshman year, she had found Kunal attractive in a way that was difficult to explain and often negated by her friends. He wasn't the kind of boy most girls would look at, more likely to be described as "cute" than "hot" but still distinctive, with a babyish face on a manly body. An anatomical paradox. He also didn't match the complete list she had made of qualities a guy had to have, but those were influenced by Bollywood movies; Kunal was real, so naturally, he had a leg up.

For months, she was happy to keep her emotions confined in the margins of her class notes and in whispered conversations with her girlfriends. She and Sheila had to give him a code name—"Sonya"—so her family wouldn't find out. She did what any other girl touched with unrequited love did: fantasized about him, overanalyzed their interactions, told herself no girl would ever like him the way she did, and memorized tiny details about him, like the heart-shaped birthmark under his left ear and the way he always shifted back and forth on his white Nikes when he was talking to someone.

Sure, they were friends—*good* friends—but she knew as well as anyone that people had lower expectations for their friends than for a potential significant other. And it wasn't a cliché-dorky-girl-liking-popular-guy scenario; if anything, it was almost the opposite: girl liking nerd and not feeling brainy enough for him, considering his last girlfriend had been the Science Olympiad champion and first chair of the orchestra.

On some level, she was aware that she was special in her own way, should not want anyone who did not want her, and all those other lessons she metabolized through the final seconds of *Full House* episodes. She tried her best to tuck her hope away and find gratitude in their friendship. Perhaps she was too influenced by *Kuch Kuch Hota Hai*, the revered Bollywood movie where two friends end up together after not seeing each other for years, but she imagined that, at the very least, Kunal would look back on her one day—preferably when she was worldly and accomplished—and see her as "the one who got away."

But things changed sophomore year, two weeks before finals. She raced to the park from a newspaper editor meeting so that she could watch Kunal's lacrosse game. That day was the championship game, so a lot of their mutual friends were there, which gave her an excuse to show her face and see him play for the first time.

Unfortunately, her meeting ran late and she got to the park just as the game was ending. The place smelled like a mixture of sweat and freshly cut grass. After the clusters of parents and players cleared the field, she jumped off the squeaky bleachers to congratulate Kunal. Instead of running to the bench, she dawdled at the base of the first bleacher, determined to wait until he was alone. Out of the corner of her eye, she watched him remove his helmet and shake his curly hair in a way that reminded her of a Gatorade commercial.

She approached him and blurted that she thought he played well.

"Thanks," he said, his dark eyes almost appearing lighter with the residual adrenaline rush.

As he removed his gloves, he exchanged a quick "good game" with two of the other players. The rest of the team usually went out for pizza or ice cream after each game, but Kunal headed straight home to study.

Before she could think of anything else to say, his best friend, Edward, approached them. Edward had a massive overbite and hunched shoulders, thanks to a perpetually overstuffed L.L.Bean book bag. He and Kunal often bored the rest of the group with their geeky science-is-the-reason-life-exists conversations. They compared—and often competed with—report cards, SAT scores, and, later, college applications. But unlike Kunal, Edward never cared for sports and spent most of his after-school time with the debate team.

They all usually hung out in a large group on weekends, playing board games in someone's basement or wolfing down French fries at Chili's. But that day, Edward was acting more awkward than usual and immediately mumbled something about needing to get home once he noticed that Kunal and Simran were talking.

"What's up with him?" she asked Kunal.

Kunal tucked his lacrosse stick under his arm and looked down at her. "I think he felt weird."

"Weird? About what?"

He shifted his eyes, uncomfortable with the question. "He thinks we flirt a lot."

Really?!

This wasn't the first time someone had shared this sentiment, but it *was* the first time she heard it from Kunal.

"That *is* weird," she said, trying to be nonchalant by avoiding his gaze.

"I don't think it is."

"You don't?"

"No," he affirmed. "Because it's true."

There they were—clear, simple, to the point; three words she had been fantasizing about for over sixty days. Her legs vibrated, and she was pretty sure that the people in the parking lot could hear her heartbeat.

It's true? It's true that we flirt?

How long has that been happening?

OH! MY! GOD!

Then, before she could bombard herself with more questions, he leaned down and kissed her. She debated with herself on what to do, how to stand, where to look, but by the time she settled on a coy smile that would make Jane Austen proud, he grabbed her chin and planted another kiss on the tip of her nose. This time, she felt his salty sweat as everything around them faded.

She had no idea what to say or expect (in television shows, a loud "wooooo" usually erupted from the audience after a romantic adolescent moment). She knew she would rush home and try to preserve the moment in her diary. And even though her writing would never do it justice, she also knew that those seconds would always remain with her, glued in her mental scrapbook, safely protected behind laminated pages with the perfect accessory stickers.

Instead of slicing the silence, Kunal wrapped his large hand over hers, without interlacing their fingers. Even his hand clasping was assertive.

It was crazy, but Simran could already see their future unrolling before them. She thought of how they would be the perfect husband and wife; a power team. She saw him speaking at his medical school graduation—they'd probably be married by then—and saying, "Lastly, I'd like to thank the woman who made it all possible," and with his large hands motioning to her, in her Jackie O–inspired dress. They would probably live in a charmingly tiny apartment for a few years before settling in a Westchester mansion.

She saw all of this, but what she didn't see were the moments in between. She didn't see them meeting around their suburb after school, just for a chance to cuddle in his beaten-up back seat. She didn't see them holding on when the other couples around them chose to let go. She didn't see them sneaking in phone calls when everyone in their houses was asleep. She didn't see them sharing a dance as prom king and queen and later, their nakedness. And she definitely didn't see them returning to that same spot in the park, year after year, takeout and wine in hand, just to remind themselves of where they began.

Nandini

Nandini jams her keys into the door. Another twelve-hour day at the office and still more paperwork to finish at home: prescriptions, lab orders, phone notes. She now spends more time in front of the computer than with patients.

There was a time when all she wanted was to be a physician. In India, there was no undergraduate education before medical school. There was just one test with one chance to take it. Her best friend failed it and committed suicide three days later. Everyone blamed his parents.

"Don't be like me," her mother said on a weekly basis. "Have a job so you never have to be reliant on anyone." Nandini would hear her ask Papa before doing anything. Inviting her sister over. Giving the bhaji walla five extra rupees when he delivered fresh okra, peppers, and onion every morning. Making poori instead of rotli for dinner.

Her mother was right. Nandini's career drew a thick line that Ranjit's family never crossed—but of course, the respect didn't excuse her from other duties.

Duties.

Years ago, Nandini tried to explain this concept to Terri, one of her nurses at work.

"How do arranged marriages even work?" Terri had asked.

Older family members suggested a match based on everything from horoscopes to family backgrounds to socioeconomics. The families met at the girl's house. Sometimes, the girl was asked to perform something. A song or poem. Nandini had asked Mami if she could talk about a patient. Of course Mami said no. So Nandini recited a story, the same one Mami told during her own arrangement, of a woman who travels to find God and save her husband. It was a tale of wifely sacrifice and persistence, virtues that both Nandini and Mami didn't really believe but had to embrace, like a starched, stuffy sari.

Then, over chai, both sets of parents would discuss everything from family lineages to traditions, expectations about

grandchildren, and potential wedding plans. With so many fac-
tors aligned, the idea was that the couple would be compatible.

Duties.

Responsibilities.

Family.

These were a marriage's foundation. Love would come later.

Terri's jaw dropped. No dates? No romance? No ability to
choose? Wasn't that a huge risk?

If she had been young, Nandini would have laughed. Arranged marriages were the common way. She grew up knowing
she would have one, just like all the other women she knew. And
any marriage was a risk, arranged or not. Without the expectation of romance or chemistry, there was supposed to be less of a
chance of disappointment or growing apart or, as Terri once said
when discussing her ex-husband, "losing the spark."

Nandini runs through this conversation now, wondering if
she would still say the same things. She walks through the dark
house, toward the kitchen. The brass pots and pans hanging
above the stove give off a faint glow. All she can see is the blue
halo from Ranjit's Mac in the living room. He's floating in his
usual post-work routine: sitting in front of his laptop, scanning
through God-knows-what with CNN on in the background.

That was the way things had become over the years, both of
them retreating to separate corners, similar to the plastic figures
she placed in her dollhouse as a little girl. Division within unity.
With Ronak and Simran gone, it may have made sense to downsize to another house, but there were too many people coming
through, making their home a lazy Susan for every Indian in
New Jersey. The nieces who spent summers with Nandini so she
could discipline them. Ranjit's entire family, who stopped by un-

announced for extended periods of time. Friends of friends of friends who needed a bed to sleep in. She always knew Indians didn't believe in boundaries when it came to relationships, but being married to the most successful son in a family means that they can never move.

"Hi." She approaches Ranjit behind the brown leather recliner and touches his shoulder in a manner that's both clinical and comforting. His browser is on LinkedIn. He recently found out his officer manager had been stealing money from the practice for the past nine months and told Nandini he'd planned to find a replacement by the end of the week.

He lowers the screen and faces Nandini. "How was your day?"

"Same as always. Any luck with the manager position?"

"None yet." He's wearing navy blue scrubs and brown house slippers.

Ranjit started his own surgical clinic years ago. It took him only three months to realize that he hated the administrative tasks. Nandini helped him find his first office manager, who moved to California two years ago for a job at Google. Since then, they've struggled to find someone stable. Nandini doesn't let herself think about how even her husband's struggle is a privilege. *He* gets to make the decisions on who works in *his* place. He's the boss.

A cup of chai, the watery kind from a tea bag, is on the side table. Nandini puts a coaster underneath it. "Can I help?"

"Not with anything right now, but I'll need you over the next couple weeks. We both know you're better at interviewing someone for a job," he says, referring to the string of jobs she herself interviewed for at the beginning of their marriage: Walmart cashier, bank teller, and nanny. The money from those jobs allowed Ranjit to complete his residency training and their family to live in a friend's unheated, moldy basement. Nandini drove a used Camry with one duct-taped window. That car somehow lasted until her own residency.

Ranjit glances at the grandfather clock in their living room. "You ready to make the phone call?"

"Hm," she says, nodding. "It's a good time in India now."

She takes the black phone off its charger and dials their calling card number, followed by the astrologer's phone number. She realizes they are being old-fashioned by depending on an astrologer to confirm that Simran's wedding date is auspicious, the way her mother did for her, and her mother before that. It was thought that by studying the patterns of the stars and planets, an astrologer could determine which date would ensure that a marriage was destined for success. *Blessed*.

The operators' accents switch from American to Indian. Static fills the line.

Beep, beep. Beep, beep. Beep, beep.

"Not there. We'll try later." She puts the phone back.

Ranjit follows her to the kitchen. There are onions and carrots that can be put into a soup. It's all she has energy for. Ranjit won't complain about her lack of cooking. She's one of the lucky ones, she knows, now having to spend days in the kitchen only when his family stops by.

But soon that amicability will be over. Years ago, Ranjit showed he could handle the worst of her. She couldn't expect him to do it again. She still hasn't figured out how to tell Ranjit about the phone call she received two months ago. She still hasn't decided when she's going to break her news to him.

"Has Simran called you today?" Ranjit asks, his lean shape becoming clearer in her periphery.

Nandini shakes her head. "Not yet. She must be busy with school. She usually calls by now."

There was always one child who loved from a distance and one who cared a little more. Ronak sent an occasional text every few days, but it was Simran who made sure to get cards for Mother's and Father's Day, who checked on Nandini when guests were coming over.

"I wish the astrologer picked up," Nandini says as she takes a chef's knife and slices an onion down the middle. "Meghna Ben has already asked me if she can order a mangal sutra. After what just happened with Simran, I don't want anything ruining or delaying plans."

Nandini reaches beneath her shirt collar to touch her own black-and-gold mangal sutra, the necklace indicating a woman is married. Although Indians didn't traditionally have engagement rings, many American customs became commonplace in Indian weddings over the years: proposals, bridesmaids and groomsmen, first dances, cake cutting. Some Indian girls even wore white wedding gowns after seeing them in movies and television shows throughout their childhoods. Simran had yet to ask Nandini about lenghas or tikas or mandap colors.

"I don't know what's gotten into Simran lately," Nandini says.

Ranjit plucks a flaccid grape from a ceramic bowl on the counter. "She's always been this way."

"Yes, but something's different. In some ways, she's surprisingly ambivalent, and in others, she's curious. She keeps asking questions," Nandini says. "About our engagement."

He walks toward her and places his hands on the counter. "What if we just told her everything?"

"Everything? Your side or mine?"

He shrugs. "Both."

When she doesn't respond, he adds, "I think she can handle it. She's almost someone's wife. An adult. Isn't it okay to treat her like one?"

Simran's wedding is coming too quickly and not quickly enough. Nandini remembers what Mami told her years ago: a daughter is yours for so many years, and then suddenly, she's gone, belonging to another family, and there's nothing that ever seems right about it.

Mami noted this while teaching Nandini how to make rotlis in preparation for the move to her in-laws' home. The impending separation made their exchanges tender that final month. She can still see it: the way she had to roll the dough into a tiny ball, douse it with flour, and then press it flat. Soon, she would have to show Simran how to do the same. Soon, it wouldn't be appropriate for her to call her daughter every night and tell her the latest story about Ranjit's family or her patients.

It seems that just yesterday Simran was five years old, visiting India for the first time, giving the beggars in the Bombay airport her bags of Tootsie Rolls, unaware of why that would only cause more problems. And now, she'll be in a red-and-white sari, pretending to be docile as the maharaja chants hymns.

"What's wrong?" Ranjit asks, squinting at her face in the way he would at one of his patients.

"It's just the onions."

He nods and turns around before putting his teacup in the sink. "Danesh Bhai called to ask about her wedding. He wanted to congratulate us."

"That's great," Nandini says, now used to people calling and mentioning her children's weddings. "We'll stop by their house when the invitations are done."

"Of course," Ranjit says.

In India, a bride's parents hand-delivered wedding invitations to community members who were older. Ranjit and Nandini somehow managed this for Ronak's wedding. Maybe they should have held back from upholding that exhausting tradition in New Jersey in the first place. But now, there was no way they could act differently for Simran's. People would already be expecting it.

Despite all the changes that occurred from living in America, some traditions of the arranged marriage process remained. Elders had to be respected. Community had to be impressed. The bride's family was responsible for maintaining relationships and reputations.

You care so much about what people think, Simran would say, shaking her head. But was it so terrible to want the well wishes of others? It was easy for Simran to complain when she had no idea how rejection felt, when she had no idea how so many things felt.

Nandini and Ranjit settle at the dining table. There's only the sound of their spoons hitting the bowls and Ranjit's hand reaching into a giant paper box for saltine crackers. He takes his bowl to the stove and gets seconds.

She watches his hands grip the ladle with precision, as though he's in one of his surgeries. Ranjit handles everything in a manner that is both delicate and firm. They don't disappear for weekend getaways or exchange a kiss before work, but there is something palpable between them, as though their duty has smuggled pockets of respect with it. She has a newfound appreciation for it lately, when they reminisce about the kids' childhoods or gossip about close friends on car rides back from dinner parties.

When they're finished, she stacks one bowl inside the other, takes them to the sink, and washes them and his teacup with lemon Palmolive soap. She plays a Dev Anand album on the iPod and wipes the stovetop with a sponge. Ranjit heads back toward the living room.

Nandini dries her hands on a maroon dish towel and darkens the iPod screen.

She turns off the light and walks toward the curved dual staircase that overlooks their high-ceilinged foyer. Simran insisted they put a table with a giant vase there.

Nandini's steps make the wooden floors groan. She reaches the second floor, passes the three guest bedrooms, and does a quick check of Ronak's and Simran's rooms out of habit. When Simran left for college, Nandini sat on her canopy bed every evening, and hugged her daughter's large stuffed animals.

Now, she continues to the master bedroom. Once she shuts the door, she tiptoes to the closet and removes a shoe box that's buried under a pile of clothes.

The official papers came from him last week. Nandini flips through them, frantically and then one at a time. Maybe if she stares at the pages long enough, she'll know what to do, what the right answer is. She scans the Times New Roman font again and again. Two hours pass this way until she surrenders to fatigue. She washes her face, puts on the same Oil of Olay moisturizer she's used for three decades, and brushes her teeth. Her eyes close as she whispers a prayer to Ganesha for the things she will soon reveal.

Four

Simran

The next morning in lab, Simran reviews research study after research study until the computer screen makes her eyes sore.

Her master's in psychology program is a mixture of lectures and research. People complete the program to apply for a PhD or do further clinical research, since the program isn't enough to be a licensed psychologist.

She only has one month left in the spring semester, and after the summer, she'll be done. The date, October 1, has been circled on her calendar since she started. Simran thought becoming a therapist would mean she'd someday see patients in her cozy Park Avenue office and say things like, "So, tell me about your mother," before jotting down their responses into a leather-bound notebook and helping them arrive at a life-changing breakthrough.

Instead, she spends most of her days sitting in lectures, analyzing research papers about psychotherapy, and wondering about which greasy food cart she'll pick up lunch from.

She scrolls through her text messages. The last one is from Neil.

Neil: How are the article ideas going?

Simran: Actually about to do some research
now. At school so have to be shady about it
since I should be working on my psychology
project.

Neil: Ah, got it. Good luck being shady!

Simran: That's so nice of you to even check
in. Thank you.

Neil: I was wondering how you were
doing . . .

Simran: I was wondering how you were
doing, too ☺

She puts her phone away just as she hears some footsteps behind her.

"Everything okay there, Simran?" Dr. Bond, the head of the
lab, asks while clearing his throat.

"Oh, hi!" Simran swirls her chair around, almost knocking
over a mug of lukewarm coffee. Her eyes meet his brown, short-
sleeved, flannel button-down shirt as she keeps a sheepish grin
on her face.

He glances at her computer screen. A HuffPost article about
how women are perceived in the workplace is prominently dis-
played. This is her luck: her adviser doesn't stop by while she's
sifting through research studies. He comes in during the one
minute she's doing research for a potential article. At least she
closed the one from *Cosmopolitan* titled "The Complete Evolution
of Kim Kardashian's Hair."

Dr. Bond is usually in his office or off at meetings where he
creates dozens of new project ideas. He stays at school until eight

every night and then takes the train back to Westchester. When anyone meets with him, he offers them a cup of Earl Grey and biscuits from his hometown of Newcastle, England.

He raises a graying eyebrow and motions to Simran's screen. The man never expresses blatant anger, and she still can't decide if that's scary or commendable.

Kunal would freak out if she told him about this. He believes it's inexcusable to not focus at school. His mind doesn't even wander during hours of medical school lectures, so he wouldn't understand why she had to read random articles when she should be doing her project. She wonders if that's why she hasn't told him that school's felt a little tougher lately.

"I'm sorry," she blurts to Dr. Bond. "I was just . . . finishing something up before I got started on my data analysis."

Translation: *I'm bored.*

"Okay," he says in an I-don't-believe-you tone, holding out the second syllable of "okay" so it sounds like more "okaaaaaaaaaaay."

Simran considers offering a guilty laugh but decides she's not graceful or cute enough to pull one off. Before she turns her head back to the (now-blank) computer screen, he pulls up a chair next to her.

"Oh, hello," she says, as if seeing him for the first time.

The clock says it's almost eleven fifty. In ten minutes, she's supposed to meet Sheila, who is in a neighboring lab doing human rights research.

"Simran, I've been meaning to talk to you," Dr. Bond says. He takes a quick glance around the room to make sure it's empty. "There has been some concern about the way you've been lately."

"The way I've *been*? What do you mean?"

"I was at lunch with some of the professors, and your name

came up," he says. "There was more than one who thought you haven't been as focused."

"Really? Me?"

He nods and gives her a look that's a mixture of sympathy and something she's never seen on him before: disappointment. For a second, her parents' faces flash through her mind.

"I, um, I'm sorry," she says, slumping in the chair. "I've just had a lot going on lately."

Dr. Bond and Simran exchange a tight smile. He buttons his tweed jacket. Dr. Bond must shop at a store called Tweed Daily. She's often pictured his closet as the tweed version of Doug Funnie's, the cartoon character she loved as a kid who had twenty versions of the same outfit.

"I promise I won't let any concerns come up again," she says.

"Well, it's getting a little late for that."

"What do you mean?" she asks.

"I'm afraid you're in danger of being on academic probation."

"What?" she whispers. "How is that possible?"

"For starters, your exams didn't go so well last week, and as far as your research evaluation goes . . . well, you missed the last two meetings."

She turns away from him. Even though Ronak has been the star student of the family, she's never had a teacher be concerned about her schoolwork. Sure, her report cards always said something along the lines of, *Simran is interesting in that she either reads books or talks too much. There's no middle ground.* But nothing like this. Plus, her neat handwriting and punctual completion of assignments showed that she was motivated and wanted to make something of herself. And academic *probation*? Indian kids don't get put on academic probation.

Dr. Bond leans forward. "Simran, you and I both know that I've always raved about you: your potential, your connection with others. God knows we don't have enough people here with a real personality. I know you can do great things for this field. However, if you don't start improving, then we will have no choice . . . but to let you go."

"*Go?* I can't go," she insists.

"I know that's a difficult thing to hear. But our program is competitive, and we have to have faith that our students will represent us well once they matriculate. A big part of your next step—whether that's a job, a PhD, what have you—is the recommendations you get from the faculty. You know that the deadline for deciding what you want to do is coming up. None of the professors will want to write recommendations for clinical work *or* further schooling for a student who isn't able to keep up. If your performance isn't to par, you won't be able to graduate with a degree from here."

Dr. Bond keeps talking, but Simran shuts him out. Not graduate? There's no coming back from that type of low blow. Her stomach churns as she pictures telling her family and friends she doesn't have a career.

"Please," she begs, cutting him off. "Please let me make this up somehow. I can turn all of this around. I *will*."

"Do you like it here?" he asks. "Really like it?"

"Yes," she blurts. "Of course."

It's true. She's enjoyed learning about everything from organizational psychology to generalized anxiety disorder. Dr. Bond has been a supportive mentor. Her classmates are compassionate, never cutthroat. And in many ways, she's found the environment to be more laid-back than undergrad.

So then what the hell has been wrong with her lately? First, the Neil situation, and now this? Has she been more out of it than she thought? This is the period of her life when she's supposed to step it up and become a real adult. She can't believe she's allowed herself to slack *now*.

Dr. Bond is still looking at her, probably analyzing her shifting facial expressions. Psychology classes have taught her how to read body language. Right now, Dr. Bond's downturned eyes and his hand propped under his chin reminds her of the way Kunal looks when watching that commercial about abandoned kittens and puppies needing a home.

She faces him and says, "I want to be here and finish what I started. Please."

"I hear what you're saying. It takes a lot of work to become a therapist. Think about everything you've already invested. The undergraduate classes, applying here, starting research, preparing for exams. I don't want all of that to disappear for you. But it's not all up to me, Simran. You know that."

"I do," she says, her pulse quickening. "But I can fix this."

"We'll see," he says as he gets up to leave the lab. "I think we should talk again soon. There's a lot you and I can discuss."

"I agree," she says. "Can we meet sometime this week? I'm going to come up with a plan to handle this, and it would be helpful to go through it with you."

He nods. "I think that sounds like a great idea."

She clenches her fists around a stack of paper. She needed this kick in the ass. Sure, things with school may be monotonous now, but just like any relationship, it's not right to let complacency erode the future. She needs to get to work.

The words circulate through her mind. *Academic probation. Academic probation. Academic probation.* She texts Sheila about rescheduling lunch. Then she removes a piece of paper from the printer and makes lists. One for how to improve on the last set of exams, another of the professors she can meet with during office hours, and lastly, points for the next time she speaks to Dr. Bond.

Forty-five minutes later, Sheila approaches Simran's desk.

"Hey, sorry I had to cancel lunch. Can we meet sometime later?"

She nods. "Sure."

Simran glances up at her. Sheila's cheeks are flushed, and her eyes appear swollen.

"What's wrong?" Simran asks.

"My parents definitely know I'm dating someone," Sheila says. "They just don't know who."

"That's a good thing," Simran says. "They'd freak out if they knew who."

"Yeah, I know," she agrees glumly. "But it's just weird. I mean, it's *been* weird, and I didn't really expect anything else. Like yesterday, we're hanging out, having this great conversation, and my dad calls and I had to tell Alex not to talk or make any noise, so my dad couldn't hear him. It's so fucking shady."

Simran scans the lab. No sign of Dr. Bond. She still shouldn't leave.

"Sorry I'm having a major meltdown," Sheila says. "It's just been a really rough day. Are you okay to talk about this now?"

"I can talk for a little bit," Simran says. "Let's get some food. You shouldn't keep all of this bottled up."

In a matter of months, Simran's program will be over and Sheila will quit her job to start law school at NYU. They had this silly idea that they could always coordinate their careers.

"Do you really think your dad knows?" Simran asks once they're in line at their go-to falafel cart. They don't have time to go to the café across the street that's famous for its Instagram-worthy avocado toasts.

"I have no idea. You know how he is," Sheila says.

Sheila's dad should have been in the CIA. The scariest part is that he'll never let on just how much he knows. He just waits for his kids to come clean. With a potbelly and full cheeks, he's always reminded Simran of a teddy bear (one who could claw the shit out of you if you deceived him, of course).

Sheila's dilemma began with an innocuous LSAT study date, which led to post-exam drinks in the West Village, and then a series of hookups in the following months. Even though Sheila never saw it getting this far, Simran knows that she secretly takes pride in the fact that, unlike her last boyfriends (all Indian), Alex is her intellectual equal, and their evolution from a friendship has made things go smoother than anything before. They're the type of couple that spends Sunday mornings drinking French-pressed coffee, reading all of the *New York Times* front-page stories, then watching the latest episode of *The Handmaid's Tale*.

Simran was there the first time Sheila tried to bring up the topic to her dad; not Alex specifically, but the idea of interracial marriage. She was received with the disheartening "after all the sacrifices we made in coming to this country, the only thing we ask for is you don't disappoint us" speech.

Simran listens to her but keeps her commentary brief. Sheila often just needs to vent and rarely takes any advice given to her. They both pretend not to notice.

Just as Simran is about to tell her that they should get back to their desks, Sheila asks, "So you're still in touch with Neil, huh?" The skin around her mouth tightens. Her eyes dart to the side.

"You're doing your judgmental face," Simran says.

"No, I'm not!" Sheila says.

"You are. Just say what you're really thinking."

Sheila faces her. "I don't know how to really say it."

Simran gives her a look that says, *Since when do you struggle with what to say?*

"I guess I'm torn," Sheila says.

"About what?"

"That night at your party, you just looked so in awe. And you get this weird smile when you mention him. I get that he's exciting and inspiring and happens to be hot in a bookish way. And I wouldn't want you to miss out on that type of connection. There's already enough drama when it comes to planning an Indian wedding, and I'd hate this to be a part of it for you and Kunal. I just want you to be careful."

"I *am* careful," Simran says.

And I love my fiancé, she says to herself, as she pictures Kunal's curly hair and rough hands. She wishes he was back home already, that their lives could be normal again.

"If you say so." Sheila's look conveys the sense of understanding that's always been the foundation of their friendship: *I don't totally get what you're doing, but I respect you figuring it out.*

Sheila squeezes her curly hair into a no-nonsense bun. She has the type of beauty that's debatable, with tiny eyes, full lips, and a five-six build that borders on what Indian aunties would call "healthy." Not tender, girl-next-door pretty, but astute, I'm-your-boss attractive, the ideal kind for an aspiring judge and women's rights advocate.

Simran tells Sheila she'll call her tomorrow. She needs to get back to work, and they could stay outside for the entire day if given the chance. They pulled an all-nighter the first time Simran stayed at Sheila's house, when they were eight years old. That was the same night Simran learned that Sheila rarely cried, not even while they watched *The Lion King*, which made Simran a sloppy mess. Sheila also hated Lisa Frank stationery, while Simran begged her parents for it. In fact, they're still so different that most people are surprised that they're friends, let alone best friends, as though friendship is something that can be plugged into an algebraic formula. What everyone doesn't see is that in addition to the potent power of history, they also have some of the same contradictions: a love for trashy reality television and classic literature, a need to be career- and family-oriented, and a tendency to take on too many side projects.

Simran's steps back to lab are swift, ready to prove Dr. Bond wrong. Columbia's campus makes her wish she was a photographer. They pass the empowered statue of Athena sitting on her throne with a leafed crown. Her arms are raised, and her palms face the sky, as if to say, *Welcome to my place*.

Simran's phone buzzes with a text message.

> Kunal: Got a little Internet access! See you in one week.

Simran: Can't wait for you to be back.

> Kunal: I know. I miss you.

Simran: I miss you, too.

> Kunal: I miss your body. Need to grab your butt right when I see you.

Simran: LOL, you're ridiculous . . . but I miss
your butt too.

She inserts a heart emoji into her last text. If she could call Kunal, he'd know what to say, how to comfort her. She reads her texts again. He'll be back in seven days. Her life will make sense again.

Outside the lab window, there's only New York and the unimposing, soft pink of spring. A group of fit, chic twenty-something girls, all in Alo workout clothes, probably walking from their SoulCycle class to Sweetgreen. The day hangs on to her shoulders the way all heavy things do.

If Simran's parents heard her conversation with Dr. Bond, she doesn't know if they'd yell or sit back in shock, wondering what they had done wrong. Kunal would start coming up with an action plan. It would probably be a distilled version of the one he made for himself in high school to ensure the highest GPA in their school's history. *Meet with teachers outside of class. Ask about extra credit. Double up on courses to add more A's to your transcript.*

She sits in front of the computer and reviews the list she made earlier. She clicks on the tab for the Internet and prepares to send out a slew of e-mails. She types and revises and types and revises, unaware that slowly, things will fall apart.

Nandini

"Remind me to pray that in my next life, I come back as a white man," Nandini says as she scans the long wine list.

Greg, her former attending from residency, tilts his head back and laughs, the same low-pitched chuckle that he had in residency. "It's not all that it's cracked up to be."

"Please." Nandini rolls her eyes. "When I walked in here, the hostess took one look at me and I knew she was thinking that I was in the wrong place."

Greg raises his eyebrows. "Are you sure that wasn't just in your head?"

"No! Even when we've been meeting vendors for Simran's wedding, I can tell that they're judging us, maybe comparing us to some Indian family that was terrible to work with, since, you know, we're all the same. The discrimination never ends."

She turns back to the wine list. When she and Ranjit moved to America, they and so many of their friends were doubted because of their accents. After 9/11, the racism took on a new texture, one that became laced with fear. Not to mention that being a woman meant even more judgment and questioning from peers and patients than Ranjit ever had. The sheer audacity of people, to think they kne—

"Nandini," Greg says, interrupting her thoughts. "Your mind is racing. I can see it on your face."

"You're right. I need to take a breath," she says. "I read this quote that said, 'If you want to imagine what a woman's brain is like, imagine a browser with three thousand tabs open.' Couldn't be more accurate."

She didn't expect Greg to understand. He had been raised in Westchester by parents who were on the board of every big museum in Manhattan. His family portraits, all pressed shirts and light and bright colors, reminded her of Polo Ralph Lauren ads. Before he had gone to medical school and later become her attending in residency, he had been a professional football player.

But despite his life of privilege, or maybe even because of it, she was shocked when he took her aside after her first patient presentation and said, "You're smart, Nandini. Really smart. I know it's tough here, especially for you. But you can go really far if you want, and I'm going to do my best to make sure you're given the opportunities you deserve." In India, there were so few women in scientific fields that mentors were unheard of. But here, an older white man stuck to his promise for her. Greg made sure Nandini had access to the best mentors for her research projects and then nominated her as Resident of the Year.

"So is that why you still haven't officially accepted my offer?" Greg asks now. "Because you think you'll be discriminated against?"

"That is a part of it, yes," Nandini says before she tells the waiter she'd like a glass of Malbec. "We both know your patients and your entire office staff would be shocked to go from having you as a head doctor to having me. But there's also that *tiny* part about me having to relocate to Baltimore while, you know, my entire life is in New Jersey."

"There is that," Greg says. "What did your family say? I'm sure they'd want you to make the right decision for your career."

Nandini faces the empty plate in front of her.

"You still haven't told them?" Greg asks. "Why?"

"I can't. I want to so badly. And I thought that once my kids were settled, it would finally be my time. But there's so much going on right now. Ronak just got married. Now it's Simran's turn, and things aren't quite as . . . smooth. I don't know if I can throw this at my family right now."

"They'll understand. They know you've hit a wall at your job. And I understand why you feel indecisive and hesitant. I get it.

But this is a chance to practice medicine in the way you always wanted, the way you were meant to."

"I know," she admits. "But as much as ideas like 'lean in' and 'women's equality' have become mainstream, it's different with Indians."

"Meaning what?" Greg challenges. "That you think people will talk about you?"

"Not think. I *know* they will."

"So what? Let them talk."

"It's really not that simple," Nandini says.

Greg has no idea what happened in India all those years ago. Like Simran, he's blissfully unaware of the corrosive damage that could come from people talking, how it can ruin everything you worked for, everything you thought you could become.

"All I know is that we don't have that much time. You're going to have to tell me yes or no soon." Greg extends both of his palms. "My hands feel even weaker than they did last week."

Nandini takes a large gulp of wine. "I promise I'll have an answer for you soon."

"There she is!" Payal yells as Nandini walks into her living room.

"Sorry I'm late. Can I get anybody more tea or food?" Nandini removes her gold stud earrings, a family heirloom Mami gave her on her last trip to India.

"We're fine." Payal pats her stomach to indicate she's full.

"I see that," Nandini says.

They've certainly made themselves at home. Nandini and Ranjit's living room has been transformed into a Baroda sari shop, complete with the multiple cups of chai. Yards of bright orange, turquoise blue, and deep purple saris are unfolded across the sofas. The floor is covered with red velvet boxes, each one nestling gold-and-crystal jewelry.

"Is *that* your new set from Delhi?" Charu points to a pair of enormous diamond-and-gold necklaces between Payal and Preeti.

"You know me. I couldn't resist." Payal beams and tilts her face downward in a gesture of feigned modesty. She rubs her face. Her eyeliner and lipstick remain intact. She often provides a loud thank-you to the power of Chanel's makeup, but everyone knows she had permanent makeup tattooing done two years ago.

"Hmph." Charu runs her fingers across the rows of winking diamonds.

Nandini suppresses a laugh. Charu pretends not to be affected by expensive jewelry when really, she's impressed by plenty of things, whether that's how much her peer's children make at their first job, the number of letters after someone's name, or how many likes can be collected on filtered Facebook photos.

"You must be so excited about Simran's engagement party," Sonali, Payal's permanent sidekick, says. Preeti nods in agreement.

"We are," Nandini says. "I think it'll be fun. And so many people are flying into town!"

"What color is Simran wearing?" Payal asks. "Please don't say something neon. I'll have a heart attack if I see another Indian girl in that ridiculousness. Since when did resembling Gatorade become classy?"

Nandini laughs. "Don't you worry. Simran will be in pale pink."

Payal leans back in relief. "*Haaaash.*"

Sonali's hands sweep over two silk saris as if they're her precious pets. "I wish my Dinesh would just settle down already. These kids now just keep swiping right or swiping left or doing other good-for-nothing things. When I ask him, he has the audacity to say, 'Mom, you just want to plan a wedding.' Now when was that considered a crime? And think about it for me. I have three sons. I'm ready for a girl in my home!"

"It'll work out. Just be patient, and have faith," Payal says as she rubs Sonali's back. Nandini can picture her real thoughts in the air in front of them: *If you pray enough, Krishna will make sure your son marries a woman who kisses your ass and only expresses anger in the most passive-aggressive forms.*

Sonali smiles. "You're lucky to have a daughter, Nandini. They care more. They want to make sure the parents are okay."

"That's true," Nandini agrees. "The way a daughter shows love is different. Incomparable."

Charu raises her nose into the air and gives Nandini a side-eyed glance. "And everything is going okay with the wedding planning so far? No issues?"

She knows what happened with Simran and Meghna. She knows. She knows. She knows.

Nandini gives her a cold, hard stare. "No issues. We are just fine."

The next hours are filled with the women exchanging opinions on one another's saris, cooking tips, and run-of-the-mill resentment toward their mothers-in-law. Nandini laughs along with their stories.

It occurs to her that she would have liked this years ago. Not as much as the other women, but it would have still been pleasant, nice. But she's felt different lately—as though she no longer fits. There's a divide between her outside and inside now. Not that anyone can tell. They may even think she's fully in the moment, not thinking of anything else. Lying, she's realized, is like most things. It gets easier with practice.

She excuses herself to start cleaning up. In the quiet, large kitchen, she starts rinsing the dishes. The remnants of Gujarati food—serrated cilantro leaves, the greenish brown sauce of curry, and thick, yellow trails of daal—swirl down each plate and coalesce before disappearing into the drain.

Our food was designed for women to be bound to the kitchen, Mami often said. There was the binding of the dough, the cutting of the vegetables, the spicing, the cleaning, the arranging . . . Nandini was exhausted just thinking about it.

Charu approaches the sink. "Let me help you."

"I'm fine, really." Nandini wants some more time alone. She hasn't even had a chance to process her dinner with Greg.

"It'll go faster this way. You rinse. I'll load." Charu opens the dishwasher and holds out her hand.

Nandini gives in, too tired to put up a fight. She passes Charu the rinsed dishes until all the plates and bowls are finished. Nandini gets the larger pots from the stovetop. She turns on the overhead fan to air out the lingering smell of cumin and turmeric.

"You know," Charu says, "everyone is so excited for the engagement party and, of course, the wedding. I can't believe the entire extended family is coming. Even the ones who've never been to America! So things really *are* going well?"

"Like I said before, yes." Nandini forces her voice to keep a light, pleasant tone. "Things are fine."

She glances at Charu and notes the difference between her and the other women here. Sonali and Preeti are quiet and simple, which makes them ideal company for social events but also

guarantee she'll never be very close to them. Payal may be superficial, but even still, she's sincere. Charu has a subtle, dangerous
manipulation about her. Nandini finds this interesting considering that Ranjit doesn't have this trait at all. Then again, his relationship with his sister works because they keep their interactions
light and pleasant, never going below the surface.

"Good. Both your kids are getting married within a year.
That's a big deal," Charu says.

Nandini nods. Yes, a wedding is the last large occasion she
will throw for her children, but it is more than that. It is the cul-
mination of what they all built in America, the struggles they
overcame.

Charu leans against the dishwasher door and tosses the light
pink dupatta of her salwar kameez over her shoulder. "Ranjit told
me Simran has been asking you a lot of questions?"

"Such as?" Nandini pretends to focus on soaking pots in the
sink.

"She's curious about your marriage. Naturally, right?"

Her words make the evening take a sharp turn.

"Simran's fine." Nandini's voice lowers into a murmur. "And
we know how to deal with things as they come up."

Scrub, scrub, scrub. Squirt soap onto a sponge.

"You know," Charu says, no longer loading any dishes, "it's
important that certain incidents are kept in the past. We wouldn't
want anything to ruin her engagement. She still has one *entire*
year before she's married."

"Why would anything ruin my daughter's engagement?"

Nandini can already hear Ranjit's voice: *She's just trying to help.*
He is perpetually blind to his sister's intentions, the same way he
never notices his brothers nudging the check in his direction

when they go to restaurants. Charu sponsored Ranjit and Nandini to America, and ever since she's cashed in one favor for a lifetime of obligation.

And she could never talk to Ranjit about it, at least, not to the extent that she would have preferred. That was one of the many things nobody ever told her about an arranged marriage. There was no expectation to communicate, to expose one's emotional exoskeleton for the sake of connection.

And why were people constantly telling her what to do? Whether it was Meghna or Charu, she was always answering to others.

She forces herself to think of her future. There's a chance she could have something greater than this. Something of her own. Something she's hoped for for so many years.

"You of all people know how a boy's parents can get," Charu says, interrupting Nandini's thoughts. "If they think a girl comes from an *improper* family, they can cut things off. All my brother wants is for his children to be happy. Settled."

"That's all I want, too."

"And it's important to me that he's content. That you aren't planning to do or say anything that will jeopardize plans. What happened in India should be kept in India. If the wrong things get out, everything can be broken. Obviously, you already know that." She says this as if she's a strict schoolteacher and Nandini is an eager first-grade student.

Charu can remind her of the scandal as much as she wants. She doesn't know what really changed Nandini from the inside.

"And anyway," Charu continues, "I know Simran is very attached to her cousins. It would be a shame if they all drifted apart because of things they're better off not knowing."

Years ago, hearing something like this would've terrified Nandini. But now, she places her hands on her hips and leans closer to Charu. "Nobody would dare take things out on Simran that aren't her fault. I'll make sure of that. And she will, too. My daughter won't be pushed around by anyone. And I won't let you threaten her future with my past."

Nandini wants to scream at Charu, *Get that stick out of your ass!* She has imaginary arguments with Charu in the shower, where she pelts her with a slew of curse words she's learned from American shows.

Charu gazes at Nandini, as if trying to study her face. "You must be relieved. After everything you've all been through, Simran has grown into such a kind young woman. I know she had her ups and dow—"

"Like I said, she's fine," Nandini says, remembering that Simran still hasn't called her back today.

She soaks a yellow-and-green sponge in the sink. "I'm going to finish cleaning up. Please, go sit and enjoy your tea."

Charu doesn't move.

Nandini faces her. "I'm not kidding. You should leave. Now."

Five

Simran

"Thank God you're here," Vishal says as Simran walks into Wicked Willy's, their go-to grungy bar on Bleecker and Sullivan. "I've been such an awkward third wheel with Sheila and Alex. Trying not to fall asleep."

"Nobody can tell. You need to go into politics," Simran says. "Or rather, anything that requires constantly masking boredom and fatigue."

"You mean like my current, soul-sucking job?" he asks, referring to his position as a financial analyst at Goldman Sachs. "Ah, that's the privilege of our generation, right? To be entitled and bitch about our jobs and flirt with the idea of doing something else, something grander, only to jump back on the goddamned hamster wheel the next morning."

"You're ridiculous." Simran laughs and sits on a barstool next to him as Vishal orders their drinks. "Where's your girl? Ami, right?"

He nods. "We haven't caught up about her, or anything, in so long."

"I know! There's been so much going on," she says.

"Yeah? Wedding planning been crazy? You're practically at the one-year mark."

"Oh, I *know*," she says. "Yeah, the planning has been crazy, and I've also been working a lot for school. It's really picked up, and I've had to buckle down. Make sure all my shit's together."

"How's that going?" Vishal asks.

"Fine," Simran says. "I'm putting together my final project for the program. It's been a lot of work. Sometimes, I lose motivation—"

"Don't we all?" Vishal asks, raising his eyebrows.

"Definitely. But it's fine. I'm getting through it."

"Well, you're almost done," Vishal says. "It's a big year for you, isn't it?"

"Yeah. There are so many things going on. And it almost feels like they're happening so quickly that I can't process them all. Or really grasp how much is really going to be different soon."

"What do you mean?"

"I don't know," she says. "I'm excited, and I've prepared for all of this for so many years. But I guess I'm beginning to see that there are expected things I have to do . . . for work and the wedding. I just want to make sure that in the midst of all that, I'm still me. That I don't let parts of myself slip away in the name of being a good Indian girl."

"Ah, a *good* Indian girl." Vishal leans back and peers at Simran as though he's seeing straight into her thoughts. He has that ability to be an active, nonjudgmental listener, something Sheila often lacks. Simran's worried that if he keeps his eyes on her, if she keeps talking, they'll stumble into a territory she won't be able to climb out of.

"Anyway, this is way too heavy of a talk for a place like this," Simran says as she motions toward a group of college kids taking tequila shots. "Tell me about you and Ami."

Vishal has been on every app and matchmaking site that exists. Simran and Sheila have heard stories about his adventures everywhere from Dil Mil, Coffee Meets Bagel, and his favorite, Bumble. Though Simran commends his persistence, she's worried those apps make it easier to assume there's always another option close by. Her uncle Rajan Kaka claims many of these sites work similarly to arranged marriages in India, by aligning people based on their values, family backgrounds, views on finances, etc.

Vishal and Ami met through Tinder of all ways. To be fair, it was sort of an accident. He signed up as a dare, and Ami made a profile before realizing it was a full-on hook-up app. (Simran had made a note to herself to remind Rajan Kaka that Tinder was nothing like an arranged marriage setup.) They've been dating for two months, and tonight will be the first time Sheila and Simran meet her.

"Ha-ha. She's not here yet. And she's not my girl. Yet." He drums his palms against the bottom of his light green polo.

"Ooh, so things are going in that direction?"

"Yeah, our last date went really well. And so far, there's nothing wrong with her. She's really bubbly, always talks to strangers. I like that."

"That's great. You need someone social. Just don't go looking for things to pick on now," Simran says, pointing a stern finger in his face. She and Sheila have heard of too many instances where Vishal rejected someone for some minor "issues." Vishal's parents remind him every chance they get that if he would just be a *little* more open-minded and a *little* less picky, they could help him meet the perfect Indian girl who meets all their standards.

"Where's your fiancé?" Vishal asks, looking over Simran's shoulder. "How are you guys?"

"Yeah, things have been great since he's been back from Africa." She nods. "I can't believe it's already been a month. He's getting ready to study for his finals. I guess everything that happened while he was gone could just be attributed to a rough patch. We've gotten our rhythm back. And he appreciates that I've been essentially living at his place, making him snacks while he studies. He really has been trying, for the wedding and us. He even watched *Miss Congeniality* with me on Sunday for the millionth time."

She reminds herself of a quote she once picked up from an episode of *Oprah*, her go-to source for wisdom when she came home from school. *In a relationship, always trust that the other person is doing the best they can.*

"You both always make it through," Vishal says. "I mean, shit, that's why you've been together this long. So then I take it you're no longer talking to Neil?"

"Uh, well, not really." Simran turns toward Vishal.

Vishal raises his eyebrows. "Seriously? You *are* still talking to him?"

"Sort of," Simran says.

"What does that mean?"

"I don't feel like I can just stop talking to him," Simran says. "There's something about him. He's brilliant and inspiring, yes. And he makes me want to do more. Think outside the box. But he's also the kind of person I'd want to be best friends with."

"I do get that." Vishal motions to the bartender for another bottle of Sam Adams. "Is there any harm in being friends with Neil?"

"No harm, I guess, except Kunal's still uncomfortable. That's part of the reason things have been going well. Neil and I have dwindled down to texts," she says.

Simran's mom and Nani used to tell her that men didn't have

to give up much for marriages to work. Women had to leave their family, join another one, put aside their own aspirations on a whim, and sever any ties from their pasts.

"Neil's actually at a place close by," she tells Vishal. "Asked if we want to join."

"Why don't we go and say hi?"

"And have Kunal freak out? No, thank you. We're supposed to be wedding planning, and you know what a beast that is. You'd think it would be easy for my family because we've already done this for Ronak, but it's an entirely new ball game when you're the bride's side."

"Don't even get me started. I've had enough of that crap," Vishal says, referring to his older sister's wedding from the previous year. "These Indian weddings are out of control. We decide we want to go all out and have the traditional events and then it just becomes overwhelming as shit. In some ways, we take the worst of Indian and American customs."

"But that's the thing. You can't just half-ass any of it," she says. "Like, for Ronak's wedding, my parents couldn't leave anyone off their guest list. People get so offended. And then, when they say they're coming, you have to take care of them. We had two guests call and say they couldn't drink tea-bag chai. It *had* to be fresh. And the world apparently stops if Indians don't have their chai three times a day, so my mom had to teach the chef at the Plaza how to make proper Indian chai. Can you believe that?"

"Sadly, I can," Vishal says, and we both chuckle. "Our parents get so caught up in what other people think, how we'll look. If we looked past all of that, we'd see a lot of fear."

"I agree. In that way, wedding planning has just been an exaggerated version of my typical life plus Excel spreadsheets. And of course some unavoidable family drama," she says, chugging her vodka cranberry.

"Jesus, the family drama."

"I guess it's inevitable. You don't really have a chance to learn all the shit about someone's family, or your own, until it's time to plan a wedding. I didn't know Kunal's mother cared so much about what dishes should be served at the wedding lunch or where we would do the mehndi, because we need enough space for the henna tattoo artists to set up stations. And then the bride and groom have to be the messengers of their parents and balance everyone's needs. It's so awkward."

"Have your parents and his been fighting?"

"They're definitely on the verge. I know my parents can be crazy, but they're mine, so it still makes me defensive if Kunal points out anything." She laughs. "But I think we may need to stage an intervention with our moms. They're disagreeing about everything. I can talk to my mom openly and tell her to calm down. But it's a lot harder for Kunal. He's not used to talking back to his parents. But we've promised each other again and again that we'll be a team with our parents. We're thinking of planning a meeting with them, because no matter what happens, they *cannot* meet by themselves."

"You know, it's weird," Simran says. "Everything seems to be back to normal. School, Kunal, my family. So I don't know why it feels like things could just fall apart any second . . . or get worse if I make one wrong move. Maybe I'm just being one of those annoying Millennials who can't deal with adulthood."

"Maybe it's fear?" Vishal suggests. "Or adjustment? There are a lot of things going on at once. I mean, you're about to finish your master's program, you're planning your wedding, and your brother just got married, so of course your entire family is on edge."

She considers his point. With so much going on, maybe some anxiety and uncertainty are inevitable.

Before Simran can answer, they're interrupted by Kunal's arrival. For a few minutes, everyone asks him about Africa, medical school, his family, and wedding planning, all out of pure politeness since they've already heard about all of these from Simran. He discusses his life with expansive hand gestures, the knowledge that the world is his to take.

Kunal kisses her when they're alone. "Are you having fun?"

"Of course I am." She gazes around the room. "I can't believe we're actually planning our *wedding*."

Kunal wraps both of his arms around her and places his head on top of hers. It's one of those easy, intimate gestures that can only happen with someone who's familiar with your body. She sinks into him and relishes his firm grip.

"I can't believe it, either," he says, shifting his gaze toward the ground. "I haven't thanked you for calling my mom and checking in with her about wedding stuff. It means a lot to me that you're doing that."

She takes a sip of her vodka cranberry. "Sure. It's no problem. And you can call my parents sometime, too. I'm sure they'd love to hear from you."

He nods. "You're right. I'll do that."

She forces herself not to ask him why this never occurred to him before, when it was so clear to him that she should be calling his mother. Then she reminds herself that this isn't even all his fault. Their parents and even a lot of their friends still abide by the idea that a daughter-in-law should be putting in more effort toward her in-laws than a son-in-law.

Always trust that the other person is doing the best they can.

Kunal ruffles her hair. "I think my mom finally feels like she has something to look forward to that doesn't depend on my dad's approval. Not that he's been able to focus on anything, anyway, with his job hunt and all."

Pratik Uncle has mastered the art of having his kids crave his affection because of how much he withholds it. Since high school, Simran's seen Kunal caught between resenting his dad while still needing his approval.

"How is that going, by the way?"

Kunal shakes his head. "No luck yet."

"It'll work out, sweetie. An opportunity will come," she says.

"I want to believe that," he says. "But it's hard seeing all of the stress it's causing for him . . . and my mom."

"I know," she says. "But you'll keep being strong for them. I know you will."

"I hope so." He kisses her forehead and gives her a we're-in-this-together type of look.

She leans against his chest and recaptures the feeling she's always had with him, the one that makes her excited for the future, for a time when they can be a real team.

From the beginning of their relationship, there was a connection that allowed both of them to confide more in each other than they ever could to anyone else. It's a freedom Simran's parents are missing. Even though they routinely discuss the intricate details of their work—frustrating patients, insurance issues, the other hospital staff members—there has always been a strict, almost professional, level of distance with their disclosures.

She tucks her head under Kunal's chin and relaxes, feeling like a chubby, satisfied cat. Things can start going back to the way they were supposed to be.

Kunal nods and motions to the door. "Jigar and Rekha just got here. Let's say hi quickly and head out. I'm ready to get to bed."

Kunal always jokes that he needs Simran to socialize, even with his two closest med school friends. *You're better at talking to people than I am.* She often reminds him that there's nothing wrong with taking a few minutes to ask someone how they're doing. At his med school winter formal, she ended up in a twenty-minute discussion with the dean and his wife, which then led to them going to their Upper East Side apartment for dinner.

Simran turns around to see Jigar and Rekha handing their IDs to the apathetic, tattooed bouncer.

The conversation among the four of them takes its usual route, which starts at small talk and ends at medicine. With the all-consuming nature of medical school, she can understand why many of their classmates broke up with their significant others. (When she went out with them after their first exam, Jigar provided her a very drunk explanation of his own breakup . . . and the mechanisms behind alcohol metabolism.)

Simran clears her throat, hoping that they'll switch to a topic that she can contribute to. "So, what are you guys doing this summer?"

Jigar mentions something about the dean's coveted sponsored Costa Rica trip being full and claims that Kunal is the "top choice" on the waiting list.

"You know you'll get it," Jigar says. "I bet your fiancée will even help you write the perfect follow-up letter to the dean that'll convince him. Right, Simran? Of course, if you wrote the letter yourself, it would probably work, since the dean loves *you.*"

What the hell is he talking about?

"Of course she'll help," Rekha says. "She even packs Kunal's lunch sometimes! I don't know how he got a woman who is so much hotter *and* nicer than him."

She pats Kunal's shoulder. "You're really out of your league, buddy."

Kunal smiles. "I've always known that."

If Simran met Rekha in any other setting, she'd want to be her friend.

Damn her.

Simran prays that her face isn't flushed. "Wait, are you guys talking about *the* big dean's trip? The one that's for the whole summer?"

She thinks back and remembers that at some point in the last six months, Kunal mentioned the dean's yearly medical mission trip. The med students are handpicked, usually only third- or fourth-years. The selected students are always eventually inducted into the school's two honor societies—AOA and Gold Humanism—which then ensures they'll match into their top-choice residency program. Kunal's plan was to apply next year.

"But you're going to go next year, after the wedding. We discussed us going on a mini-moon and then a real honeymoon later just to fit the trip in for you. Why are you talking about this now?"

She inhales deeply, waiting for Kunal to tell her that all of this just happened. They share big things with each other. They have to.

Jigar grabs her shoulder. "We made him apply for *this* summer."

The bar becomes quiet and blurry. Thoughts burst in her mind, one after another.

She turns to Kunal. "You applied for a trip this summer? Are you serious?"

Kunal is buzzed and relaxed, which only irritates her more. "I'm sorry I didn't tell you. It all happened so randomly. Honestly, it was a joke because there was no way I thought I'd get in this year."

"When were you going to tell me this?"

"I'm so sorry. I . . . forget to tell you."

"You forgot?" She means to raise her voice but can only emit a whisper. "Seriously?"

"There was so much going on while I was there, and you and I barely spoke." His face stiffens. "But of course I wanted to let you know. I really did. I promise you I didn't think I had a chance for this at all."

She struggles to keep her facial expression intact. "Kunal, can you help me with something?"

She guides them outside the bar. There's a sign boasting one-dollar Jell-O shots in neon green chalk. People are being spit out of clubs and into twenty-four-hour pizza shops. A girl bends over a trash can as her boyfriend makes a frantic bun with her hair.

"Weren't you going to apply for that trip next year?" She feels a stab of sadness, then worry. Is her fiancé really planning to be away again? And without telling her?

"I was. I *am*. I just thought I'd take a chance this year. Just to show interest."

They stand by a filthy window. She pictures their acne-skinned, bright-eyed high school selves staring at them through it. What would they think of older Simran and Kunal?

"How could you apply for a trip like that without even talking to me? I don't get it."

I want to spend more time with you. I want to matter more, she wants to say but doesn't. Can't.

"I really didn't mean to," he says. "I told you I'm sorry I forgot. I really am."

"That's it? You just *forgot* to mention a trip that takes up an entire season? Not to mention, we're supposed to be planning our wedding! I thought we would be doing it all together, as partners. I thought you cared about doing it that way, too."

"I *do* care." He shrugs and tilts his head down. "I'm sorry. Look, I love you, and I made a mistake by not telling you. Please, let's just have fun and discuss this later."

"Discuss what exactly? When did you submit the paperwork for this?"

She almost retracts her question. Maybe she doesn't want to know. Maybe she cares about him too much to be angry about something that makes him happy.

"Simran, this is no—"

"WHEN?"

"In Africa." Kunal refuses to look at her. "Around five weeks ago."

She tells herself to take a deep breath, to remind herself that she loves him, and that's what actually matters.

But she hears herself blurt, "Five weeks? Five *weeks*? You've got to be kidding me."

Kunal stays silent. He is not kidding.

"I can't take this shit." She raises her hands in the air.

A group of drunk college students saunter past them, unfazed. That's the nice thing about New York: privacy in public.

"Can't take what?" Kunal asks, as if to say, *What now?*

"There's always something. I love you so much, but I don't

know. Is this how it's going to be? You doing things without even considering telling me?"

She tries to tell herself she's just had too many drinks. It's not that she's becoming the type of woman she swore she'd never be.

Kunal clenches his fists and paces toward the curb. "No, it isn't always going to be like this. God, Simran, do you always have to make a problem out of everything? You always make me feel like I'm screwing up. Not doing enough. Whether it's for you or the wedding, it never ends. I'm stressed enough right now. And you know I'd never want to hurt you. I. Just. Forgot."

The rational part of her tells her to stop talking. Stop thinking. Because when she's drunk, her anger takes on a magnetic quality and tends to attract all the frustrations she's been storing inside. She thinks about how she's been living out of a drawer in Kunal's room since he's come back from Africa. They order takeout and eat it in front of the television when he isn't studying. They visit his family when he's free. His life. His way. His time.

"No. No, no, no, I will not let you make this my fault," she says, stomping toward him. "I will *not!*"

There's a staccato of high heels and leather shoes against the sidewalk. The air is heavy with summer and sweat. Things that usually signal a carefree time but for them now only manage to make the atmosphere more charged.

"I can't deal with you right now," Kunal says. "I have too many other things going on."

Kunal has refused to fight at night since he started medical school. A fight makes it too difficult for him to go to sleep, which makes it too difficult for him to study the next day. So when things start to escalate, he shuts down.

"I know you have a lot going on. Things way more important than KEEPING YOUR FIANCÉE IN THE LOOP."

It's official: she's lost it.

Kunal gazes at her, then kicks a stray beer can out of his way. "I should go. We can't talk like this. It isn't going to go anywhere."

"So you're really going to just walk away?" She watches the beer can roll and let out a low-pitched rumble until it hits the side of a brick building.

When he doesn't say anything, she adds, "Please, Kunal. I just want to talk. Please."

She stares at him and waits for him to say, *Yes, okay, let's talk* or *Why don't we cool down and talk later?*

"I need some sleep. Good night, Simran." He shoves his hands into his pockets and starts to walk down Bleecker Street, covering twice as much ground as she could with his long strides.

She leans against the rough brick and waits for him to look back.

He doesn't.

Her breaths become quick and shallow. She walks back into Wicked Willy's, where everyone is now more sluggish and glassy-eyed versions of themselves. The entire place reeks of body odor and alcohol breath. She can already hear her future self cursing for drinking like she's still in college.

Vishal and Ami are pressed against each other in one corner. Sheila's draped over Alex's shoulder, in danger of being kicked out by a bouncer. Jigar has ordered yet another round of cheap tequila shots for Rekha and some other people Simran assumes are their classmates.

They'd all tell her to let Kunal cool off. Wait until the morning.

She opens her phone and scrolls to the text message from over three hours ago. Before she knows it, her thumbs are moving at record speed.

Simran: Still out?

Her phone flickers from 1:45 to 1:46. She's texting Neil Desai in the middle of the night. *The* Neil Desai. After what happened with Kunal.

She pictures Neil twisting out of Egyptian cotton sheets to check his phone and frowning when he sees her name.

As she's putting her phone away, she feels it vibrate. Her stomach jumps.

Neil: Still out but starting to fade. Want to
join?

She paces through groups of people laughing and yelling and smoking and singing. The entire damn city is a party. She's past the point of thinking. She just walks.

In a few minutes, Simran is inside Le Souk, a place that's half hookah lounge, half club. Luckily, the thump of music makes it hard to think, or do anything, besides navigate through the film of smoke.

Neil is wearing a white button-down over jeans, with his lean arms resting over the side of the bar. His sleeves are rolled to his elbow, where Kunal told her the radius and ulna bones meet.

Maybe she should leave. She checks her phone and ignores the nausea twisting her stomach. No missed calls, no anything, from Kunal. She takes a deep breath and adjusts the top of her dress.

Neil turns to the side, his square shoulders straight but re-laxed as he laughs with a stocky Indian guy.

"Hi, you!"

She wants to smack herself the second the syllables come out. What happened to being calm and cool? It's like when she was six years old and Dad's boss invited them to dinner. Her parents told her to stay quiet three times on the way over, and she under-stood. The second their host opened the door, Simran took note of his forty-inch waist and gray beard and yelled, "OH MY GOD, IT'S SANTA!" She would later find out that he was an Ortho-dox Jew.

"You made it!" Neil says.

He orders her another vodka cranberry from the bartender.

"Where are your friends?" Neil asks, and then adds, "And your fiancé?"

"They couldn't make it," she says, swirling her straw.

"That's too bad. Here," Neil says, holding out his arm for her to grab. The gesture makes her think of scenes from black-and-white movies, when women wore fabulous gloves up to their elbows. "I want to introduce you to some people."

Her eyes dart to a cluster of tables near the entrance where his friends are sitting. What the hell is she doing here, in all her non-journalism, lack-of-prestige glory?

Neil's friends turn out to be a mix of people he went to college with, other *New York Times* writers, and some from his home-town of Kansas City. He tells everyone about how they met, about her "potential." All his friends have careers inspired by something they enjoyed and worked their asses off for: an online jewelry start-up, a self-help book line, a human rights reporter, an editor at a small publishing house.

Her concerns about coming to Le Souk were unnecessary. Within an hour, she feels as though she's known everyone for years. It's refreshing to leave the world of wedding planning and judgment and expectations and never-good-enough. Everything from Wicked Willy's recedes into the darkness.

Neil returns from the bar, his hands full with the drinks that he just ordered for everyone. She's never seen someone who can pluck friends from every corner, like fresh berries—unlike Kunal, who stands in the periphery and knows that, sooner or later, people will come to him.

After Neil passes the drinks around, he squeezes into a chair next to Simran.

"Neil, your friends are all so *cool*, for lack of a better word."

He folds his hands together and squints at her. "I think they'd say the same about you."

"No, I mean, they've all made something of themselves in different ways, without worrying about stability or prestige or any of that."

"Yeah, I think some people get to a point where they stop chasing approval."

Stop chasing approval. She rolls the thought in her mind and lets it collect momentum.

"What's it like doing your job? Writing stories for people?" she asks. "Getting their trust?"

"It's sloppy. A lot of learning by trying and falling on my face. You just can't be afraid to look like a dumbass for a while, maybe forever . . . you know, you could do that. There's nothing stopping you."

"I don't even know what I'd do," she says. "In high school, I thought I'd join NYU's creative writing program and then write and teach and travel and help other girls do the same." She doesn't know what made her think of that. Maybe it's being around all these creative people.

"So why didn't you?" he asks.

"I didn't get in." She lowers her voice and remembers the letter informing her she had been wait-listed. The official rejection came two weeks later in a sad, thin envelope. The type of envelope that only ever carries bad news. Her parents and Kunal were right. Some things were better left as hobbies.

"But I've been thinking about it lately," she says. "What it would be like to get away for a bit."

"You should."

"How?"

"Don't you have time between graduation and starting work? Hell, I don't even have the time, but I'm thinking of getting away, too. But then again, I can't stay in one place for too long," he says, and she wonders what it would be like to pick up whenever she pleased, be free of any anchors. Maybe the world is made up of two types of people: the Neils and the ones whose destinies are dictated by mob mentality.

"On a more profound note," Neil says, "I tipped a busker today because of you."

"You did? No way."

"Yeah . . . a guy playing the saxophone at the Forty-Second Street Times Square stop. I put a dollar in his ripped case. You know, I always wonder how those guys learned how to play."

"Yeah, I wonder that, too. I like to pretend that they're all on the verge of making it big. What made you tip this guy?"

"Thought of you," he says, his hazel eyes focusing on hers. "I remembered in that one text, you told me you always tip buskers.

You're probably getting scammed every day, but still. Most people would keep walking past them. At least, most people in New York would."

"Well, I'm glad you didn't," she says. Her cheeks hurt from smiling too much. She made Neil Desai do something different in his day?

"Who are your other New Yorker soft spots? Besides the musically inclined performers?"

She bites her bottom lip. "Hm, let's see. Cab and Uber drivers. Waiters. The men who own street carts and fruit stands. All of the Indian people I see who are the same age as my parents and are busting their butts at tough jobs so their families can have a better life."

She loves that conversations with Neil are a pure unspooling of thoughts.

"Yeah, I see so many people and wonder, what's this person's story?" Neil says. "Where is he going? Where does her family live?"

She nods. "Same here. I wonder that all the time."

He grins, putting his arm around her. "I'm glad you came out."

"Me too." She lets herself lean into him and almost pretends he's her boyfriend, that they spend their mornings writing and their nights having a great time with great people.

Simran's face becomes warmer as the pull from earlier rushes back. And then, she leans forward and kisses the man who isn't her fiancé on his cheek.

He looks at her.

Music thumps around them, and the entire room is bathed in darkness. Each second is satiated, choking with possibility, and she realizes that there are two contradictory women residing in her who can have two contradictory desires.

She tells herself to stop, to leave. She's already breaking so many rules. She could end this now.

You're engaged! a voice inside of her head screams.

But then another one emerges. *You want to know what this feels like. You need to.*

Something inside of her anchors her to the couch. Being closer to Neil makes her feel safe and on edge at the same time. Is this what breaking rules feels like? Is this what she's been missing?

She shifts toward him. Their lips meet.

Everything else becomes blurry.

There's only Neil's woodsy scent and Simran's fingers sliding through his hair, his hand gripping her forearms, his lips against her earlobes. Nobody's ever touched her this way. A mixture of freedom and excitement churn inside her. What the fuck is wrong with her? Kissing someone other than her fiancé should twist her stomach with guilt, make her realize that nobody could ever compare to Kunal, the only other guy she's ever kissed.

But none of those sentiments come. Instead, she feels another electric rush of adrenaline. And that scares the shit out of her.

Neil's lips are softer than Kunal's; his tongue, more aggressive. He's different in every way but feels right. With each second an entire life unfolds before her, one with passion and drive and encouragement and motion.

"I can't," she says, pulling away from him. Her lips are tingling the way they do after she eats too many jalapeños.

"God, you're right. I'm sorry. I don't know what I was thinking."

Her fingers graze his palms. "No, I'm sorry. I really am."

Before Neil can say anything else, she stands up and runs through the thinning crowd, not stopping until she steps into a cab.

Nandini

Nandini stands as Meghna approaches her. Meghna scans her from head to toe, not even bothering to be subtle. Her small, round eyes seem to say, *You are so American.*

Nandini motions to the chair across from her. "Please, Meghna Ben, have a seat."

Meghna sits down without cracking a smile.

She takes note of Meghna Patel's salwar kameez, low bun, and disapproving eyes. She should have picked a different place to meet her daughter's future mother-in-law. Why did she ever think that a woman like Meghna would enjoy bruschetta and Pinot Noir?

But it was too late. They're both here. Plus, the Indian restaurants in Edison would take too long to get to (and likely require a shared car ride).

Nandini opens the black leather menu and pretends to study the appetizers.

"I'll have whatever you're having," Meghna says before she gazes around the restaurant and focuses on a table of middle-aged women, all tanned, toned, and wearing tennis whites.

After Nandini has ordered them both spinach salads and a mushroom risotto, she takes a sip of water and clears her throat. "So, how are things?"

Meghna keeps her face straight. "Fine. Just fine."

"That's good," Nandini says.

Meghna also had an arranged marriage, immigrated to the United States, and spent years adjusting to life in New Jersey. Nandini thinks of how Meghna doesn't believe in nannies, prefers her husband managing all of their family's finances, and looks forward to cooking a new meal every evening.

They have so much in common.

They have so little in common.

The waiter brings the salads. Meghna slowly pushes the spinach leaves with her fork. This is going to be a long meal.

"Do you want to order something else?"

"No, this is fine," Meghna says before taking a bite.

In just these few moments, Nandini can tell that Meghna is the kind of woman whose emotions simmer below the surface. It takes a closer look to notice her slight frown and clipped words.

Is this really the woman Nandini will be sharing her daughter with? Is she good enough for Simran? Will she treat her with respect? With tenderness?

She hears Simran's loud voice: *Stop being so judgmental. Let me make my own decisions.*

Simran would be furious if she knew this was happening. Should she ask Meghna to keep this meeting between them? Or would that look bad?

Nandini breaks off a piece of bread. "So, the wedding details are coming along well."

"Yes . . . things are starting to come together."

"Are you getting excited?"

Meghna nods, but her lips stay in a straight line.

"I wanted to address some of the issues that came up before, on our phone calls."

"Okay?" Meghna says this as if there weren't any issues, as if they haven't had multiple calls about multiple details.

Nandini folds her hands together and leans forward. It's the same stance she takes when she's about to give a patient bad news. "I know you have your own ideas on how you want the wedding to be. . . ."

Her voice fades. It doesn't matter that they're in America or that Nandini and Ranjit are paying for everything. The boy's side still holds the power. Pleasing them is the top priority. Ranjit had told her earlier today to "just do whatever you need to keep them happy."

"I do have my ideas," Meghna says. "And I didn't think that would be such a problem."

"It's not that it's a problem; it's that, you know."

"You know what?"

"Well, we are putting it on. What I mean is, our family is hosting. So, we thought it would just be easier for us to manage things."

"Manage everything yourselves? You mean, control the show."

Nandini widens her eyes. She can't decide if she should be offended by Meghna's words or relieved that she had a sincere emotional response.

"I wouldn't use the word 'control.'"

Meghna stares at her plate, which is still full. "I always had a plan for how Kunal's wedding would be. I've been thinking about this since he was a little boy. And there are some traditions that are very important to us. To our entire family."

"I understand. But there are some that are also important to ours. And this isn't India. We can't have ceremonies that are several hours long or invite thousands of guests the way people did when we were growing up. It just doesn't work here."

"It's not just about what works," Meghna says. "It's about what's good for my son."

She stares at her plate and inhales deeply. Nandini watches

this, the rising and falling of her chest, the accordion-like wrinkles on her forehead. Suddenly, behind her own bitterness for this woman, something else pokes through, and she can see the place they're both coming from. Love. Love for their children. Love for their culture.

She wonders if the arguments over these details are happening because they're both trying to make sure this wedding belongs to them. If they were friends, she might even share this thought with Meghna. She's always wondered what it meant to belong, to a country, to a job, to an event, to a self.

Nandini takes a deep breath. "Listen, I think we can ta—"

Meghna cuts her off. "So have you decided to use the same priest who conducted Ronak's ceremony?"

"Yes, we are. He's very close to our family and always does a great job of explaining of all the Hindu traditions in English."

Meghna scowls. "What if we had another priest in mind?"

Who was this woman to keep challenging her? She grips her fork and knife in a way that says, *I will not be pushed around by you.* "Meghna, I'm sorry if you had another priest in mind, but this is who we've chosen. Perhaps you could host your own religious ceremony on another day with your priest?"

Meghna pushes her chair back. "I think I've had enough wedding talk for one day."

But before Nandini can suggest they change the subject, Meghna grabs her purse and rushes out of the restaurant.

Six

Simran

"Don't tell anyone I'm not coming to your engagement party. Especially your mom," Nani says on the phone while Simran is still caught in that blurry space between sleeping and waking up.

"They're going to find out soon enough." Simran buries her head into the pillow. Images from last night flash before her like a silent film. The contours of Neil's lips. His strong grip.

Fuck.

She sits up in bed. She's still in her strapless dress, but her bra shifted during the night and created two boob-shaped lumps on her stomach. A wave of nausea rises inside her throat. She clutches her stomach and leans forward. She can't decide if she needs to puke, eat carbs, or drink water. So she takes a deep breath and fans her face. The nausea starts to subside.

"Simran, are you there?"

"Yeah, sorry." Her head pounds every time she inhales. Boom, boom, boom. "Nani, you realize that everyone's going to freak out, right?"

"I can handle them. They don't scare me," she says, sounding more like a middle-school girl playing Truth or Dare than Simran's wise Indian grandmother who prays to Ganesha first thing every morning.

Simran rearranges the books that she knocked onto the floor last night: *Their Eyes Were Watching God*, *The Awakening*, *This Side of Paradise*, and some yellowing Judy Blume titles.

She looks around her one-bedroom apartment. It's small even by New York standards. But it's become the perfect place to be when she doesn't want to socialize with people, when Netflix, flannel pajamas, and a fluffy blanket are all she needs. The living room only fits one love seat. Her wooden coffee table is a discard from her parents' basement. She shoved a tiny white IKEA desk against the window. Framed postcards from the Met are hung on the walls.

Her parents are paying for her rent and tuition until she graduates. In a matter of months, she'll have to make sure she has some kind of income.

Stop dwelling, Simran.

She lowers the blinds in her bedroom and living room. She needs darkness. She stumbles into the kitchen and plugs in the coffeepot. It starts to gurgle.

"Nani, I'm still not clear about why you can't come to the party. What exactly did the doctor say was wrong?"

"I haven't been feeling well for the past week. Nothing serious. He just wants me to be cautious. All that time in the air can be dangerous for someone my age, flying alone, trapped with everyone's germs."

"But you've done that plenty of times. Why is this any different?"

"Oh, it doesn't matter."

"Yes, it does. You never tell us if anything is going on with you."

"Because I don't want you to be concerned about me." Simran hears Nani turning down the volume of a Fair and Lovely commercial, the kind that used to convince she and her friends that they could be hot if their complexions were ten shades lighter. She wonders how much money and time Indian women have spent in pursuit of fairness.

"You have your own life," Nani says. "Your brother's new marriage. Your wedding. Your parents. And I'm fine. More than fine. I couldn't ask for anything else. Everything's perfect."

"But it won't be the same without you," Simran says.

Simran takes out a Styrofoam bowl and plastic spoon for cereal. Anything to do fewer dishes. Her future mother-in-law would be so proud.

"I know. I wish I could be there. And no, not just because I wanted to dance to rap songs that I can't listen to here," she says, referring to her newfound love for American hip-hop or, specifically, to "that talented artist named Cardi B."

Simran writes a mental note to herself: *Look forward to becoming an old lady so I can say whatever I want and it can't be held against me.*

"But you're okay? In general? How is everything going with the girls at school?"

Nani goes to the all-girls school near her house every afternoon to read stories to the students about the Indian goddesses. Some of the teachers at the school found her ideas too "progressive" and stopped her from coming during recess, so now she goes after the last class.

"Yes," she says. "Just, you know, the same nonsense from the principal but the girls themselves are doing well. I think they're learning a lot. I never feel as though there's enough time with them, but everything has limits. It's more than I could do when I was married, so I can't complain."

She chuckles, and her voice seems lighter than usual. Simran thinks back to what both she and her mother have noticed over the past month with Nani. Unanswered phone calls. Her being out of the house more. The lightened mood.

"Oh my god," Simran says, her voice lowering to a whisper. "Do you have a boyfriend?"

"What?!"

"Sorry, you just sound so *zen*." She actually wants to tell Nani that she sounds high. "And you've been distracted. Tough to reach. Something's going on."

"And you think it has to do with a *man*? Please, Simi. You know I loved your nana very much, but men can't take care of themselves. They need someone picking up after them, cooking for them, everything. They're babies. I paid my respects as a widow in the way I was supposed to. What's the phrase? Been there, done that."

"Okay, I was wrong. Sorry," Simran says.

"It's fine. Just fine," she says, in a way that's not fine at all. "Anyway, enough about me. How is Kunal?"

"Okay." Simran leans against the kitchen counter and splays her toes on the cool, smooth tile. "I think we should take a break from wedding planning."

"*What?*" Simran can see Nani sitting up, placing a wrinkled palm over her mouth. "What *break*? What does that even mean?"

"It means that I wanted us to get through this smoothly, and I know he did, too. But things aren't going the way I thought they would. And we need to change the way we're thinking; other-wise, this process is going to ruin us. So maybe taking a step back from wedding planning would be helpful. I mean, we still have about a year until our actual wedding date, so there's time. . . ."

She doesn't tell Nani the rest of what she's thinking. Maybe taking a break from *them* would be helpful. She can't let herself complete that thought even in her own mind.

But Nani reads through Simran's words. "Simi, running away isn't the answer. Nobody said this would be easy. And you've been . . . *friends* for so many years." (Nani still can't say the words "boyfriend," "girlfriend," or "dating.")

"That's the thing, though. We've been with each other for such a long time, and practically grew up together. And through each new phase, we just kept going and going and going. It's as though I've dated five different guys along the way because of how much we've both been through. But now, with the wed-ding, all these things are coming out from both of us that we didn't expect. And everything is a mess. Things just don't feel . . . *right*."

"So? You think the answer is to just walk away? When your wedding is in almost *one year*?" Nani asks.

"It's not walking away at all. It's just taking a second to think. He and I really need to talk. We have so many things to discuss, *really* discuss. There are things that we need to establish. And things we both have to work on. I don't want to be quiet or pas-sive about what doesn't feel right in my life. And if putting off our wedding date for sometime, for a while, will be better for us in the long run, then we should do it."

Simran opens a bottle of Aleve and shuffles the tiny blue pills among her fingers. She imagines herself going to Kunal's Stuy-

Town apartment right now, walking up the five flights of narrow stairs, and telling him about what happened with Neil.

"Putting off your wedding date? Please tell me your mom doesn't know about this," Nani says.

"No. There's no way I'd tell her right now. She's been so stressed lately, even more than usual."

"She's dealing with a lot. You all are. I know there were some things she wanted to talk to you about soon."

"Well, she isn't telling me anything."

"Do you think she's happy? She constantly seems distracted. Maybe she's always been that way and I never noticed."

When Simran thinks of her mother, she has a vision of her cooking rotlis at four a.m. for her dad's family. Every day the same combination of rushing, folding, tucking, pleasing emerging from the pliable contours of her memory.

"She needs to take it easy for once," Nani says, as if reading Simran's mind. "Not that I can tell her that. She takes anything I say so personally."

"Same here."

Mom often says Simran should have been Nani's daughter. Nani was struggling with major depressive disorder when Simran was born. She couldn't sleep at night, so Nani would wrap her in a hand-embroidered Indian blanket and walk through their house for hours. There's a picture of two-month-old Simran screaming while Nani clutches her, a proud smile stretched across her face.

"I know how overwhelming it is to have your husband's family around all the time. When you have to constantly be diplomatic, put on a polite face, it changes you over time," Nani says. "How could it not? Why else are the women in India, the ones in joint family households, so exhausted? You'll see, when you and Kunal are married, even though you don't have to deal with the same things we did, things will be different. You'll *feel* different."

"It seems like that's just what marriage does," Simran whispers, wondering if there's a part of yourself you simply have to give up before joining someone else.

When Simran was younger, she and her female cousins would fast for one week a year in the hopes of finding a good husband. The idea never made sense to her, the idea that a woman had to sustain on less in the present to gain more in the future.

"I should get going," Nani says. "And remember, don't worry about anything. I'm fine. And everything's going to work out."

"Right. I know that," Simran say, unsure which one of them she's trying to convince.

Cognitive dissonance: the discomfort and mental stress experienced by someone who has contradictory beliefs at the same time. Simran's professor writes the words on the whiteboard in bulbous, cursive letters that seem to dance.

"Individuals want their expectations to align with their reality," Doctor Griffin explains. "In the right position, anyone can justify his or her behavior. This is nothing more than a defense mechanism to preserve one's identity."

After class, Simran sits in the lab and soaks in the sound of fingers diligently hitting keys. Undistracted, focused fingers. She's surrounded by people who are compassionate, insightful, and willing to do whatever it takes to become therapists. She wishes she could be like them. Instead, she thinks about the dumbest things. Her mind wanders like it's a self-made Wikipedia maze.

She pushes her chair back and walks down the hallway, arriving ten minutes early for her meeting with Dr. Bond.

She takes a deep breath. Despite the multiple times she's rehearsed the words in her bathroom mirror, she needs to muster up this final push of courage. *Spit it out, Simran. Just spit it out.*

"Do you know why I wanted to meet?" she asks Dr. Bond after she's sat down and declined a cup of Earl Grey.

He nods. "So you can tell me why you missed the deadline for, well, everything and see what we can do about it. I have no idea whether you've even prepared an application for a job or PhD."

When Simran doesn't answer, he says, "What exactly is the problem, Simran? It's as though I just can't get through to you. You know a master's in psychology isn't enough these days to get a good job, yet, you still do nothing about your situation. You're about to start the summer semester. Your *last* one. And if you're still planning to graduate at the beginning of the fall, these things should already be figured out."

She clears her throat and steadies her hands. This conversation has to happen. Now. "I know. I've tried to do what it takes, I really have, but there's a disconnect. And it's been there for longer than I've wanted to admit. That's why I had to meet with you."

She can't pinpoint any particular emotion on his face. He doesn't appear angry or surprised or even irritated.

She wishes he'd just yell at her. She glances at a picture of him with his kids at the Jersey Shore, with red buckets and a sandcastle in the background. Maybe this is how he disciplines them, by allowing them to wallow in their own disappointment. A direct contrast to how Indian parents freely express their dismay.

"I want to tell you a story," Dr. Bond says. "There was a stu-

dent here six or seven years ago. Smart. Charismatic. The kind
people opened up to and leaned on. A lot like you. She had so
much potential. But for some reason, she kept doubting herself.
That led to her not completing her assignments on time or speaking up in class. She just never gave it her all. And of course, then
some faculty members told her she wasn't cut out for this. They
spoke about her to others, discussed the way she was perpetually
at the bottom. Hopeless. Not good enough."

"The way they've said that about me?" Simran asks, picturing
everyone talking about her in the stuffy faculty lounge that always smells like bread.

Dr. Bond doesn't answer her question, which is an answer
on its own. "After some time, it became clear that her heart just
wasn't in it."

She doesn't look at him. She can't. She never thought she
would become *that* type of student. That type of person. She
pictures herself drifting from the present to the future like a dan-
delion seed.

Dr. Bond continues. "It wasn't because she *couldn't*, which is
what everyone else and she thought, but rather, because she
wouldn't. I realized that she had come straight from college, just
like you. Had never seen anything outside the classroom."

She has no idea how she'd be outside a school building. This
place has been her home for the last year and a half. She's stepped
in and out of these doors for various reasons, and she knows
everything there is to know: which water fountain has the strongest blast, what time the coffee stand on the first floor runs out
of cream, when the lounge is empty and peaceful.

"What happened to her?" Simran asks.

"She took a leave of absence—after a lot of paperwork—worked in the outside world for a little bit, and came back refreshed. Now she's one of the top child therapists in Manhattan."

He nods at her. Simran nods her head back to mirror his gesture, so he thinks she agrees with what he's saying.

"Just like that?" she asks, picturing this girl and the plot points in her happily-ever-after career story.

Dr. Bond shrugs. "She needed to get away to realize what she was missing. And perhaps it would do you well to engage in some, what do you call it? soul-searching."

Soul-searching. The phrase conjures up images of vast beaches, solitary bus rides through western Europe, or days filled with luxury carbohydrates and literature, like Elizabeth Gilbert in *Eat Pray Love.* What Simran really needs is a vacation from her life.

"Look," he says. "We can try and work around you missing the deadline. I'm going to be honest and tell you, this type of setback might change your graduation date, but there's always a way if you're willing to make it work."

Simran takes a deep breath and squeezes her eyes shut. "You're right."

He nods. "Okay. Then let's ju—"

"I'm not going to do it," she blurts. "Any of it. At all."

There. The words she rehearsed all morning. As soon as they escape, their truth becomes palpable. She can't be the type of person who lives from happy hour to happy hour, dreads Monday mornings, and counts down the years until retirement.

"What does that mean, Simran? Do you not see yourself as a therapist?"

Simran settles on the image she used to have of her future self: wearing a chic black dress and leaning back in a light gray armchair as she listened to a variety of people tell her their darkest secrets.

"I used to, but now I don't. I've realized that the part of therapy that excited me the most was being able to listen to other people's stories. But now I know that I also want to share things I've learned from others. And explore their lives and issues in a way that's not so clinical. This"—she points around the office—"isn't the right fit for me. It's just not working. It hasn't been for a while. And I should have done this a long time ago."

Dr. Bond leans back in his chair and rubs his forehead. This is harder than she thought it would be.

Although a part of Simran wants to disappear, a larger part of her feels a sense of relief. Is this what it's like to be honest with someone? With herself?

She tells Dr. Bond it's not his fault. It's all hers. It's her unhealthy relationship with achievement. The parasitic nature of expectations. The way she's somehow become okay with slipping tasteless, poisonous lies into her coffee.

Simran sighs. "You have every reason to be upset with me."

He folds his hands together and looks at her. "You came here to get an education for you, not me. The last thing I'd ever want for you is to be here out of obligation. That's not fair to anybody, especially you."

"I'm so sorry," she says, biting her bottom lip. She will not cry. "I don't know what's been wrong with me lately. Or maybe this was always an issue and I'm only facing it now. But either way, this is the right choice. I know it is."

"Have you thought about what else you could do as a career?"

"No . . . maybe I could be . . . a journalist," she says, her voice trailing off as she pictures her unfinished articles.

"Do you have connections in the field? Opportunities in mind?"

"No." She shakes her head. "But I can start learning what it even means to be a journalist. And maybe in the meantime, I'll find a job somewhere. I guess this is really the first time, *ever*, that I don't have a plan."

I don't have a plan. I don't have a plan. I don't have a plan.

He uncaps a black Montblanc pen. "And you're sure you aren't deciding this because of other shifts in your life?"

Simran gives him a swift nod but considers his question on the inside. Is anyone ever entirely sure when they decide to let go of something big?

"Whether or not this is influenced by the other shifts, I know this is what I need to do."

She stays in Dr. Bond's office for over an hour, and they dissect her feelings behind why she picked psychology, why it isn't the right choice. *Thattagirl, Simran. End your time here like a real therapy patient.*

"Your parents will understand one day," he says at the end.

Yeah, right. For her entire life, she's been taught that professional success equated to acceptance. It told their community that her parents had done well, that she was worthy of respect. Maybe all of that should be enough for her. She almost wants to call her parents and tell them how much she loves them and still wants to make them proud.

Columbia is a blur on her walk home. She looks forward, avoiding eye contact with any students rushing past her, with their notebooks and leather laptop sleeves and excitement. The man who sells roasted peanuts smiles at her. She waves back.

And just like that, it's over.

She won't be a therapist.

Images of a future she'll never have flash before her: sitting in a sunlit office with a patient, learning about different cases at conferences, feeling a sense of stability about her career, having conversations about it with her family and friends. . . .

And then a thought emerges as she passes her favorite deli: *Fuck, Simran, what the hell is wrong with you?*

She can feel her heartbeat. Everything around her seems to disappear. She clutches her chest. Takes deep breaths. How will she break this to everyone? What will she say when people ask her what she does? Did she just make the biggest mistake . . . and without a backup plan at that?

She looks back at Columbia's campus. She could cross the gates, march back into Dr. Bond's office, tell him this was all a mistake.

Or she could move forward.

She stands still, not knowing what to do.

Cognitive dissonance: when you've got only yourself to blame.

Nandini

"We've always had to worry about Simran, haven't we?" Charu sneers. "We saw warning signs and should have been better prepared for this. What is it these Americans suggest when someone starts acting like this? Therapy? A new exercise regimen? A facial?"

"*We* have things under control." Nandini points to herself and Ranjit to tell Charu, *You are not part of us.* "Simran doesn't need anything."

"God, that Meghna Ben and Pratik Bhai." Charu rolls her eyes. "Who do they think they are, behaving this way? They should know where *we* come from, for God's sake. We're *Mehtas*."

Nandini rolls her eyes. The entire family knows Charu's system of judging Indian people: last name, parents' profession (extra points for doctor/lawyer/engineer, demerits for anything artistic), place of origin in India, skin color, house size, and, lastly, children's professional accomplishments.

Charu rambles until she tires herself out.

"Let me know if there's anything at all I can do," she tells her brother in the accent she usually reserves for when she talks to American people.

After she leaves, Ranjit settles onto the recliner and pulls out his laptop from beneath a stack of medical journals.

"Do you have to tell Charu Ben everything?"

Ranjit keeps his gaze on his laptop. "What are you talking about?"

Nandini points to her cell phone. "Why does she have to know about what happened with Meghna Ben? It's bad enough as it is without her being involved."

"I thought she could help. Maybe she could have suggested something we hadn't thought of, since clearly these people are difficult to plan a wedding with," Ranjit says. "Besides, what's wrong with Charu knowing?"

Mothers lie. For her whole life, Nandini thought pushing Simran to do well, work hard, and have high expectations would guide her in the right direction. Instead, she was preparing her to be exhausted, overwhelmed, and confused. All she could hope for was a partner who understood her, and once she found that, it was important for her to not taint that, out of youthful recklessness or the inability to realize what mattered for the long-term.

"Well, if you think she's so helpful, you'll like to know that she judges everything that happens between us and our kids. I don't understand what type of joy she could possibly get from all this meddling. We need to keep things that concern our family between us. Nobody else needs to know. Nobody."

Ranjit stands up and kicks the recliner's foot stand. "I know. I know. It's always my family's fault. They're the bad ones."

"I've never said that."

"You don't have to. It's written all over your face. You're in the worst mood whenever they leave our house, call us, talk to us."

She takes a deep breath. "You can't deny that your family's . . . *needs* . . . have interfered with my own."

Marriage etched away at the person you once were, forced you to grope for whatever remnants you could get of your old self: a conversation with a childhood friend, yellowing photographs, compliments. Nandini felt herself becoming tinier, almost nonexistent, with each polite nod or stifled complaint or ambivalent surrender.

"This *again*?" Ranjit asks. "Yes, Nandini, I know you wanted to start your own practice, but we couldn't afford for you to take out the time or money."

"Because you expected me to take care of everyone," she says. "Literally. They're all somehow my patients. Even when they're not! When I've said I shouldn't see family members and help refer them to someone else, it's expected that I oversee their medications, give them opinions on their labs, or see their friends that they bring to my office without any advance notice. I'm literally their doctor on demand no matter how hard I've tried not to be. How could I ever expect to advance if there were continuous demands placed on me outside of work?"

Nandini thought a career in medicine would be about building long-term relationships with patients and teaching training doctors and adding to the field in creative, stimulating ways, not watching the clock and documenting visits so that her numbers could be compared to the other doctors'. Competition was fierce in their family medicine clinic, and if the staff thought she wasn't contributing her portion, she would lose her job. It had already happened to two other women, even after they discovered they were paid less than their male counterparts. Forget that they never asked for maternity leave or flexibility with child care. Even with the sacrifices the female physicians made, it was never enough. There was no way for Nandini to spend extra time with Mr. K after his pancreatic cancer diagnosis or celebrate Mrs. L's first pregnancy. Instead, she was another cog in the wheel, a white coat with legs. On her days off, she woke up wondering if she had prescribed Ms. B the right dose of blood pressure medication or if she had read Mr. M's lab results properly.

Ranjit slams his laptop shut. Nandini looks down at the red hand-embroidered rug they got from Delhi. It was the only trip they ever took as a couple, the first time they saw northern India. For five days, they posed for photographs, filled themselves up on street food, and shopped for new clothes. In the evenings, they slipped under crisp hotel sheets and reflected on their day.

On their last train ride, she thought, *This is how light we can be, without having to schedule anything around others*. They had two identities: the vacation Ranjit and Nandini, novel and daring, and the day-to-day Ranjit and Nandini, who walked side by side, guided by habit more than anything else. Over time, she told

herself they would be able to make the most of the delicate contradictions embedded in their marriage.

Ranjit scoffs. "It's easy for you to make everyone *I'm* related
to the culprits. As if your own sisters don't do the same things
to you."

"You're right," she says now. "I allow everyone to do this to
me at my expense."

"Okay, go ahead and have your pity party. Just don't go pointing fingers at my family and me for why things didn't work out."

"You'll never understand." She snaps her head up. "You got to
have your practice. Hire your own staff. Work in the way you
want, when you want. And then even become the president of
the Indian American Association! It must be nice knowing you
could make mistakes—*big* mistakes—and still have everyone's
support. Even after your family found out what *you* did, they still
paraded you as the most eligible bachelor around."

She shouldn't blame him. It was the culture's fault. Women
were supposed to be accustomed to nursing guilt and blame.
They had to keep their husbands sane. Teach children manners.
Make the perfect daal. In some parts of India, mothers were still
faulted for giving birth to daughters instead of sons, even though
Nandini learned in high school that it was the male who determined the sex of a baby.

"They're my family," Ranjit says. "They'll always support me
and vice versa. And I'm allowed to make mistakes. We all are."

Nandini tries to ignore the resentment building up inside her,
a resentment she's tried to let go of for decades.

"Mistakes?" she asks. "Our kids have a *half-sister*."

She watches her husband's expression shift from anger to surprise as the words come out of her. They rarely bring this up. For

a while, she even thought she might have gotten over it. But she realizes that a lot of her life has been about ignoring rage and hoping it disappears, then learning it never does.

Rage lives in the body, Mami used to tell her. *You just learn to deal with it differently as you get older. But it doesn't really go away.*

And the rage of double standards was even tougher for her. Why did her husband—*men*—get away with everything? Why was she always apologizing and making amends for her past while theirs got to disappear?

"Had . . . had a half-sister." Ranjit's voice is soft, as though he's worried someone could hear them.

"Oh, right, of course. *Had*," Nandini says, recalling the way she had found out about her husband's other child.

Six months into their marriage, Nandini noticed something in their bank statements. Money was being sent to an address in southern New Jersey every month. When she confronted Ranjit, he didn't even bother covering it up. Instead, he sat next to her and told her about his first love, a Muslim girl, and how they had had to break things off because her family threatened to disown her. He knew his own family would have never approved of her, so in some sense, the decision was easy, until the girl missed her next two menstrual cycles.

The girl's family married her off in weeks. She was able to pass the baby off as her new husband's. They settled in New Jersey, where Ranjit followed so he could visit the baby. The girl's husband, a rotund fellow who was ten years older than her, worked two jobs: pumping gas and tending the register at Kmart. Ranjit began sending them money every month, which the girl passed off as tokens from family back home. One month after the baby turned five, the entire family died in a car accident.

She shouldn't have felt betrayed after he told her. After all, who was she to hold someone's past against them? And as much as it bothered her, she always had to remind herself of what they both needed: a chance to start over.

"How many times are we going to have this conversation?" Ranjit asks.

Nandini squeezes her hands together. "You're right. My fault. I should be *used* to us overlooking your past. How *dare* I ever bring this up?"

"You and I know that we *both* let things go from the past," Ranjit says now.

"You can hardly compare the situations!" Nandini says. "I can't believe you would even mention that now."

"I can't believe I thought we may actually have a peaceful night tonight . . . for once," he says. "But no, things just *had* to be taken in this direction."

She wants to laugh when she remembers that tonight is the night she was going to tell Ranjit the things she has been keeping from him for months.

She considers stopping him as he paces toward the kitchen, pours milk into a sky blue mug, and puts it in the microwave. Nandini had observed this part of her husband's bedtime routine during their first week of marriage, when they were still strangers, waiting for their inevitable intimacy to arrive like a package on the front porch.

But then she glimpses him drinking his warm milk, like a child. There was no use in hurting him tonight. They were too heated already. Her husband may irritate her, but he isn't vindictive, deserving to be hurt. Her news will have to wait.

She walks up the stairs and slams the guest room door. It is hard to imagine that their first apartment was smaller than this bedroom. They never had heat or air conditioning. When Nandini told the management company about a roach infestation, they told her she was lucky not to have to worry about rats. Their neighbor's son went missing after school one day. Another was involved in a shooting. Ronak took his first steps in that dump, too young and carefree to notice his surroundings.

Her phone lights up.

Can you talk right now? Is it too late?

She walks into the bathroom and studies herself in the mirror in the way people sometimes do, taking note of fresh shadows and emerging gray roots.

After she dials the number, she sits on the floor and waits for his voice.

She's finally ready.

Seven

Simran

Kunal's phone goes straight to voicemail.

"Hey, I really need to talk to you. Call me back as soon as you get this. Please."

Simran hangs up and curses at herself for leaving the type of vague, ominous message she hates receiving.

She brightens her phone screen and dials Mom's phone number.

Mom picks up after the first ring.

"Mom, can we talk?" Simran asks.

"Yes." She pauses. "I need to talk to you, too, Simran. There's something we should discuss as a family."

"Uh, about what, exactly?"

"You should come home tonight. Text Dad and me when you're on the train. One of us will pick you up from the station."

"Can you be more specific about wh—"

Mom hangs up.

Hours later, she's at the train station with her Sole Society gray overnight bag, which is stuffed with the essentials: granny panties, Cookie Monster pajamas, Snickers bars, and a decoy psychology textbook in case anyone "accidentally" peeks into her bag, the way Mom used to "accidentally" stumble into Simran's diaries while she was at school.

Mom is already waiting in her silver Mercedes. Simran stands still and observes her laughing into her cell phone.

She deserves so much better than Simran for a daughter. Each step toward the car emits another truth:

Step: I'm a fuckup.
Step: My career no longer exists.
Step: Kunal and I need to take a break.

Simran knocks on the passenger's-side window. Mom glances up and shakes her head, the way she used to when Simran would wake her up from her power naps between hospital shifts. Mom's finger darts to end the call.

Simran climbs inside, tosses her bag into the back seat, and motions to her phone. "You didn't have to hang up."

"It's fine," Mom says, waving her hand. Simran catches a whiff of the lavender lotion she keeps in the car. "How was the train ride, *beta?*"

"Fine. Who were you talking to?"

"Just someone from work."

"Okay," Simran says, focusing on her mother's face, her long slim nose, which she inherited, waiting for her to elaborate.

There's no way Mom can know about school or Kunal, not just because Nani wouldn't have told her, but because unlike Dad, Mom is incapable of keeping things that piss her, off all to herself. Ever since Ronak and Simran were little, Mom preferred the confront-as-soon-as-possible method, while Dad could let his anger settle down.

They pull away from the station and drive deeper into suburbia, with its tree-lined streets and wide sidewalks. Simran's parents chose Livingston for its good schools even though it lengthened their commutes to work. They pass her elementary school's playground. It still has the same green monkey bars and tilted tire swing. Simran thinks back to who she was then. Did she ever see any of this coming? When was the moment that she veered off path?

Mom starts humming to herself, seemingly unaware that Simran is in the car with her. Her hair is in waves across her shoulders instead of in its usual tired bun. Simran looks at her the way a stranger might. Her slim build, thick hair, and large, almond-shaped eyes. When she was younger and they'd visit the city, men whistled at Mom whenever they passed construction sites. Simran learned how to flip them off.

"So, how is everything?" Simran asks the question as though she's talking to an acquaintance, not the woman who gave birth to her.

"Everything's going well," Mom says. "There are still so many last-minute things to do for the engagement party. It never ends. We still have to get snacks for the welcome bags, go through the final timeline for each event, iron the gift saris, make sure our outfits and jewelry are labeled, and go—"

"Mom, don't worry. I've got it. What was it that you wanted us to talk about?" Simran's stomach churns as they pull into the driveway.

Mom turns off the ignition and gazes at the steering wheel. "There's something I've always wanted to do. At one point, I thought it could wait until you and Ronak were settled. But then, as the years passed, I gave up on it ever working out. And then a few months ago, things changed and, well, I knew it was important to tell all of you as soon as possible."

"Is everything okay?"

She moves her stethoscope from the dashboard to the console. "Yes, for the first time in a long time, things are better than okay. Let's go inside. I'm sure Dad is waiting for us."

Beneath the perpetual stress and need for everything to be in order, Simran catches a glimpse of something lighter inside her mother. For a second, Simran thinks, *I can actually tell her everything and it'll be okay. We understand each other.*

They pull into the garage. The newspapers, which are usually stacked by the side door, are gone. So are Ronak's old baseball bats and the piles of everyone's shoes and the broken lawnmower. Their lives tucked away. Set to impress.

Dad's jade green BMW is next to them, with the same expired Christmas tree air freshener hanging from the rearview mirror. He installed one of those devices from India that plays "Jingle Bells" when he puts the car in reverse. Ronak and Simran begged him to remove it after they got dirty looks in the mall parking lot.

Simran takes a deep breath and opens the car door. The garage doesn't have its usual scent of gasoline.

She has three options:

Tell them about her idea to put the engagement on hold.
Tell them about school.
Tell them about both.

The first choice is the most logical. They can all start damage control, make the necessary phone calls. The second can wait until later, say, after she's had time to run away and establish a new identity.

Simran walks toward the door. All she wants to do is run upstairs and reread *Their Eyes Were Watching God*. She loves the way Janie searches for her identity and becomes independent after years of being afraid and unsure.

There's a rumble of laughter on the other side of the garage door.

"Is Dad watching a movie?"

Mom shrugs. "I haven't seen him today. He left early this morning to meet with a potential new office manager."

Simran removes her cream Tory Burch flats and steps into the house. The television is turned off. Two pairs of unfamiliar brown men's loafers are side by side in the kitchen.

She pokes her head back into the garage, where Mom is still standing by the car, dazed. "Who came over?"

"I didn't even realize someone was here," Mom says.

"Someone's *always* here," Simran says, and they scoff. Since she was little, they've joked about how Mom's a constant hostess, whether she wants to be or not.

"You're telling me," Mom says. "Oh, well. They'll leave—eventually—and then we can all talk."

Typically, when an uninvited guest comes over, Mom rushes to the kitchen to boil a fresh pot of chai and arrange snacks in tiny glass bowls. Today, she slips off her faded black flats and slings her arm through Simran's.

"Come. Let's go say hi."

A knot of dread tightens in Simran's stomach. The same type of dread she used to have in PE class when they'd have to climb the rope in front of everyone. She'd feel her loose, unstylish shorts clinging to her sweaty legs and pray for the entire thing to end.

She steps into their house. Before she can call her dad, she hears it: the deep bass, the quick sentences.

Simran paces toward the living room.

"Kunal?"

He stands up. "Simran. Hey."

He's sitting on the beige sofa, *their* beige sofa, next to his dad, Pratik Uncle. Simran's dad is across from them on an armchair.

"What's going on?" Simran asks, standing still, taking note of the Parle-G biscuits on the coffee table. She and Mom have joked about how after so many years, Dad still can't host properly.

"Yes, what brings you here?" Mom stands behind Simran. And then, as if noticing her own raised eyebrows, she adds, "What a pleasant surprise."

Dad and Pratik Uncle motion for them to join the conversation.

Simran and Mom avoid eye contact and sit on the love seat.

"Nandini Ben, please know that Meghna and I want this time to be as pleasant as possible." Pratik Uncle leans forward and clasps his hands together. He's wearing a short-sleeved button-down shirt, starched no doubt by Meghna Auntie. It's the kind Simran's dad has on in sepia-toned pictures, the ones her mom lost or threw out in a fit of Diwali cleaning.

Mom nods and offers a smile that's more a stretch of her lips than anything else. "That's what we always hoped for."

"Then let me say that we should not have any more misunderstandings during this process," he says.

Kunal and Simran exchange a questioning glance. Did their moms talk without them?

"Since it's clear we are all on the same page, I thought it would be good for us to show our commitment. To becoming one family," Dad says.

Simran grips her knees. "What does that mean?"

"That means that Pratik Bhai has agreed to be my new office manager."

Mom doesn't bother keeping her voice soft. "Excuse me?"

"I don't know why I didn't think of it earlier," Dad says. "Isn't it a great idea, Nandini? And you can even help him learn about the practice."

"We can't thank you enough," Pratik Uncle says. "Ranjit and I were also discussing something else. Since your family is coming into town soon, how do you feel about making an official announcement to everyone about this at the engagement party?"

Arranged marriages were traditionally run in one manner: the parents met, introduced the children to each other, and made plans. Somehow, Kunal and Simran have gone in the opposite direction. She wonders if things would have been the same if they had met through Shaadi.com, the Indian online matchmaking site that Ronak used, where parents often write profiles for their daughters that say, "Fair-skinned, docile girl seeks nice man," regardless of whether that's true. She pictures Kunal reading her honest profile: "Stubborn, confused bookworm seeks intelligent, patient man who wants to live in a big city."

Pratik Uncle smiles. "I'm just sorry we didn't do anything like this earlier. Not that I can count on Kunal to be on top of these types of things."

Kunal offers a nervous laugh and keeps his back straight. Simran wants to give him a hug, assure him that he hasn't done anything wrong. Kunal's dad has always had a way of bringing him down. While her mother's words have a similar way of stabbing, she and Simran share a friendship that Kunal and his dad lack.

"Well, if these are the plans, then we'd better get started," Mom says, staring at her feet, the color draining from her face. "Let me get you all something proper to eat."

"Also, we have a list of some of the Hindu traditions that our family has in every puja. I'm sure you and Meghna can go through those together and decide which ones are most appropriate," Pratik Uncle says.

While Dad and Pratik Uncle talk, Simran stretches toward Mom. "What about the thing you wanted to talk to us about?"

She puts her hand on Simran's wrist. "It was nothing."

"Really? It seemed like something."

"There are more important things happening now," Mom mutters. "There are always more important things."

"Ranjit, Pratik Bhai." She clears her throat. "About those traditions for the engagement puja, of course, we'll want to respect the wishes of our families. But I think it would be right for Simran to decide what she is or isn't comfortable with. I'm sure Meghna Ben would agree with me that it's not fun to be a bride and have no choice in anything, right? It certainly wasn't fun for us."

"Nandini, we can finalize those little details later," Dad says.

Translation: *Let's not sound too forceful in front of them. They're still the in-laws, the ones we have to look good in front of.*

"Yes, of course," Mom says, her voice polite but firm. "I just wanted to say that while the kids are here."

Simran always expected her mother to micromanage every

detail of the wedding, making it more about her as Simran's part became smaller and smaller, like a house you drive away from but still watch in the rearview mirror.

But now, for the first time, Simran sees another side of the woman her mother is, two versions sitting side by side. She's the woman who encourages Simran to call her future mother-in-law three times a week. She's also the woman who pushes Simran to have a career, something of her own. The woman who visits Dad's family every evening but also refused to quit her job, even when it may have been the easier thing to do.

Maybe her mother is also in a constant battle. Simran wonders how many times Mom was trying to protect her and she misunderstood. She wonders if men always held her back, in one way or another, and if her choices simply came down to what was best for Ronak and Simran instead of what would have fulfilled her.

Simran stands up and races to the kitchen. She needs to get out of here. "Mom, I'll get the snacks. You stay here."

"I'll help you," Kunal says as he stands up.

"No, it's okay," Simran says, rushing ahead of him. Before he catches up with her, she yells, "I just have to get something from my room!" and leaves him in the kitchen.

Simran runs up the staircase. Her heartbeat quickens. *Lub-dub, lub-dub, lub-dub.*

She slams her room door, sits down on her bed, with its white canopy and lavender sheets, and puts her head between her knees. There's a stack of Baby-Sitters Club books at the foot of her bed. She remembers how those books made her want her own group of cool female friends. She was even inspired to start her own babysitting club. Okay, fine, it ended up being a club comprised of only her, but still. She studies her walls and examines the posters of boy bands and chubby babies that have been there since elementary school.

Maybe her life has always been like this bedroom: unchanged in the hopes of preservation but now just out of place. She's had the same best friend and boyfriend for years. She's always been near New York City, to the point where saying "the city" couldn't mean any other city. What would it be like to blow up her life, start over?

She reaches for her cell phone and scrolls toward Neil's contact information.

"Hello?" His voice is lower than usual.

"Hey. I'm sorry, did I bother you at work?"

"It's fine. Give me a second to step out."

Her throat tightens as she hears his background change from a murmur of conversation to silence. She pictures him in a conference room with a long mahogany table and gaping windows that overlook a Tetris-like Manhattan. A grand space for grand people with grand ideas.

"I'm sorry," Simran says again. "I thought we should talk."

Neil clears his throat. "Yeah, I didn't really know what to do after that."

"I didn't, either."

"And it's been a while since we talked," he says. "So I figured you didn't want to be in touch."

It's been weeks since we kissed, Simran thinks. *I've kept track of every day that's gone by since then.*

"I shouldn't have let that happen," she says. "I wasn't thinking clearly. I know that's the cliché people use when they do something fucked up, but it's true. I've never done anything like that before. And I'm sorry."

"Does your fiancé know about what happened?" Neil asks.

Your fiancé. The words seem to come out in slow motion.

"I was going to tell him today and talk to him about taking a break, but then some other things came up that I wasn't expecting."

"So, then, no, right? He doesn't know?"

"No, he doesn't." Simran grabs a throw pillow from her bed and wraps her arms around it. "I'm sorry for everything. I've never met anyone like you, and I didn't think it was possible to have such an instant connection with anyone. And now, things are complicated. I thought I could cut everything off with you, but I can't."

"You don't get to have it both ways, Simran," Neil says, his voice becoming quiet.

"I know I don't."

She hears him walking back and forth. She bets he's wearing shiny designer loafers. "You need to figure out what you want. With this situation and with all the other shit in your life. You claim you want to do certain things, but then you just end up doing what everyone expects you to do."

"You're right. And I wish it were simple to just *do* that," Simran says.

"Of course it isn't simple. That's the point. But I'm . . . older than you, in case you didn't notice," he says, and she laughs. "I'm not going to sit around and wait for you to make up your mind."

"You shouldn't. I'd never expect you to," she says. Of course men like Neil Desai don't need to sit around and wait for anyone. "There's a lot going on right now, and I don't know what to do."

"I can see that. Well, I wasn't sure if I was going to tell you this, but maybe it'll make things easier for you."

"What?"

"I'm leaving for China this week."

"*China?* Why?"

"They want me to put a more global focus on my column, not just focus on American economics. The managing editor suggested I start there. And if I like it, I might stay."

Neil was about to live on the other side of the world, and Simran would get married, live a quiet life, and dig him from her memories whenever she and Kunal had a low moment.

They hang up a few seconds later. Simran buries her head into her pillows.

There's a knock at her door.

"Just one second!" She sits up.

Dad walks inside her room and closes the door. His mouth is turned downward, and his shoulders are slumped.

"Dad, I was just talking to my fr—"

"Don't," he says, holding up his palm. "I've been wanting to talk to you. Alone."

"Why?" Simran asks.

Dad never asked to talk to her alone unless something was concerning. When she was younger, it happened more, for everything from her report cards to her failed driver's license test to college rejections. Mom was always harsher when Simran didn't accomplish something. She'd lecture Simran about the importance of discipline and hard work before rushing off to her clinic. Dad could approach these things with a calmer, more curious angle. He'd ask to talk to her in her room, turn off his pager, and sit on the edge of her bed, waiting for an explanation. He seemed more like a therapist than a surgeon during those moments, and Simran often wondered if that sense of calm guided him in the operating room.

"You haven't been yourself lately," Dad says now. "I know you think I probably haven't noticed, but I have."

Simran frowns. "You have?"

Dad nods. "More than you realize. You've been distant on the phone. And, I don't know, not as excited as I thought you'd be. There's something off. And I don't even want to get into who you were talking to."

"No, that was just . . . nobody." Simran's voice is strained and hushed.

Dad sits on the corner of her bed the way he used to, the way he hasn't in years. "I've never told you this, but after your mother and I got married, we had to forgive each other, let a lot of things go from our pasts, in order to move forward."

"Okay . . . ," Simran says, even though he doesn't seem to be waiting for her acknowledgment.

"And really, she had to do more of that for me," he says. "And was it tough? Yes, it was. Were there times we wondered if we'd make it? Yes. If someone is willing to put in the hard work to deal with life—real life—with you, you can't just take that for granted."

He squints. Simran and her dad have never discussed romantic relationships or love or anything in that realm. Their care for each other tends to emerge in the form of logistics: *Did you eat today? How much sleep have you gotten?*

He stands up and walks toward her room door. "Just think about it, *beta*. Really consider what you're willing to throw away and if it's worth it."

He keeps her door open. The floorboards groan as he descends the stairs.

Her phone buzzes with a text message alert.

Mom. Did you get the snacks together? Pratik Bhai and Kunal are still waiting.

Simran goes back to the kitchen, where there is no sign of Kunal, and removes plastic bags of chakri and sev from the section of the pantry that's reserved for Indian snacks.

"There you are. Finally." Kunal comes behind her and puts his arms around her waist. He smells like the Axe body wash his mom buys in bulk from Costco.

"It's weird that you can be this close to me here," Simran says. "I'm so used to sneaking around with you in this house."

"Sneaking around in person *and* on the phone," he reminds her. "I'll never forget how quiet your voice was whenever you called from your closet . . . after your parents were asleep. You were always so scared of getting caught."

"Yeah," she says, pretending to focus on removing plates from a cabinet. "So, how have you been?"

"Don't make small talk like that. I've missed you. And I know I've been wrong."

"No, I have," she says, all of a sudden feeling heavy. Kunal's always had a way of eroding her emotional calluses.

His voice softens. "I'm sorry about everything. I should have told you I applied for the dean's summer trip. I don't mean to take you for granted. I really don't."

Simran checks the hallway between the kitchen and the formal living room. The coast is clear. "I know you don't. It's my fault."

"No, don't say that. Look, I'm sorry about my dad and me coming over here, and now our dads working together. It was a surprise, and I think our parents just wanted to move things along. You know it's always been hard for my parents that our family is not as well-off as yours. Maybe I've always had a chip on my shoulder about that and didn't realize that. My dad's always made me feel not good enough because that's what he thinks about himself. But it's hard balancing that and feeling like I have to take care of my mom. Sometimes, growing up, I felt so lonely and isolated. I would have drowned in that if it wasn't for you and how you've supported me."

Simran touches his forearm. "I can't imagine how difficult it's been with you and your parents, in so many ways. You do so much for your family, and I really respect that."

Kunal smiles. "Trust me, I know there's a lot our parents won't ever get about our relationship, but there are things we can learn from them."

"Such as?" she asks.

"They didn't give their marriages any choice but to work. I want that. And we could even look at what they haven't done and learn from that. Wouldn't it have been nice if your parents went on real dates? Alone?"

She nods. Her parents have only ever taken one vacation alone. A trip around northern India, years ago. She's never even seen them kiss.

"So would I. And I know you've mentioned that I want someone like my mom—traditional, tolerant—but that's just not true."

"It *is* true," she says. "You think that's the way women are supposed to be."

Kunal shakes his head. "No. I'm glad you aren't like her. You're vivacious and fun. You always make me relax and have a good time. Relationships—marriages—work because people decide they'll work. It's a matter of perspective and what you're willing to put in."

Maybe he has a point. Maybe some things haven't really changed since their parents' generation, and building a life with someone is a practical decision, a function of attitude, and not some fleeting rush of oxytocin.

Kunal lowers his shoulders and exhales. "You know what I realized the other day? You're the only person in my life who really understands me."

"What about your family? And med school friends?"

He scrunches his face, considering this. "They know me well enough, sure. But you're the only one I can be myself around. With everyone else, there's some distance, in one way or another. But you take me the way I am. You make things fun, for God's sake. Sometimes I get scared of my own issues and then I get pissed and don't know what to do. And everything with Neil freaked me out because I thought, *What if this guy is better than me? Better for you and better in general?*"

"We should talk about some things." Simran moves to another cabinet to avoid looking at him.

Kunal leans against the cabinets as if he's here all the time, when really, it's Simran who always goes over to his family's house.

"No," he says, walking over to her. "I don't care about all of the crap that's happened so far. Neil, our fighting, whatever. You know that seven-year-itch theory? It says that when relationships reach seven years, they'll hit this breaking point, where two people will realize they're better off going their own separate ways, or they'll stay together. If they stay, they can reach this new place that's even better than what they had before."

A wave of fondness passes over her as she processes Kunal's

words. He's always believed in them in a manner that's logical but still infused with hope. He may be an adult in so many ways—being the man of the house when his father works long hours, tutoring his classmates—but there's a part of him that stays vulnerable with her.

They hold each other, anchored to her parents' kitchen floor.

When she doesn't say anything, Kunal whispers, "I love you."

"I love you, too." Simran pulls away from him, her heart rate quickening. "But there's a lot I need to tell you about."

He clutches both of her hands. "Like what?"

"Well, after we got into that fight at Wicked Willy's, I we—"

"Simran, where are those snacks?" Mom walks into the kitchen. Kunal jumps away from Simran as though he was electrocuted.

Simran points to the bags. "I'll bring them out now. Sorry, we were just talking."

"It's fine. I'll take care of it." Mom darts from one corner of the kitchen to another. Simran helps her stack plates onto a tray. Mom's breathing is heavier than before.

"Mom, are you okay?"

She nods. "Let's get this food to everyone."

Kunal smiles at her. "How's work going?"

Poor Kunal. He's just trying to make conversation and has no idea that speaking to Mom when she's in this mode will only made her more frantic.

"Work is fine," she says. "But I might leave for India after things for your wedding are wrapped up."

Simran picks up the tray. "Why?"

"I want to check on Mami. Something is going on, but I need to see her myself to make sure everything's okay. And we have so many SkyMiles. I should use them. I don't know how I'll get off work since I'm already taking so much time off for the wedding, but I'll figure it out.

"If Mami would stop being so stubborn for five minutes, life would be easier for everyone. She knows it looks bad that she isn't staying with family and is just living alone. In India, people stay with their families. That's why nursing homes are such a foreign concept and are only now starting to be used. She would never agree to stay in one, but at least it would give her company. . . ."

Mom continues to ramble to herself. Simran watches her scanning the kitchen, making sure she didn't forget anything.

"I'll go," Simran blurts.

"You'll what?" she asks.

"I'll go see Nani. I can leave after the engagement party. You stay. You'll have to keep some guests here and wrap everything up. I can go."

And with those words, she feels a stirring, a pull she can't ignore. She has to get away from here for a little bit. Get some space to breathe. Escape.

"What?" Kunal asks at the same time Mom says, "What about school?"

Kunal looks at Simran with raised eyebrows, as if to repeat her question.

"I have some time off," Simran says. "And I'm, um, just finishing up a project that can be done from anywhere. This won't interfere with anything. I want to see Nani, too."

"You would go to India?" Kunal asks. "Just like that?"

"Yeah. I would," she says.

India, where nobody knows her except Nani. She pictures herself on a plane, flying away from all of this.

"How long would you stay there for?"

"I'm not really sure. I can use the trip to get some of my wedding shopping done," she says, throwing in a final bargaining chip.

"Well, okay," Mom says. "We should be planning your shopping soon anyway. If you're sure it's manageable with school and everything, we'll book a ticket for you this weekend. Now come on, let's go back and sit together."

Mom walks ahead of them. Kunal and Simran sneak in a quick kiss, the type that somehow still makes her feel distant from him. She lets out a sigh of relief she didn't realize she was holding. She's getting away soon.

As Kunal weaves his fingers through hers, she realizes they didn't discuss anything that was on her mind. They walk out of the kitchen, and she wonders why it was so much easier to be open with Neil than the man she's going to marry.

Nandini

"Have you thought about what you're doing to do?" Greg asks.

"I've been thinking about it nonstop." Nandini keeps her voice soft and closes her office door. There are already five patients waiting to see her at the clinic. She takes deep, steady breaths. There's no need to get overwhelmed.

"And . . ." Greg trails off for her to fill in.

"It's a lot to take on."

On his end, Nandini hears the *beep, beep, beep* of heart rate monitors and a series of overhead pages. She pictures Greg wandering through the gray hospital halls with purpose, the same halls where he taught her the things she needed to know about patient care, about herself.

"I've been worried. I *am* worried," she says.

Greg sighs. "It's never going to be easy or simple. But you just have to do it. Decide. Commit."

"I know."

"Do you?"

"Of course," she lies.

How could he understand the self-doubt that hums in her mind? Therapy taught her how to turn down its volume, but it's still there every day, waiting to invade her thoughts.

"You know, I've constantly been doing things for other people," Nandini says. "And when you've been that way for so long, you forget how to even decide what the right thing is. You question yourself."

"I hear you," he says. "But if you stay there, you'll keep living for other people. You know that."

There's a knock at her door from Suzanne, her nurse. "Dr. Mehta, your ten-o'clock patient wants you to write her a letter that says she has to bring her golden retriever on flights for emotional support."

Nandini presses the mute button on her phone. "Can you tell her I won't be able to write that? Those letters take time and require a lot of information."

"Got it," Suzanne says.

Nandini hears the squeak of Suzanne's sneakers as she saunters toward the waiting room.

"Sorry about that. I should get going."

Before she can hang up, she's interrupted by another knock

from Suzanne. "Sorry, Dr. Mehta. The patient is insisting that you write the letter and she isn't leaving until you do."

Nandini tells Greg she'll call him back.

"I'm sorry," Suzanne says after Nandini has stepped out of her office. "I tried to explain everything to her."

"It's okay. Just another day. Let me go talk to her now." Nandini keeps a smile on her face, but inside, she can feel the frustration churning and building.

The patient, a girl with freckles and curly hair, is already standing near the reception desk instead of sitting in one of the chairs and reading a magazine. It's as if she knew Nandini would be looking for her.

"Are you Dr. Mehta?" The girl adjusts her Rutgers University sweatshirt. She must be around Simran's age, maybe a couple of years younger.

"Yes, nice to meet you."

When the girl doesn't say her name, Nandini says, "Now, let's go back into one of the rooms and ta—"

"I need a support letter for my dog."

Nandini points toward the exam rooms. "I think it's better if we discuss this privately instead of in the waiting area."

"I need the letter, like, *now*," she says.

"It's really better if we go to t—"

"Why? Can you even speak English? I need a letter so my dog can get on the flight."

Years ago, Nandini would have held on to these words and replayed them over and over on the car ride home. Now, she feels a mixture of sadness and helplessness and anger. The girl is scared and lashing out at her. It isn't personal. She can see things like that now, things that would have bothered her before.

"I understand you're frustrated, but I think we should talk in another place," she says.

"Dr. Mehta, are you really going to see her before me? It's already time for my appointment."

Nandini turns to face Kevin, one of her geriatric patients. "I'll be with you soon, I promise."

She can't tell Kevin that the clinic double booked her throughout the day so she can see more patients. *Keep the visits short and focused*, the director told her. *There's no need to get into long conversations with your patients. They have to be in and out.*

Maria, a fifty-year-old woman Nandini has been seeing for ten years, stands up. "I need to see you soon, too, Dr. Mehta, but if you want me to come back tomorrow, that's fine."

Nandini scans the rest of the waiting area. Their family friend Arun is waiting with his mother, who is visiting from Canada.

Every day, she thinks. *Every day there's someone from my personal life who shows up without an appointment and expects me to drop everything to see them.*

"I'll meet with everyone as soon as I can. I promise," she says, loud enough for the entire waiting room to hear.

The girl who needs the support letter storms out of the clinic, muttering things under her breath.

Nandini starts seeing her patients in fifteen-minute blocks. A blur of images come to her mind throughout the day. Nandini, serving tea to her future in-laws while Mami nodded with approval. Nandini, chopping ginger and garlic in the dark morning hours before she went to the clinic, so that Ranjit's family would have a fresh Indian breakfast. Nandini, going to parent-teacher conferences alone, because it was expected for her to leave her job for the children and not for her husband. Nandini, wiping and crying and soothing and serving.

Nine hours later, she shuffles back toward her office and calls Greg.

"I'm done with it," she says. "All of it."

"What? What do you mean?"

"This place isn't working for me. It never did. Every day, I wake up with this dread in the pit of my stomach. And then I get here and I'm just going through the motions, trying to make it to the end. I've lost touch with why I even became a doctor. I can't do this anymore."

Her voice starts to break. She can't cry. She's given too much of herself, of her emotions, her hope, her potential, to this place.

"I'll take the job," she says. The words hang heavy around her.

"You're serious." Greg says the words as more of a statement than anything else, almost as if to confirm Nandini realizes what she's saying.

"I'm serious. Enough is enough. I need to do what I've always wanted to do. Be the type of doctor I thought I was working to be in residency, before I lost myself to . . . life."

They talk for a few more minutes, and when she hangs up the phone, she feels a sense of relief for the first time in years.

Eight

Simran

The engagement puja is a blur. Kunal and Simran sit side by side in front of a mahajara priest, who chants Sanskrit hymns and gives them instructions for the rituals, steps to ensure a healthy marriage, which they conduct in fixed, robotic movements. Their parents and siblings sit behind them. Everyone else is arranged around the room, their legs folded and palms clasped together.

Simran feels like an outsider, suspended above the room, watching herself audition for the role of a good Indian wife. Polite smile. Shaking legs that are concealed under an eggplant-colored sari. Being an Indian bride is a careful game of addition and subtraction.

Add: eyelash extensions, fake smile, layers of makeup, and clothes that weigh as much as an eight-year-old child.

Subtract: hair anywhere except from the head and a minimum of five pounds. Every time she says a prayer, she feels a mixture of gratitude, relief, and confusion. This is what her life was always supposed to look like. Things are finally working out. She didn't screw everything up. There's no time to focus on why it doesn't feel the way she thought it would.

After the puja, Kunal and Simran bow down to all their elders and ask for their blessings. Some give them cash folded in tattered envelopes. Large plates of panda and ghor papdi sweets are passed around the room. The extinguished incense spreads the smell of jasmine through the house. Songs from nineties Bollywood movies blast through the speakers, each one its own pocket of time travel. They pose for professional photographs with their families.

At one point, Kunal squeezes her hand and whispers, "We made it."

"We really did. All the way from the lacrosse field to here," Simran says as she tries to refrain from kissing him and getting cursed by all the uncles and aunties who think only married people should have physical contact.

Many of the aunties stop her to offer their precious wisdom.

Do not get Samiya as your wedding decorator. She is our friend, but she is a beetch. Your entire reception will look like peacocks exploded all over it. Blue! Green! Blue! Green!

Please make sure the venue has good Wi-Fi. I need to tag my Facebook photos ASAP!

My aunt's sister's friend's son wants to come to the wedding. That's okay, right? Nobody should feel left out.

Kejal Auntie, one of Simran's favorite family friends, puts both of her arms around her. "Simi, *beta*, you're going to have a royal wedding!"

"I'm not sure about that, but thank you," she says.

"No, it'll be better than any of the royal weddings, I know it. Those brides have nothing on you!"

"Well, I love them and think they've all got a lot on me, which is great." Simran knows all too well that Kejal Auntie and so many of their other friends obsessed over every detail of every royal wedding. They still watch parts from Diana's, Kate's, and Meghan's ceremonies.

"Hm, well, are you going to do one of those crazy wedding diets?"

"I don't know. Probably not," she says.

"Really? You're not?" Kejal Auntie asks.

Marital status and weight are two of the most popular topics among Indian aunties. Simran thinks Kejal Auntie can't even help herself.

"It's not in my plans right now," Simran says as she recalls some of the miserable and unhealthy practices her married friends endured, from 1,100-calorie days to Atkins diets to creating Pinterest boards just for "thin-spiration."

"Good for you, *beta*. No need to make yourself miserable during a time of your life that's supposed to be happy. And speaking of, I also wanted to talk to you about some other things. . . ."

"Such as?" Simran asks, not sure if she wants to know.

"You know, marriage tips. Things to keep in mind in the *bedroom*."

"Wow, that's so . . . um, nice," she says. "Maybe another time."

"Ah, I see. You already know about all that, don't you? No tips needed for you!"

A warmth spreads to Simran's face. This can't be real.

Kejal Auntie leans closer and lowers her voice. "Good for you, *beta*. Do you know how much all of us had to suffer with these men who had no idea what they were doing? It's always better to test a man out before sealing the deal."

She winks and adjusts her sky blue sari, which makes her look like an Indian version of the chubby, grumpy fairy from *Sleeping Beauty*.

The Indian *Sleeping Beauty* fairy with sex tips.

Simran wipes a bead of sweat off her stomach. "Thank you, auntie. That sounds really um, exciting. I should go change out of this sari."

Time passes in a blur of sensory overload. Grilled onions, cumin, and chili powder permeate the room. Some uncles and aunties stop her to take a selfie. Others form clusters around the table of dosas and uttapam. Glasses of red wine sparkle like rubies. Adults split pistachio-filled Indian sweets and sing along to the Bollywood songs. Everyone is intoxicated—no, overdosed—on wedding fever. There's nothing like a big group of overbearing Indians to remind you that shit is real.

Simran scans the crowded room and finds Sheila.

"Are you okay?" Sheila asks.

"Fine," Simran says, guiding them toward the staircase. Her armpits are damp. "I just need to get out of this outfit. Can you help me with the safety pins?"

Most Indian outfits require around three thousand safety pins, all of which disappear when you need them again.

"Of course." Sheila nods and pulls up the skirt of her tan salwaar kameez, the one she wears to every Indian function, regardless of how formal it is.

"Incoming," Simran says, pointing in the direction of Sheila's mom, Anita Auntie, who is approaching them. She's tugging the wrist of an olive-skinned, lanky guy who looks like he doesn't know whether to laugh or cry. Simran recognizes him as Kunal's distant cousin Karan.

"Sheila, I've been looking for you! This is Karan Shah. I told him he had to meet you."

Sheila shoots her mom a look of death.

Anita Auntie pretends not to notice.

Behind them, a cluster of guests motions for Anita Auntie to join them at their table. She swats in their direction, like they're mosquitos, and keeps her eyes on Karan. Her waist-length hair is swept into a loose braid, and unlike her daughter, she's wearing blush and a teal eye shadow that matches her sari. The final remnants of her berry lipstick linger on the perimeter of her lips, which now resemble a shriveled prune.

"He's a lawyer. About to move to New York City. You can help him get adjusted, *na*?"

Karan raises his eyebrows and focuses on the ground.

Sheila grinds her teeth. Her voice says, "Sure," while her eyes say, *Fuck no*. She adds in a low voice, "Nice to meet you. I'll see you la—"

"Sheila, don't be rude!" Anita Auntie exclaims, maintaining her smile. "You should at least offer to show Karan a good restaurant or something. How about on Monday night?"

"Mom, just don't."

"Don't what?" Anita Auntie is the queen of knowing when to play dumb.

"Don't arrange a date for us."

"Why not?" Anita Auntie laughs. "Clearly you're unable to do so yourself."

"I can set up dates just fine, actually," Sheila says. "Enough with all of this. You already made that profile for me on Shaadi .com behind my back."

Sheila showed Simran the list of people Anita Auntie found, all Indian guys who described themselves as "tall, handsome, fair skinned, and well educated" (what else?).

"As if that wasn't bad enough, you have the audacity to tell me there's no pressure to find a guy. There's *always* pressure with you!" Sheila says. "And how do you even know what's best for me? We have different standards for marriage, because you and Dad never dated. Are your glorified arranged marriages even healthy?"

"*Bas,*" Anita Auntie says, holding up her hand. "I told you before that this weekend was a chance for you to meet someone. Look at Simran! She's got her life together. And you! I asked your father what crime I committed to deserve such a stubborn *dikri* who refuses to settle down."

Sheila and Simran have spent many afternoons analyzing Anita Auntie's histrionic tendencies. Simran thinks she got them from loyally watching *The Bold and the Beautiful* and *The Young and the Restless* for the past two decades. Sheila thinks she does it for fun.

"*Bapre,* if I left everything up to you, then you'd ne—"

"I don't want to meet ANYONE!" Sheila says. "I'm dating someone already!"

Simran looks around the room. Luckily, the chatter has prevented anyone from hearing the exchange.

"What did you just say?" Anita Auntie's eyes widen, resembling a bull ready to go after a red waving flag. "You're what? Who?!"

Sheila rolls her eyes. "I was going to tell you later this weekend. Can we not make a scene here?"

"Ha." Anita Auntie grabs Sheila's wrist and lets go of poor Karan, who runs away, likely heading for the nearest bar.

"We're going outside. Right. Now," Anita Auntie says, looking for Sheila's dad.

Sheila and Simran make eye contact. Simran mouths a quick

I'm so sorry. But it doesn't matter. Sheila's hands are shaking as she follows her parents outside.

Simran looks around the kitchen at all their guests, people who know what they're doing and where they're heading in life. In the kitchen, the aunties are dividing the mundane tasks of wiping the countertops, packing food into empty yogurt containers, washing dishes, and running the Swiffer across the floor. Are they content with where their lives went? Or did they just do what was expected of them—or worse, what was safe?

The house starts to close in. Simran takes deep breaths to stop herself from throwing up. The nearest exit is only a few steps away. She can be in her bedroom in twenty seconds if she runs.

"Simran!"

She turns around to see Mom in her gold sari, her hair in a chignon. "How do you feel?"

Simran smiles. "Great."

Mom steps closer to her. "You know, I was just telling your brother that you might be the youngest in our house, but so many times, you are the strength. My Durga. Nani always told me that when a daughter grows up, she starts to truly become your friend. But when she is more like that, then it also means that it's time for her to leave you.

"Everything's finally settled. Ronak's wedding. Yours. I never thought this time would come."

The lines around her eyes soften. It's strange to start seeing your parents as people.

"But I wouldn't take any of it back. Look at how you turned out. I know that if anything ever happened to me, I wouldn't have to worry," she continues. "You'd take care of everyone."

"I would," Simran says.

Mom glances at the guests in their living room. "Did you invite Dr. Bond for this?"

"No, I mean, he wouldn't be interested in attending something like this," Simran says, the entire sentence coming out in one breath.

"Even if that's true, you should extend the courtesy. It shows initiative. Remember what I've always told you. You may have been born in Livingston, but to everyone else, you're always Indian, an outsider, and because of that, you'll always have to work harder than the American next to you to establish your career."

One of Mom's favorite carpool stories was about how she would speak to patients' family members during morning rounds. After night shifts, she wore scrubs and kept her hair in a ponytail. When she'd ask how they were doing, they'd sometimes say things like, "We're happy now that the janitor is here to take out the trash!"

They pace toward the kitchen, passing guests who smile and say congratulations as if she has so much to be happy about. Kunal is in a conversation with his mom and Charu Foi.

There's a gray-haired man standing by their refrigerator. He's around six feet tall with broad shoulders, the kind of man who likely played football when he was younger. He's gripping a plastic compartment plate with both hands. When he turns around, Simran notices his long face and sharp nose, which remind her of George Clooney.

"Simran, this is Dr. Dalton," Mom says. "My attending from residency."

"Oh wow . . . ," she says. "I've heard so much about you."

"Same here."

"I, uh, didn't think you'd be . . . here." She gives Mom a questioning glance.

Mom ignores it.

Mom always told Simran about her senior attending at Hopkins, who let her moonlight in the emergency room to make extra money, challenged her to lead grand rounds presentations, and insisted she apply to be chief resident.

"Yes, well, I was in town, and once your mother told me about this, I knew I couldn't miss it." He gives Nandini a playful jab with his elbow, which she returns. Simran didn't even know they were still in touch.

"Well, that's sweet of you," Simran says. "It's so nice to finally meet you in person."

"Likewise," he says, putting down his plate and extending his arm for an unsteady handshake. "Your mother was—*is*—something else. Of course, she always doubted herself, but I like to think that was part of the reason she succeeded."

"I'm sure. Do you ever practice in Jersey?"

Mom turns toward a group of aunties who are asking if she needs any help bringing out dessert.

Greg scoffs. "No, I'm still in Baltimore. Where your mom will be soon."

Simran chokes on her mango lassi. "What do you mean?"

"For her new job." He says this nonchalantly, as if it's well-known information.

"What new job?" Simran tugs on Mom's sari. "What new job is he talking about?"

The color drains from Mom's face. She makes a face at Greg that says, *Don't say any more.*

Greg doesn't notice. "Her dream job. The one in Baltimore to take over my practice and teach Hopkins residents at the hospital. Didn't she tel—"

"I haven't had a chance to fill her in on anything yet," Mom says, cutting Greg off, then turns to face him and whispers something, their heads curving inward. "You enjoy your food. Simran and I will get some extra dessert from the garage."

She guides them to the garage and closes the door behind them. There's a rumble of chatter on the other side of the garage door.

"What the heck was he talking about?" The floor is cool against Simran's bare feet. She lifts up her chaniyo, which keeps getting caught in her anklets.

Mom leans against her car. "Greg has an opportunity for me in Baltimore. At Hopkins. I was going to tell you about it last time you were home, but then Dad hired Pratik Bhai as his office manager, and I knew he'd need me here to make sure things went smoothly. And, well, I was going back and forth, but things became more time sensitive. Critical, really."

"Meaning?" Simran puts the ice cream back in the freezer. How long has her mom been thinking about this?

"I'm taking the job," she says, her eyes on the garage door, in case anyone walks in. She rubs off the remnants of the red kumkum powder and dried rice on her forehead.

"What? Seriously? In *Baltimore*? What does Dad think of you doing that?"

"He doesn't know yet." She keeps her shoulders straight, her voice clear. Simran sees, for the first time, how she's become a little more outspoken, less afraid.

"You haven't told him?"

"No, I was going to tell him after your engagement party. I'm not sure how he'll react."

Simran raises her eyebrows.

"Look, Simran . . . your dad and I have set up a dynamic that helps everyone except us. There's a lot you don't know about him, about what I've had to deal with. Don't get me wrong: over the years, I've seen how he's changed and accommodated, I really have. And there are so many times, especially since you and Ronak moved out, when we've established something that seems, well, nice. But how much do you keep giving and giving for the family? Am I supposed to just spend my life putting everyone else first?"

"No, you're not," Simran says. "But Dad at least deserves to be kept in the loop about what's going on."

How could you be married to someone for years but still be unable to say the simplest things to them? *I'm unhappy. I want something else. I need more.*

Mom checks her hair, adjusts the gold-and-black mangal sutra on her neck, the necklace she got during her wedding ceremony. She looks fit to play the role of "dignified mother" in a Bollywood movie, the pristine lady who has to be the best hostess, the best everything. "I know that, Simran. But even if he doesn't approve of this, I'm thinking of going. Without him."

"You'd leave Dad?" Simran asks.

She glances at her daughter with the look of someone who has realized they've revealed too much. They hear a deep laugh, the kind that comes from the pit of the stomach. Dad. He's on the other side of the door, oblivious.

"I really can't process this right now," Simran says.

She takes the tubs of kulfi back out from the freezer, scampers into the kitchen, dumps them on the granite counter, and runs to her room. The house is filled with people, but there's nobody she can talk to. It's like that cliché people use about living in New York City: *loneliness among millions.*

How long has her mom plotted this part of her life? How many times was she looking for a way out from this, from them?

She goes into her bathroom and splashes cold water on her face. Her eyeliner is smeared, and there are splotches of pink across her cheeks. So much for being the put-together bride.

Her phone buzzes with a text from Kunal: Where are you? I miss you.

She adjusts the folds of her sari, which still has the earthy, damp scent of India on it.

Charu Foi approaches her as she comes down the stairs. "Simran, where have you been? Kunal's looking for you. You know, he's so smart and humble. And his parents seem to be the same."

She motions toward Kunal, who is handing his mom a glass of water. He introduces her to a family friend, and for the first time, Simran sees his attachment to his mother as a form of compassion. He's mindful of her struggle making friends and building a life outside of their family, which are things only he can help her with.

"And it's so nice you're marrying a doctor," Charu Foi continues. "You'll never need to worry about working."

That's one of the most irritating phrases Simran has heard all day, second only to "you're picking a good career for a woman."

Simran watches Charu Foi squint, as though she's trying to stretch her insult so it can accommodate more than one person.

Sure enough, she continues. "Look at how your mom runs around all day, every day. What's the point of doing that just to prove something?"

Simran keeps a steady gaze on Charu Foi and refuses to smile. "Well, I *want* to work, even though I'm marrying a doctor. And my mom's the reason I understand the importance of having something that's my own."

"Oh? So you have a good job lined up after graduation?" Charu Foi asks.

"No," she says, keeping her voice clear and calm. "Not yet. I'm still working on that."

"Hm," Charu Foi says, looking at Kunal, who will surely cure cancer before he's thirty. "Anyway, I can just tell you're ready for marriage now."

"How's that?" Simran asks, wishing she could leave this conversation. This house.

"You're different from when you were younger. You used to be spunky and outspoken, and now, you're just so eager to please!"

"That's not true," Simran says, resenting not just that she said that, but also that she might be right.

She wishes she could think of something clever to respond to her with. That always happens to her during uncomfortable conversations: in the moment, she freezes and then sometime in the following decade, she thinks of something perfect she could have said.

Mom steps in between them. "Charu, I need to speak with Simran. Now."

She pulls on Simran's wrists and guides her into the home office, with its mahogany desk and stone fireplace. There's a twenty-year-old picture of Ronak and Simran with Santa Claus on the mantel.

Simran puts her hands on her hips. "Oh, so *now* you're ready to tel—"

"YOU DROPPED OUT OF YOUR PSYCHOLOGY PROGRAM?"

Fuck.

"Who told you that?"

"Dr. Bond called the house. He was trying to reach you and

was surprised I didn't know what you did. But no, I'm a fool, thanks to my lying daughter. What have you been doing all this time? Obviously not studying."

Simran keeps her face straight. She will not cry. It doesn't matter how much confidence she saves up—just a few words from her mother can whittle her down into someone else, into nobody. "I was going to tell you when I came back from India and had figured things out."

When Simran says nothing else, Mom asks, "WHAT HAVE YOU BEEN DOING, THEN?!"

"I've just been figuring some things out," Simran says.

It's probably not the best time to tell her that over the past few weeks, in the midst of trying to write articles, Simran applied to a multitude of jobs, including a Starbucks barista, a hostess at Ilili, a candy woman at Dylan's Candy Bar, and lastly, one of those human sandwiches for Subway. She almost laughs at the thought of her parents explaining the final one. *Yes, our daughter went to Columbia and then became two pieces of bread. We couldn't be more proud.*

"Like *what*?" Mom challenges. "How we sacrificed so much to provide *everything* for you? What a *mistake* on our part."

"I have *never* taken your sacrifices for granted," Simran says. "You're one to talk about secrets. You just dropped the bomb on me about leaving Dad!"

"That is not relevant right now. And my situation is different."

"How?"

"Because you *chose* this, Simran. You've chosen your career and the person you're going to marry and, frankly, everything else. Nothing was forced on you, and you were fully aware of what you signed up for."

"So I'm not allowed to change my mind? Because I'm supposed to just swallow my misery like a *real* woman? Don't you want me to do what I want?" Simran yells, not noticing the hush that's washed over the house.

"Please. You don't know what you want. You're a child. You have no idea what it means to build a life."

Mom turns around, faces the mantel, and avoids Simran's childhood photos.

"You're right. I don't," Simran says, raising her voice. "But it's not like *you're* easy to talk to. I've had to deal with so many things alone! And you think *nothing* was forced on me? Really? God, all you've ever expected is for me to be like you."

Mom shifts toward her. There's a brief drop in her face, as though she may be considering this. But then her features tighten again.

Simran opens the study door. It takes her a second to register everyone lined up in the hallway outside: Kunal's family, her aunts, uncles, cousins, Ronak, Namita, and her dad. Nobody says a word. They just look at her as if she's some foreign creature they're trying to identify. Maybe because she is and always will be an outsider. Someone who doesn't belong. The one to be embarrassed and entertained by.

Mom steps out after her.

"You dropped out of school?" Kunal asks. "How could you do that? And not tell me?"

"I wanted to. I really did. There's a lot we need to talk about. We just haven't had a chance."

He puts his face in his palms, unable to look at her.

"It's not worth it to throw away your life just to be defiant, Simran," Dad says, tilting his head downward in the same way he used to when she was little and asked to eat dessert before dinner.

"You think this is some act of rebellion?"

"Isn't that what it always is with you?" he asks, the calmness in his voice somehow stinging more than anger would. "You're always trying to prove to us, to everyone, that you don't have to listen."

Her dad's three brothers, each one heavier than the last, stand around him. It's a running joke that they're the living version of those Russian dolls that fit inside one another.

"She'll come to her senses," Kaushal Kaka says.

Rajan Kaka shrugs. "Maybe not."

"I'm standing right here," Simran says. "Please don't talk about me in the third person."

"You love psychology. It has everything you need," says another voice whose owner she can't find. Should she get a microphone? Stand behind a podium?

"No, it doesn't," Simran says. "And it never did. Maybe I can be something else, like a journalist."

Everyone starts moving toward her and talking at the same time, as though she suggested becoming a stripper. She almost expects a stampede like the one in *The Lion King*.

What does that even mean, a journalist?

You'll sit at your desk and make pretty sentences about strangers while your friends actually become something?

You are almost at the finish line for becoming a psychologist. It makes no sense to quit now.

You just need a break. What's that word you American kids use? Sabbatical!

I thought she was over her nonsense. I told you she was aiming too high. She should have tried for something easier.

Poor Ranjit and Nandini. Just when they thought they could celebrate. . . .

"Look," Simran says, facing the crowd. Now would be a good time to use one of those power poses she's read about. "I'm sorry my news came out this way. But I do believe that I did the right thing. And I have to figure out the next steps on my own, in a way that feels honest to me."

Everyone murmurs, not knowing how to respond to her. Simran keeps her head held high and chokes back a few threatening tears. She can't let her outside reflect her inside. She won't.

"You've been lying to me," Kunal says.

"No. I mean, yes," Simran says. "I'm sorry. I'm so, so sorry. I should have told you earlier. You deserved that much."

He turns and walks toward the kitchen, his mom behind him.

Simran start to follow them. Dad goes up to Mom. "What was Simran saying about you leaving?"

"Ranjit, I will not discuss this in front of everyone. I. Will. *Not*."

"Well, I will not be made a fool in my *own* house!"

"I'm not trying to make you a fool. I'm trying to keep it together."

"Dad, let's take a walk," Ronak suggests before facing his relatives. "Thank you for coming today, everyone."

Simran's brother might as well have a superhero cape blowing behind him. *Don't worry about that fuckup, people. The perfect child is here!*

Dad puts his hand up before Ronak can come any closer to him. He repeats the gesture when his brothers and sister start talking to him.

He grabs his wallet and keys from the front desk. "I need to get out of this place."

Simran sees his green BMW screech out of their neighborhood through the nearest window.

Nandini

"NOT NOW, PLEASE!" Nandini screams.

She double-checks that the master bedroom door is locked.

Another knock.

"Just leave me alone!" she yells like a little girl.

One floor below her, guests are starting to trickle out. At least, the considerate ones are. The rest are lurking in the kitchen and living room, rehashing what they just saw.

Nandini pictures herself opening the door, standing in the hallway overlooking the living room, and saying, *Yes, please feel free to keep talking about my family in our house. Can I serve you some chai while you're at it?*

At least Greg left before this scene. How would she explain any of this to him? He wouldn't be able to understand. *She* doesn't even understand.

She checks her phone. Sure enough, there's a text from him:

Greg: I'm sorry if I caused any trouble. I
thought you told them. We really need to
talk.

She walks toward the bed, rips off the plush white down comforter, and punches the throw pillows. Then she sits at the foot of the bed and rests her face in her palms. If she stays here, she can pretend that this was all a bad dream, a mistake.

It doesn't matter that she did everything right, everything she possibly could. Things went to complete shit. Her emotions are a tangled knot of contradictions. She wants to yell at Simran again. She wants to make sure she's okay. She wants to tell her she's worried about her future.

How could this have happened? How could Simran have not told her? Could she have done something to prevent all of this? Where did she go wrong?

She takes a deep breath. Her questions don't matter. The truth matters. And the truth is clear: Simran deceived her. After everything, her daughter felt the need to lie.

A voice from within her speaks back: *But aren't you lying to her by keeping things from her? What about the fact that you've never told her about what happened in India or about your job offer with Greg or even meeting Kunal's mom for lunch?*

She tells the voice that she withheld those things to protect her daughter.

The master bedroom is just as she remembers it from this morning, minus the king bed that had tight hospital corners before she ripped it apart. Brightly colored artwork from India, including a burnt orange tapestry Mami bought, hangs on the walls. The floors are shiny and wooden. Simran and Ronak used to wear socks and slide across them on weekend mornings, when Nandini and Ranjit were hoping to catch up on sleep. Where did those times go? How did they get here?

Her thoughts start racing, and she struggles to keep up with them.

You're a disappointment.

You screwed up all those years ago, and here you still are, screwing up.

Just because your kids don't know about what happened doesn't mean it's behind you. You're always going to pay for that.

You deserve this.

How dare you think that things were about to change?

She stands up. Blood thumps through her ears. Her breaths quicken.

Do not give in to the panic. Do not let it control you.

She inhales and wraps her arms across her body, the way her therapist taught her to all those years ago. Her sari is suddenly too tight and itchy. She removes all the safety pins holding the folds together. Yards of gold silk fall to the floor in a heap. She wishes she could remain there, with her sari billowing around her feet like a shimmering puddle.

Her stomach twists. Does she need to throw up? She runs into the bathroom, avoids the mirror, and hunches over the toilet. Nothing.

From here, she can make out the faint buzz of Gujarati downstairs. People are cleaning and gossiping.

She turns on the shower to drown out the noise. In five seconds, her bra and underwear are in a pile on the floor. The hot water hits her body like a smack. She savors the heat, the pain. She clasps her hands together and prays for the gift of being able to forget.

Nine

Simran

Anyone who has ever flown to India knows they've arrived by the smell: a mixture of gasoline, oil, and stubborn humidity. The pilot announces Baroda's weather in English and Hindi. Simran realizes she's slept the entire flight, thanks to too many glasses of red wine. So much for exchanging life stories and gaining tough-love wisdom from her neighbor, the way Rachel did in Simran's favorite *Friends* episode, when she was going to London to break up Ross's wedding.

Everyone cheers when the plane lands, all of them tired of the plastic cups and stale air. (That and Indians love to cheer. The first time Simran went to a movie theater in Baroda, she was thrown off by the lasers people brought to point toward the screen whenever a beloved actress came on, each appearance followed by a barrage of whistles and claps. *That's the way to watch a movie*, Nani said, appalled by the decorum of American theaters as she munched on the candy she snuck in.)

The heavy air feels like a wall between her and her life. She can almost pretend nothing ever happened. Slap a temporary Band-Aid over her post-dramatic stress disorder.

Simran almost forgot about how different the Baroda airport

is from JFK. Here, she steps off the plane, gets onto a crowded bus to the airport, and then struggles to find her luggage on the carousel.

She gets off the bus and follows the signs to baggage claim. There are already dozens of people waiting for their bags. A mother links her pinky with her toddler's. A pair of grandparents spot their suitcases with matching labels.

She is the loneliest person here.

There's a family of four next to her. The mom and dad count their luggage. The dad asks his daughter, who can't be more than six years old, if she has her passport. She pulls it out of her teal book bag and yells, "I told you I'd remember, Daddy!" He lifts her up for a kiss. Simran wonders if she'll ever disappoint her parents.

A memory comes to mind. A trip to India when Simran was in elementary school. Her dad couldn't take time off from the hospital, so Simran, Mom, and Ronak trekked the journey together. Mom was managing three massive suitcases, two children, and a delayed flight. One of the suitcases fell off the cart Ronak was pushing. A lady bumped into it, glanced at Mom, and yelled, "Hey, watch it!"

Mom didn't say anything.

The lady yelled again: "I said, WATCH IT! Jeez, why are you traveling if you can't even manage your own shit?"

Simran looked up at the lady and yelled, "Why don't *you* watch it?"

Within seconds, Mom grabbed her hand, faced the lady, and said, "My daughter has a point. There's no need to be so rude."

Mom put the suitcase back on the cart and, when the lady wouldn't move, said, "I'm sorry. Maybe I wasn't clear. Get out of my way. Now."

Ronak tugged on Simran's arm, and the three of them kept going. Mom only started crying once they boarded the plane.

The story is often recalled by their family to laugh about how outspoken Simran is, but she knew the real point. That with her mother, they would make it to India. They would make it anywhere.

Now, Simran sneaks a peek at an old man's wristwatch. It's around seven p.m. in America, which means her parents have likely dispersed to different compartments of the house, back to not speaking. Kunal might still be at the hospital. And Neil, Neil is just one country over.

Whenever Simran's family visits India, Dad beckons for someone to stack their bags on top of a black taxi, while Mom calls Nani from a phone booth that says "STD." She should call home. Check in.

Instead, she goes outside. Within seconds, there are beads of sweat rolling down her stomach and back. There seem to be a thousand people waiting behind the metal bars, some of them holding signs, others shrieking as they spot their loved ones emerging from the double doors.

Three boys and a girl dressed in rags surround Simran, their palms clasped together. "Please, please, please."

Simran removes the bag of Reese's Peanut Butter Cups she remembered to grab from Duane Reade. The girl grabs the bag and rips it open. The chocolates spill onto the concrete and roll in different directions. The kids run after them and hide them in the folds of their clothes.

A group of men motion toward her bag. "Help, madam?"

Simran shakes her head. She doesn't have enough rupees to give an adequate tip.

She finds the driver Nani hired, a thin, short man holding a sign that reads, SIMI. She puts on her resting bitch face again. He flings her bags into the tiny trunk with ease, which is a feat considering his build.

They drive on the highway for half an hour. It's the first time she can't point things out to Ronak or her parents. For ten miles, there's a pickup truck *and* a cart of bulls riding on either side of the car. Baroda is similar to New York in that way, both of them manic cities, infused with impulses. The roads become narrower and bumpier. They pass tiny shops that have packets of paan and Cadbury chocolates hanging in their doorways. Rows of scooters and motorcycles are parked on dirt roads. Dogs with protruding ribs nap outside of bungalows. There are billboards of Bollywood movies, the latest iPhone, and a McDonald's that sells chicken tikka burgers.

All Simran sees are her parents' faces, the blur of the engagement party, her solitary Uber ride to the airport.

"We're here," the driver tells her in Gujarati as they pull up to Nani's house, the same one Simran's mother grew up in. The barred windows are closed. Outside the entrance, a brown cow chews on a mixture of grass and banana peels.

The driver retrieves Simran's massive green suitcase, the one that their family usually stuffs with gifts and American candies for relatives.

After her bags are arranged on the dirt road, Simran hands him some flaccid rupees and takes quick steps to the entrance. "Nani!"

"Simi!" Nani says as she opens the groaning wooden doors. *"Tu ketli saras lagech."* You look so nice.

Simran drops her bag. "Oh my god, what happened to you?" she asks as she comes close enough to inhale Nani's signature scent: incense and fresh basil.

"Nothing." Nani pulls her into a hug, and Simran feels her

vertebrae, like beads on a string, through her starched sari blouse.

"You've lost so much weight. Too much," Simran says, soaking in the angles of Nani's face. It's as though someone sucked the life out of her. She looks like Nani through a funhouse mirror. Or is it that Simran is suddenly noticing her age because she hasn't seen her in too long?

"I've always said I needed to," Nani says, laughing.

"But you didn't. And this, this is just crazy. Too much."

"You're starting to sound like your mother. I'm *fine*. Come, I've already gotten everything ready for you."

Simran removes her shoes and follows Nani's slow steps into the dining room.

There's a photo of the goddess Durga at the entrance. She's sitting on a lion. Despite the weapons in her hands, her expression is serene. Maybe that's true strength: maintaining a sense of peace but having all the tools to fight whatever might be hurled at you.

The rest of the house is still the same: no decorations and walls that are cracked and yellowed from time. They pass the living room, with black couches that are now spitting up cloud-like stuffing. A black-and-white portrait of Nana is on the main wall, above a cupboard where Nani keeps all the poems and short stories Simran's ever written.

Memories are splattered throughout the place. There, near the twenty-year-old television, is six-year-old Simran, dancing to the songs from *Dilwale Dulhania Le Jayenge*, and then twelve-year-old Simran, sitting at Nana's dusty desk, sifting through his plastic-wrapped books with their permanent library smell.

Simran thinks back to one of her favorite quotes by Maya Angelou: *Every woman should know where to go when her soul needs some soothing.*

The dining table is covered with bowls of her favorite Indian street food: bhel, shakarpara, chakri, chaat. Two cups of chai are on plastic floral tablemats. The cups used to have designs of pink flowers with long stems, but over time, the flowers have been distilled to specks. Simran sips directly from her cup. Nani pours the tea into a saucer, blows on it, and then drinks.

At the end of the table, there's a purple pillbox, the kind with tiny compartments for each day of the week. Simran thought Nani took only the one blood pressure medication Mom ships to her.

"What do you want to do today?" Nani asks after they've been eating for a few minutes.

Simran shrugs. "Doesn't matter. Whatever you want. Maybe we can go to the school."

Mom told Simran her geriatric patients' lives always eventually revolved around their health. Appointments. Bowel movements. Memory loss. Simran could never picture Nani living that way.

Nani's hands shake as she brings the saucer to her lips. "Let's decide in an hour. The girls will be having lunch then. And so will the teachers, so nobody can bother us."

They talk about the girls: which ones are keeping up with their reading assignments, which ones are falling behind, and which one's parents can afford after-school lessons, an essential component of passing the year-end exams.

Simran shows her pictures from the engagement party, including family portraits where, at a quick glance, they look content.

Nani's servant, Kavita, a fifty-year-old woman who has been coming to her house for three decades, takes their plates and refills the chai cups. It doesn't matter how many times Ronak and

Simran visit India; they've never gotten used to the idea of servants. Even their parents have trouble adjusting to that now.

"It's so different being here alone," Simran says. "Quiet."

"Of course," Nani says. "Are you talking to your family yet?"

"You know what happened?"

"I think everyone in India and America knows. You made quite the show," she says. "Your mom called."

Simran rolls her eyes. "I don't even want to know what she said."

Nani smiles. "She's just worried about you."

"No, she isn't. None of them are. They just want me to live like them, instead of doing what I want."

"And what is that?"

Simran wraps her fingers around her teacup and absorbs its warmth. "To do something that's authentic to me. Have a sense of purpose."

"How do you plan to do that?"

"I have no idea. All I know is that I need to read and learn more right now. See where I can contribute to something. Twenty-six was supposed to be the year I had everything figured out. Instead, I just feel like I'm wearing some strange version of myself."

Before Simran met Neil, Nani was the only person she could tell that to without being judged.

"Oh, Simi," Nani says, shaking her head in the same way she did when Simran was in third grade and cried to her after Matt Fowler yelled about her "stinky Indian food" to the entire cafeteria.

"I know. I know," Simran says. "It's just that for my entire life, I thought I did everything I was supposed to do. But maybe I was some insufficient combination of rebellious and risk-averse, and now it's all catching up to me."

Unlike Neil, Simran was never strong enough to accept anyone's disapproval or any job without guaranteed health insurance.

"I was bored with school for a long time, so I wasn't giving it my all," she tells Nani. "I saw it as this thing I was told—pushed—to do. And I thought it would work because it was about knowing people. But it wasn't enough. I didn't like collecting data and making experiments out of human nature. I only liked that people approved of it. Understood what I was doing."

"So do something else," Nani says.

"That's what I tried to explain to everyone at home. I told them that I could maybe give journalism a thought. Research some topics for articles. They didn't get it. Mom was the worst out of everyone. I can't do anything properly in her mind."

"That's not true. She just doesn't want you to make things harder than they need to be, the way she did."

"The way she did? She's *always* done what she's supposed to. At least, until now. Did she tell you about how she's thinking of leaving Dad? Moving away?"

Nani looks out the window, toward the potted basil plants in her garden. "You should let her explain that to you, when the time is right."

Before they can continue on the subject, Nani asks, "How is Kunal?"

"I don't know," Simran says. "He's leaving for Costa Rica in a few days. He told me he doesn't know who I am anymore or how to be around me. He's never said anything like that before. He's always said that we balance each other out. He's practical, I'm emotional. He's a straight shooter, I meander around everything. But I've never heard him question anything between us, about us, like that. Not that I blame him. But . . . our relationship has been through so much, and I don't know if this entire mess is because we're supposed to be tested on whether we can make it through."

"So that was the last contact you had with him?"

Simran nods. "We agreed to take a little time to think, get some space, since we'll both be out of the country. We set a date to talk about everything after he's back from Costa Rica. August 20. Exactly ten months before our wedding date."

"I see." Nani nudges another plate of chakri toward Simran. "Am I allowed to ask if you are still in touch with Neil?"

Simran pictures Neil's head shot alongside his latest column, which she might have read a dozen times on the flight. "I thought all of this would make it easier to stop thinking about him, but it hasn't. In a way, I think he's the only person who would understand why I had to do what I did. But right now, it's better for me to have some space from everyone."

"Simi, what happened to you?"

Simran props her hands under her chin. "What do you mean?"

"You used to be so much more—what's the word?—brave. Regardless, now you're just so 'Oh, my life is hard' and 'I'm just going to sit here and feel sorry for myself.'"

"No, I'm not!"

"Sure you are," Nani says, giving the table a light slap. "Of course, I guess I should be glad that you aren't handling your problems by drinking scotch or dating too many people at once or sleeping at work and not caring about family."

"Are you referring to me or the characters in *Mad Men*?"

"Ah, right," Nani says, as if it's perfectly reasonable to confuse her granddaughter with Don Draper.

Nani reaches across the table and puts her cool palm over Simran's. "Now buck up. Stop being such a weakling. You have some difficult things you need to figure out, choices you need to make. And the way to do that isn't to cower. You're better than that.

"You stood up to your entire family. That's not easy. Your mother and I couldn't do it. And even now, do you know how many people just take the life that's handed to them, and then regret it when it's too late?"

Simran shakes her head.

"Nobody can do the work you'll have to do in order to grow and accept yourself. Only you can take that journey. But you're not going to get anywhere by moping and feeling sorry for yourself." Nani lowers her voice. "Now, come, let's get ready to go to the school. I have your clothes in the bedroom."

They stop at the garden, which is now occupied with its standard afternoon members: black sparrows that flock from one clothesline to the next, gray monkeys with tails that curl like question marks, and Kavita squatting to wash the dishes and arrange them in the sun to dry. Many people around Baroda will stretch out for their afternoon naps.

Nani guides Simran into her drafty bedroom. It's dark and warm, with low ceilings.

Specks of dust float in the sunlight. There are two short beds with stiff mattresses and folded cotton and polyester blankets. The floor is cluttered with cardboard boxes.

"What's going on here?" Simran asks.

"I'm finally trying to organize everything. You accumulate so much junk over the years. Those"—Nani points to boxes labeled *Simi*—"have some things you can take back home."

Simran nods, and Nani says, "And I have your salwar kameezes in the bottom drawer of the *kabaat*."

Simran wears cotton salwar kameezes whenever she comes to India, partially because they're comfortable and partially because they decrease the number of stares she receives for being an obvious foreigner.

On their walk to the school, Nani waves at her neighbors and stops to talk to everyone. She introduces Simran to the tailor at the end of her street. They say hi to the owner of the local DVD store. (Nani knows about his three scandalous affairs, his mother's irritable bowel syndrome, and where he gets his pirated DVDs, but she forgot his name.) She yells at the corner paan dealer for overcharging her yesterday. Mom told Simran that despite the expectations of widows in India, Nani only became more social after Nana passed away.

Simran's grandmother: charismatic, cultured, and capable of beating the shit out of you if you offend her.

There's more sweat trickling down Simran's stomach by the time they reach the school's playground, which is a sea of dirt patches and rusty swing sets. The girls are dressed in navy blue and white uniforms, their hair slicked back with coconut oil and tied into pigtails.

"Mimi Masi!" One of the girls runs toward Nani and gives her a hug.

"Hi, Pallavi," Nani says. "This is my granddaughter, Simran."

Pallavi waves and offers a shy smile.

"Pallavi is the top student in her class."

"That's great," Simran says. "What do you want to be when you grow up?"

"A doctor," she says, pointing her nose in the air, reminding Simran of what Mom may have been like at that age. Self-assured. Unaware of limits.

"She's learning how to read the story of Sita," Nani tells Simran as Pallavi nods. "The right version, of course, not the one where Rama is esteemed for being perfect."

Out of all the Hindu stories Nani's shared with Ronak and Simran, the *Ramayana* is her favorite, because of how it showed a man's devotion to his duties and a woman's ability to sacrifice.

Rama, the king of Ayodhya, is forced to spend a period of exile in the forest. His wife, Sita, devotedly joins him but is kidnapped by Ravana, the conniving king of Lanka, and Rama's enemy. Sita is eventually rescued, but she has to perform a series of tests that confirm her purity. She passes the trials, asserting that she didn't have any inappropriate relations with Ravana, and Rama welcomes her back to the kingdom.

Unfortunately, the local citizens start to doubt her and, in turn, criticize Rama for keeping a wife who had lived with another man. Despite his own faith in Sita, Rama realizes that he can't be an effective ruler when his people discredit his choices. His dharma as a king overruled his dharma as a husband, and ultimately, he drives Sita out of the kingdom. She obeys and eventually raises two boys as a single mother. Her resilience and unwavering strength became the virtues that Indian women revered over generations.

Pallavi finishes summarizing the story for Simran. When she walks away, Simran turns to Nani. "It's amazing you've taught her all of that. She knows every detail."

Nani shrugs. "I try. She's at the top of her class, but her parents can't pay for her English lessons, so there's a good chance she won't get that far in school. She had an older sister here. They took her out of school once she started her period. Now she's married. They could barely afford her dowry. That's my main problem with our country. The minute a girl bleeds, she no longer belongs to herself."

Nani introduces Simran to some of the other girls. "Simran, do you want to tell them a story?"

"Sure," Simran says, moving away from Nani.

Simran motions for the girls to come closer to her, but only two of them listen. The others rush to play hopscotch or sit on the dirt, their hands in their laps.

"So, uh, have either of you heard of Goddess Kali?"

Simran tries to remember the details Nani taught her about Kali years ago. But before she even starts, the two girls run away.

"Hey!" she yells.

Neither of them looks back toward her. Pallavi is leading her own discussion at the far end of the playground.

Nani touches her arm. "You have to get started right away or they lose interest. Sometimes, their teachers don't show up, so they stay out here for the entire day, waiting for their parents to pick them up. They're fed up by now. Bored out of their minds."

"I don't know how you do this." Simran slumps her shoulders.

Nani throws back her head and laughs. It's the first time Simran has heard her laugh since she got here. "Come. I'll show you the rest of this place."

They take a tour through the hallways, where a janitor asks Nani if Simran's the granddaughter she's been talking about.

"I used to bring your mom here," Nani says. "She was the only one of my kids who cared to come with me. The other ones were always bored. But she would walk around with me. When she was eight or nine years old, I told her not to tell my in-laws about these visits. She kept that secret without asking any questions."

"You never thought about working here after your in-laws passed away?"

She looks over the playground, considering this. "By that point, it had been so long that I don't even think it occurred to me. You see, most people eventually make peace with their lives, but that doesn't mean that things turned out the way they wanted. And when you've been living in a certain way for so many years, you lose that faith you used to have in yourself when you were younger."

Just before Simran can tell her that might be one of the most depressing things she's ever heard, Nani says, "But I'm happy with my life now. I have regrets, yes, but who doesn't? Don't trust anyone who tells you they don't have regrets."

"You really are doing so much for these girls. Have you ever thought of doing more?"

She furrows her thin, gray eyebrows. "Oh, no."

"Why not?"

"I don't want to get any more involved in the politics of teaching at this school. All that corruption and fighting and getting pushed around. The administration is already watching me."

She shades her eyes with her hands and squints at the school's entrance. "Let's go before some annoying administrative person shows up to make fake small talk."

They say goodbye to the girls and head home. Simran realizes she hasn't thought of home or Kunal or Neil all afternoon.

At home, they slip off their chappals. Simran unlocks the wooden doors. She's always loved the large double doors in old Indian bungalows, with their barrel-bolt locks that are on the top instead of the side, like American doors.

Nani sits on her leather recliner. "Simi, can you get me some water?"

Simran goes to the kitchen and opens the fridge. The inside door has bottles of boiled water, which Nani always has ready when they visit. During their first trip to India, Ronak drank water at a neighbor's house straight out of a pot and battled a miserable, endless cycle of diarrhea and vomiting for the rest of the trip. Since then, he and Simran never drank water that wasn't from Nani's fridge.

Simran pours some water into a steel glass. When she comes back in the living room, Nani is horizontal on the recliner.

"I'm going to take a nap for a little bit. You'll be fine, right?"

"Of course," Simran says. "Are you feeling okay?"

"Yes, yes," Nani says. "I didn't sleep very well last night, so I just need a little rest."

"Okay," Simran says, giving her a quick kiss on her forehead.

Simran goes into her bedroom, closes the double doors, and unclasps her suitcase. In the inside pocket, she takes out an article she started last month: "Things Nobody Ever Told You About Being an Indian Adolescent Girl" by Simran Mehta.

She spent three paragraphs talking about how Indian girls have to balance academic success, abide by their parents' strict rules, and deny any desire to want a relationship. Then, she discussed how those things change when an Indian girl enters her twenties, and all of a sudden, if she isn't thinking about a relationship, something is wrong with her. She included lines from celebrity media interviews and novels.

Simran's not sure if it's being in India or time or a mixture of both, but she suddenly sees that the piece isn't working. The message is strong, but the execution is poor. She folds it in thirds and tucks it into the bottom of her suitcase.

A puff of dust fills the air when she puts her notebook on top of the dresser, next to tubes of Tiger Balm and Pond's talcum powder. She starts opening the boxes labeled *Simi*. Two are filled with antique jewelry, Bollywood cassettes, and frayed Enid Blyton books, the ones she used to read on her family's trips to India. All of the boxes are stuffed with ghosts, items that have lost their purpose.

On the other side of the room, there's a pile of unlabeled boxes. Two of the boxes have faded kurta tops and saris. The box underneath them has black-and-white pictures of Mom and her sisters when they were younger.

In one of the pictures, Mom is wearing a navy blue cotton frock and doing a curtsey. She's grinning, and her baby teeth are missing. In another, she's sticking out her tongue at the camera. Simran doesn't remember her ever being this carefree.

She looks at the picture again. There her mother is, playful and confident at once. This little girl had no idea she would move across the world, have an arranged marriage, find herself stressed and overwhelmed as she tried to balance the needs of the world with her own.

Maybe Simran has seen glimpses of this little girl sometimes. In the car when she lets her hair down and hums to old Hindi songs or when she stretches out on the recliner and pretends not to be watching a marathon of *Golden Girls*.

Simran puts the picture back into the box. There are also black-and-white pictures of the extended family, where Nana and Nani sit in the middle and nobody is smiling. Underneath them is a portrait of Mom and her sisters. They're all wearing school uniforms similar to the ones she saw today.

A few stray sheets of paper and dried fountain pens are amid the photos. Her mother's old homework. Simran reads through her mother's analysis of *The Scarlet Letter*, with her long, looped handwriting that has since flattened into exhausted doctor script.

At the bottom of the stack, there's a photo of Mom in her wedding sari. Simran lifts it up and studies the red dupatta over her head, the gold naath on her nose. Her smile is straighter than in the earlier pictures.

Below that picture, there's one of Mom during her wedding ceremony.

Sitting next to a man who isn't Dad.

Simran stares at the picture again. At first, she's confused. It can't be real. Her mom, with her hands draped in maroon henna and the man who isn't her dad, wearing a cream sherwani and bifocals. *Bifocals.* The fire between them. Nani and Nana on one side. His parents on another.

But then, as she stares at the picture again and again, the confusion lifts and is replaced with shock. The type of shock that makes it hard to think or feel or even see. The picture becomes blurry, just a constellation of shapes. But it *is* real. That *is* Mom next to another man.

Simran stares at the man. He doesn't look familiar. Who the heck is he?

Mom's husband, that's who, a voice in her head says.

She feels a wave of sickness rising in her stomach. Her mother was someone else's wife. What else has she been hiding? What if Simran doesn't even know her? What if her life has been a lie?

Simran grips the picture and runs to the living room. "Nani!"

Nani doesn't move. Simran nudges her shoulder.

"Nani, wake up."

It takes Simran a few more seconds to realize that Nani isn't breathing.

Nandini

She ran away from her first husband three times.

The first time, she went to the market to buy okra for dinner. A black rickshaw was dropping off a young mother and her son. Nandini saw their hooked pinky fingers, told the driver to wait, and then stepped in, one chappal at a time. She tucked her dupatta into her lap. She reached Mami and Papa's house in twenty minutes. After she paid, the driver settled in front of their neighbor's veranda to take a nap.

Her parents were drinking afternoon chai in the living room. She covered her head with her dupatta and approached the barred window. There was a mound of dirt next to her feet, speckled with Cadbury candy wrappers, guava skins, and cigarette butts. She stood on top of it and waved.

At first, their faces lit up.

Is everything okay?

Are you hurt?

She explained everything in hushed Gujarati and flashed a smile whenever neighbors walked by. Papa told her to come inside. Portraits of his mother and father hung above the bookshelf, both of them framed with a white garland.

I can't stay there, she told Papa after she told them how things had been for her. *Let me come back home.*

Papa kept his voice steady. *You have to learn to honor your commitments. They're your family now, and your duty is to them. Don't embarrass us.*

Nandini pretended she didn't hear him and walked toward her bedroom.

Papa blocked the door. *You should go home. Your home.*

I can't. Nandini tried to say the words as if there was no room for an argument.

Papa shook his head. He refused to hear any more.

When Nandini tried to walk past him, he said, *I will drag you back there myself if I have to.*

He opened the front door. *I mean it. You're going back now.*

Mami started crying and repeating something Nandini couldn't understand. Before Nandini could say anything else, Papa grabbed her wrist and guided her down the concrete steps. Papa shook the driver awake and pushed Nandini inside the rickshaw. He paid the driver double the fare to not bring her back.

Her in-laws' house was ready for dinner when she shuffled in. Nobody suspected anything thanks to Papa's explanation over the phone, but her father-in-law told her it was no longer appropriate to visit her parents whenever she pleased.

Her following mornings were spent cutting vegetables, feeding leftovers to the cows, washing clothes, and pinning them across the thick rope in the backyard to dry. Her mother-in-law barked orders like clockwork from her rocking chair. *Don't burn the onions! If you care about your husband, you'll feed him properly! Gain some weight if you want healthy babies!* Nandini's husband would watch the exchanges with his arms crossed.

By lunchtime, her sister-in-law's one-year-old son would need another diaper change. Nandini would unpin the cloth from his doughy waist and soak it in the leftover water. Everyone else in the house—her father-in-law, mother-in-law, sister-in-law, and brother-in-law—would leave for languid strolls in the park and mutter questions about lunch when they returned.

We don't need you to work, her mother-in-law said after Nandini couldn't find a part-time position at the local hospital. Her new family found her education impressive, but it was to remain on paper. She had already waited for her parents to set up the marriage until she was done with medical school, which made her an "old bride." But now, she was no better than the girls she lamented growing up, who went to school just to increase their eligibility for a groom.

She ran away the second time in a manner similar to the first with the same results.

It didn't take her long for her to realize she was waning. Her husband had told her about his parents' requests, so they had begun having procedural sex. Thrust, thrust, collapse.

Within two months, she felt her stomach churn and saw bright red blood in the toilet. Five minutes later, something that looked like a liver emerged between her legs.

Her husband slapped her when she lost the baby. He demanded that a doctor confirm what Nandini said.

On the way back from the hospital, she caught her reflection in the mirror and was surprised at what she saw. There was something ablaze inside her, kernels that deserved to glow. The death of her baby reminded her of her own life.

The third time she ran away, her friend from medical school picked her up on a motorcycle in the middle of the night. She never told her parents why she left: her brother-in-law began crawling into her bed at night, while her husband was at work. When she told her in-laws, they called her a liar.

Papa didn't have the energy to send her back again. Friends stopped calling. Invitations for Diwali parties and weddings never arrived. Everywhere they went, they ran into diverted eyes and whispers.

For the following months, Nandini helped the maids with the

housework so Mami could rest. She found potential grooms for her sisters. They sat for nightly dinners where nobody spoke. It was a long process, transforming into another person.

But none of it mattered. Her parents had lost their place in the community and were still trying to earn back the money they gave for Nandini's dowry. She once saw Papa pacing in the park, his eyes pointed toward the ground as though he dropped something he could no longer find. None of the men Nandini's age were interested in a woman who left her husband. Family members suggested they move to another city. Change their name.

Papa began having trouble breathing. They took him to the hospital Nandini never worked in. He was diagnosed within one hour. *Congestive heart failure.* She set up a bed for him at home and gave him his medicines, checked his vitals every thirty minutes. His socks left imprints on his ankles. *Pitting edema.* On days she wasn't there, the maids told her Papa refused to take his medicine or eat. The doctors diagnosed him with depression.

She approached Papa's room after dinner one night.

He wrapped his clammy hand around hers and pointed to a black-and-white photo of a man.

What do you think?

He couldn't manage two words before coughing. Hack, hack. Fist over mouth.

Nandini liked the man in the picture, his side part, the mustache that curled at the ends. Ranjit.

He wants a doctor, Papa said. *We know the family. They are in America. New Jersey. He wants to move there, with a wife.*

The man also had a past. Something about being with a Muslim girl.

When she didn't answer, her father sat up.

Tell me, Nandini, where did I go wrong with you?

Nowhere, she insisted, thinking of the way he woke up at four a.m. to sell brass pots and pans, how he used an entire week's pay to buy Nandini and her sisters tickets to *The Sound of Music*.

She thought about Papa's question. She thought about her life at that moment, a life of endless rejection from family, a life of dissolving everything her parents worked to maintain. She thought she was strong enough to accept all of that.

Call his parents, she told Papa.

At the end of the month and after three "Swaha" chants by the local priest, she was married. Ranjit never once asked about her past.

Papa passed away two weeks later. She hung a fresh garland around his photo.

Ranjit saved Papa from spending his last weeks in distress. He took his final breaths in his bedroom, surrounded by family, a smile deepening the lines around his eyes.

Nandini and Ranjit moved to America, where they both redid their residencies in order to practice. The first years were spent in a studio apartment in downtown Baltimore. Their car was broken into three times, and they slept on a mattress in the middle of the floor. After their thirty-six-hour shifts at the hospital, they would eat milk and cookies for dinner.

There weren't many Indian families in Baltimore yet, and they couldn't afford frequent phone calls to India, so Nandini wrote letters to her mom, sisters, and friends. She waited for their replies to arrive in sky blue envelopes that were coated with India's damp and earthy scent. Sometimes she cried out of pure loneliness.

It started slowly; or maybe it was there all along. Ranjit was the first member of his family to have a furnished apartment. It was understood that he and Nandini would pay for everyone's sandwiches at Subway and all of their nieces' and nephews' Six Flags tickets. When Nandini's sisters moved to America years later, they sent their kids to stay at their house for months at a time. *You're better at keeping them in line than I am*, they'd say, as if the compliment insulated the imposition.

Nandini's position as one of the only three doctors at the family medicine practice allowed her to manage everyone's healthcare. She could see people as her patients, had access to medication samples, and was home by seven every night. But she knew, just before Ronak was born, that she was ready for another job. Working in primary care had become corrosive. She wasn't getting through to patients or practicing in the manner she envisioned. Maybe she could work at a teaching hospital, where she could conduct research and present at case conferences.

Ranjit held up his palm before she could finish. His family needed her to have stable hours. Nandini went over to their homes on a daily basis, to drop off cholesterol and samples of high blood pressure medication, examine a new rash on someone's leg, or refer someone to a specialist. She knew Ranjit wanted to marry a doctor so she could take care of his family, while he could focus on being a surgeon. They were both doctors, but she was the one who handled any family health concerns, managed their children's schedules, and took care of the housework while he could focus on becoming a boss, the owner of a practice. Even professional ambition could become a vector for subservience. The women in his family talked behind her back, wondering why he settled. But her job, their dependence on her, kept them in line toward her face.

All around her, Indian women in America were leading parallel lives. Becoming friends with their husbands' friends' wives. Crouching over stovetops while the men sat at the table, waiting to be served. Ironing button-down shirts from the clearance rack at Marshalls. Wiping down the kitchen counters and packing food into Tupperware containers after a party.

Nandini knew she was in a better position than other women. Ranjit was even-tempered and easygoing. A man who let both of their pasts recede into oblivion. They treaded through garden-variety marital issues: control, money, time.

By the time Ronak was born, she and Ranjit had established an understanding where she thought love would be. He became president of the local Indian American Association and was encouraged to think about the national position. They had guests stay over multiple times a week. They were interviewed in the local paper for embodying ideal Indian values. It was possible to start over, she realized, the days of her first marriage sometimes visiting her in faded flashes, as though they were memories within memories.

Ranjit had given her too much to be grateful for. Whenever she questioned her life, she forced herself to think about something else, but the doubt always lingered in the corner, its arms outstretched, waiting to be picked up again. She had two selves: one going through the daily motions, another that was always elsewhere. Over time, she realized it wasn't Ranjit's fault that their marriage felt like a dress that never quite fit. It was their marriage's fault.

Nandini told herself she wouldn't be one of those wives, like her mother or sisters. When the time was right, she would pursue her goals. She couldn't accept the possibility that her aspirations were larger than her capabilities, that she would have to downsize her dreams and accept an ordinary life. No, once her duties were fulfilled, she would move on from all of this.

But everything changed after Simran. Ranjit's family gossip

about her no longer mattered. Nandini would be damned if her daughter suffered from a fate that resembled her own.

After a certain point, she forgot where her life ended and Simran's life began. During the teenage years, she realized there were many Simrans: the one who was her best friend, the one she emotionally relied on, the one she worried for, the one she needed to guide. They slipped in and out of these roles with a simple mixture of words, intonations in opposing directions. It was only Simran who knew the lies Nandini told others, the truths she told herself. They exchanged glances across the table when Ranjit's family was over. They laughed when Ranjit and Ronak couldn't boil a pot of rice.

As much as Nandini liked to think of herself as an evolved mother, improved from the generations before her, she knew there were certain mistakes she repeated.

There were occasions when she considered telling Simran about her first marriage. Late at night after Ranjit and Ronak had gone to sleep and she and Simran sat in front of the television. On car rides back from school.

The confession lingered on her tongue but refused to enter the air in front of her. Even as a mother, she couldn't be sure that her daughter would still accept her, if she revealed all of herself.

And now she had failed her, just when she thought things were in place. She thought she did everything right, but it didn't matter. People always blamed the mother when kids weren't doing well.

Maybe she should have stayed home more.

Maybe she shouldn't have been so exhausted, so distracted.

Maybe she shouldn't have let parts of herself dissolve, until there was nothing left.

Ten

Simran

The hospital reeks of rubbing alcohol and latex. Nurses rush in and out to check on the Nani's pulse or tighten the white blood pressure cuff around her twiglike arm.

There's a fluorescent tube light over the bed that gives the entire room a jaundiced tint.

Simran rests her head against the bed. Fiddles with her dupatta. Watches the clock on the faded wall. Tick, tick, tick.

Some amount of time later, Nani stirs under her sterile blue blanket and sits up in bed, noticing her surroundings. "What happened?"

"You weren't waking up," Simran says, afraid that if she clutches Nani's hand too tightly, it'll snap.

"I was tired," Nani says, her voice barely audible over the monitor, with its continuous mountain-like designs that Kunal taught Simran represent heart rate and rhythm.

"It wasn't just that," Simran says.

"Ugh." Nani presses her hands to her forehead. "I have a headache."

"Let me call the doctor."

The doctor is a short chubby man with a gray comb-over. He

takes out his stethoscope and presses it against Nani's chest, then her back. She takes deep breaths whenever she feels the silver disc touch her skin.

"Your labs haven't come back, but your blood pressure has been very low. I think you were dehydrated. I would tell you to drink more fluids, but you already know how important that is." He slings his stethoscope around his neck and raises an eyebrow at Simran.

"What are you talking about?" Simran asks.

The doctor clears his throat and breaks his gaze with Simran.

Nani sits up in bed and says, "You can tell her. She's going to find out soon enough, anyway."

"Tell me what?"

"Are you sure?" he asks, his eyes shifting from left to right. "Really sure?"

"Yes. I am," she says.

Even though Simran's grandmother is the one pale, weak, and in bed, he's scared of her. The woman has a gift.

"Tell me what?"

Simran looks back and forth between them, as though she's watching a tennis match. "TELL ME WHAT?"

Nani turns onto her side. "Simi, I've been sick for some time."

"Sick? Sick how?"

Her lips become straight. "I have ovarian cancer."

"You . . . what?"

The air in Simran's lungs disappears, as though someone just punched her chest. "How? How is that possible?"

Nani scoffs. "You know these types of things are always possible."

"No, I don't . . . I don't understand. It doesn't make any sense."

But then Simran thinks about how it does make sense. Nani missing the engagement party. Mom saying she's been hearing from her less. The purple pillbox.

"Now, look," Nani says. "Do *not* get weak about this. The last thing I need is for my granddaughter to be whimpering when she's with me."

Simran wants to tell her that she can't process this right now, that they need to rewind back one day and go back to normal.

Instead, she takes a deep breath and straightens her shoulders. Her grandmother and mother both have the ability to maintain discipline even when they should be in distress.

Simran faces the doctor. "Tell me everything."

He glances at Nani for approval, which she provides with a nod.

"She was having abdominal pain for a few months. When she finally agreed to see me, I thought she was just constipated. But things didn't get better with standard treatments. So I decided to run some tests and we found a small mass on her right ovary."

"What is her prognosis?" Simran asks.

He looks at the ground, and his voice softens. "This type of cancer is aggressive. We were fortunate to find it before it spread, but in most cases, things wi—"

Simran stands up. "How much time does she have?"

"Without treatment, maybe a year."

"And with treatment? She *will* have treatment."

"Please," Nani says, holding up her hand. "I have no desire to be poked and prodded and harassed just for a few more months. I want to go in peace."

"*Go?* How can you just say that as if you're heading to a coffee shop?"

Simran runs through the Kübler-Ross stages of grief: denial, anger, bargaining, depression, acceptance. Which stage is appropriate for her right now?

"Because I can," Nani says, crossing her arms like a four-year-old not getting her way.

"So you're not even going to try to fight it?"

She shakes her head. "You won't understand this yet, but when you're my age, and at peace, you'll know when it's your time."

"No. I'm not buying into any of that. It's not your time now."

Nani turns away from her.

"At least tell Mom," Simran says, knowing that Mom would make it her mission to consult the most aggressive surgeons and oncologists in the world.

"She has enough going on. You all do. What's the point of me being eighty years old if I'm going to burden my family?"

"You're never a burden," Simran says.

"And you know I prefer my space," Nani says. "I don't want any of you hovering around me and feeling sorry for me all day."

"At least tr—"

"Simran, *no*."

"It's important you stay calm, Mimi Ben," the doctor says. "You're still weak."

"Then we need to not discuss this anymore," Nani says. "It's only going to make me more irritated."

So they don't.

The doctor shuffles outside, muttering something about waiting for the lab results. A nurse in a periwinkle sari comes into the room. She rolls a rusty cart that has a tray of steaming daal baath. Nani waves her hand. The nurse takes it away.

"Now, tell me something else," Nani says, turning toward Simran. "*Anything* else."

Simran stares at her. How is she supposed to talk about any-thing else? How can she pos—

"Simran, *now*. I mean it," she says.

Simran brings up whatever comes to her mind: the latest Am-itabh Bachchan movie, Indian politics, the newest gossip about her friends. She even tells Nani she's thinking of writing an ar-ticle about girls' education in India.

Somewhere between Sheila's mom trying to set her up with Karan and Vishal's latest date, Simran blurts, "I found pictures of Mom from her first wedding."

To her surprise, Nani turns to her and says in a calm voice, "I thought you would."

"You did?" Simran asks. "Why's that?"

"Because I know your habit of looking through things. And that this would all come out anyway. I told your mom to tell you sooner."

"Tell me what, exactly? That she neglected to mention an-other *husband*?"

And before her grandmother answers, Simran says, "Oh my god. She left him the way she's going to leave Dad. This is what she does, isn't it? She's one of those Madame Bovary type of women."

Maybe her mother's the way Vishal used to be, before he started dating Ami: with one eye on the present and the other elsewhere, always on the lookout for something better.

Simran can't look at Nani so she focuses on the wall behind her, with its extra sockets and knobs for oxygen tubing.

"She's not one of those women, Simi," Nani says. "There's a lot that you don't know."

She tells Simran everything: her mother's arranged marriage to a controlling man, how she ran away multiple times, their family's social isolation, Simran's dad meeting her, with his own baggage, and the life they built together after Nana passed away.

Simran listens to Nani in silence, as though she's talking about someone else, and is overcome with a mixture of betrayal and anger. She doesn't know her mother. Maybe she never did. She feels a part of her sinking as an array of childhood memories run through her mind. All those times Mom pressured Simran to be this way or that way and she was hiding *this*? How easy it was, to just see her mother for who she claimed to be, to not ever consider the history she left behind.

A heavy pang of sadness settles over her chest as other thoughts come into focus. Her mother tried to protect her from her past. She lived in pain, in a way Simran would never have to and could never fully understand. Simran wishes she could replay every conversation, every piece of advice, every moment of disappointment. Maybe there's more to every single thing Mom ever told her.

"This doesn't make any sense." Simran slumps into her wooden chair. "I need to call her."

"No, not yet," Nani says. "She's going to be livid with me when she finds out I told you, and I'd rather not hear any of that today."

Nani looks toward the other side of the room, where there's a pale blue curtain pushed to the wall, an empty bed on the other side of it. "You know, *I'm* the one who made the mistake. She didn't know what she was doing. None of us did. We all jumped from our father's house to our husband's. And we were taught not to defy anyone, to just deal with everything and keep it to ourselves. Was she depressed? Of course she was. But people in India barely believe in depression now, and they definitely didn't then. She was trapped. I should have realized it earlier. Done something."

"Do you think there was anything you could have done?"

Nani sighs. "I like to think there was something I could have done, but I really don't know if that's true. We . . . *women* . . . are raised to be polite. To change our shapes and be accommodating and not threatening. And as much as I liked to think that I was a good role model for her, I now see that maybe at the time, I wasn't strong enough to teach her how to be honest with herself. Have a sense of conviction. Forget about pleasing others. So, despite what was against both of our true characters, Nandini became like me as a married woman. Obliging. Deferential. But she seemed better, stronger, when she became a mother. She was so determined to make sure that you didn't have to struggle, even if that meant she had to put aside some of her own things for a while. But then again, she also felt the need to prove to everyone that she was an adequate mother. She was always torn that way."

The last few months flash through Simran's mind like a silent film: her mother's reaction to Neil, her insistence Simran get married before anything catastrophic could happen, the contradictory advice toward dealing with in-laws and her career.

Simran folds her hands over Nani's. She leans back and closes her eyes. She looks at the empty bed, unable to process anything, except the beep, beep, beep of the monitor.

Nani refuses to let the cancer impede her for the rest of Simran's trip. Not when she has to stop during their morning walks to catch her breath. Not when she can't finish a small bowl of daal baath because her stomach is bloated. Not when pangs of pain and nausea wake her up every night.

By the end of Simran's second week, the girls at school are used to her being at Nani's side. Simran and Nani come and leave at different times each day, both of them in charge of their own tasks. Nani knows how to keep the girls entertained. She lets them interrupt her with questions, follows their tangents.

Simran helps them practice English and stay focused. They establish a rhythm Nani struggled with maintaining. Sometimes, they review essays that were assigned earlier that day. Other times, they discuss the boys they have a crush on. There's no structure or analysis or measurement to their methods. The only certainty of each day is that most of their time will be filled with the girls sharing their opinions on everything: the latest Shah Rukh Khan movie they hope to see, arranged marriage, what it's like to get their period and be pulled out of school, their parents' stress over their dowries, what they hope to be when they grow up.

In the evenings, while Nani watches soap operas, Simran looks up these topics online. Hours pass in a blur of essays and articles and interviews. Nani and Simran debate over the lack of data on girls in rural India and how likely it is for things to change. Simran starts to feel something in her take root and sprout in a way that hasn't happened in a long time.

"Are you married?" Pallavi asks one day. She's the clear alpha of the group.

Simran pictures Kunal's bushy eyebrows, the scruff around his lips. "No, I'm not yet."

"But you're . . . old," she says, covering her mouth after the words come out.

Simran laughs. "I know it seems that way, but there's never a right age to get married."

"My sister used to say that, too," Pallavi says. "So she said no to this guy who asked her for marriage. And then he tried to throw that stuff in her face."

"Stuff?" Simran asks, and Nani mouths, *Acid*.

"Is your sister okay?" Simran asks, picturing the horrific images she's seen of victims of acid attacks.

Pallavi nods. "She didn't get hurt on her face, only her neck. We thought she was lucky."

"It's too common. Unfortunately," Nani says.

"So is your sister married now?" Simran asks Pallavi.

Her coconut-oiled braids sway as she shakes her head. "Nobody wants to marry her with the burns on her neck. She helps my parents make clothes, but that's all she can do in her life. Mummy and Papa paid dowry to one family, but they just stole it and then pulled out of the wedding deal. . . . That's why my parents said I have to get married soon."

"What do you mean, 'soon'? How soon?"

Pallavi glances at Nani, then Simran. "Mummy and Papa said I have to leave school by the end of the year."

"What? Why?"

She looks at the ground and starts making circles in the dirt with her feet.

"Pallavi, why?"

"I have to get married and help out at home. They can't pay for school anymore. We don't have any money left."

"But you want to be a doctor," Simran says, leaning down to be at Pallavi's eye level. "Don't you?"

Pallavi shrugs. "They said I can't."

Before Simran can say anything else, Nani grabs her arm. "We have to go."

Nani motions toward the school entrance, where a man is watching them.

Simran uses both of her hands to help Nani stand up. They walk as quickly as they can with Nani's shuffled steps.

"*Ek* minute, Mimi Ben! Mimi Ben!"

"*Are bapre*, what now?" Nani mutters as she prepares her fake smile.

Simran turns around to see Deepak Bhai, the school's principal, approaching them. He has a shiny, black, middle-parted toupee and a round red rose that make him resemble the guy from the game Operation. With his toupee, wrinkled hands, and shiny cheeks, he could either be thirty-four or fifty years old.

"*Kem cho*, Mimi Ben?" *How are you?*

Nani nods. "*Majama*. And you?"

"Fine. Can we talk for a second? If you don't mind?" He motions toward the empty part of the playground. With his protruding stomach and thick wrists, he could be the poster man for how fast food has ruined India.

"Yes. Simran can come with us," Nani says.

Once they're away from the girls, Deepak Bhai says, "I know we've had this conversation before, but, well, I don't know how to say this. Again."

Nani cranes her neck toward him. "Just say it."

Deepak Bhai looks at his feet. "Some of the parents are very concerned with your . . . role . . . with the girls. They have been, and you know that. But now the complaints are getting worse. More, eh, aggressive."

"And why is that?" Nani asks, placing her hands on her hips.

Deepak Bhai is sweating bullets. You'd think the guy was under one of those bright interrogation lights they show during suspect interviews on television.

He reaches into his breast pocket, pulls out an off-white handkerchief, and dabs his forehead. He closes his eyes. Rocks back and forth. Has he fallen asleep standing up?

Simran sees Nani trying to stifle a laugh. She refuses to look at her. That's one thing she, Mom, and Nani have in common: they are incapable of holding in their laughter when it's inappropriate. Once, at a wedding, the groom's father farted during his speech. Mom glanced at Simran, and within seconds, they both ran out of the room like complete idiots.

Simran clears her throat.

Deepak Bhai opens his eyes. "They, the parents, don't know what you're teaching them. You see, for the other *official* teachers, there's a clear curriculum. The parents know what the girls are learning. Whereas for you, it's not as straightforward. And it has come to my knowledge that some of the things you're going over with them are not so, how do you say it, conventional."

"What does that even mean?" Simran asks. Nani raises her hand, as an indication for Simran to stop talking, but she doesn't listen. "My grandmother has done more for these girls than any of these teachers. They don't even show up to school most of the time! And thanks to her, some of them are starting to learn how to write in English."

"Simi, I can handle this," Nani says, her voice quiet but firm.

"No," Simran says. "You've been devoted to these girls, day in and day out." She looks at Deepak Bhai. "Who is in charge here?"

He dips his head down, and Simran's worried his toupee will slip off. "I am."

"And who is *your* boss?"

"He's, eh, not here."

"What's his name?" Simran takes out her notebook and a pen from her bag. "Write down his contact information for me."

Deepak Bhai's hand shakes as he writes his supervisor's name and phone number.

Bharat Narayan
+91-263-6377

Simran rips out the page from her notebook and puts it into the front pocket of her bag.

"We'll be going now," Nani says, grabbing Simran's hand as they walk away.

The phone is ringing when they get home. It attempts to pronounce the name of the caller. Ronak and Dad had installed the feature during their last trip to India.

Simran runs toward it and presses the "talk" button.

"Mom?"

"Simran, is that you?"

"Sheila?" Simran steps toward the barred window, the one her mother stood on the other side of after she ran away from her first husband. Now, on the other side, a thin lady with silver hair and a large maroon bindi is pushing a giant cart stacked with eggplant, radishes, cabbages, and peppers.

"I got this number from Ronak," Sheila says.

"Oh," Simran says. "What's up?"

"What's up? What's *up*? What the fuck is up with you? I haven't heard from you since the engagement party. You told me you were going to India, and the next thing I know, you're on a plane. I'm really worried about you."

"There's nothing to worry about," Simran says. She mouths *Sheila* to Nani, who nods.

"What are you even doing there?"

"Just hanging out with Nani. Getting some space," Simran says, not knowing how to tell Sheila that she's literally living the life of an old lady.

"And? What about Kunal? You know, that guy who gave you a ring?"

Simran looks at her left hand, which has been bare since the day she left for India. "I'm sure he's getting his space, too."

Sheila sighs. "Please tell me that this doesn't have to do with Neil, that you're over all of that. You are, right?"

"I haven't talked to Neil," Simran says.

"That's not what I asked."

When Simran doesn't say anything, Sheila adds, "Simran, I don't understand what's gotten into you. One second, everything is fine. Normal. And the next, your engagement party is a mess, you've dropped out of school, you don't have a job, you can't give me a straight answer about Neil, and you just run away?"

Simran moves into Nani's bedroom and closes the door. "I'm not running. I just needed to get away from everything."

"Well, shit's hit the fan since you left. Have you seen Facebook?"

"No," Simran says, grateful that Nani doesn't have a strong Internet connection (except for the living-without-Netflix part).

"There are people from NYU who've written on Kunal's wall, saying they're sorry for what he's dealing with and things like that."

"Seriously?"

Damn social media. Can't anyone fuck up privately anymore?

"Yeah," Sheila says. "I ran into Priyal and Neha and that whole group the other day. They all were like, 'What the hell happened to Simran?' and 'I didn't know she was that kind of person.' Even Rahul was talking shit."

"Rahul?" Simran asks.

Rahul went to NYU with them and now works at a tech start-up. He has the unfortunate habit of telling too many bad jokes and following each one with a Woody Woodpecker laugh.

"Don't worry. I bitched at all of them," Sheila says.

Simran pictures her scandal spreading through Manhattan, a force growing with each person it comes to. The worst part is what it's done to Kunal. She thinks of him the way an acquaintance would. He's hardworking. Practical. Guided by principle. A good man who does good things. Someone who doesn't deserve this.

"It's been really weird not talking to Kunal," Simran says. "Like a feeling in the back of my mind that I'm forgetting something."

"So call him," Sheila says.

"I don't know. I don't know what to say. I don't know what *he'd* say. We both set that August 20 date. I don't know how he'll react if I try to contact him before then. But, man. . . ."

"You miss him?"

"I do," Simran says.

"Of course you do. How could you not? You've been talking to him almost every day since high school."

"True. . . . Ugh, let's change the subject," Simran says. "How are things with you?"

Sheila grunts. "I don't know. At your engagement party, I told my parents everything about Alex."

"And?"

"At first, my mom acted like she didn't hear me, so then I had to repeat myself. Then she turned to my dad, who basically took over after that, because my mom was stunned. God, she was so freaking dramatic. She started laying down and *fanning* her face and mumbling some bullshit about her blood pressure. Then my dad began firing all these questions, which I think were supposed to be rhetorical but I answered anyway."

"Like what?"

"Like, 'Why did we ever move to this country?' and 'Where did we go wrong as parents?' and 'How could you do this to us?'"

"That's terrible," Simran says. "I'm sorry. But that took a lot of courage on your part to be straightforward with them."

Simran has always pushed Sheila to stand up for herself when it comes to her parents. They know she gets guilt-tripped easily into doing whatever they think she should be doing.

"It's fine," Sheila says. "I wouldn't tell them this but they made me doubt things with Alex. They asked me what it would be like to have an 'outsider' with me at all family events and what that would mean for our kids. They think I could get anyone and don't know why I'm settling, so to speak. Then, of course, my dad kept going. He thinks our generation is going to have a lot of divorce because we don't know how to pick partners. But I don't know. I'm just not going to talk to them."

Sheila and Simran, all grown up and not on good terms with their parents. Simran can see their ten-year-old selves looking at them, shaking their frizzy-haired heads in disappointment.

They talk for a little longer, and then Sheila says, "I know you probably have to go, but there are some other things I forgot to tell you. You'll see this soon enough anyway, but I think Neil might be dating someone."

"How do you know that?"

"It was in some gossip blog that the NYU people were reading. Apparently another writer."

Simran stops herself from asking any questions, questions she has no right to. Instead, she pictures the female equivalent of Neil: a girl who is beautiful in an I-read-a-lot sort of way, who wears mascara and crisp, white button-down shirts. She has a sinking feeling in the pit of her stomach as she pictures them flipping through the Sunday *New York Times*, holding hands inside a hipster coffee shop, or taking a selfie on the steps of the New York Public Library.

"Also," Sheila says, "you should check in with your family. Ronak told me some things have happened since the party. He wouldn't get into it with me over the phone, but, I don't know, he sounded off."

Simran hangs up with Sheila. But before she calls her parents, she dials Bharat Narayan's phone number.

Nandini

Dear Simran,

For years, I thought you could look into my eyes and see that I've been lying. You could see past the facade I put up for the world. You could tell there are gruesome, shameful stories I've kept locked in a box, stored deep inside myself. But I concealed it. The way I learned to do. The way I've done since. It's taken me years to realize that the things I've hidden have had a far bigger impact than the ones I've revealed.

I was scared then. But I've only been more scared since. Becoming a mother has a way of coating your life with a thin layer of fear. Every day, I feel as though I'm running from it—what happened and everything else that's been with me since. Self-hatred. Lies. The way people looked at me. Shame.

It consumed my identity more than anything else, especially the things I took pride in. More than being my strong mother's daughter, or an older sister, or a doctor. Everything that made me me seemed to crumble and no longer mattered. I spent years running or hiding or running and hiding. I hated myself for bringing this on my family, for what this did to my parents' sense of stability.

That's what a secret like this does to you. It corrodes you. I used to have large aspirations. Images of my future that were infused with possibility. I used to think of movies where women had British accents and men had shiny shoes. I was starting to become a strong new woman, someone I could be proud of. And then she got taken away from me and I wondered if I only dreamt of her existence in the first place, if she was ever real. Because once she left, the only thing I had was the feeling that I was to blame for all of it. I learned to accept whatever was handed to me instead of fighting for more. Sooner or later, the world shows you what you deserve. And I knew I didn't deserve anything.

After I met your father, I felt something that seemed like hope. I thought I could start over. That's what you and Ronak were to me. A fresh start. A chance.

But I know now that nobody can run away from their past.

If I ever give you this letter, that's what I want you to take away from it. Don't ever run away from anything. Run after what you want. Run toward something greater than anything I could ever give you.

Love,
Mom

Eleven

Simran

Bharat Narayan has to be at least seventy years old, with white Einstein hair that spreads in every direction like a cloud. He wears a navy blue kurta top with white linen pants and looks like he meditates every morning.

"So, what can I do for you?" he asks, folding his veiny hands together.

Simran gave herself a little pep talk on the way here. *You can do it, Simran. You're confident. You're capable.* It was inspired by one of her favorite episodes of *30 Rock*. Liz Lemon always knows how to pump her up.

She shifts in her chair. "I'm not sure yet. My understanding is that my grandmother, Nani, Mimi Ben, is concerning some of the students' parents because of her visits."

Simran gives him a quick recap of their conversation with Deepak Bhai. Her Gujarati has become stronger, more accurate. A sign that she's been in India for three weeks.

He nods and folds his hands together. Simran wonders if he's telling himself that Indian girls from America are too outspoken.

But a second glance reveals that he's interested, not appalled.

"Yes, I am aware of that," he says. "Did Mimi Ben ask you to come here on her behalf?"

"No, not at all."

Nani thinks Simran is at the bookstore down the street, not in Alkapuri, a town that's a fifteen-minute rickshaw ride from her house.

Bharat Narayan's entire office is covered with trinkets from around the world: a miniature black-and-yellow rickshaw, a blue porcelain baboon covering its eyes; a paper fan with a watercolor of two women in high buns and kimonos. A stark contrast to the orderly books and humming computers in the psychology building. Simran wonders if staying calm amid the clutter is some type of mental experiment for him.

"What doesn't make any sense to me," Simran says, "is how some of these teachers don't even show up, and then my grandmother, who shows up every day because she *wants* to, has to deal with opposition."

Bharat Bhai leans back. "It's complicated."

"Meaning?" Simran asks.

He raises his eyebrows. "Xavier's has a high need. People—young, qualified people—are not willing to live near the school. We can't take the best of the best teachers in Gujarat. They all want to go to bigger schools in bigger cities. There isn't enough staff to monitor how much the teachers teach and if they show up or not. We simply don't have that luxury. So we have to take who we can get and then we *have* to keep them."

"And the curriculum? The things the girls are taught in the classroom? Who decides that?"

"Designed by the school board. Look," he says, fiddling with a blue fountain pen on his desk. Surely a token from one of his trips. "I'm sure you know we have enough trouble keeping enrollment at our school. Girls leave for all sorts of reasons: their families want them to get married or help at home or can't afford sanitary napkins and school tuition once they start menstruating. It's all unfortunate, yes. But if we make their parents uncomfortable with what they're learning, then we risk getting to a point where we don't have a school left."

"So, what are you saying?"

"We are going to have to ask Mimi Ben to stop coming."

Simran slams her hand on the scarred desk, surprising both of them. "You can't do that! That's ridiculous."

"I don't want to. I really don't."

"Then don't," Simran says.

"I might not have a choice," he says, his eyes widening. She thinks she believes him. But she can't digest what he's saying. She won't.

"There must be something you can do. Anything." Simran's mouth becomes dry as she pictures Nani's reaction.

And even though she knows that it probably won't help to argue with Bharat Bhai, she can't accept this. Her mother would know what to do right now. She'd manage to bitch out the school board while still getting her message across.

Bharat Bhai shrugs and leans forward without saying a word, which conveys enough. Simran gazes at the wall above him, with its framed degrees from some school in Delhi.

"I'm going to look into some things. I'll be in touch." She stands up and wishes she was wearing a blazer or something she can button. A gesture like that would make a confident and conclusive statement right about now.

Instead, she says, "I should go."

The rest of the office building is a conglomeration of cubicles and computers, employees in off-white button-downs and black slacks, dashing to their next tasks like fruit flies. Simran pushes open the double doors, which are opaque from dirt and rain stains.

The air outside is heavy with dust and heat. There's a Havmor café across the street, nestled in between shops that have sari-draped mannequins in their windows. Simran pictures her mother walking on this exact road.

She can't go back home and face Nani yet, so she sits inside Havmor and orders a glass of Indian cold coffee: coffee blended with vanilla ice cream.

How is she going to break this to Nani? Simran knows how she'll handle it. On the outside, Nani will act like she's fine, as though she was prepared for this. But really, she'll be crushed.

Families collect around Simran, enjoying butterscotch ice cream, Nani's favorite flavor. She considers getting some to take to Nani but decides against it. It'll melt before she's home.

Simran steps out of Havmor and walks toward the busy street, where all sorts of vehicles are going in every direction. In India, drivers honk more to assert their presence rather than to scold, so there's a constant cacophony of honk, honk, honk. There are no accidents despite the lack of traffic lights or marked lanes. Several rickshaw drivers are sitting on the sidewalk and smoking cigarettes.

She's hit with a pang of nostalgia for New York. For her old life. For Seamless delivery and Sephora. People her own age. Knowing how to get from one place to the next.

Simran considers raising her hand for a rickshaw but finds herself crossing the street, back toward Bharat Bhai's office.

· · ·

An hour later, Simran tiptoes back in the house. Nani's asleep on her recliner and doesn't hear Simran. Five issues of *Stardust* magazine are on the table next to her. They have pictures of Indian celebrities on the cover, with stories in large hot pink font that make *People* magazine look like high-class literature:

Will the Katrina and Salman Love Story Ever End?

Abhishek: "I Know What I Want."

Who Really Caused the Rift Between Sanjay and Shah Rukh?

Simran covers Nani with a thin, beige blanket.

She'll tell her about her idea later.

"I think it's time we call Mom," Nani says that evening as they're eating bhindi shaak that's been simmered until each piece of okra is soft and charred.

"You're ready to tell her about your you-know-what?"

"No. But you should talk to her. About everything. And then maybe she can tell you about her matters."

"I don't know. It might be too soon."

"It'll never feel like the right time," Nani says, the mixture of encouragement and tenderness in her eyes bringing back memories of when she used to help Simran with her homework. "She should be awake by now. I used to always call her at this hour."

"I don't even know what to say. Where to start."

Simran hears the last words she and Mom exchanged. The resentment coalesces into sadness and confusion.

Kavita takes the dinner dishes into the outdoor sink in the garden as Nani and Simran go into the living room. A gecko's outline appears behind the light. It scurries toward the cracked ceiling when it hears them.

Simran removes the cordless phone from its charger and punch the digits for Mom's cell phone, which goes straight to voicemail. She dials their home phone number. Her stomach seems light, as though there's air under it.

Five rings.

Simran checks the time again. Her parents couldn't have left for work yet.

"Hello?"

"Daddy?"

"Simi—Simran. Hi."

I miss you, she wants to say.

Pressure builds behind her eyes. She takes a deep breath. "How are you?"

"Okay. Fine. And how are you? How is India?" His tone is even, with a forced detachment.

"Fine. I'm having a good time with Nani."

I'm sorry for everything.

"Are you going to work soon?" she asks.

"In a little bit," he says.

"Anybody still discussing the party? I mean, I've been here for a month, so I hope it's out of everyone's system. . . ."

Dad sighs.

They both know the real answer. Of course everyone's still discussing the engagement party. Their out-of-town guests left right away, as though their family's shit show could be contagious.

"Well, okay then," Simran says.

Silence.

More silence.

She waits for him to say everything will be fine. She needs to hear him say it.

Simran glances at Nani. "Is Mom there?"

Dad sighs. "No. Mom is not here."

"But it's not even seven there. Did she go into the office early?"

"I'm not sure."

"Not sure?"

On his end, Simran hears the sigh of a closing door. "It's hard for me to know Mom's schedule when Mom hasn't been here."

"What? Where has she been?"

His voice becomes soft. Strained. "Somewhere else. She moved out."

"When?"

"Earlier this week."

She almost expects him to say he's joking, that Mom's just in the living room, reading the Health section of the *New York Times*.

But when he doesn't say anything, her hand starts to shake.

"She just left?" Simran asks, picturing her mother at home, how she runs their family, the way she accounts for everything in a manner that's exhausting but inevitable, as though she never knew any other way.

"Well, she did say she's coming back tomorrow. That she just needed a little space for a few days. So I guess I should be grateful for that."

"Is she going to Baltimore?" Simran asks.

Dad sighs. "At some point, yes. I overheard her making plans with her *friend*"—his voice catches when he says "friend"—"but I don't know when she's leaving."

This is Simran's fault. They both know it. If she could have just kept her shit together, her mother wouldn't have been compelled to stay in a hotel for a few days. The thought of her dad sitting alone at home, eating day old Taco Bell, waiting to hear from her mom, is too much to bear.

"Have you tried calling her?" Simran pictures her mother slipping into a car with Dr. Dalton. It doesn't make any sense. She knows her mother cares about Dad; maybe not in the way Simran cares about Kunal, but still, she wouldn't just leave.

"Just once," he says. "But she's an adult. She knows what she's doing. How her actions affect other people."

"Do you think she's been unhappy?"

"I'm sure a part of me realized she had been . . . absent . . . for some time. But I don't know. Maybe I overlooked it. Or ignored it."

He keeps going, and Simran wonders if he's talking more to himself than to her.

"You know, when I met her, she was so different from any other woman I'd known. Confident. Fearless. And now, she's worn down. Indifferent."

"I don't see her being indifferent," Simran says.

Dad doesn't respond.

Simran tells him she has to go, hangs up the phone, and calls her mom's office. She waits through the standard menu options and presses "1" to make an appointment. It's the only way to speak to a human being at a doctor's office.

"Livingston Family Medicine," says a chirpy voice on the other end.

"Susie, hi. It's Simran. Can you tell my mom I'm on the phone?"

"You want to speak with Dr. Mehta?"

"Yes. I can wait if she's with patients."

Susie lowers her voice to a whisper. "Are you sure you meant to call *here*?"

"Yes," Simran says. "I know she's busy, but it's important."

Simran pictures her mother at work, whisking past hand sanitizer dispensers and stacks of patient charts and nurses in flowered scrubs. She feels a quick pang of sadness. *My* mother. *Her* patients.

On Susie's end, the background shifts from chatter to silence. "Simran, your mom isn't in the office. She already quit."

"She *what*?"

"Quit. Uh, were you not aware of this?"

"No, of course I was." She clenches her fists. "I just didn't realize things were already, um, official."

"Well, we guessed that she got another opportunity. She'll be in and out to wrap things up with her last patient appointments this week. I'll tell her you called when I see her, if that's okay?"

Simran hangs up the phone, wanting to tell Susie she's not sure if anything will ever be okay again.

Nandini

Nandini rehearsed her farewell speech for the hundredth time. *I'm leaving the practice. Dr. Goldstein will be taking over your care. We'll review your labs, medications, and follow-up appointments to make sure everything is in place.*

It was the same speech she had given all her patients this week—105 down, 45 to go, and then she'd be done with her work here.

Her first patient, Ms. Morris, comes in with blurry vision. Her blood sugar is over four hundred, so Nandini calls her family to drive her to the emergency room. The next patient asks Nandini to examine all five of his children. The afternoon passes this way, in a blur of dosage adjustments, referrals to specialists, and the sound of forty pairs of lungs inhaling and exhaling. Nandini steps out of the building for twenty seconds to scarf down a bag of almonds. Three of her late-afternoon patients are smoking in the parking lot. She realizes she hasn't given her farewell speech to anyone.

There's a dull throb in her lower back that she's become used to. When she paces back into the office, Terri, one of her nurses, is waving her arms and pointing to three doors that have a red tag on them, indicating they have a patient waiting to be seen.

The last patient comes thirty minutes late for an annual well check. Nandini waits in the exam room and inhales the scent of rubbing alcohol and Lysol. There are jars of cotton balls and gauze pads next to the sink. Everything in its place. Sterile.

After the patient leaves, Nandini checks the hallway and ducks into the closet at the back of the office. It's stuffed with two large filing cabinets, one swivel chair, and stacks of patient charts across the floor that resemble a game of dominos.

She slumps in the chair, her head against her knees as she spins around. Her phone vibrates every two minutes. She holds down the power button until the screen is dark.

This is my last time in this stuffy place. I'm never going to sit here again.

The thought loops around in her mind, as if to make sure she really is ready to leave. Every decision in her life has been this way: certain until that last second, that last sliver of doubt.

She jumps at the knock on the door.

Three no-nonsense thumps of knuckle.

"I'll be right out!" she yells.

Three more thumps.

Nandini opens the door.

Ranjit is on the other side, still in the black scrubs he wears on surgery days. He looks older. Or maybe she never bothered to notice that his hair had become more salt than pepper.

"Oh." Her breath catches in her throat. "Hi."

"Hi," he grunts.

She steps outside the closet. Two nurses pretend they're not watching them.

"Let's step into my office," she says, pacing in front of him, and closing the door after they're both inside.

Nandini scoots into the black armchair behind her desk while Ranjit settles into the tan one in front of it. It's strange seeing her husband sitting where she's counseled countless patients and their families on labs, CT scan results, and treatment plans.

"I don't know what to say to you," she says.

Ranjit stands up and clenches his fists. "*You* don't know what to *say* to *me*? Why don't you start with what the hell you're doing? You have the audacity to GALLIVANT WITH THAT *DHORIYO* and then tell me you have nothing to say to me?!"

"That's what you think all of this is? That I'm having an *affair* with Greg?" She snickers once. Twice.

Ranjit sneers and narrows his eyes. "I'm glad you find it hilarious that you're an unfaithful wife. No wonder our daughter's life is the way it is. Look at her mother."

Now Nandini stands up. She doesn't care who can hear them. "I've done everything for Ronak and Simran. They know that.

And you know that. Don't you dare start with me about my parenting. Or anything else, for that matter. You have no idea what it's like for me."

"Really? What don't I know?"

"All of it. Your sister and brothers watching and judging every single thing I do. You refusing to see any fault with them. Because it's just expected for me put up with all of that with a smile on my face. Even if that means working at a job that drains me. I've revolved my entire life around our family, and I will *not* listen to you say otherwise."

She suddenly recalls something she told Simran years ago: arranged marriages come with their own brand of insecurity, a stark awareness that there are always things that will remain unshared.

"Really?" Ranjit asks. "You won't listen to me say otherwise when you walk out on our family because you're with another man?"

"I'm *not* with him, god damn it," she says, gripping the edge of her desk. Her hands are chapped from years of washing and sanitizing. "Dr. Dalton—Greg—is sick. He has ALS."

"ALS?" Ranjit takes a step backward.

"Yes. It's rapidly progressive. That's why he wants me to take over his job."

"The Baltimore job," Ranjit says, as if understanding her for the first time since they started talking.

Nandini nods and takes a deep breath. "Yes, the job is at Hopkins. In Baltimore. I wanted to tell you this before. I tried at the engagement party and then you just stormed out and we haven't really spoken that much since."

"And that's all because of me?" Ranjit challenges.

"It's also because of me," she admits. "I didn't want you or Simran to find out about this that way, at the party of all places. But Greg didn't realize that, and it came out. Anyway, it's not easy for me to talk to you, and I wasn't sure how you'd take this."

Ranjit falls back into the chair and gazes at the wall. "You're actually telling me that you were, *are*, taking a job in Baltimore?"

Just spit it out, Nandini, the voice in her head says. *Say what you're really thinking for once instead of worrying how you'll be perceived.*

"I've wanted something like this for years, for so long that I didn't even think it was possible anymore. And then, when I thought it was the right time, so much happened. Pratik Bhai became your office manager. Everything with Simran. It's always my life, my wants, that are put on hold. And you don't seem to get that. Nobody does."

"So that makes it okay that you kept it from me?"

Nandini shakes her head. "No. I've tried to tell you before that I've needed something different. But you've always said I need to keep this job, so I can take care of the family. And, you know, I think I finally accepted that I wasn't able to connect with patients or practice medicine in the way I thought I would. But then Greg reached out because he needed someone to take over his job. I said no at first, but he was persistent. And when I learned more about the job, it was harder to look away. It's a light patient load, with some afternoons free for giving lectures, or doing research, or advising residents. I mean, a chance to work in the way I've always wanted!"

"So, what?" Ranjit asks, wringing his hands together. "You just accepted something in another state? What were you going to do? Send me a postcard after you arrived?"

She bites her bottom lip. "I was going to talk to you about it after the party. But when I saw your reaction, I knew you wouldn't understand. You never did. I thought that at least if the kids were settled, it would make things easier for everyone."

Maybe she needed both of her children to be married for the same reasons she needed them to be polite and get good grades. It told her that she had given them a good life. It told others that she had done her job.

"Anyway, it doesn't matter," she says. "Everything's more complicated now, especially after the fiasco with Simran. And I know none of this is your fault. I was never meant for this type of life. You've been good to me. You really have. It's just always about everyone else. Kids. Family. Patients. You and I have barely ever focused on anything else, let alone each other."

Ranjit sighs. The lines around his eyes deepen. He always appears refined. Nandini remembers the first time they were allowed to be alone, one hour after they first met. They sat on the swing on her parents' veranda, the warm wind pushing through the windows, bringing in the scent of jasmine flowers and chili powder.

She faced him. "I'm difficult. You won't be able to handle it."

He chuckled. "I like that you're difficult."

Now he places his face in his hands, which are as equally chapped as hers. "I'm going home. Clearly you still have a lot to do."

"Can't we talk some more?" she asks as he steps toward the door.

"I think we've talked enough," he says, closing the door behind him.

Twelve

Simran

"A re you ready?"

Simran turns to Nani. She's wearing her favorite peach cotton sari. Her hair, streaked with gray and white, is tied into a low bun, and is sealed in place by the string of jasmine flowers Simran bought this morning.

"I don't know if we should do this," Nani says.

Simran removes Nani's tan chappals from the rickety shoe rack. They're imprinted with the outlines of her size-5 feet, her long toes.

"Yes, you should. They're waiting for you. Come *on*." Simran links her arm through Nani's, which seems frailer compared to even one week ago. The gate groans as Nani closes it behind them. Everyone else on the street is taking an afternoon nap.

In the rickshaw, Simran hands Nani the folders they've put together over the past week. "Do you want to go over anything?"

Nani shakes her head. "Whatever's meant to happen will happen."

"Don't think that way. If there's anything I've realized over the past several months, it's that nothing's going to change just by sitting around and throwing pity parties."

"That's what I used to tell you. Does that officially mean I'm irrelevant? Have you and I switched roles?"

"No, of course not. Never." Simran studies the contours of her grandmother's face, wondering if its details will ever fade from her memory.

Baroda whirls by during their rickshaw ride: men in faded kurtas pushing vegetable carts, women in saris balancing brass pots of water on their heads, the occasional pair of cows along the perimeter of the street. Simran wraps her dupatta around their mouths and noses to block out the puffs of exhaust and dust.

The rickshaw's engine putters into a decrescendo as they reach Alkapuri.

"That's it, right?" Nani asks, pointing to the building Simran was in just two weeks ago. It seems smaller today. More likely to cave in. Trap them both.

Simran nods, and they walk toward the steps. Nani puts both of her hands in Simran's. They climb step by step. Nani doesn't lose her breath once.

"Are you sure you're okay?" Simran asks.

Nani holds her hand up.

Translation: *Don't ask me that again.*

Bharat Bhai's secretary asks them to wait in two gray chairs, the kind with thin, pointless armrests. The carpet is puke green. Simran inhales and squeezes her hands together until her knuckles are white. It's better not to say anything to Nani right now. This is no time for a pep talk.

Five minutes later, Nani and Simran walk toward a door that says CONFERENCE in black letters. There's a long mahogany table with six people on either side of it, Bharat Bhai at the head. Shafts of sunlight poke through the opaque windows.

"Welcome, Mimi Ben," he says, clasping his palms together, bowing his head.

Nani returns the gesture.

"Shall we start?" he asks, and Nani nods.

The room is quiet as everyone on the school board faces them. Simran's underarms start to sweat.

Nani makes her way to the front of the room. "Good afternoon. My name is Mimi Kadakia. There are a lot of reasons why I should be an official teacher at Xavier's school."

Within seconds, she's rattling off all the things Simran has discovered through her evenings reading. Simran compiled everything into two separate documents, one for Nani, another for her to reference as she works on her own article about these issues.

Nani starts with the facts. The value of educating a young woman in India. The way girls who work outside of their homes end up earning more money for their entire community, have decreased risks of dying from early pregnancy, and are less likely to be victims of domestic violence.

Then she transitions to the specifics. How her course would be designed, from the exams to the essays to the weekly syllabi. The lessons of the Indian goddesses tied to modern-day life. She talks about Pallavi, her goals and potential, how she's getting pulled out of school.

She's a natural.

Simran's heartbeat slows down. Everyone in the room is paying attention, nodding their heads, unbothered by Nani's strained voice, her heavy breaths. It's the type of magic that only exists when you watch someone doing what they were always meant to do.

Bharat Bhai stands up. "That was wonderful, Mimi Ben."

Nani bows her head in a gesture that's both triumphant and grateful.

One of the board members, a thirty-something woman with thick eyebrows and glasses that remind Simran of a fly, raises her hand. "I just have one question: How can you guarantee that you'll be able to, how do you say, handle the rigors of teaching all day?"

Nani furrows her brow. "I don't understand?"

"Most of our teachers are young. Energetic. Yes, you have been coming to the school every day for some amount of time. But without any official experience in teaching, we do have to make sure you can do the job."

"I guarantee that she's more energetic and committed than any of the other teachers you have," Simran says.

The woman doesn't look at her. "I'm sure you understand. We've had *unconventional* teachers before. It has been a liability."

"A liability? Like the *conventional* teachers who skip their own classes?" Simran asks, and Nani grabs her wrist. Simran can hear her mother telling her to shut up.

"Mimi Ben, do you feel comfortable signing a one-year contract?" The woman peers at both of them, almost as if she knows that within one year, Nani's delicate cells will have already betrayed her.

Nani looks toward Simran and then back at everyone else. "Well, I guess if I have to commit to one year, it's better that I don—that I think about this for some time and get back to you later."

"So, you're not sure?" Bharat Bhai asks. "Really?"

"No." Nani faces the ground and lowers her voice. "I can't sign a one-year contract."

The board members stare back at her.

"I, well, am not able to—"

"What she's trying to say," Simran interrupts, "is that she can't sign it herself. We both have to sign it. Because we are going to teach the class together."

Nani turns to her. "Simi?"

Simran clutches her shoulder and faces the board. "I know. I know. I should have jumped in earlier and told them I'm going to help you start the class. Once it's established, you'll be able to manage on your own."

Bharat Bhai raises his eyebrows. "Is this true?"

"It is," Simran say. "We've been working together to make the ideal curriculum. The thing is, nobody expects anything from these girls. They need encouragement from as many people as possible. People who believe in them to be something besides wives."

The way Neil believed in her. She pretends he's in the room, telling her to keep going.

"That sounds nice in theory, Simran," Bharat Bhai says. "But we don't have enough staff to follow that type of long-term plan. And what about payment? We can't afford to pay both you and Mimi Ben a full-time salary."

"That's fine," Simran says.

"It is?" Nani asks.

"We'll figure it out. How about I e-mail you our curriculum, and in the meantime, you'll put the contract together?"

Bharat Bhai nods. "Yes, I think that sounds good."

"Okay, we'll be in touch!"

Despite the silence and somber surroundings, Simran feels like she and Nani were just announced as winners at the Oscars. They should be making a tearful and touching acceptance speech. Any second now, someone from *Fashion Police* will push a microphone in their faces and ask, "So, how does it really feel?"

And then she thinks, *Neil. I am embodying Neil. Neil is the reason I thought any of this was possible.*

Before anyone else can interject, Simran says, "We should be going now. Thank you!"

She pulls Nani's wrist and guides them out of the room.

They buy glass bottles of Limca and bars of Dairy Milk chocolate to celebrate. The shop owner gives them a complimentary packet of Indian-spiced hard candies when they tell him the news.

My grandmother, Simran says. *A teacher.*

Getting her first job while her mother quit everything she worked for.

"You know you can't stay in India," Nani says as she breaks off a large piece of Dairy Milk.

"Yes, I ca—"

"Don't be ridiculous! You have too much going on in New York right now."

"But I want to help you get started. If we create a strong foundation for the girls with your knowledge and insight now, then we can make it sustainable. Whoever comes after us will be able to implement your ideas and make sure the girls are always getting the education they need."

Nani squints as she thinks through the process. "So, while I'm teaching this to the girls now, we need to find other people to learn the curriculum, so they can teach it after. . . ."

"After we both leave," Simran says. She won't say after Nani's gone. She just can't. "Through my research, I've realized there are people all around India who would love to join something like this. There are even teachers in this community who feel jaded by the current education plans. Let me reach out and see if we can find people to come and work with us."

"If that works, then I won't be abandoning the girls."

"Yes. And I'm going to write about all of it, in the way I've always wanted to," Simran says, realizing the truth of her words as they evaporate in the heat. "It's the first time a decision's felt right, which is strange, because I didn't plan any of this out."

"But what about everything else back home?"

Simran picks up their drained bottles and puts them at the end of the table. "I'll go back once you're established here, after this is all figured out."

"So then does that mean you've decided what you're going to do?"

Simran nods. "I was scared at first about going back. But I guess when you've messed up enough, you can handle anything that comes along."

Before she came to India, everything made her cry, to the point where she began giving herself pep talks in the mirror. But she's ready, or really, as ready as anyone can be who is unemployed, has few friends, and is a laughingstock of the South Asian community.

"Being here with you has been better than I even thought it would be," Simran says, reaching across the table to clutch her hand. "I'm so, so proud of you."

Nani's eyes become moist.

Simran changes the subject. "And I know Mom. She won't do what she wants with her life if she thinks mine is still a mess. She's been through enough in her life. I can't let her sacrifice any more or allow Dad's practice to suffer just because I don't have my shit together."

Nani wipes her hands with a napkin. "And so, what about Kunal?"

"I need to talk to him," Simran says. "See where we can go from here."

She stares at the wooden table, wondering how long it'll take for her to forget Neil. Forget how he showed her how safe she'd been with her life choices. Forget their kiss.

"Simran, you're not the reason your mom is going through all of this," Nani says.

"Of course I am. And you know what the crazy part is? For my entire life, I always got so frustrated whenever she seemed impossible to please. But now I see that she just didn't want me to suffer the way she did."

A teenage boy wipes the neighboring tables with a faded white rag. The shop owner waves goodbye as Nani and Simran approach the row of rickshaws parked against the curb. Simran scans the sidewalk for their driver.

Nani notices him across the street. "Cigarette *piyech*."

They settle into the hot, squeaky rickshaw seat. Simran begins to tell the driver Nani's address, but Nani cuts her off. "I need to make a quick stop before we go home."

"Where?"

"A place you should see while you're here."

She spouts off directions in curt Gujarati to the driver. *Left here. Down this road. That neighborhood on the end.*

Twenty minutes later, the rickshaw turns onto a dusty side street. There are no cows, cars, or people anywhere.

"You can stop now," Nani tells the driver as they approach a beige, one-story house.

Simran soaks in the sterile concrete, the closed windows. "Who lives here?"

"Your mother did."

"What? When?"

She's unable to picture a younger version of her mother opening the faded burgundy front door or climbing out of a window.

"During her first marriage. Her husband—her *ex*-husband's family lived here. Can you imagine? Twelve people in this tiny space, and she did all the housework. This is what she would have had to deal with if she didn't run away."

Simran's face becomes warm.

Nani turns back to her. "What she has with you, your dad, Ronak . . . that's the life she fought for. You are her blessing. You could never be the one to ruin her life."

Nani tells Simran about the first time she saw this house, the way Mom was going to live. She went home and cried all night after Nana went to sleep.

"I guess I didn't even realize how lucky I am to have Kunal," Simran says.

Nani gives her a look that says, *What do you mean?*

"He's smart, supportive . . . would never put me through anything near this hell that Mom dealt with. Maybe that's why Mom's pushed me to make it work, because a life with him would be good. Loving."

She wishes she could call Kunal and tell him this.

I was wrong, she'd say. *I shouldn't have treated you the way I did, or doubted us.*

One minute later, they're interrupted by a thump of knuckles against the windshield. "Mimi Ben? Is that you?"

A woman cranes her neck into the rickshaw. She's around Nani's age, but everything about her seems stiffer, as though she could unravel at any moment. Even her sari folds are starched and tightly pleated.

Nani's fist clenches around Simran's. "Pushpa Ben. *Kem cho? Boj varas taigya!*" *How are you? It has been so many years!*

The woman's eyes are scrunched as though she's licked a lemon. Her lips are turned downward. *"Majama. Tha me?"* *Fine. You?*

Simran leans back into the seat as Nani says, "Good. This is Simran."

The woman takes a deep breath and puts her hand on her chest. "Is this . . . your . . . *hers? Are bapre*, she looks exactly like her."

Nani clears her throat. "Yes, this is *Nandini's* daughter."

"Ha. Must be nice."

"It is," Nani says.

Pushpa Ben scoffs. "Your daughter did what she did, and she still got to have everything."

Nani taps the rickshaw driver's shoulder and asks him to turn off the engine. She turns back to Pushpa Ben. "Everything? Everything? My daughter went through hell here. And last I heard, your son was more than fine in America."

Mom's ex-husband lives in *America*? For some reason, Simran pictured him as a lonely, old, miserable oaf in Baroda. Has he seen her since then? Seen them?

The driver steps out of the rickshaw and paces down the dusty street under the guise of needing another cigarette break. Poor guy couldn't have seen this coming.

"Yes, he is fine. Now. No thanks to you or Nandini."

"Enough." Nani grinds her teeth. "We'll be leaving now."

She cups her hands around her mouth and yells for the rick-shaw driver, who scurries back toward them like a frightened puppy.

Nani grunts. "That woman has some nerve."

The tires screech as they putter away from the house. Nani grabs Simran's hand, and Simran misses her mother so much that it's hard to speak.

Nandini

"It's only a matter of time now," Greg says. "I know you know that."

Nandini squeezes his stiff, dry hand that once used to throw a football and suture people's limbs. She can't speak. If she lets any sounds escape from her mouth, she'll break down. Greg doesn't need that.

"The doctor becomes the patient in the exact hospital he trained and taught at," he says with a soft laugh. "What a cliché I've become! But really, no wonder patients complain all the time. Being a patient is the worst."

"I'm sure it is," she says, and he looks relieved that she's finally spoken.

"How are your first days here? Do you like being back in Bal-timore?"

"I do." She leans back in the stiff armchair reserved for family members visiting patients. "So much is coming back to me from when I was here before. The intern and resident Nandini is still in here somewhere. But I've had lifetimes since then. I feel like everything's changed, and yet there are parts from my past that seem to keep coming back in one way or another."

She stops herself from saying more. He doesn't need to know about India. Nobody else does.

"Well, you are the hardest working resident I ever had, so if that old Nandini is in there, I don't know that that's a bad thing. How's the staff treating you? And the residents?"

"Everyone's been very nice, for the most part."

"But?" he asks.

"It's just been interesting to see how women are treated in medicine. Of course, I understand it's hard for your colleagues to go from you to me, but even some of the patients would rather have a male intern tell them what's going on over me. I used to think it was something that only happened when I was training or at the practice in Livingston. But no, it's everywhere. Women have it rough. Did you know there was a study that came out about how in some households, women are the primary bread-winners but still handle most of the housework and parenting? I mean, what is that?"

"I hope you never change." Greg gives her a look that's a mixture of exasperation and amusement. "So, minus the sexism—that I know needs to change and is unacceptable—how is it?"

"Other than that, it's been amazing. Beyond what I could have even hoped. It's harder work than I thought. I have to read on the cases every night to make sure I'm up-to-date on the latest research. And it's energizing to teach every morning, then see patients at your clinic after. I get to do everything I wanted. And *enjoy* it."

"Good. Everything will work out, then. I'm sure of it," he says, and they both know he's referring to her family and not the new job.

"I really hope so." She tries to ignore the knotted panic that has built a home in her stomach. "I don't know if everything with my family can be fixed . . . or if I ruined them all."

Greg's voice thins to a whisper. "I know that *you* know that isn't possible."

She can't face Simran yet. Ronak is the only one who calls. Ranjit refuses to speak with her. She can only imagine what Charu has been telling him.

Greg gives her a tired smile and reclines back in the bed. He's lost weight over the summer, so now the skin of his face has started to hang off his high cheekbones. Dark circles encompass his still-vibrant blue eyes. He gets tired from just one long conversation now. Sometimes he doesn't have the strength to drink water.

As much as Greg seemed strict and intimidating when she was in training, she saw the gentleness underneath the facade, like Ranjit, like her father.

Her father. If only he could see how she's doing now. She pictures him with his swollen ankles and nagging cough. He was exhausted when he showed her the picture of Ranjit. Exhausted and hopeful.

A part of her wants to tell Greg that this *has* to be temporary. He *has* to get better. He can't just be in this bulky bed with buttons on the side, wearing a flimsy gown that's open in the back, and waiting for a tray of food that includes fruit suffocating in plastic wrap.

She remembers the first time she was in a patient room with

him, one that's just down the hall from them now. She stood around the patient's bed with the other residents. In front of everyone, Greg asked her to name the causes of anion gap metabolic acidosis. *Pimping.* That was the ridiculous word used to describe attendings asking residents to recall information on the spot.

She went blank. *Oh no, I forgot. Everyone's going to think I'm stupid. I know even less than the medical student. I shouldn't be here, and now everyone else is going to figure that out, too.* Her thoughts continued to spiral downward. The stares of her co-residents and the patient bore into her chest. Her heart started racing.

"Nandini, just take one second to think about it," Greg said as he buttoned his white coat. "The answer will still be there if you give yourself time."

She took the deep breaths her therapist taught her, and within one minute, the words came back to her. She listed every cause and even threw in a couple of points from a recent journal article she had read the week before.

This has been a constant in her life, she realizes now: moments of chaos that seem impossible to navigate at first but then somehow lead her to a place of confidence. And faith.

"You've done more for me than you'll ever realize," she says now.

She monitors the tone of her voice. She doesn't want to seem too emotional. Even after their relationship crossed the border from colleagues to friends, she never stopped wanting to seem put together in front of him.

"Now, now, don't act like I'm going just yet," Greg says.

"I'm not." Nandini stares out the window at the dark parking lot. She turns back toward Greg as he's reclining the bed.

Greg closes his eyes. "I'm going to get some rest."

"Okay." Nandini reaches for the *JAMA* journal she brought to keep her company.

"No," Greg says, his voice thin but firm. "Go home."

"I'm fine here," Nandini says without looking up from the journal.

"No, *I'm* fine. And you are, too. You just need to understand that."

She leans toward him for a quick hug. He smells like aftershave and the strawberry popsicles he keeps sweet-talking the nurses into bringing him. She basks in all of it. The sterile, gray walls. An old *Law & Order* episode droning on the television. The surreal realization that someone other than her thought she could be greater than herself.

Thirteen

Simran

I'm home, Nani," Simran says one month later.

"Good, Simi." Nani's voice comes through the phone. "Now go make some things happen."

"Nobody's here. It's so weird and quiet."

"I'm sure they'll be back soon."

Simran arranges a pile of wedding invitations on the counter. "I feel bad for leaving you."

"But I'm fine." Nani's voice becomes softer. "You helped me set everything up for the girls. Because of you, we've made a splash with the right people. . . . Okay, and some of the wrong ones as well, but who cares about them? There are organizations now donating menstrual pads and notebooks for the girls so they can stay in school. And we have four teachers ready to continue this next year and the year after. It doesn't even sound real. I'm not alone in this!"

"You're not alone. And neither are the girls. They finally have the support they need to pursue their educations. I still can't believe it," Simran says as she thinks back to the nonprofits that contacted them after news of Nani teaching spread through Baroda. One of them even did a write-up about her in their newsletter. Another linked her with teachers who have always wanted to provide girls with what they called "an empowered education."

"You should believe it," Nani says. "You've researched it. You've written about it. And soon, you're going to bring their issues to the limelight."

"That's the dream. They're all rough drafts right now, but hopefully they'll find a home," Simran says, referring to the collection of articles she's since written about girls' education, menstrual hygiene, economic empowerment, and the dangers of early marriage. It's been a raw process of learning as she goes along, a combination of fear and faith that's nothing like the protocols of psychology.

"Yes, they will. I know they will, Simi. And now it's all good," Nani says. "I'm good. Great. Really."

Simran thinks back to the discussion she and Nani had with the girls' parents. Pallavi's family is now putting off on getting her married. She's still the top student in their class.

"I'm proud of us. Of you," Simran says.

"I am, too, Simi."

"How are you feeling?"

"Fine."

"Really? *Fine?*"

Nani doesn't say anything for a couple of seconds. "I've struggled with my energy a little. But it's nothing for you to worry about. Really. I feel like a different person because of everything you set up for me here."

"Hey, you're the one who did it."

"No, I couldn't have without you. I didn't."

"I knew you always could. I really did," Simran says.

Simran hangs up and wheels her India bags into the living

room, puts on a pair of rubber gloves, and sprays the countertops with Lysol. Then she washes the dishes with her mother's lemon dishwashing soap and yellow sponge.

The garage door opens as she's tying up a trash bag.

"It's me!" Simran yells before anyone has the chance to be startled.

"Simran," Dad says, stepping into the kitchen. "I didn't know you were back."

"Just got here an hour ago," Simran says, not knowing how to tell him that it was strange to text only Ronak, and not her parents, when she boarded the plane or landed or got into an Uber.

"Oh, I see," he says.

When Simran was younger, she often came home from school to him napping on the couch, only waking up to the sound of his pager with a Pavlovian dog–type jolt, murmuring some medication or wound care order into the phone, and drifting back to sleep.

Today, he's in the same black scrubs that he always wears on operating days, but there are more shadows on his face, deeper lines under his eyes. He suddenly looks older. Defeated.

"How are you?" he asks.

"Fine. How are you?" Simran refrains from giving him a hug. "The house is a mess. Mom would not approve."

He makes a sound that's a cross between a snort and chuckle. "When your mother decides she's done with her little vacation and wants to be an adult, then she can decide what the house should look like."

"I don't think this is really a vacation. It's her dream job."

Dad doesn't say anything.

"Has she been gone since I called you from India?" Simran asks.

He nods. "She was in a hotel here at first. And then, this week, she left me a message saying she was going to Baltimore. Didn't know when she was coming back."

"Didn't know? Have you talked to her since she left?"

He shrugs. "What's there to talk about?"

"Um, everything? How she's doing? How you are? What her life there is like?"

He lowers his voice and faces the ground. "This is just what she does, I guess. Runs away. I should have expected it."

Simran looks down, not wanting to show that she knows what he means.

Her mother left her first marriage because she felt alone. Trapped. Could they have pushed her to do the same thing? She wonders how some families make it seem so easy to be happy. Drama-free. Like those white families in movies.

Simran removes the rubber gloves, washes her hands, and calls Mom's cell phone. It goes straight to voicemail.

Dad paces around the island in their kitchen, muttering things under his breath.

Simran once told Ronak she knew their parents were perfect for each other. They were saying goodbye to people after a party at their house. From her bedroom window, she watched them standing on the driveway, their bodies glowing from the head-lights of cars pulling away. They leaned in toward each other and were talking, laughing. She heard them come back into the house and settle on the recliners in the living room. They rehashed the entire evening, her mother imitating the ridiculous things their friends and families had said, her father listening, chuckling.

"My family warned me she was fickle. That it would be a problem," he says.

Simran's not sure if he's talking to her or to himself.

He leans forward onto the counter. Simran goes to the cabinet and removes his favorite mug, the one that says DR. DAD, an old Father's Day gift from Ronak and her. She fills it with coffee. He seems to need something stronger than tea.

"I thought all the other women were boring. Typical. I didn't want typical. They told me to be careful, that boring can be okay, but no, I had to try and prove them wrong. I always had to prove. Ha," he says, taking a large gulp. "Ridiculous. Just ridiculous."

"What is?" Simran asks.

"All of it. She thinks I don't ever need a break from all of this shit? I've worked hard, I became a doctor, always took care of our family, and everyone else's half the time. And she gets to just walk away? What the hell kind of nonsense is that? As if my life is so easy to deal with? As if *she's* always so easy to deal with?"

It occurs to her that as much as Simran's mother felt her life was constricted by others' expectations, it's possible that her father felt the same way. And while Mom could unload to Simran, he didn't have anyone. He was raised to believe he had to keep a strong, neutral front in the midst of Mom's stress and mood swings, his family's dependence on him, and a grueling job. Like her, he was also exhausted and frustrated, was also craving understanding and support. He just couldn't show it.

"Dad, it's been crazy around here. And hard. But we—you—should try to talk to her. Maybe there's more to what she's doing than you understand," Simran says.

Dad puts his mug in the (now empty and clean) sink. "Well, like I said, she made her decision."

"Yes, but I don't know if it's as simple as you think it is," Simran says. "And not talking to her isn't going to solve anything."

He doesn't say anything.

Simran hears her mother's voice. *Your father's just not one of those men who is easy to open up to.*

You have to at least give him a chance, Simran said at the time.

"Dad, she needs to hear from you. It'll make a difference, I promise. But you have to be willing to take that first step," Simran says now.

He looks at her, his lips tight, as if he may consider taking her advice.

But then he turns around.

"Come on. At least *think* about it." Simran hands him the phone.

Can he not just take it? Make the call? Or did their arranged marriage leave them both too emotionally stunted to put their pride aside when necessary? How would they have been different if they had dated?

When it's clear that he isn't going to call, Simran walks toward their living room and sits on the leather recliner. The mantel is still lined with photos that they had framed for the wedding guests. One of Ronak's proposal in Central Park, him on bended knee, Namita, with her hands around her mouth in surprise. Another of Kunal and Simran from their college graduation, where they are smiling in purple robes.

Inside Simran, there's a longing for opposing things, for stepping away from her old life, building something new, the way she started to in India, but also needing her mother to come home, their family to feel like them again. It's like being caught in a Chinese finger trap. The more she tries to push out, the more she suffocates.

"She'll come back when I tell her I need her for the wedding. My wedding. She *has* to for that."

He raises his eyebrows. "Is that still on as scheduled?"

"It will be."

"Really? Pratik Bhai and I have been avoiding the topic at the office, which has also been so pleasant," he says.

"Sorry," Simran says. She regrets the word the second it comes out. Why is that a reflex for her? To say sorry when she senses someone is getting upset over her actions, even if she thinks she did the right thing?

"So you and Kunal have discussed it?"

Simran nods. "We will. Kunal and I are supposed to meet when he's back from Costa Rica. I just need to talk to him."

"And when will you do that?"

"I don't know. Soon," Simran says, not wanting him to know just how soon.

Nandini

Adam Davenport, the chair of Internal Medicine at Johns Hopkins, motions toward a brown leather chair in the corner of his office. "I hear you've had a strong start here."

Nandini nods. "That's great."

She glances around the room. It had been decades since she was in this exact seat, meeting with the former chair, who now lives in Spain. The walls are covered with framed diplomas from Adam's training programs, Harvard and Hopkins. He was promoted to chair just two years ago and is known for his no-nonsense, progressive leadership style. His graying sideburns, firm handshake, and charm remind Nandini of a young Bill Clinton.

"We're happy to have you back with us," he says. "Of course, there are things we'll have to review since the department has changed since you were here."

"I've noticed that already," Nandini says.

Adam sits in the chair next to hers. He reviews the nuances of her contract, including how many hours she's supposed to spend teaching every week, the number of residents she'll directly supervise, and her expected administrative tasks.

"It's very busy here, as I'm sure you've already seen," Adam says. "People have gotten overwhelmed in the past. Now, you just started, so I know there's a learning curve, but these are things I need you to be aware of, so we can all ensure you're the right . . . *fit* for the position."

Adam says the word "fit" as if it's painful. He darts his eyes to the side. It occurs to Nandini that he's trying to scare her. She recently read a few articles about why there were so few female physicians in leadership positions. Everything from grueling work hours to lower pay than their male colleagues to shady politics to lack of support were mentioned. Hospitals are eager to hire people they pick, and here she is, just because of Greg. Maybe Adam had someone else in mind. Maybe people had already expressed disappointment toward Greg choosing her. Maybe in the few weeks since she started, they thought she wasn't good enough.

Nandini feels a pressure building on her chest as Adam keeps talking. Can she really handle this? Will she be able to prove herself? Is she too young? Too old? Will people wonder why a middle-aged Indian woman got this job?

Stop that. You deserve to be here, she tells herself. *Show him that.*

She pictures all the women who struggled in medicine before

her. All the times they worked toward things but were denied what they deserved.

She's met plenty of Adams throughout her training, men who were kind to her face but underneath were still trying to figure her out, decide if she was worthy of respect. Men like him needed to know she wasn't going to back down.

"Adam." She puts up her hand. "I understand everything you're saying. And I'm doing well here. If you'd like to check in with the residents and other attendings, you should."

She keeps her neck straight, her facial expression even.

Translation: *I dare you to mess with me.*

"Greg did rave about you," he says as he shifts in his chair.

She nods. She often forgets the impact of Greg's influence. This is the problem with feeling powerless for so many years. You forget how to accept power even when it comes to you.

The rest of the conversation is filled with superficial small talk about Adam's job, Nandini's schedule, and other logistics. It's clear by the end that he's gotten the point, that he won't try to have a conversation like this with her again.

Thirty minutes later, Nandini walks toward her car. She's proud of herself for standing up to Adam, but still, confrontation has always been difficult for her. Maybe it'll never be easy to talk back to people who try to make her feel small. Maybe that is the point.

She unlocks the car and checks her phone. Two missed calls from Simran.

I don't feel like talking to you, she thinks. A ripple of guilt travels through her for the thought.

Her therapist taught her how to breathe when she feels the threat of a panic attack. She grips her steering wheel and sits up straight. She inhales slowly and lets the air fill her body for several seconds. When she exhales, she tells herself she'll be okay.

She's interrupted by Simran calling again. She takes one more deep breath and picks up.

"Mom!" Simran sounds startled, the way she did when she was in elementary school and woke up from nightmares. "You picked up!"

"How are you, *beta*?"

"Uh, fine. How are *you*? What are you doing?"

"I was just meeting with the chair here at Hopkins."

Simran's voice becomes quiet. "Oh. Wow. So, you're just there, ready to work?"

"Uh-huh," Nandini says. *Please, let's not fight. Not today.*

"How was the meeting? Did you like the chair?" Simran's voice is hollow, hesitant.

She has to be careful how she responds. One wrong word could set off an emotional landmine between them. She gives Simran a quick rundown of the meeting. She waits for Simran's disappointment, for her to say, *Come home already.*

But to her surprise, Simran says, "Mom, are you serious? You showed the chair that you're a boss? That's amazing."

"Really?"

"Yes, really."

Nandini leans back and smiles. This is something she learned about Simran when she was a teenager: just when she worried they were on the verge of an argument, Simran could find a way to make Nandini feel understood. She thinks about the line between daughter and friend, how it becomes blurrier with time.

Nandini starts the car. "Thank you . . . for saying that."

"You don't have to thank me. I mean it."

Nandini hears Simran sigh.

"What is it?"

"Nothing," Simran says. "I just hope you're proud of what you've been able to overcome, you know?"

"Are you talking about the meeting or something else?"

"The, uh"—Simran hesitates—"meeting. And just anything, in general. Everything. You're really . . . strong."

"Ah, *beta*," Nanini says. "Where is this coming from?"

"I don't know. It's the truth. And I should tell you that more. You should tell *yourself*. Don't let that guy or anyone else scare you. You can take them any day."

As Simran keeps talking, Nandini stops herself from telling her daughter that she misses her, that she wishes she was here with her, in this dim parking lot. Something about her seems different.

"*Beta*, are you sure you're ok—"

"I'm fine," Simran says.

Before Nandini can ask anything, Simran says, "I've gotta go. Sorry."

Fourteen

Simran

Simran hangs up with Mom the second she sees Kunal approaching his building. Her eyes take time to adjust to him, the way they do to darkness when the lights are suddenly turned off.

She studies him as though he's a stranger. Green scrubs. Tattered brown carry-on bag. He seems tanner. Taller. The kind of man who is always on a mission. Then her view shifts, and she sees him as though he's the self-assured but vulnerable high school boy she fell for.

A thought emerges as he comes closer.

I love you.

His smile is only visible after he's walked a few steps. So he's looking forward to seeing her. Maybe he's even excited.

He glances behind him, which is when Simran sees Rekha.

The air leaves her body. Rekha was in Costa Rica with Kunal? Did he tell Simran that Rekha was going on the trip? She's also pulling her own tattered carry-on, also in green scrubs, but manages to look respectable and gazelle-like.

Simran angles her head away from them, just enough to watch them hug from her periphery. Rekha saunters into the neighboring apartment building.

"Hey," Kunal says as he approaches her.

"Hi. How was your trip?" Simran stands up, wishing she was wearing something cuter than her black cotton maxi dress. (Thanks to all the butterscotch ice cream she shared with Nani, it's one of the only things that fit. She should have tried her first juice cleanse. Or at least attended a couple of those barre classes where she always ends up hiding from the instructor.)

"Fine," he says. "Good."

"That's good," Simran says. "Did you have fun?"

He nods.

"Did Rekha? I didn't know she was going to be there."

He tilts his head down and gives Simran a look as if to say, *I didn't know a lot of things about you.*

"Well, I'm glad you're back," Simran says.

"Yeah," he says. "You too."

They take a slow step toward each other. Kunal gives her a side hug. Simran rests her head against his shoulder. From the outside, they could be auditioning for a scene from a terrible Hindi movie.

They climb the five flights of narrow stairs to his apartment and settle into his bedroom. The space is a shrine to all the furniture New Yorkers have dumped onto the sidewalk. There's a twin bed and chipped dresser against the back wall. The only cluttered surface is his desk, which is drowning in anatomy textbooks and loose-leaf sheets of notes in his shitty handwriting. His laptop is on top of a crate that's filled with Rold Gold pretzels, Clif Bars, and ramen noodles, a sign that Meghna Auntie made a recent Costco run. The only picture is a framed one of them from NYU graduation. It's also been Kunal's Facebook profile picture for the past year.

"So, tell me about your trip," Simran says.

Kunal sits on his desk and gives her a brief rundown about the mobile health clinics their team set up, the families who traveled dozens of miles on foot to see them, how he learned to screen for cervical cancer. He had a lot of one-on-one time with Dr. Maude, he says, and can see himself becoming dean of a medical school later, you know, after he can no longer spend entire days operating on brains and can "just take it easy."

His phone rings for the second time since they've been in his room. He silences it.

"Who was that?"

"Just my mom," he says, tucking it into the front pocket of his scrubs. "Anyway, what about you? How was India?"

Simran stares at his feet, the only part of his body he hates. Her throat tightens.

"What's wrong?" he asks.

Everything spills out: Nani's cancer, her mother's first marriage, Nani becoming an official teacher for the girls at school. It's cathartic to release the past months from her mind.

Kunal doesn't say anything at first. He shifts from his desk to be next to Simran on the twin bed. Rubs the small of her back. She forgot how he always maintains a sense of calm when someone is having a crisis. It used to be one of her favorite things about him.

"Wow, that's just crazy. I don't even know what to say." He holds both of her hands. "I can't imagine what that must have been like for you."

Simran is jolted back to their senior prom night, when they snuck away from their friends just to drink Oreo milk shakes and cuddle in the back seat of his beat-up Honda Accord. He held her hands the same way then. How do people get from that place to where they are now? Is it a single moment that changes the trajectory of a relationship, or is it always multiple events, which go unnoticed at the time but somehow add up?

"I guess we have a lot to discuss," Simran says. "About us. I made a list."

"Of course you did," Kunal says, laughing for the first time since they've been together.

He jumps off the bed and closes the door. Not that there's any point. The walls are so thin that his three roommates will likely hear every bit of their conversation anyway.

When he comes back onto the bed, Simran says, "Before I went to India, everything in my life felt off. I was restless. And confused. And then, being there showed me that I really needed to get away from everyone to remember who I am, what I want."

"And that is?"

She pulls away from him. "I want to have my own life that I'm proud of. I don't know exactly where the next few years are going to take me, but for the first time, I don't care. I don't care about not knowing. I just want to find work that feels challenging and fulfills me. Something where I can write about people and make an impact in a way that aligns with me, not you or my parents."

Kunal's gaze moves from Simran to the floor. "I see."

"And really, I owe you an apology, because I realized how you must always feel when you go on your trips. I'm sorry for not understanding that before."

"That means a lot coming from you." Kunal smiles. "And I'm glad you were able to experience that."

"I can see now how great it must have been for you to connect with everyone during your trips. Feel like you were making a difference."

His phone rings again. This time he quiets it without looking at it. He clicks the tiny side button down so it will be silent from now on.

"I guess we should get through this," Simran says, removing her list.

"Wait," he says. "I just need to know one thing from you. Do you want us to work?"

"It's not that simple."

"Yes, it is. Do you *want* us to work?"

"I do," Simran says.

"Okay." He's entering full-on planning mode. "I've been thinking about everything a lot. I really believe we can start over and that there's no need to get into everything from the past."

"There isn't?" Simran asks. "At all?"

The blur of the past year enlarges before her. Meeting Neil, eating dessert with him, kissing him, going to India, being with Nani, going to the school, her mother leaving their house . . .

Kunal straightens his shoulders and looks at her. "I don't think it'll help either of us to keep dwelling on anything that's already happened. I want to move on."

"I do, too," Simran says.

He squeezes her hands. "Simran, if we're going to do that, I need to know you're serious. Really committed to us."

"I am," Simran says.

"You can understand why I have my doubts after everything."

"I do."

"So I think we should establish things going forward."

"Such as?"

He runs his thumb down her arm in a swirling pattern. "How do you feel about premarital counseling?"

"What?"

"We would talk to so—"

"I know what it is. I just didn't think you'd ever want to do it. You're serious?"

"I am."

"*You* would want to sit in front of a stranger and talk about your feelings for an hour? You don't even like being on the phone for more than ten minutes."

"Yes, but I think it would help." His face drops. "And I think we need it. I really do. We have so many issues that we should work through in the next ten months. And we've talked about this before. Real relationships take work. Hard work."

Simran takes a deep breath. "Then where would you like to start with the, uh, work?"

"How about we both try to make more of an effort with each other's interests? I'd like it if you could come to a dinner Dr. Maude is hosting next week."

"For everyone from the trip?"

He nods. "And how can I do something for you?"

She stares at him, bewildered. Who is this scripted man?

At least he's trying, a stern voice in her head says.

And wasn't she just thinking that her own mother should give her father a chance? Why shouldn't she do the same?

She pictures her schedule for the next month. "I would like it if you came to a book signing with me."

"Which book signing?" he asks.

"Laura Martinez. That psychologist who writes pop psychology articles for *The New Yorker*. She has a new book out about how people become sociopaths. She's doing a reading at the Strand next month."

"Okay. I'll go. *We'll* go."

They order pizza, the food they both missed the most when they were out of the country. They watch two episodes of *Modern Family*.

And then, after they've settled back onto his twin bed, they start to kiss. It's been so long since she's felt Kunal's lips against hers. His hand slips under her shirt. She watches him slide out of his scrubs.

"I've missed you," he whispers.

"Me too," Simran says.

And it's true. She did miss him. This.

She runs her hands across his back. Lets herself relax. He throws her black lacy bra and underwear (she matched for once) on his desk.

"Damn, that was nice," he says an hour later, pressing his body even more against hers.

"Hmm," Simran says.

She feels the thump of his heartbeat and hopes it will quiet her racing thoughts.

But it doesn't.

After Kunal falls asleep, Simran stares out of his nearly opaque window. It looks dirty no matter how much it's cleaned. An ambulance wails every half hour. Yellow and red lights reflect into the bedroom. A cluster of men argue in Italian.

She considers calling her mother and leaving her eighth voice-mail of the week. But there's no private space to talk without the risk of waking up Kunal or his roommates. Somewhere around one a.m., Kunal gets up and goes to the bathroom. Simran sees a light winking in the spot where he was sleeping. She digs under the twisted sheets and retrieves his phone.

Three missed calls from Rekha.

Nandini

"Did they try to scare you, too?" Yuwa Oni asks Nandini during lunch.

Nandini takes a sip of sparkling water. "Adam tried when he met with me, yes."

Yuwa and Nandini first met last month during a department meeting. Yuwa went to medical school in Nigeria, moved to Baltimore with her husband, and is now the head of the Nephrology department at Hopkins. She stopped Nandini after the meeting and asked her to grab coffee. Nandini was taken aback by her initiative. The only friends she made in America were Ranjit's friends' wives. But Yuwa was the type of woman she wished she had known in medical school in India or at the clinic in New Jersey. The type who shared her ambition, her desire to be something more. She wishes Mami could meet her.

Mami. She's not returning Nandini's calls or posting on Facebook. Has Simran spoken to her?

"Fucking asshole," Yuwa says. "I guess that's what one has to be to get to the position of department chair, but still, what an asshole."

Typically, Nandini would have flinched at the curse words, but today, she laughs. Yuwa's freedom with words is refreshing.

They are sitting in the cafeteria. Every few seconds, someone's pager beeps. Clusters of residents and attendings in white coats are in the tables around them. To her pleasant surprise, Nandini noted two weeks ago that a majority of the medicine interns are women, a stark contrast from when she was doing her training. The medicine interns are wearing their house staff ties and scarves, a Friday tradition that has been at Hopkins for as long as Nandini can remember. Nandini still keeps her Osler scarf from residency inside her purse, folded up, hidden from view.

"My daughter gave me pep talks after I first told her about Adam," Nandini says. "Suddenly, she's so much more under-standing and supportive."

"Don't you love how kids do that?" Yuwa asks. "Right when you think they can't possibly annoy you more, they surprise you."

Yuwa has two daughters in their twenties. One is doing mi-crobiology research at Boston University and the other is a ballet instructor in New York City. Nandini pictures them as younger versions of Yuwa, brazen and outspoken and fierce.

"So true," Nandini agrees. "But you know, I haven't talked to Simran as much as I'd want to since I've been here. I'm sure she's concerned. And sometimes, I pull up her name on my phone and then, I just can't make the call."

"Why is that?"

"I guess I'm worried she won't entirely get what I'm doing here. I don't know if anybody does. I've been so out of the loop with my family and everything happening with them. It's just been so busy here."

And my husband certainly doesn't understand, she thinks. She is going to New Jersey next weekend and can't imagine what Ranjit will have to say to her. Can she even blame him for being angry?

She still feels guilty for not being home, not being available, for everyone.

"Why do you need anybody to get it?" Yuwa gazes at her, waiting for Nandini to answer.

Yuwa has a point. Why *does* she need anybody to get it?

"It's just the way things have always been for me. I don't even know how to be without people's approval. I guess that's how I've defined myself for so many years," Nandini says, surprised at her own honesty. Being around Yuwa reminds her of how people describe dating: a sense of excitement intertwined with being understood. In just one month, she is beginning to see that true friendship has little to do with how long you've known someone and everything to do with faith. The faith that you can expose your rawest thoughts and still be accepted.

"It's the way we're raised, to always care about being accepted and not making ourselves a hassle. But you can't worry about any of them right now, not your family, not Adam. *Especially* Adam. You of all people don't even need to think about him." Yuwa fiddles with the long silver necklace that she wears every day. She always wears vibrant accessories: silk scarves in bold jewel tones, fringed earrings that dance when she moves her head, turquoise enamel bangles that peek out from underneath the sleeves of her white coat. She inspires Nandini to wear eyeliner and brighter colors, to be seen.

"What does that mean, I don't need to think about Adam?"

"Well"—Yuwa smiles at her—"I've heard that the residents are already so impressed with your teaching."

"Really? That's nice to hear," Nandini says. She feels proud whenever she is able to show someone how to review labs or press an abdomen to feel for the edge of the liver.

"I'm sure. *And* I think they're going to nominate you to speak at the AMA conference."

"What? *Me?*" Nandini has been reading the American Medical Association newsletter routinely over the past two decades. Sometimes, she and Ranjit even considered attending the yearly conference. But speaking? The thought of being in front of a room full of doctors fills Nandini with a thrill she hasn't experienced in years, maybe ever.

In medical school and even residency, she imagined her future would be full of hours spent at a podium, educating and inspiring people about what she learned. But over time, the image became smaller and blurrier, like a childhood memory, and she learned to let it go.

"Yes!" Yuwa says. "Look, I've only just heard it from a couple of them, so I don't know what'll happen, but you know how things are around here. The way people talk about you is *everything* in this political place."

"That is true," Nandini says. "And even being considered for this makes me happy."

Is it possible that people have noticed her hard work? She's been getting to the hospital by six every morning, rounding with the residents, and rushing to Greg's private practice. From there, she picks up an arugula salad and black bean soup from the local deli, which she enjoys in the solitude of the apartment she is leasing this month. Her evenings are spent reading the latest research studies and making study guides to review with the residents the following morning. The clinic in New Jersey, which had drained her, had also taught her how to work fast and under pressure. And while she has still been tired over the past month, it is a satisfying type of exhaustion, not the corrosive burnout she experienced in New Jersey.

"I'll have to tell my daughter about that. And Greg! He'll be so happy," Nandini says.

She visits Greg in between rounds and then at night, before he drifts off into a disturbed, fragmented sleep. It is hard for him to finish his meals or even sit through an entire comedy sitcom.

Nandini finishes the remainder of her soup. "Maybe I'll go see him now."

Is it bad that she is excited to tell Greg about something good for her, when his body is breaking down? Maybe she should wait.

She says goodbye to Yuwa and walks out of the cafeteria, unsure where to go next.

Fifteen

Simran

Laura Martinez is even better than Simran had predicted. She talks about the most famous sociopaths in history, the way her audience can identify one in their personal lives, and reads excerpts from her book.

Simran looks over at Kunal, who is slumped forward, scrolling through some medical article on his iPhone, his eyes glazed over.

She nudges him with her elbow.

Kunal looks up. "Sorry. Paying attention now. Promise."

She keeps a neutral facial expression. "It's okay. I know sitting through an hour of couples counseling before coming here isn't your ideal day."

He shrugs, as if to say, *Good point.*

"But just try to pay attention for a second. It's not your type of science, but it's still interesting."

He nods and straightens his shoulders.

In the past months, they've booked almost all their wedding vendors. They've sat in meetings, reviewed contracts, and had conference calls. They've looked at flights for their shopping trip to India. They've managed to keep their parents calm.

Forward motion, that's what their therapist recommends. Keep moving, keep looking ahead. That's how you prepare for marriage. That's how you become an adult.

Simran and Kunal are sitting in the back row. The top floor of the Strand, the one reserved for readings, is packed. The walls are lined with filled, mahogany bookshelves. Lights are strung across the ceiling. The crowd is an eclectic assortment of thick black glasses and crisp button-downs and bold lipsticks and even bolder hair colors.

After Laura is finished with the reading, she sits behind a petite brown desk. A man wearing all black asks everyone to make a line. He tells them they will all have an opportunity to have their books signed and take a quick picture with her. He goes to each person in line, writes their name on a yellow Post-it note, and attaches it to the front of their book.

Kunal opens the front cover of the book and whistles. "Wow, you'd think they would at least give you a discount for coming here."

"It doesn't really work that way," Simran says. "Besides, people don't value books anymore. I don't mind splurging on one I know will be good."

"But you have so many you haven't even read."

"That's because I haven't had the chance."

"Yeah, and then they just collect and take up space."

Simran halts their discussion by pointing out the spines of books on the shelves next to them. The line inches forward. Kunal yawns.

"Hey, I just realized I never got to see all your pictures from the trip. I've only been able to look at the ones other people posted on Facebook. Want to show me now?" Simran asks, with the eagerness of a mother hoping her baby will stay quiet during a long flight.

Kunal pulls out his phone and shows her photos of him with young children and mothers, the rest of the medical students, a couple of him and Dr. Maude. There's one selfie of him and Rekha in a restaurant, a plate of plantains, black beans, and rice behind them. Kunal is sitting up straight, his arm extended for the selfie. But Rekha is leaning toward him, a dopey grin on her face, almost as though the picture interrupted a joke between them.

"Where was that?"

"Random café," he says as he swipes to the next one.

"Those were great," Simran says after they've looked through all of them.

When it's finally their turn, Laura looks in their direction, stands up, and extends her arms. "I can't believe *you* made it!"

Kunal turns to Simran. "Do you know each other?"

Simran shakes her head. "I mean, I've been to another signing of hers before. Do you think she remembers me?"

Simran waves at her. Laura walks toward them. Simran keeps waving. So does Laura.

And then, Laura walks past them.

She was looking behind them the entire time.

It's like that time in middle school, when Simran thought the dashing Ben Kleinman was gesturing to her in the cafeteria for a full five minutes before she realized he was motioning to the cheerleader sitting ten feet behind her.

Simran follows Laura's low-pitched voice, as does everyone else in line.

"Come on! You can hang out with me at the desk," Laura says.

In five seconds, she's back at her desk, with a guy who dresses like Neil Desai by her side.

Simran takes a second glance.

It *is* Neil Desai.

But could it really be him? No, that's not possible. Simran looks again. He seems a little older than she remembered. Refined. The stubble across his chin gives his face a novel ruggedness. She's taken back to the feel of his lips. His woodsy scent. He takes a generous sip of champagne and flashes a Crest-commercial-worthy grin at some people in the back of the room. He always knew how to charm, even from afar.

Everything around her becomes blurry. Kunal starts talking about how they should go on their honeymoon before he starts rotations.

"Oh my god," Simran says.

"What?" Kunal asks.

Simran doesn't process him. She only hears syllables in slow motion.

Kunal looks at Simran, then follows her gaze toward Neil. "You've got to be fucking kidding me. Is that *him*?"

"I didn't know he'd be here," Simran says. "I thought he was in China."

But Neil Desai, *the* Neil Desai, is standing here, in New York City, as if everything is, well, normal. Simran forgot about the way he always stood with his thumbs slung into his pants pockets. Casual. Confident. She forgot about the way his eyes crinkled at the corners when he smiles.

She holds her breath. Neil looks like he's about to face them.

No, no, no. We can't just talk.

But then, he turns the other way and starts speaking to the

man in all black, who Simran has now figured out is Laura's agent. Hearing Neil's voice reminds her of the night they first met. The way her eyes hung on him before she knew who he was.

A tremor starts to develop in both of her hands. She has a window to get them out. She prepares to pull Kunal's arm. Make them dash to the exit.

But then Laura Martinez yells, "Next!"

Kunal and Simran approach Laura's desk. Simran focuses on the wood's swirling patterns. She will not look in Neil's direction.

"I'm sorry to keep you waiting," Laura says as she glances at the Post-it on Simran's book. "I appreciate your patience, er, Samuel."

Samuel?

"Simran," Simran says. "It's Simran."

"Oh, right. Sorry about that," Laura says.

Simran's cheeks are warm. She hands Laura her book. Laura opens the front cover. Asks if they are having fun. Kunal mumbles something. Simran says of course they are. Laura lingers over her signature. Simran's left foot starts to shake. Tap. Tap. Tap. Tap.

Simran grabs the book from Laura's hands the second she's done signing, before she's even had a chance to cap her purple Sharpie.

"Thank you," Simran says before she turns to Kunal. "Let's go."

Kunal is already facing the exit. Simran lets herself take one last glance at Neil.

He's already looking at her.

The synapses between her brain and lips freeze. She had pictured this moment for so long. Mentally played out how they would be. That she'd wear the perfect outfit. Have all the right things to say.

"Hi there," Neil says.

"Hey, how are you?" Simran asks the question as though she's run into an old friend from NYU.

"Fine, and *you*?" Neil's voice is playful and cheery.

"Great." Kunal's fingers dig into Simran's back. "I, *we*, were just leaving."

"I see that," Neil says as he runs his hands through his wavy black hair.

They stare at each other in silence. Simran waits for something to break their interaction. Another friend of his coming to speak with him. Laura asking him a question. A phone call.

But nothing happens.

Neil offers a tight, polite smile, and something inside of Simran crumples.

She motions toward Kunal. "This is Kunal."

"Of course," Neil says, extending his hand. "Nice to meet you, man."

"You too," Kunal says, his tone akin to hospital bed corners: rigid, crisp.

Neil lowers his head and takes a sip of his champagne, aware that Kunal thinks it's *not* nice to meet him at all.

This can't really be happening. Simran takes yoga-class-worthy breaths. Now would be a great time to leave.

"So, you're in med school, right?" Neil asks.

"That's right," Kunal says.

"How's it going?"

"Fine."

They stand side by side, avoiding eye contact, Kunal, in a faded polo and khaki shorts, and Neil, in a light blue button-down and navy blue blazer. They would never be friends: one man who goes to bars where people wear jeans and hoodies, another who attends galas in a perfectly tailored tuxedo.

There's more silence, except for a grunt from Kunal. Unlike Neil, he doesn't have a baseline level of panache with people, whether he likes them or not (which is also why he cowers away from most social interactions unless, of course, they're related to medicine). Simran used to admire that he marched to the beat of his own drum, didn't feel the need to put on a show for anyone, but sometimes she wishes he'd just be a little friendlier.

Neil takes a subtle peek at Simran's left ring finger and then looks at both of them. "Congratulations."

Kunal slings his arm across Simran's shoulder, a gesture that's a mixture of sweet and territorial.

"Thanks." Simran puts her hands behind her back, her heart still pounding. "Wedding planning has been busy."

Do not talk about wedding planning with Neil Desai, you idiot.

The line dwindles as everyone gets their books signed and pictures taken. A couple of twenty-something girls wearing crop tops and pencil skirts are watching them. They're probably wondering how someone like Simran knows someone like Neil.

Simran wants to say, *It was good to see you. We should get going now.*

But she hears herself offering something else. "I didn't know you'd be here. Did you come back from China early?"

"I did," Neil says. "I'm going to be back and forth between China and Manhattan for at least the next year. But I'm glad I made it for this. Laura's been a good friend for a long time. Remember? I told you that when we were at Milk Bar."

He looks at Simran in a way that's wistful. Wistful and sad. A look she'll have to analyze in her diary later.

"That's right. You did," Simran says, remembering when they discussed all their favorite writers, how Neil was friends with several of them. "And I forgot that you're the one who told me about this book. I read the preview on Amazon weeks ago and couldn't wait for it to come out. And then she goes ahead and does an event at my favorite bookstore! I used to come here almost every weekend in college."

Her heart rate slows down. What should she ask about next? Every word matters. Everything about *him* matters.

"Yes, your love of bookstores is endearing, Samuel."

"Shut up! I can't believe you heard her call me that."

"I think a lot of people did." He gives Simran a knowing smile. It makes her want to tell him about everything. India. Nani. Her mother still being in Baltimore. That she's gotten a better idea about what she wants to do with her life.

For a split second, she wonders what it would be like to be engaged to Neil. Would they be one of those annoying couples who posts too much on Facebook? Would she discuss his proposal with anyone who would listen? Would they always be giddy, counting down to their wedding?

She snaps back to reality and grabs Kunal's hand.

Neil looks at Simran and laughs. "And by the way, I told you about this event, too."

"Did you?" Kunal asks, offering his contribution for the night.

"Oh yeah. I forgot about that," Simran says to both of them.

Kunal peers at her. "*Really?* You forgot he told you?"

"Yes, I *really* did," Simran says, before turning back to Neil. "We should go."

Only a dozen or so people are left in the room. Laura is now mingling, a glass of champagne in her delicate hand, her smile fixed and ready for photographs. Simran watches her eyes meet them. She walks over. Neil introduces her to Kunal and Simran. Simran freezes in the way she always does when she's up close to someone fabulous and successful.

"We're going to that spot I love on Irving," Laura says to Neil. "You're coming, right?"

Neil shrugs. "I hadn't decided yet."

"You have to!" Laura slings her arms around Neil's waist, grazes his shoulder with her freshly blown-out hair. "And you know it's close to my apartment."

Neil turns red, as though he doesn't receive this type of attention from women all the time.

Then Laura links her fingers through his and gives his hand a tight squeeze.

Of course they're together. Of course he'd be enamored of a woman like her. She's still vivacious and alluring even when she can't finish her sentences. Simran pictures their matching Warby Parker glasses on his nightstand, and her stomach twists into a knot.

She waves a quick goodbye to Laura and Neil. Kunal has already turned around.

Kunal and Simran don't talk on the elevator ride to the ground floor. Once they're outside, they walk to the corner of Thirteenth and Broadway to hail a cab. If this was any other night, she would have suggested they get dessert from Max Brenner's or take a walk around Union Square.

"I'm sorry. I didn't know that would happen."

"Whatever," he mutters.

"You know that, right? I didn't know and I *am* sorry. Please let's not let this ruin our night. We've come so far with therapy, even you said that, and I don't want to go backward."

"This isn't about going backward. It was right in front of us. I saw the way you looked at him, talked to him. Fucking ridiculous."

Simran shakes her head and whispers *no*, but she is unable to elaborate any further, because he's right. Being around Neil puts her in a state of awe and ease at the same time.

"Everything was fine, more than fine, before he stepped into the picture," Kunal says. "We were on our way to planning our wedding, our lives, and then he comes and shits all over it."

Simran looks up at him. "I thought that, too, but there were a lot of things we needed to work on. And now we are."

She can't deny that in one way or another, Neil made her question everything in her life, that everything that seemed secure started to feel out of place, that a new restlessness took shape.

A group of tourists pass them and snap photos on large Canon cameras of the Empire State Building in the distance. Some of them start to sift through the books in the three-dollar bin.

"You can't talk to him again," Kunal says. "Ever."

"I don't need you to set rules with me, Kunal. I wasn't planning to talk to him. We haven't communicated since before I went to India."

"So then we're clear, right? You're not going to talk to him again."

"I'm not going to talk to him again."

Saying it out loud makes her limbs heavy. She will never talk to Neil Desai again. She can't.

"Fine." Kunal shoves his large hands into his shorts pockets. "I was actually going to bring that up in therapy next week."

"You were going to discuss Neil during therapy?"

"Well, yeah, him and just the general question of how we want to handle people who may be a threat to our relationship."

"Who are these so-called people besides him?" Simran scans every other guy in her life and can't figure out who he's referring to.

A cab slows down for them and they both shake their heads. It joins the swelling traffic.

Kunal stares at a cigarette butt on the sidewalk. "In Costa Rica, Rekha told me she had feelings for me."

Simran's head jerks up. "What? Rekha told you *what*?"

"That she's liked me for a while."

"When during your trip was this?"

He keeps staring at the cigarette butt. "On the last day."

"You're kidding," Simran says.

Kunal shakes his head. "I was so thrown off guard. I mean, she just blurted it out, and I told her she was confused because of everything I've helped her out with. And she said sorry. She knew you and I were having problems and she felt bad about trying to take advantage of the situation. I told her it was fine an—"

"You told her it was *fine*? *Fine* that she told you she's been in love with you this entire time?"

He holds up a palm. "No, it was fine that she mistook our friendship for something more. It happens. And she said I was right. That she was sorry. And"—he faces her and takes a deep breath—"she kissed me."

"She *what*?!"

"After she told me. In Costa Rica. I pushed her away."

"And you're telling me this *now*?" Simran wraps her arms across her belly. Sweat starts to form on her palms, under her arms. Simran pictures the selfie of them at the restaurant in Costa Rica, the hopeful look in Rekha's eyes. She tries to imagine the moment between her fiancé and Rekha. She wants to know everything about their kiss. She wants to know nothing about their kiss.

"I told her she can't do or say anything like that with me ever again. She was really drunk, so I wasn't even sure if it registered. And then, after we came back to New York, she called me and said the same things again."

"Is that why she called you multiple times that night I was over there? When you got back?"

"She kept trying to reach me to talk." Kunal nods. "I listened to her voicemails the next day and told her we can't be friends anymore."

"I don't even know what to say. . . ." Simran says as she wonders why she didn't bring the missed calls up until now. Maybe a part of her knew and didn't want to acknowledge the truth.

He grabs Simran's arm. "I really did push her away. I promise."

"I believe you." Simran waits for pangs of jealousy or anger to arrive. But she feels nothing. She can't even cry. Instead, she finds herself feeling sorry for Rekha. Simran knows what it's like to be intrigued and comforted by Kunal, his self-assured way of always having a plan and solution for everything.

She waits for herself to yell, but it doesn't happen.

Instead, her voice is steady as she says, "Well, thanks for telling me."

"I wanted to and just didn't know the right time." He steps closer to her for a hug. "Let me grab a cab for us."

She puts out her hand. "I need to be by myself tonight."

"Seriously?" Kunal asks. "You're not going to come back with me? You're going to be like that?"

A few months ago, that type of questioning would have made Simran retract her statement. *No,* she'd have said. *I'll get over my emotions and do what you ask.*

But now, she holds her ground. "I have a lot on my mind right now. I just need some space."

"What's on your mind? Are you upset because of what I just told you?"

"No, not just that. There are other things."

"You're different, Simran. You know that? You've changed," he says.

Simran takes a few seconds to repeat his words in her head. "You're right. I am. And I'm fine right now. Really. I just need some space."

"You're sure?"

"Yes. I'll call you tomorrow."

Kunal takes that as enough reassurance to not probe any further, which only confirms that Simran made the right decision. It doesn't matter how much therapy they get. He still doesn't know when she needs him to try.

Simran tells Kunal goodbye as she steps into a cab. She asks the driver to stop only three blocks later. She needs to walk the twenty blocks to her apartment, bleed into the city. She gazes down Park Avenue, where everything is visible for miles, as if someone unrolled Manhattan like a giant carpet.

As she walks uptown, she thinks about the shifts in her life. Six months ago, everything was set. Stable. Nani was healthy. She and Kunal were excited to plan their wedding. She was ready to become a therapist. Her parents were thrilled that their kids were finally going to be settled in their own lives. Her mother seemed okay, or rather, the same as always. But at least she was home. Simran had good friends, a good fiancé, a good future job, a good life.

So, why has everything unraveled? All that time, trying to measure up to who she thought she was supposed to be. If she was a better granddaughter, maybe she could have helped Nani, encouraged her to get treatment when there was still time. She should have taken the initiative to help her get established as a teacher years ago. She knew that Nani was living alone and didn't know how to ask for help, but she chose not to get involved.

And her relationship with Kunal already felt like it was calming down. They fought, yes, but it was the type of harmless banter she thought accompanied all couples who were in long-term relationships. Would they be in the same place if she hadn't met Neil? Neil, the guy she couldn't stop thinking about, who is now dating one of the most talented writers she knows. What was the point of everything they went through?

And what about grad school? Dad was right. She *was* on the home stretch when she quit. She could have pushed through for a few more months. It wouldn't have been the worst thing to have a job she liked *enough*.

Then there's her mother. Simran thought Mom knew she could always rely on her. But maybe Mom was hoping for this departure long before Dr. Dalton got in touch with her and Kunal proposed. Maybe she knew, after her first marriage, that tradition wasn't for her, but she didn't have another choice, until now. But still, how could she just *leave*? Was everything Simran did enough to push her over the edge?

Simran so wants to be that type of carefree woman who takes things as they come without overthinking. But she still can't figure out if everything happened because she was too immature to appreciate what she had or because it was all wrong for her. What she does know is that there's a gradual gnawing occurring inside her, a sense that there's more to this than she understands.

It starts to rain once she's on Twenty-Ninth Street. The streetlights blur and change sizes under the water, turning her surroundings into a giant kaleidoscope. The subway is a thunderstorm under the sidewalk. Wind tunnels through the street, like a harsh truth, and she's hit with nostalgia, not for a particular place or time but for the woman she no longer is.

She turns onto her block in Midtown East, where all the offices have closed down and bars have opened up. She thinks about her bedtime routine. Washing her face, brushing her teeth, falling asleep to Netflix. To silence.

But as she approaches her building, there's someone waiting for her at the entrance.

Sixteen

Simran

Simran's mother is leaning against the brick building. She's wearing her favorite little black dress from Barneys, a splurge that took Simran six months to convince her to make. They took a cab up Fifth Avenue after her English class that day. Simran told Mom to take the time to try it on, throw in a pair of shoes. Mom was always rushing, stressing, never doing anything for herself.

Now, she's typing a text message on her iPhone.

"Mom?!"

Simran runs toward Mom. She can't decide if she wants to hug her or scream at her.

Mom looks up. "Hi."

"Hi? Hi?! What are you doing here? Where have you been?"

A couple, likely on their first date by the sheepish looks on their faces, stares at them. Simran smiles at them. They keep walking.

Simran grips Mom's shoulders. It's really her. Her *mom*. Her hair's thrown into a messy bun, and her maroon-rimmed reading glasses are slung in the front of her dress. A gray satchel, an old birthday gift from Ronak and Simran, hangs off her slim wrist.

Mom reaches forward to hug her. Simran squeezes her and

takes a deep breath. She smells like her L'Occitane lavender hand lotion.

When Simran pulls away, Mom's face is moist with tears.

"Mom, what's wrong? What's been going on? You haven't responded to my calls. God, I've been so worried about you. We all have. We thought you left us."

"No, I, well, I . . ."

"You what?"

Mom looks down. As the glare of the streetlight hits her face, Simran sees she's still crying.

"What is it?"

Mom sighs. "I don't even know where to start."

"Start anywhere." Simran is more yelling than speaking. "Really. *Anywhere.*"

"Greg died last night," Mom whispers.

The second the words come out, Mom starts sobbing. Simran has never heard her cry like that, with loud wails and quick breaths. She puts her arms around Mom again.

"Oh my god. He died?" Simran stops herself from saying more because she can't think of anything that will help.

"He stopped breathing. Felt himself suffocate to death. Can you imagine?"

"No," Simran says. "That's the most horrifying thing I've ever heard."

"It can happen with the disease. He knew that. We both did. But he didn't want to be put on a ventilator. He was gone before I got to the hospital."

"I'm so sorry," Simran says.

"We knew it would happen."

"Still, that doesn't make it any easier."

Mom nods and inhales deeply. Simran thinks she's about to cry again, but to her surprise, Mom reaches into her purse for a tissue and dabs the corners of her eyes. She stands up straight and adjusts her dress. It's as though something in her brain told her to go back to being tough, put-together Nandini.

Simran motions to the lobby. "Let's go inside."

She considers giving Mom a warning about her apartment as she pictures her laundry hamper choking with dirty clothes, the job applications scattered across her coffee table, and the empty bottles of wine lining the sink.

Mom crumples the tissue with her hands. "Actually, if you don't mind, I'd like to go to that coffee shop you took me to before. I need to eat."

"Okay." Simran guides them to the corner of Thirty-Second and Lexington.

The coffee shop is closed, so Simran suggests a twenty-four-hour diner on Park. It's where she, Sheila, and Vishal go when they aren't in the mood for Kati Roll or Mamoun's.

The only other customers are a group of girls in clubbing clothes, who are loud with drunkenness and the lack of inhibition that accompanies college students. They're having chocolate milk shakes and cheese fries. The walls are covered with black-and-white photos of customers. A jukebox with neon lights is in the back corner.

Simran and her mom sit in a red vinyl booth near the entrance. Whenever someone opens the door, the crisp New York air rushes in. Simran takes a quick glance at the large, laminated menu and orders a coffee. Mom also asks for a coffee along with an egg-white omelet.

As they wait for their food, Simran tries to process everything that's happened tonight. The Strand event seems so far away.

Simran looks at her mom again. It's surreal seeing her unfolding a paper napkin and laying it across her lap. She almost expects Mom to laugh, say this entire thing was a big, bad joke.

They don't talk until their coffees arrive. Both of them pour in cream and rip one white sugar packet.

Simran inhales her coffee and takes a large gulp. "Does Dad know you're back?"

Mom nods. "I dropped my things off at home before coming here."

"And? Did you talk?"

"Technically, I guess. He obviously looked surprised to see me. We said hi. He asked how Baltimore was. I said it was complicated. And that was it. You know him, he's not the type to ask a bunch of questions. Of course, he did manage to sarcastically say that he hoped I had a fun trip. And then he stayed in a huff. That was it."

"Well, you did leave out of nowhere. He's going to be angry and confused about that."

Mom's omelet arrives, and she drizzles it with hot sauce. She once told Simran that she's needed to put hot sauce on everything since she was pregnant with Simran.

"Yes, I did leave suddenly, but—"

"But *what*? You'd be so upset if Dad did anything like that to you."

Mom's fork and knife drop on her plate with a loud clank. "Did anyone stop to think for one second *why* I did what I did? That maybe it wasn't an easy, no-big-deal type of thing for me?"

"Then what was it? Why did you do it? Why did you shut all of us out?"

"Simran, this is going to be hard for you to understand right now but when"—she catches her breath—"or if, you're married and have kids, you'll realize that there are a lot of things you give up in order to make life work for everyone else."

"I know that. You've said that for a long time. But what changed now?"

"With you and Ronak getting married, it hit me. I'd just be in the house with Dad. Or with Dad and some combination of his family. And that would be that. The idea of it made me feel trapped. Maybe I'd take the occasional break with some of the other aunties, but even they've become busy with grandchildren or traveling or whatever.

"I had been frustrated with my job for a long time but wasn't ready to quit because it was the only thing I had going for me outside of the house. But then Greg got in touch with me, told me he was sick, and needed someone to take over his patients. And I thought, *Maybe this is my chance to practice medicine in the way I've always wanted.* Greg had a light patient load, and his practice was already sold to a larger group, so there would have been no pressure for me to see a certain number of patients in a tight time frame. I could spend valuable time with them, do some extra reading on their cases, and teach residents at Hopkins on some mornings, the way he did."

Simran pictures Mom in her white coat, her stethoscope slung around her neck as she teaches residents how to decide on the best antibiotic or when to consult a specialist or how to break bad news to a family. She's similar to Kunal in that way, always wanting to do more, push herself, partially because of innate ambition and partially to quiet that steady IV drip, drip, drip of a thought: *You're not good enough.*

But unlike Kunal, she didn't have people encouraging her to work, to expand. By his age, she was already with her first husband. Simran wonders who she would have become if she hadn't been born in India.

"Mom, I've always seen how difficult it's been with Dad's family around expecting so much from you. I really have. But couldn't you have tried to talk to him about this job? How do you know what he would have said?"

"I don't know," she admits. "But that's the thing. I can't let go of things from the first years of our marriage. And see, that's the problem with arranged marriages. Nobody knows how to communicate with their spouse or how to deal with issues that you kids experience earlier, since you date, so a lot of things are misunderstood or not conveyed."

Simran refrains from telling her that plenty of things are misunderstood or not conveyed, even when you have dated.

"And then people become bitter," Mom says. "That's the real danger: bitterness. Bitterness first breeds disappointment, then manipulation. Some people learn how to mold bitterness so it suits them, but I knew I couldn't be that way.

"I was at my most vulnerable when we got married. I was going through a lot of things because of—it doesn't matter, because of what—but I was going through a lot, and he didn't understand me, so I curled into myself. Tucked parts of myself away. And because of that, his family was able to control him through their demands. And now, he *is* more understanding, more aware. I see what a kind and patient person he is. But I can't let go."

"So, then that's it? You just say, 'Oh, I can't let the past go,' and decide not to even try?"

Mom reaches across the table and takes the coffee mug out of Simran's hands. "Simi, calm down."

"Right, sorry. I should stay calm as my mom tells me she just wants to give up."

"Do you know why I came back from Baltimore?"

"Because your friend passed away and you wanted to be near family?"

Mom shakes her head.

"You needed a break from your new job?"

"No, because I needed to try to talk through things with your dad. I don't want him—or you, or Ronak—to think I don't care about you. And you need to stop trying to handle this situation for your dad and me."

"Me?" Simran asks.

The drunk girls leave. Simran and Mom are now the only people here.

"I knew you would get involved and try to fix things between us. That's just how you've always been. But this is not your concern. He and I should be managing this with each other, like adults. And the only thing I've ever really wanted in my life, more than anything, is for you to not have to go through any of the struggles I did. I spent so much of my time as a little girl concerned about my parents. And then, as a married woman, I was always worried about being a perfect daughter and sister-in-law. You have the chance to discuss these things with Kunal beforehand. Make sure you don't have to deal with that."

Simran thinks back to the instances when her mother warned her about how she'd look toward Kunal's family or how important it was for Simran to have her own career. All those times when Simran thought Mom was getting angry at her for not meeting some high, preconceived expectations. Was she looking out for Simran the entire time? Was she determined that her daughter wouldn't suffer the way she did?

Simran sees her mother's life in a blur: running away from her first husband, taking care of her dying father, moving to America with Dad, waiting for letters from Nani, getting yelled at in residency, sitting in her car, exhausted, only to come home to cook for a full house. Despite everything she went through, she remained hopeful and made sacrifices so Simran's life wouldn't be like hers.

"*Beta*," Mom says, folding Simran's hands in hers, "don't cry."

"I'm not," Simran says, and they both laugh. She's had that same response since she was a little girl, even after she skinned her knees playing kickball and had snot running down her face.

And then, before Mom can comfort her any more, Simran blurts, "Mom, I know about your first marriage."

Mom yanks her hand away as if she just touched a hot stove. "What? What do you . . ." The expression on her face shifts from confusion to shock to anger. The anger sticks. "Mami told you about that? How dare she even thi—"

"It's okay." Simran reaches across the table and grabs her hand again.

"It is not okay at all!" Mom stares behind Simran, at nothing. "You were never supposed to know, and my mother is well aware of that. She had no business telling you that when I wasn't even there. She always warned me it would come out, but of course, she conveniently didn't tell me *she'd* be the reason why."

"What does it matter that you weren't even there? Who cares? She did this so I'd be aware. It's a good thing, Mom."

Mom slumps back in her booth. Simran isn't sure if she's going to scream or cry. Or both. Maybe she shouldn't have brought this up. For a second, she almost thought they resembled those harmonious white families she saw in movies growing up. They didn't fight or scream or misunderstand.

But now, she's fucked things up, as usual. Seconds stretch into minutes. Neither of them knows what to say. Mom grabs her hair, releases it, then massages her temples. Simran wonders if this is what she does when she's overwhelmed at work. As much as she and her mother know each other, there's still so much they'll never know. Simran wonders if having those divides is the only way to be a daughter.

Simran takes a deep breath. "I know you're upset . . . but I also know that I'm happy I know about this. I only wish I had known sooner. We could have talked about it, or even if we didn't, at least some things about you would have made sense to me. And look, it's still hard for me to really process it. A part of me feels like I just heard some terrible story that wasn't real. But I hope that you know it's better this way. You've been taught to keep so much locked up inside of you."

Mom stares at the table. "That's how it was for women in India. We're taught to bottle up everything and put on an 'everything's fine' face for everyone, even our own families."

"But it doesn't have to be that way anymore."

"I'm sorry you found out that way."

"I'm not," Simran says, and Mom looks up, questioning. "I mean that."

"There's so much that happened . . . so much I've tried to forget, move past. But it's impossible."

"Of course it's impossible."

Mom reaches across the table and squeezes Simran's hand again. She closes her eyes and then exhales. Something about seeing Mom so defeated breaks Simran. Her mother has always been tough and able to put on a strong face for everyone. Now she's wondering how much has been behind that facade.

"You're okay now. You're more than okay. Look at everything you've overcome," Simran says. "You can get through anything. Anything. I'm so proud of you, Mom."

"You are?" Mom looks at her in surprise.

"I really am." Simran knows she can't talk about this anymore; at least, not now.

The waiter drops off the check. It's attached to a card for free coffee on their next visit. Mom scribbles a tip and her signature, the same rushed one she writes on prescriptions.

In a feeble attempt to make small talk, Simran points out different restaurants during their walk back to her apartment.

And then, as they're crossing Park Avenue, something occurs to her. Something she needs to write down, think about. Something she should have thought of before.

Her mother's right: arranged marriages make communication hard. Impossible, even, at times.

But Simran can talk to Dad for her.

If they try to hash out everything themselves, there's too much room for misunderstandings and overreactions. Simran has to present Mom's side to Dad and then let them talk. They both need someone to explain the other person's perspective.

Her mom won't feel comfortable enough to tell him why she left. He'll be too proud to say he was hurt.

Once they're outside Simran's building, she says, "I'll get out my extra towel for you. And clean up."

Mom shakes her head. "I'm going to go back."

"This late? Just go in the morning."

"No, I'll be more comfortable at home. And my car's right there." Mom motions across the street.

"Then I'll come with you."

"Are you sure?"

"Yes, I'll just run up and pack a bag."

Simran doesn't know how to tell her that after everything they've discussed tonight, she needs to be with her parents.

Ten minutes later, they are sitting inside Mom's air-conditioned Mercedes, with a playlist of old Bollywood songs in the background. Simran shifts the seat into a recline and soaks in the soundtrack of *Dilwale Dulhania Le Jayenge*. For a second, she's ten years old again.

"I'm glad you're coming home," Mom says after they've taken the exit for their house.

"Me too," Simran says, hoping she'll still feel that way after she's talked to Dad.

Nandini

She's sitting in the home library, reading a journal article on the large Apple desktop. There was a new study that came out in *The New England Journal of Medicine* about hypothermia protocols following cardiac arrest. She saves the article, attaches it to an e-mail, and sends it to the internal medicine program director at Hopkins. *Good read for the residents*, she types into the subject line.

Ranjit knocks on the French door. "Busy?"

She fiddles with the stack of papers next to the computer. "No. Just sent an e-mail."

"I see." He leans against the door. He has a brown manila envelope in his hands.

The door was one of the first things they picked when they were building the house. Nandini liked its white-framed sections, all like tiny windows, and the way they allowed fractured sunlight to fill the library. They were so much more open and inviting than the large black doors in her parents' house.

Ranjit steps into the room, and they gaze at each other, a heavy silence falling over them.

"So, how are you?" she asks as she removes her reading glasses.

"Just fine," he scoffs, and closes the door. "You haven't asked me that since you came home."

"You haven't, either," she says.

"I'm not the one who left." Although his voice has its same characteristic low volume, there's an edge to his tone. He's always been able to keep a straight face while saying charged words. She's seen him give bad news to patients and their families in the same manner.

The computer screen is dark. She wiggles the mouse. "You're right. *You're* not the one who left. Is that why you came in here? To talk about that?"

"I don't know. Are you back for good? Or is this just a nice pit stop?"

"Are you going to keep making sarcastic comments like that, Ranjit? If you are, it's better that we talk later."

Ranjit crosses his arms and doesn't say anything. His way of conveying he'll do his best not to be sarcastic anymore.

"And, yes." Nandini leans back in the leather chair. "I'm back . . . for good . . . and we should talk about things."

"Please." He extends his arms like a gracious host. "Be my guest."

She mentally runs through the discussion she and Simran had on the car ride back from the city. "I shouldn't have left without telling you."

"Okay. . . ." He sits in the big blue armchair and puts the envelope on the windowsill.

"I'm sorry for that. I am. I was frustrated about a lot of things, at work and here, and instead of just running away, I should have at least tried to talk to you."

Ranjit raises his eyebrows. He knows how proud his wife is, how proud they both are, how difficult it is to say things like this. They've never discussed their emotions in this manner.

"There's a lot . . . a *lot* . . . that went on before Baltimore, not to mention in Baltimore. It's been hard. Harder than I anticipated."

"Well, trust me, it hasn't been easy around here, either," he says.

"I know that."

"Do you? Do you *really* realize that?"

"Yes," she says, but he doesn't seem to hear her, or care, because he turns away from her and says, "Our children and I had no idea what was going on, you quit your job, you think you're too good to let anybody know any details. Really, what kind of a grown woman behaves that way? And thinks it's okay?"

"I didn't think it was okay," she says.

"Sure you did. You thought it was okay enough to do it."

"Did you ever stop to think *what* point I had to be at to do what I did? It's not like I'm the kind of woman who does this all the time."

He gives her a knowing look, and she gives him one back that says, *Do not go there. Do not talk about my ex-husband, because you know this is different.*

"Are you going to keep being like this?" She peers at him.

"Like what?"

"You know what. It's not helping anything."

"Oh, so *you* get to walk out without saying a damn word, but God forbid I have a reaction."

Nandini clenches her fist under the desk. "Of course you're allowed to have a reaction," she tells him.

What she doesn't say is that his reaction is surprisingly refreshing. For the past few years, she thought they had both become victims of apathy. But if that was ever true, wouldn't she be at fault? She sees now that she should have put her husband first when they were married, instead of prioritizing their families and everyone's expectations. Yes, it was the arranged-marriage mentality—*when you marry the person, you marry the family*—but by putting everyone else's needs first, she neglected him. Them.

She stares at her husband now. He stands and looks out the library window, at the road he took when he left Simran and Kunal's engagement party. She later found out he parked outside of the 7-Eleven for several hours.

They don't talk for another few minutes.

Ranjit sits back down on the armchair. "Nandini, Simran told me about Greg. That's awful."

She nods and stares at the silver keyboard. Greg was gone, and in the worst way. The one person who believed she could be somebody, maybe even somebody great.

"Yes, well, I'm sure he's in a better place," she says, not believing her own words as they emerge.

"Still, I know that had to be extremely hard for you."

"Simran told you about that, too?" she asks.

Ranjit smiles for the first time since they've been speaking. It's clear Simran told him everything.

Ranjit snickers. "Do you think she'll stay this involved after she's married?"

"Who knows? Remember when we were unsure whether her wedding was going to happen?"

"I know!" Ranjit says. "I was worried there for a while, but I guess they worked everything out. No, I don't guess, I *know*. I mean, clearly they must have, if they've already booked the caterer, photographer, and videographer. But who knows how these kids operate, right?"

"Simran did all of those things herself? She didn't mention that to me."

"She started while she was in India and then finalized everything this past month, since she's been back." He nods. "She researched all the options by herself and negotiated with the vendors. She even got a couple of better bargains than we did with Ronak! I just signed the checks. We made sure to discuss things with Pratik Bhai and Meghna Ben, because you know how they are. I know she wished you were a part of all that, though."

"I do, too," she says as she rubs her forehead. "I'm just surprised she moved so . . . quickly. I wonder why she'd do that."

Months ago, this information would have excited her. Now,

she refrains from saying that she doesn't know whether to be proud or confused or worried. It doesn't add up. Her daughter coordinated the most important details of her wedding in a rush? While Nandini wasn't there? And after months of not planning anything?

"So, you're telling me that her wedding is still happening in nine months?"

"Yes, and well, it's always easier being the groom's side. Look at how Ronak just showed up while Namita worked through everything. We didn't realize how great we had it," Ranjit says.

"In a lot of ways," he adds.

They sidetrack into a discussion about Ronak and Namita's lives, their jobs, their tiny apartment in Boston. It's the easiest thing for them, to have their children as a default conversation topic. She used to mind it when they were younger, wished they could discuss other things, but now she finds it endearing. She now sees that over time, this is what a marriage becomes: a mixture of pride and gnawing resentment and comfort.

"What is Simran going to do with her life?" Ranjit asks after they've covered everything about Ronak and Namita. "She still hasn't found a stable job. She's occasionally tutoring college kids for the GRE, so it's something, but that's not a *real* job. I told her we can't keep helping her with her apartment rent. She's going to have to figure out how to pay for that . . . and everything."

"What has she told you she wants to do?"

Ranjit sighs. "Whenever I ask her, she says she's still figuring it out, but I haven't heard any indication that she's actually trying. Do you think you should ask her?"

"Why? Do you really think that's going to help?"

"I don't know. But I'm concerned. What was she even doing

for that entire time she was in India? And why isn't she doing anything with her life now? She's planning this wedding, but what comes after that?"

Nandini listens to Ranjit's concerns about Simran's career. She hears her mother's voice: men want one thing for their wives and another for their daughters. Ranjit wants Nandini to have set hours, confined ambition, while Simran still has to be as professionally accomplished as possible.

"I've wondered the same things," Nandini says as she glances at the baby pictures of Simran and Ronak along the mantel. Her favorite one is of Ronak pinching a five-year-old Simran's chubby cheeks. They're both wearing Mickey Mouse hats. Splash Mountain is in the background. Nobody would guess from that picture that one child's life would be a straight shot to traditional success while the other would stumble.

Ranjit follows her gaze. "Do you think you're setting the right example for her, by not forcing her to face reality?"

Here we go again, she thinks. *Just as I thought things could turn around.*

She stands up. "Am *I* setting the *right* example for *her*? Don't you dare imply that I've done anything except set the best example for her. I've pushed her, encouraged her, been there for her. You know that."

She walks toward Ranjit and stands in front of him. "And I've done the best I can for myself. Maybe it hasn't always worked out the way I wanted to . . . but I've tried."

She feels the pressure building behind her sternum. It was too much. Cramming all that information into her head for exams. Her ex-in-laws not allowing her to work when she was young and energetic and excited. Doing residency later, with years of living like a zombie because of the sleep deprivation and patient care and research in the name of being the best resident. All of that just to be burnt out at a family practice clinic, where she had to meet quotas and rush through patient visits and count down until her day was done. What was the point?

Ranjit seems to read her mind as he says, "So, what now?"

"What do you mean? With work?"

He shrugs. "Sure . . . with work."

She throws her hands in the air. "I don't know. Now that Greg's . . . gone, I'm not sure if the department chair will try to push me out. I've been trying to establish myself, but maybe I need to make another plan."

"Is that what you want?"

She shakes her head. "No, but I have to be realistic."

He walks to the windowsill and hands her the brown envelope he was carrying before.

"What is this?" she asks.

"Open it."

She extracts a thick wad of paper. She reads the top sheet.

Nandini Mehta Lease Agreement

She gives him a questioning glance.

"Just read it," he says, motioning to the paper.

She grabs her reading glasses from the desk and sifts through the pages one at a time. When she's finished, she keeps the envelope open. Ranjit is gazing at her, his face drawn into a question.

She walks toward him. "You got me an apartment in Baltimore? Why?"

He takes a deep breath. "Because you should have a decent

place to go after you're done with work. Not that tiny studio apartment that's so far that you've been leasing. Simran said it's a forty-minute drive from the hospital."

"And you . . . you're okay with me having a permanent place there?"

"I don't know if I am now, but let's see. I can come visit you, or you can come here, on the weekends."

"Why? Why are you doing this?"

"Because I've had time to think. And because our daughter is way too involved in our business, yes, but she had a long talk with me."

They smile at each other. Sometimes she'd remember the American television shows she watched growing up, where husbands gave their wives roses and planned candlelit dinners and held hands. *That'd be nice*, she thought. But then the sentiment would pass, like a breeze, and she'd be fine.

"What about your family?" she asks.

"I told them this was my idea. And you know what? My brothers told Charu you've done a lot for all of them. You took care of our parents for all those years. And you still watch over everyone else, whether it was at your clinic here or during your free time."

She glances outside the window. "Well, that's at least nice to hear."

"It'd be nice if you gave me the benefit of the doubt every once in a while." Ranjt faces her, his brows furrowed. "You're always so quick to criticize. You have this fixed idea in your head that I'm blind to my family's faults, but that's not true. I know, more than anyone else, that they can be a lot for you."

Nandini considers this. Of course he would know the frustrations of his own family. But hearing him say it, for the first time since she's met him, stirs something deep inside her. It is a force that can only come from discovering a new part of the man she's known for years.

"I felt so taken for granted," she says. "As if all of this is expected from me. And it never mattered whether I was exhausted or fed up or wanted to do something for myself."

She continues to vent. He listens to her without saying anything. Simran had once told her she learned about a technique called motivational interviewing in one of her psychology classes. It was based on the idea that with the right circumstances, people could change, but it *always* had to come from within them. Marriages unravel and come back together for all types of reasons, but maybe this is just what she and Ranjit needed.

The right circumstances.

Seventeen

Simran

"Penis lollipops. Perfect," Sheila says, holding up a black plastic bag with lollipops in neon colors.

"Ha, you're ridiculous. I veto any more phallic-shaped purchases. The *giant* inflatable penis with a freaking grin on its tip—*head*—is going to be embarrassing enough." Simran puts the lollipops back on the shelf, next to the other penis party favors: balloons, necklaces, cake toppers.

Sheila and Simran continue to fill their baskets with an array of bachelorette party goodies. They buy ice-breaker cards that have sexual innuendos (what else?), streamers that spell out Simran's name, and gift bags for everyone attending. They leave the mall and load their bags into the trunk of Mom's Mercedes.

Thirty minutes later, they are at Sujata's Salon, early for Simran's hair and makeup trial. Sujata tells Simran that she's finishing up with a client and asks her to sit in a black swivel chair. She offers them coffee, tea, or champagne. They take the champagne.

Sheila pulls up a seat next to Simran. "So, can you believe we're at your *wedding* hair and makeup trial?"

Simran shakes her head. "It hasn't really hit me. Maybe it only will during the actual weekend."

"How is it all going? It's only seven months away!"

Simran nods. Seven months is nothing. June will be here before she knows it. "Great. All of the big things are done, so now it's just the typical little stuff. You know, like family inviting themselves over two weeks before any of the events, my parents and I snapping at each other but then being okay. That's just what happens when there are too many strong personalities involved."

"I bet." Sheila nods and takes a generous sip of her champagne. "How's Kunal?"

"He's busy with school—has his semester finals coming up before winter break—so he can't really be that involved. Which is fine, because he doesn't give a shit about whether we have orchids or hydrangeas or whether our programs are folded in half or are just a single page."

"What about Kunal's mom? How's she with all of this?"

"She's fine." Simran sighs. "I make it a point to call her every week and check in. She gives her opinion on *everything* and has all of these things she wants. She'll probably send me over the edge during the ceremony. Or before."

"Damn, you really call her every week just to check in?"

"I do," Simran says.

"Well . . . good for you!" Something seems to shift in Sheila's eyes, but right as Simran looks at her, Sheila raises her glass as though she's giving a toast.

"Yeah, I mean I see now that everything she does comes from being lonely and scared," Simran says. "It's kind of simple when I look at it objectively. She loves her son. She's scared of losing him."

"Well, I'm sure your parents appreciate you putting in that effort for your future in-laws."

"They do. And we're ready for our India shopping trip next

month, over Kunal's winter break. His parents are joining us for a part of it." Simran gives Sheila a look that says, *God help me.*

"That'll be . . . interesting."

"Yeah," Simran says, her voice trailing off as she pictures the inevitable awkwardness of sitting in sari shops with Mom *and* Meghna Auntie, all of them sipping Thums Up as men unfold yards of fabric.

Then Simran thinks of the fact that her mother didn't have any such shopping trips. She was just asked whether she wanted a cotton or silk sari. Simran wonders if during her first or second marriage, Mom felt that things were about to change too quickly.

"But," Simran continues, "I do have to say that Kunal's stepped up in terms of dealing with her and his dad. We made this agreement in therapy that we would be the ones to communicate with our own parents instead of having each other do it."

"Wow, that's a big step. You're so, I don't know."

"What do you mean, 'you don't know'?"

Sheila shrugs. "You're so consumed with all of this. Way more than I thought you'd be."

"Is that bad?"

"No, of course not. It's just different from the way I thought you'd be. And at least you're both over all the other crap from the past year," she says.

Simran had told Sheila about how they saw Neil at the Strand. What she didn't tell Sheila is how, since then, his face has appeared during the most random moments. While she and her parents are making an Excel spreadsheet. During their reception food tasting. While she sits on the subway and sees an almost version of him in glasses and a checked button-down with a messenger bag.

If Vishal was here, Simran would have told him she doesn't

know if she's supposed to ignore any thought of Neil, or if she should send him an e-mail or text. Doing nothing doesn't seem right.

Simran asks Sheila the last time she spoke to Vishal.

"It's been a while. He's all work and Ami. And you know"— she leans closer—"he kind of told me she's not so excited about his two best friends being girls."

"He told me about that, too. And well, who can really blame her?" Simran asks Sheila. "Maybe this was always going to happen and we were spoiled with him being single."

"Yeah, I guess . . . ," Sheila says. "We're all growing up. Moving on."

"We are," Simran says. "It's weird how that happens."

"Yeah, seriously. Anyway, it's good you're doing all this planning when you have . . . time."

"I do have time right now," Simran agrees. "I mean, a little less than before, since my parents were getting antsy about how I was going to make money. They were right, so I decided to stop tutoring on my own and start teaching a GRE course with a test prep company."

"But that's not your career," Sheila says. "It's how you're paying your bills for now."

"I know," Simran says. "Obviously I'm going to have to make some significant lifestyle changes for now, but that's fine. This is how it has to be until I have a better idea of where my career is going."

Simran has noticed the different ways her friends and family have tried to mention her lack of a real job or plan. There's a unique type of rift that forms between you and everyone else when they can't figure you out, put you in a safe box.

There's no need for Simran to sugarcoat something anymore just because everyone else is uncomfortable with it. "I'm going to stay back in India for a while after our wedding shopping."

"For what?"

"To be with Nani at school."

"I don't get it," Sheila says. "You go to India . . . and then what?"

"And then . . . that's that," Simran says. "I was happy when I was there, and she and I were doing something together. Something that impacted people. I haven't ever felt that way before. About anything. And if I want to write about people, I have to learn about the world. Actually see things . . . see people."

"Yeah, but where does it all lead? What's the point?"

Simran's not sure why, but she stops herself from telling Sheila about a project she just started working on and the new applications she's filled out.

"The point is that I'll be fulfilled. That's enough of a point," Simran says, her voice becoming firmer. "This allows me to focus on the girls, which is great. I'm so sick of thinking about myself all the time. And I can do what I think is best. I really don't need to explain myself to anyone."

"Okay, okay," Sheila says. "I get it."

They both know Sheila doesn't get it. She's almost done with her first semester of law school, and like Kunal, she knows that the *point* of anything is to get to the next step.

"I'm not trying to be annoying," Sheila says. "It's just that you're so smart and could do so much. And I want to make sure you don't lose sight of that."

They're interrupted by Sujata, who whisks toward them and apologizes for the wait. She's thin, around forty years old, dressed in a black T-shirt and black leggings, and has a single streak of hot pink through her black hair. A belt of makeup brushes is slung around her waist. Everything she does is swift: the way she talks and opens the tubes of makeup, how she arranges bottles of hair product in front of the mirror. According to New Jersey Indian wedding gossip, she can get a bride *completely* ready in two hours. Namita's makeup took two hours on its own.

Simran and Sujata spend a few minutes talking about Simran's ideal makeup and hair looks for the garba, wedding, and reception. Simran shows her pictures she saved from Instagram and points out the longest fake eyelashes she's comfortable with. Sujata rubs Simran's face with a makeup-removing wipe and starts applying primer.

She gulps down her champagne before Sujata starts experimenting with lipsticks. In an attempt to change the subject, Simran asks Sheila how things are with Alex.

"Actually, they're better," Sheila says.

"Seriously? You mean, with your parents?"

"Yeah, so after that initial meltdown they had, or rather, that my mom had during your engagement puja, I told him we should just keep our distance for a while. Honestly, it was pretty embarrassing to know that they were discriminating against him and he was aware of it. But he's tough. And he was pushy about us spending time with them."

"So have you all been talking?"

"Yes. And we just went to brunch."

Simran widens her eyes. "You and your parents and Alex went to *brunch*?"

Sheila nods. "At Friend of a Farmer. Two days ago."

"Damn. How was that? Did the pumpkin pancakes help ease the tension?"

Sheila laughs. "It was awkward at first for sure. Alex and I made a list of conversation topics in case there was a lull. And I had counterarguments prepared if they started attacking him."

"Not surprised. You're already set to be an amazing lawyer," Simran says. "So, how'd the conversation flow?"

"I think my parents were taken aback by how friendly he was. And you know my mom, she's so susceptible to compliments and charm. It was my dad I was worried about, but Alex impressed him with all his finance knowledge. He even gave my dad tips. In a way, I think they respected that he took so much of an interest. Maybe I should call Shalin and thank him for that."

Shalin is Sheila's ex-boyfriend from NYU. He was the "perfect" Indian guy on paper: conventionally handsome, pre-med, from a good family, a talented Bhangra dancer. But as he and Sheila dated, she realized he was a narcissist. Everything always had to be about Shalin. He even talked about himself through an entire dinner with her parents. Their relationship was like a lot of college ones, high highs and low lows. Sheila dumped him after he told her he was a catch and she could never do any better. In a movie-worthy conclusion, Shalin didn't get into any of the medical schools he applied to and has become that sad college graduate who still goes to NYU parties every weekend, where he lurks on younger girls.

"Oh, Shalin. The Warner to your Elle Woods. All the way up to when he told you you weren't smart enough to be a lawyer," Simran says.

"Seriously," Sheila says. "I was *so* Elle Woods with him, minus the fact that I'm not girly at all. Or blond."

"True. But still. What a fucker," Simran says.

"Yeah, thank God I dodged that bullet. And I'm glad I recognize that now. You were so amazing, listening to me vent about him all the time. And then being there even through all this Alex stuff."

"That's why I'm here," Simran says.

Sheila smiles. "I'm glad all of that's figured out now. And I want to make sure you're okay, too."

Simran is glad she can't speak as Sujata applies lip liner, then a gloss. For the first time, Simran sees the connective tissue between her and Sheila fraying. Sheila's so sure about what she wants. She wants to be a judge but also has an urge to be married and have kids by a certain age.

Sujata stands in front of Simran. "You're done! Ready to look?"

Simran's stomach twists as she says, "I'm ready."

She closes her eyes as Sujata spins her chair around. When Simran opens them, a more glamorous version of her is staring back. A *bride*. She squints as if she's trying to register herself.

Sujata enhanced Simran's large, almond-shaped eyes with smoky eye shadow and fake lashes. She contoured her cheekbones with the right mixture of bronzer and highlighter. Simran pictures a tikka on her head, a dupatta draped over her bun. Kunal's going to see her this way. She's going to be a wife, for God's sake.

She takes another glance at a future her. Her brows are furrowed. She straightens them out.

"You should relax," Sujata says with a quick pat on Simran's shoulders, which she didn't realize were raised.

"Yes, I should," Simran says. "I don't even know why I'm feeling . . . uneasy all of a sudden."

"It happens with brides sometimes," Sujata says. "It can be a surreal thing for them. And if you don't get your makeup done often, you might not be used to seeing yourself like this."

"Sure," Simran says, hoping that the way she's feeling is simply a matter of extra foundation and eye shadow. "I feel like I constantly go between being excited and then being, I don't know, *this*."

"Planning an Indian wedding will do that for you," Sujata says. "They're no easy feat. I've seen every mix of emotions in this salon. Trust me, if I ever find someone, you can guarantee that I'll be eloping."

"Sounds smart," Simran says.

Sujata peers at her face. "Is there anything you want me to change? Redo?"

"No, I love it," Simran says to Sujata, her insides twisting. "This is exactly how I thought I'd look on my wedding day."

"You look perfect," Sheila says.

"Thanks," Simran says.

Sheila polishes off the remainder of her champagne. "Simran? What's wrong?"

"I'm not sure." Simran grips the edge of the makeup table. "Is this really happening? Really?"

"Yes, it *is* happening," Sheila says. "Simran, what is going on with you? You're freaking out and, I don't know, not acting the wa—"

"Not acting the way you thought I would?" Simran asks, cutting her off. "What is that supposed to mean?"

Sujata takes this as her cue to mention she should check on her new shipment of hair products.

"I don't know," Sheila says after Sujata walks away. "I just thought things would be different."

"Different? Different how?"

Sheila shakes her head. "I feel like you're morphing into the perfect Indian girl. I mean, you used to be outspoken, someone who stuck to what she wanted, like I di—"

"Like you did?"

Sheila nods. "Yes."

"Well, trust me, I'm proud of you for breaking out of the mold and being strong enough to hold on to what you wanted. But not everyone is like you."

"I agree." Sheila raises her eyebrows. "But you're not everyone. You're my best friend for a reason. And I just think you can get more from life. Is this how you thought things would turn out?"

"Wow, you're really asking me that," Simran says. She tells herself to stop talking, but she can't.

"I am. Because if I don't, I'm not sure who will."

"Do you really have to do this right now?"

"Do what?" Sheila asks.

"Any of this. Can't you just support me?"

Sheila throws her hands up in the air. "I don't even know what to support with you! You're literally all over the place. God forbid I have an opinion."

"Oh, please! You've been expressing your opinions about me nonstop. Trust me, I get it. You have opinions."

Sheila turns away, and Simran notices her chin trembling. She's trying to stop herself from crying.

The last time Simran saw her cry because of something re-lated to them was in middle school, when she thought Simran had picked Nishi, their neighbor's daughter, as her new best friend. Simran had asked Nishi to sleep over because Nishi was shy and had trouble making friends. It didn't take long for her to start coming to their house on a daily basis. Nishi's mom even bought them matching dresses. Sheila stopped Simran in school one day and asked if she was replaced. When Simran asked why Sheila thought that, Sheila started crying. It was the first time Simran caught a glimpse of the vulnerability beneath the brazen, tough image Sheila always projected.

The truth was, Simran liked Nishi, but she didn't challenge Simran the way Sheila did. Nishi went along with everything Simran wanted to do. She agreed with all her thoughts on Disney movies and Nickelodeon shows. Despite the closeness between their families, there was a level Nishi and Simran could never go beyond.

Simran faces Sheila now. "We should go."

Sheila and Simran walk to the car. And even though they may look fine to Sujata and other people in the salon, they don't talk for the entire car ride.

Nandini

"I've finished looking at all of the scans and doctors' notes," Nandini says.

Mami sighs through the phone. "I'm glad."

"Mami, how could you have kept this from me? You should have sent this to me ear—"

"Don't *you* even go there," Mami says, raising her voice. "You know exactly why I didn't. You know exactly what I've never wanted. I had to spend years being the proper, polite Indian widow. Now, I'd like to live with dignity. On my own terms, for once."

Whereas Papa and Greg felt their bodies betrayed them, Mami treated her illness like a long-lost friend finally coming to visit.

"You have to at least think about doing something else," Nandini says. "Even for a minute!"

"I've thought about everything, and my decision is final," Mami says firmly.

Nandini knows how impenetrable Mami's stubbornness is because hers is the same way. She pictures this stubbornness gene tightly packed in their cells. It always had to be handled with caution. A stubborn Indian boy was a leader. A stubborn Indian girl was a nuisance.

"If I lived there, I could have done something," Nandini says. "Stepped in earlier."

Mami turns down the volume of the psychological thriller she's been binge watching. "I wouldn't have wanted you to stay here, and you know that. I would never, ever have forgiven myself if you stayed with those horrible people or revolved your life around Papa and me. You were always too smart for that. And I should have realized that sooner, before you went through that ordeal."

"I know you wouldn't have wanted that for me, but there's so much distance between us. I hate that. I always have."

"I know, *beta*. But this is the way it was supposed to be for you. For all of us. When you get to my age, you spend so much time thinking about all the things you've been through in your life. You think and remember and wonder and reflect. And I've realized that everything really did work out. Maybe it was only at the very last minute, but things finally came through."

Nandini considers this, how she had to separate from her mother to understand her. Maybe her relationships with her mother *and* her daughter were hinged on letting go in order to become whole, a delicate dance between separating and joining, losing and finding.

"And now you get to work in the way you always wanted to," Mami says. "We both do. For years, we assumed ambition was a curse for us. Men could always wear it like a cape, while women, women were forced to tuck and hold it inside themselves. But look at us. You see, we all had to become scandals before we became ourselves."

"You are right about that."

Mami always had a way of assembling words that were like the last piece of gulab jamun on the dessert platter. Words that coated the mouth with a lingering sweetness and certainty.

Mami lowers her voice to almost a whisper. "With time, I know you'll stop going to that bad place."

"I hope so," Nandini says as she thinks of that dark, vast space both she and her mother are prone to slipping into.

But she knows she doesn't need to hope because her mother's always been right. Somehow, Mami's life became like her womb: a place that made space, became greater than it even was.

"I mean it. Don't worry about anything," Mami says. "And yes, by that, I mean Simran."

"Please don't even start, Mami. You know she's not doing well."

"That's not true at all. You're always so hard on her, the way you were on yourself. Don't you understand? Your daughter is now starting to make an impact on the world. She's gotten organizations to donate so much for the girls here. Her articles are submitted for *publication*. And she taught herself all of that on her own. She's living the way we should have years ago."

Nandini lets out a breath she didn't realize she was holding. "I'm glad you see it that way. But that doesn't mean she'll be happy or even secure. And what if, with time, she loses her connection to us?"

"What makes you even think that's a possibility?" Mami scoffs. "Haven't you ever noticed that Simran has become more intertwined with you while Ronak has built his own shape?"

"That's definitely been true."

"Okay, then, you understand." She takes a long pause and then adds, "Nandini, you have to learn . . . when to let go."

Nandini doesn't know how to respond. Instead, an image comes to her mind. Nandini, as a little girl, sitting at the vanity table with the cracked mirror in her parents' bedroom. Mami would slather coconut oil in Nandini's hair and then weave it into thick, sturdy braids. She thinks of the earthy smell of the oil, the dark blue bottle it came out of, and the swishing sound her hair made as it was crisscrossed. She'd give anything to go back to that place, have her hair pulled and folded by her mother's self-assured hands. She needs to feel Mami's steady heartbeat through her cotton sari blouse.

Nandini cries softly so her mother won't hear. As the hot tears trickle down her face, a new clarity comes to her. Sadness isn't clear or linear or logical. Yes, there is a sadness that stands naked, on its own. And there is the type of sadness that holds anger under its wings. Then there is sadness that's interlaced with pride. And in the midst of the turmoil, this is what her mother has given her.

Eighteen

Simran

A year and a half ago, Kunal barely slept the night before his first day of medical school. He switched between lying on his stomach and then his back for a few hours before giving up and going for a run. He came back around six thirty a.m., his body draped in sweat and rain, his curls seeming darker and more defiant than usual.

Holy crap, he's starting medical school, Simran thought as she tried memorizing all the details of the morning. It was too early for the New York cacophony that usually reverberated through his windows, but the stillness illuminated the reality: they were embarking on a new chapter together. Again.

Simran got out of bed during Kunal's seven-minute shower, brushed her teeth, and made him a fresh cup of green tea. His suit for the first-day orientation was already hanging in the closet. She made a whole-wheat egg-white sandwich and put it into his reusable lunch bag. Her parents usually drank their morning chai together, but if one of them had to leave early, the other would have a warm mug of it ready on the kitchen counter.

Twenty minutes later, Kunal was ready to go, thermos and anticipation in hand. Simran plucked some stray lint off his suit jacket while he slipped into his only pair of dress shoes, handed down by his father.

"You're going to be amazing," Simran said as they both stood at his door. She didn't know if it was his suit or the fact that the sun still wasn't up, but something about the moment hit her. *We're grown-ups.* Somewhere between the back seat of his Honda Accord and endless packets of Easy Mac, she and Kunal had become adults. Together.

"I hope so," he responded before squeezing Simran's hand. It was the first time she had seen him nervous about anything.

They held hands throughout the five flights of stairs. Simran wanted to be with him until he left the building. They kissed—the type of tasteful kiss she used to see wives gives their husbands in movies—and he stepped onto the sidewalk, his black umbrella releasing over his head. The rain had become even more threatening in the past hour, and every drop exploded on the sidewalk like a tiny shooting star.

"Shit," he said with a sigh as he gave the sky an irritated glance. "I hope I'm not late."

"You're more than thirty minutes ahead of schedule. You're *fine.*"

He gave Simran another kiss, this time sneakily grabbing her butt (something he always did when she wore sweat pants).

Simran watched him saunter to the intersection, eyes forward. She leaned against the doorway as she studied his straight, broad shoulders.

Kunal turned around when the "walk" signal lit up. They exchanged smiles, and Simran blew him a kiss, aware that she looked far from cute in her glasses and haphazard pajamas.

But then, in the midst of all his anxiety and rush, Kunal

started jogging back toward her. The umbrella fell to his side, and Simran screamed, "You're going to get wet!"

He kept going.

Simran stepped out of the doorway and met him on the sidewalk.

"What's wrong?" she asked, holding her arms into the air. "Did you forget something?"

"Nope." He shook his head as a grin lit up his face. "I just had to kiss you again."

"Aw, really?" she gushed, and elevated onto her tiptoes.

He lifted her face toward his. They stood there, ignoring the swollen traffic. A few minutes passed until she watched him stride back toward the intersection until he disappeared.

Now, the rain drums on Kunal's bedroom window as he and Simran lay next to each other, their chests rising and falling post-hookup.

"You know, I've really missed us feeling like *us*," Simran says, resting her bare legs on Kunal's. "And you've been putting in so much effort. It's meant a lot to me."

He shifts up, cups her chin, and kisses her. "Of course."

She pushes herself off his single, flat pillow. They twist under the sheets, their nakedness peeking out. The sunlight is split by the dusty shades. When she leans forward to kiss Kunal, he seems unfamiliar, as though her internal tectonic plates have shifted.

Simran starts dozing off later that afternoon. Kunal kisses her and shuffles out of bed, muttering something about getting a strong start preparing for the head and neck anatomy final.

Simran wakes up when it's dark outside. She steps out of bed and finds Kunal in the living room, scanning through something on her laptop. He's deep in thought and doesn't even look up when she enters the room.

"Hey, what are you doing?"

He doesn't respond and just turns her laptop around. An old online conversation between Neil and Simran is on the screen.

Simran inches closer to see the contents, but all she can manage to read is Neil saying, "You make me happy."

"Y . . . you," she stammers, "were going through my e-mail? The *archives* of my e-mail?"

"Fuck yeah I was going through your trash," Kunal confirms, his voice raising. "And I'm glad I did."

Simran digs her feet into the thin carpet. "Why would you do that?"

"Because I was curious. And you know what? I didn't think there would be anything to find. But then I come across this"—he points to the screen—"and it's just *awesome*. Fucking awesome."

"It's not like that," Simran insists, her chest heaving. "Anymore."

"Anymore? *Anymore?* What the fuck does that even mean? Are there other conversations like this?"

When Simran doesn't answer, Kunal stands up and yells, "ARE THERE?"

Blood pounds in her ears. She nods.

Kunal clutches the flimsy coffee table and hurls it backward. Simran's laptop falls on the floor, still open. He slams the lid.

"Don't do this," Simran says, hesitant to touch him. "Please."

Kunal turns to face her.

"Please," Simran says again, her voice cracking.

His eyes are wide. He's taking deep, heavy breaths. "What the *fuck* ever went on with you guys?"

The question seems to echo. Simran takes two steps backward. She could tell him everything, but then he'd be hurt, and what would really be the point? Just to make herself feel better for confessing? Or, she could put everything with Neil behind her, *them*, and they could move on. She could get over Neil with him. She pictures she and Kunal ten years from now. Both of them coming home from work, stretching out on the couch, drinking Pinot Noir out of bulbous glasses with thin stems. All of this would be so far behind them, it would be as if it never happened. Just a tiny blip in their story.

But then what would that make them? What kind of start is that to a marriage? And after everything they've been through, doesn't Kunal deserve honesty? Simran remembers the time he found out a professor gave him a C on a biology project without even looking at it, which Kunal learned after he met the professor during office hours and demanded a correction. The professor had a history of giving out arbitrary grades based on how much he liked a student. It wasn't the grade that upset Kunal; it was the unfairness. He's the type of man who has always based everything on principle.

Simran pictures Neil's glasses, the lines around his eyes, his wide smile. She stands up straight and says, "I . . . had feelings for him."

"Wow, that's just *fucking* great." Kunal pounds the sofa with his fist. "You had feelings for that asshole."

Somehow, him saying that out loud pushes her to continue. She can't stop now.

"We kissed," Simran says, the syllables spilling out. "Once."

She pictures this scene as a comic strip. Her confession captured within a cloud above their heads. Kunal and Simran frozen in space. Some moments are like that. Frozen. She is officially that kind of woman. A cheater. A liar.

"You *kissed* him?" Kunal furrows his thick brows, as if he's trying to figure out a difficult test question.

"Yes, that night we, we—"

"You've *got* to be fucking kidding me," he says, cutting her off. "You're actually standing here, telling me that you *cheated* on me?"

"Yes." Simran feels pressure behind her eyes. She wishes the ground would open up and swallow her.

She waits for him to yell or throw something or punch the wall. Or all three.

Instead, he falls backward onto the black futon. He covers his face with his large hands. Simran sits next to him as he mutters something under his breath. He presses his feet into the ground, and she sees that his socks have holes in the big-toe areas. Him showing defeat stings far more than anger would.

She rubs his lower back, surprised when he doesn't flinch away. "I'm so sorry."

Her words are stupid and weak. She had envisioned this confession over and over again but still can't think of something better to say.

Kunal shakes his head.

"Please, say something," Simran says. *Bitch me out. Call me names.*

There's a key in the front door. Kunal's roommate Vik, who works nine to two every day at a marketing firm and somehow manages to come home for a nap every afternoon.

Once they hear Vik's room door close, Kunal turns to her and says, "When Rekha kissed me, I pushed her away. But you didn't push Neil away, did you?"

Simran thinks back to that moment. Neil's woodsy scent. Her

nails digging into his arms, his thick hair. The edges of his glasses pressing against her cheek.

"No, I didn't push him away," she says.

In high school, she used to wonder how Kunal would react if he thought she cheated on him. She expected him to curse and threaten. Not talk to her ever again.

But now, he looks up. "How could you not tell me that? This whole time? The feelings, the kissing? All of it? How could I have not noticed?" His tone is more surprised than accusatory. And somehow, he even seems calm. Maybe it's a combination of counseling, age, and shock, but he's exactly the opposite of how she thought he'd be.

Simran shrugs. "You were really busy. Sometimes withdrawn. I mean, first we were fighting when you were in Africa, then you came back and we got caught up in wedding planning drama and our families and then, I don't know, we just kept going on that way."

Kunal gets up and walks to the kitchen. She hears him remove a glass from the cabinet and fill it with water. He comes back into the living room.

His Adam's apple constricts as he takes large gulps of water. "So, now where do we go from here?"

Simran raises her eyebrows. That's it? Their betrayals just evaporated into thin air? They could be angry about something as stupid as a text message for days and then this was over in a matter of minutes?

"I don't know," Simran says. "I think that because we're really different from each other, we have to put in even more effort to make the other person happy, and that can be tough, but when we don't, we open ourselves up to a lot of . . . issues. Maybe that's just what it comes down to: how hard you're willing to try. And I know you have been trying, with counseling and all."

Kunal nods, considering this. "I guess that's why you were drawn to Neil. Maybe you just needed someone who listened to you. Understood you."

"Maybe," Simran says, thinking that there is no single reason to pinpoint why you can have an instant and intense connection with someone.

"But I don't want to constantly fight when I leave for my trips," Kunal says. "Or think that something bad is going to happen just because I have a demanding job. What about when I do Doctors Without Borders after residency? Am I going to have to worry about something like this happening again?"

"No," Simran says. "We'll take those incidents as they come, and we'll be married by then, so we'll be taking both of our schedules into account when you make those type of trips."

Kunal frowns. "You know, when people are married, they don't have to put their lives on hold."

She glares at him. "Who's talking about putting anything on hold?"

"Nobody. I'm just telling you this now so you can't throw it back in my face later. You shouldn't expect me to stop everything just because we make a commitment."

He walks around the coffee table. "In Africa and Costa Rica, I met people who stay there for big chunks of time and some others who live there for good. I could see us doing that one day. It would let me practice the way I always imagined."

"Now you want to *live* in one of these places?"

"Sure," he says, as though he just suggested they move to Jersey City. "A lot of people do it. Their wives are all friends with one another. The kids play together. It's not so bad."

Kunal sent Simran a *New Yorker* article the other day about Paul Farmer. In the body of his e-mail, Kunal wrote, "This guy is incredible." Which he was (it's difficult not to be incredible when you devote your life to treating sick people in Haiti). But with Kunal's ideal arrangement, only *he* gets to be the Paul Farmer.

Simran's problem this entire time hasn't been Kunal's absence. It's been his attitude. He's content with her being one of the tinier accessories of his life. He's okay with them simply filling their default roles.

"What about my career?" Simran asks. "I'm going to stay in India after our shopping trip."

"But that's just this time. And because we're already going for our wedding shopping. I didn't think being in India was going to be a regular thing."

"Maybe it will be a regular thing," she says. "I could see things going that way."

"I wasn't aware that's what you had in mind," he says, frowning.

"Well, now you are aware," she says.

"Where is this coming from?" he asks.

Simran refuses to back down. "It's always been there. I've just suppressed all this stuff for years to try to be someone I'm not. And I'm sick of it. I'm not doing it anymore. So I'm asking you, after we're married, if I also need to travel so I can teach and write, will you be okay with that? Will you be okay with us having a long-distance marriage because of *my* ambitions?"

"Simran, I don't understand why you always have to stir the pot for circumstances that aren't even occurring."

"So now I'm stirring the pot because I'm asking if things will be fair?"

"No, it's just that I didn't think you'd be this way. I mean, my mom handled everything with my dad's job, and I don't remember her bitching every chance she could. Why can't you just learn how to deal?"

"Why can't *I*?" Simran asks, her voice raising more than she'd like it to. "Maybe because I'm not your mom, Kunal. I wasn't raised that way. Hell, you know my own mom isn't even like that."

"You're right," Kunal agrees. "Your mom's controlling. Whatever she wants, goes."

"Fuck you," Simran blurts, smug when he raises his eyebrows in surprise. "You have no idea what my parents' marriage is like."

"Maybe I don't entirely," he says. "But I get worried that that's how you'll want to live your life in the future. I want to do things for the world and lead a simple life. Have someone to come home to who I can rely on. I'd hope you would respect that. And I've always needed you to make things happen."

Yes, you get to be the honorable doctor who gives free services to dying children. I should be so grateful to just be next to you while your noble needs are catered to.

"I want to do things for the world, too," Simran says. "I know I don't travel to all these places to treat sick people, but I'm also planning my own ways to contribute."

"But it's still different," he insists. "You know that I don't care to live in a big house or drive a nice car or take a lot of extravagant vacations to God knows where. I mean, I've thought about even getting a job in med school because of all the loans I've had to take out. And when it comes to an opulent life, I just . . . I don't respect that. Not at all."

A new life sprawls out in front of her, one spent justifying her tastes and interests, proving herself day in and out. She feels the blood rushing to her face as she soaks in the truth, *his* truth.

Simran glances at her outstretched hand. The diamond ring appears lifeless under this fluorescent light, like it's trying too hard.

"Both of us seem to want incompatible things in life," Simran says, her voice becoming hushed.

He sighs. "Look, people have differences and they figure them out. It's not a big deal."

Simran raises her now-quivering voice. "It's a big deal to me. I want someone who *wants* to call me and make me a priority. Make my career a priority. Someone who loves and respects my family. And you know, at times, you do that, a lot of that . . . but it always seems to go away. The other day, Sheila was telling me about all these things Alex does for her, and I started feeling jealous. *Jealous.* Of my friend who is going through something so difficult."

"Seriously? This again?" Kunal asks, and she almost wishes she could retract her words. Almost. "It's *so* fucking annoying when you compare me to other guys. It's like I can never be good enough. You act as if you're doing me such a big fucking favor by putting up with me. But you know what? You're no walk in the park, either, Simran. The other day, I was in such a good mood and then I thought, 'Damn it, I have to go see her tonight. She's probably going to be pissed about something. But of course she won't tell me what it is; she'll just bottle it all up.'"

He catches Simran blinking away tears but continues talking. "You know, if you want things to change, then why don't you go ahead and be the fucking change? Did you ever think about that?"

"Seriously? SERIOUSLY?!" She hears herself crossing into dangerous territory but keeps treading.

She wonders what it would feel like to beat her fists against his shoulder. Her voice breaks, but she keeps rambling. "Did *I* ever think about that? What do you think I've been doing?! I drop *everything* when you're free. For God's sake, I live out of a fucking drawer in your tiny room where I'm not even comfortable half the time because I don't have most of my stuff. I call your mom routinely because I want her to know she doesn't have to worry about losing you when we're married. And you? You usually can't even send me a text during the day! And now, I tell you I see myself traveling and actually doing something with my life, and you can't even promise me you'll be supportive!"

Both of them stay quiet but keep eye contact.

"You know what, Simran?" he asks. The anger from before is clearly there in his eyes, but it's distilled with a layer of sadness, which is even more heartbreaking. "I looked through all of your Facebook pictures the other day, and I realized that you smile differently with me than you do with other people."

"What do you mean?" Simran asks, surprised that he even took the time to do this. Kunal rarely goes on Facebook.

"You just look forced with me, but in other pictures, you tilt your head, laugh. . . ."

She shakes her head. "I don't want it to be that way. But what if we're just not right for each other?"

"Ugh," he grumbles, as if to say, *Not* this *melodramatic crap again*.

"No, I'm being serious. Don't you ever wonder that?"

Kunal lowers his eyebrows. "No, I don't. You know why? Because I love you. I know I want to be with you. I always have."

"I love you, too," Simran whispers.

He lowers his shoulders and exhales.

Suddenly, he seems to morph into his younger self. He's the

boy waving at her before scoring the winning lacrosse goal, the boy who snuck into his basement to call her late at night, the boy who kissed her in the back seat of his beat-up Honda Accord. And that's when it occurs to her: a relationship can be at its most beautiful and raw at its most desperate point.

Simran can tell by his soft expression that he isn't taking her seriously, so she takes a deep, nervous breath. "We should break up."

"Just stop," he urges. "Okay? You can't pull these threats whenever we hit a rough patch. Sweetie, you're emotional, and you're just jumping to an extreme that we both know you aren't going to follow through with. I mean, look at your whole situation with school and how you quit. Damn it, you can't just quit—or say you'll quit—on things when they get difficult."

She runs her hands through her overly dry-shampooed hair. Sure, they will both make more of an effort . . . at first. But with enough time, their usual equilibrium will ensue: Kunal will slowly inch back into complacency, and she'll keep picking fights to try to kick him out of it. Despite this, they'll still find a way to remain pathologically committed, more out of a fear of failure than anything else.

Simran says some of this to Kunal, and he shakes his head while squeezing her hand. "That's not going to happen. I promise you it won't be that way. You're my future *wife*. God, I need you."

Within minutes, their emotions translate into something physical. He runs his hands down her waist, lingers on her neck. She doesn't want to fight. She doesn't want to say these things. She loves this boy. This *man*. Her man.

Their kisses are ravenous and desperate, in vivid contrast to their shy first one. Kunal tastes like green tea and cherry Chap-Stick. She digs her nails through his hair and feels his large hands cup her butt and pick her up off the ground. He wraps her legs around his hips.

Simran gets off him. She squeezes her eyes shut and opens them. Kunal's still standing there. His shoulders are lower now, and she draws an imaginary line down them with her eyes. Seven years of her life stuffed into this guy's shoulders.

"I have to go." Simran slips the ring off and places it on his desk. The tears start to come when she sees it against the dull wood. She never thought they'd get to this place, but who ever really does?

"Simran," he says, finally registering her gesture. "Don't do this."

He digs his fingers into her arm as a mechanical plea. They pull her toward one direction while something inside her points toward another.

"I'm going," Simran says.

She loves Kunal. He knows her in ways nobody else ever will. But if she doesn't go, they'll both hold each other back. She takes a deep breath and stabilizes her legs as every part of her seems to lunge into a free fall. And for the first time since they've met, she walks out on them without looking back.

Nandini

"How exactly does this all work?" Charu asks Nandini.

"It just does." Nandini shrugs her shoulders as if Charu asked her about an appliance and not her life.

"So, you're still going back and forth between New Jersey and Baltimore while Ranjit stays here?" Charu asks the question with disbelief, as if she wasn't already aware of this, as if asking again and again would make Nandini change her answer.

Nandini empties a bag of Indian snacks into tiny, hand-painted bowls. "Correct."

She hates to admit that it still stings when people judge her. But over the past several months, it has affected her less.

Nandini invited Charu, Payal, Sonali, and Preeti over for dance practice. They're supposed to find two Bollywood songs to perform at Simran and Kunal's reception. So far, Payal has insisted on "anything Priyanka Chopra starred in," and the others seem fine taking her lead.

"I think that's so nice!" Payal exclaims. "Can you imagine? A new life once the kids leave the house? We all dream of it"—she gives Charu a look as if to say, *You do it, too, don't lie*—"but you're the only one who has done it! I mean, I always said I'd move back to India or get back into my singing, but here I am, still in the same place. Tell me, are you enjoying this?"

"I am." Nandini feels the weight of her words. *I am enjoying my life.* "I'm learning a lot. And I actually just found out that I'll be speaking at the national American Medical Association conference."

"Wow!" Sonali says. "Congratulations! I wish I could do something like that."

Nandini had a panic attack when she first heard she had been picked to speak. Luckily, she was alone, so nobody saw her as she became dizzy and disoriented. Her breathing quickened as she thought of how Greg would never know, that her own mother wouldn't be able to hear her. Then she pictured herself at a podium, stumbling over her words and not knowing how to answer any questions from the audience.

"I think it's possible for all of us to do the things we wished to do. It won't look the way we thought it would, but it can happen," Nandini says now.

"But some of us consider our children and families," Charu chimes in. "I think it's important that we're there for them and making sure we're not being *selfish*."

The word "selfish" hangs in the air. Sonali's eyes dart toward Preeti.

Ignore her, a voice in her head says. *She's trying to get to you.* Mami and Nandini's therapist used to tell her that she had to choose what to give her energy to. And in this moment, she could choose not to give anything to Charu.

But then she remembers when Charu gave Simran a bottle of Fair and Lovely and warned her to "not become too dark" and how she told her to hold on to Kunal because he was "out of her league." For years, Charu has been trying to scare Nandini and her daughter. Enough is enough.

"Just bitch her out already," Simran told Nandini on the phone the other day. "She needs to be put in her place."

At the time, Nandini told Simran to remember to be respectful. But now, she thinks her daughter had a point.

"Oh! Another dig at me. That is what you do best, Charu, isn't it? Good for you." Nandini hears the words come out of her mouth like a verbal avalanche.

Mami and Simran would have said, *Good, shut her up for once.* Yuwa would have been proud of her and given her a high five.

But Sonali and Preeti have their mouths open in disbelief. Payal has a gleam in her eyes. Is she giving Nandini a nod of approval? Was it possible she wanted this to happen?

Nandini hears the creak of the basement steps. Two seconds later, Ranjit approaches them, holding a tray of mango lassi.

"Why is it so quiet in here? Where's the music? Aren't you supposed to be practicing a dance?"

The women's eyes dart between Nandini and Charu. Just as Charu is about to say something, Payal interjects. "We were just talking about how wonderful it is that Nandini was chosen to speak at a conference. And that she's doing what she's always wanted to do."

"She is," Ranjit says. "It's been a fun change for us. What do the kids who date call it? A *long-distance* relationship! We're in a long-distance relationship."

"Yes, we are," Nandini says. She refuses to look at Charu. Let her scowl. Let her give her brother heat for supporting his wife.

To her surprise, Charu clears her throat and says, "I've got to get home."

Nobody protests, and Ranjit doesn't even seem to notice any tension. Nandini breathes a sigh of relief as she hears Charu's quick footsteps going up the stairs and then out the front door.

Later, Nandini will go through what happened with Simran, Mami, and Yuwa. All of them will find their own ways to encourage and congratulate her. Over the past months, she's realized that she doesn't have to go through everything alone. It's okay to have a tribe.

"Everything okay?" Ranjit asks.

Sonali, Preeti, and Payal nod.

"It's more than fine," Nandini says, and for the first time in a long time, she means it.

Nineteen

Simran

Once Simran is outside Kunal's apartment, she strides from street to sidewalk, feeling unrecognizable, like a stranger to everyone, even to her own self. She clutches the side of a brick building and grabs her stomach. *Don't throw up*. She sits on the sidewalk and tucks her head into her hands. It suddenly seems too warm for December in New York. She unzips her coat, airs out her sweater dress.

Manhattan swirls around her. A middle-aged Hispanic man arranges vegetables in their brown boxes as if they're gems on display. Children are bundled in winter jackets and drinking hot chocolate. A young, brunette couple sits on a bench, their gloved hands intertwined. They've definitely had sex.

Yes, go be happy. At least someone should.

Simran's not sure what she's thinking as she pulls out her phone and dials her parents' number.

Dad picks up on the first ring. "What's going on, *beta*?"

Time to rip off the Band-Aid. "Kunal and I are over. For good."

"What?" Simran hears a click that indicates their conversation is now on speakerphone.

"Hi, Mom. Dad, I was saying that I broke up with Kunal.

We're not engaged anymore." Simran hears the words come out of her mouth and hang in the air. Everything's slower, as if she's drunk. She even throws in a "cancel your India tickets" statement, in case anything is unclear.

"Why is this happening?" Dad asks. Simran knows she won't hear her mom's voice.

"It just is. There were things we'd been ignoring for a really long time. Things that would have been difficult for both of us to live with."

"So then Kunal also wanted this?"

Simran sighs. She must be sick. Yes, that's it. That's the only reason she can say this so quickly. "Not exactly. I made the decision. But it's right for both of us."

"Why don't we all talk? You, Kunal, us? We ca—"

"No," Simran says, cutting her dad off. "There's nothing left to talk about. I'll call his parents myself and talk to them."

"Is there . . . someone else?" he asks.

"No, this has nothing to do with anyone else," Simran says.

"What will we tell everyone?" Dad whispers to Mom.

Maybe Mom will get it. After everything they've been through this year, everything she's been through in her life, this can't possibly rattle her.

Mom clears her throat. "Oh, just forget it, Ranjit. We don't need to worry about everyone. Obviously Simran isn't worrying, so why should we? Simran, I don't understand. You picked the person you wanted to marry, all on your own. You went behind our backs, for years, to date him, and then we accepted that, because you were so determined. We never pushed an arranged marriage on you because we thought we taught you the value of commitment. And now you just decide to walk away? Because things are difficult?"

"Mom, we literally had a discussion when we were at that diner months ago, you know, about how you didn't want me to struggle with anything the way you did."

She scoffs. "And you haven't! You think you've had to deal with anything *close* to what I've been through?"

There are so many times when Simran thinks her mom understands her, they understand each other, and then, poof! They're back to square one. She doesn't see the contradictions in her own words, the impossibility of pleasing her.

"Do you think the chance to marry someone comes every day?" Mom asks. "Do you realize what this means for any future potential man who may come into your life? What you'll have to explain?"

"I do," Simran says, and then adds, "And don't worry. This doesn't mean you've failed as a parent."

Simran regrets her words the second they come out. She shouldn't provoke Mom. She hears Dad sighing as if he's thinking the exact same thing.

"Ha, as if *you* know anything about parenting. What's the point of even having children, Ranjit? And sacrificing everything to give them a life here? They take all of the wrong values from America. We were better off staying in Baroda. At least then our daughter could have had a sense of right and wrong."

Simran's surprised by her own sudden sense of calm. She doesn't need to react to anything Mom's saying. This is a natural, expected consequence of telling her shocking news. And as strange as it seems, it's reassuring to hear her parents interacting with each other, aligning, being normal for once.

"Mom, Dad, I know you're going to be angry—*livid*—with me for a long time. Maybe even longer than I realize right now.

But at some point, I know you'll understand that I had to do this. Not to hurt or disrespect you but to stand up for myself and have the type of life that's right for me."

There. Simran stuck to the script. She hangs up and stays in her spot, staring at the phone. Nobody tells you that when your identity begins to betray you, every part of you revolts.

When she and Ronak used to attend Hinduism classes at the mandir, they'd often learn about the theory of reincarnation, the idea that you can come back with an entirely different self. She wonders if people are also capable of being reborn emotionally throughout each lifetime.

Simran stumbles into her apartment. The first thing she notices is Kunal's old anatomy textbook. It's one of his slimmer ones, only a couple hundred pages, none of them highlighted or tabbed (he finds that distracting).

His go-to pen is inside the book. She thumbs the engraving. *NYU School of Medicine.* That's when the pain grows roots. It stretches across her chest and infiltrates her organs. She collapses onto the floor and hears her sobs as if they're coming from someone else.

There's a very good chance that her life will never be okay. She's read those stories of people who took a turn for the worse with just a few events. There's a thin line between a life to be proud of and a life that destroys you.

Then there's a banging at her door. Assertive knuckles against concrete.

Kunal.

She takes brisk steps toward her door. Everything can be okay again. Who cares if they have deep-rooted issues? Anything has to feel better than this. There are millions of women in this world, even in just New York, who would die to marry a future doctor who loves his mom.

Simran opens the door. It takes her a second to register the frizzy hair on the other side.

Sheila. She's wearing a light blue sweater and brown dress pants, no jewelry, and some eyeliner that has smeared.

"I know you're still mad at me," she says. "But I need to talk to you."

"Did Kunal call you?" Simran asks, standing to the side to let her in.

Sheila frowns. "Kunal? Why would he call me?"

"No reason."

They stare at each other for a couple of seconds.

"So, what's up?"

"Are you okay?" Sheila's eyes move from Simran's hairline to her cheeks, which Simran knows must be some shade of pink.

"Uh, yeah. Long day."

"You sure that's all?"

"Uh-huh." Simran can't form words without the risk of crying. "Why?"

"Well . . ."

Sheila smiles and places her left hand against her cheek, just slowly enough for Simran to catch a wink on her ring finger.

"OH MY GOD," Simran says with a gasp, at the same time that Sheila yells, "ALEX PROPOSED!"

They both shriek, and Simran grabs Sheila's hand to examine the one-carat emerald-cut diamond set within a halo.

"When did this happen?"

"Just this morning. He asked me while we were reading the

Times and eating breakfast. It was perfect. No big performance or flashy scene. Just us."

"And your parents?"

"Oh my god, that's the even crazier part! You know how Alex and I had met up with my parents a few times? Apparently he had been calling them on the phone and even saw them twice without me. Then, my dad's best friend from med school, whose daughter married a German guy, reasoned with my dad about why this was a good idea and how even an Indian guy can be shit and blah blah blah."

"Wow," Simran says, motioning to her sofa. "That's just . . . wow. I'm so happy for you."

"Me too!" Sheila says, in the giddy bride-to-be voice that she swore she'd never have. "I can't believe it! After all the bullshit, it finally worked out. I guess things have a way of coming together, right?"

Simran nods.

"You're the first person I wanted to tell," Sheila says as she hugs Simran.

She gazes at Simran's floor, and her voice becomes quieter. "I'm so sorry for what happened at the salon. I want to move on."

"I want to move on, too," Simran says.

Sheila smiles. "And now, we can plan our weddings together, the way we always thought we would when we were younger."

"Sure," Simran mutters. "But more than anything, I'm really proud of you for fighting through this. I know it wasn't easy for you at all."

"No, it was hell. You more than anyone know how distraught I was. I can't believe that I even thought of breaking things off altogether."

"Nobody would have blamed you either way, Sheila. It was an impossible situation."

"I know, but I couldn't have gotten through it without you," Sheila says.

As Sheila walks to Simran's kitchen, Simran mentally replays everything that happened at Kunal's apartment. The anger builds as she hears him insulting her mother, her future plans. He needs to know that he also contributed to things getting fucked up. He made her feel inadequate. He became the type of person who wanted a traditional, subservient wife.

But then she takes another peek at Sheila's left ring finger. Did Simran give up too easily? Did she let the heat of an argument lead her to a decision she'll always regret?

"Do you, by any chance, have champagne?" Sheila asks.

"I do." Simran straightens her face and takes a deep breath. Gives herself a psychological dose of Xanax. There's no need to ruin this moment.

Simran opens her silver refrigerator. She doesn't tell Sheila that she had picked out the bottle for her and Kunal to share before they left for India, so they could toast to their wedding shopping.

Simran removes two glasses from the cabinet. She and Kunal were going to put white wineglasses, red wineglasses, and champagne flutes on their registry. She guesses she's stuck with one type of glass for now.

After Simran hands Sheila her glass, Sheila says, "There's so much to celebrate!"

"Cheers." Simran raises her glass and feels a surge of relief and excitement. The future materializes in front of her, one that's new and scary and different than anything she's ever known.

Sheila walks toward the sofa. Simran joins her. She yearns for a conversation with her best friend, a chance to be open and understood, and also to feel new.

Nandini

"Really? That's it?" Nandini scoots to the edge of her new sofa in Baltimore.

Simran nods. "Yes, that's it."

"So you aren't even going to try to see if things can work?"

Simran's head snaps up. "I *have* tried. A lot. No, more than a lot. More than you realize. And I'm done. Aren't we supposed to be here to focus on you, anyway? The entire reason Dad and I drove to Baltimore for the day was to be able to see how *you're* doing, not me."

"I see. So I can't even ask if you're sure about breaking off your engagement."

"God, Mom, I'm telling you I've made a decision that is already hard enough for me, and all you can do is challenge that? Make me feel worse?" Simran stands up and starts folding her chair. Nandini hadn't found time to pick out anything besides the sofa, so Ranjit and Simran brought the folding chairs usually reserved for parties.

"Oh, right. I'm supposed to just accept whatever you say." Nandini's heart beats quicker. "If I don't tell you certain things, then who will? Do you think anyone in the world is going to care enough to challenge you?"

"I don't *need* challenging right now! How do you not get that?"

Ranjit comes back into the tiny living room. Both Simran and Nandini have pursed lips, tightened fists. As if even one more word could lead to an explosion. Two plastic cups of chai are on the coffee table, untouched. Nandini hadn't found time to buy dishes, either.

Nandini widens her eyes at him. *Say something to her.*

Ranjit sits on the other folding chair. "Simran, are you saying you don't want to get married at all? *Ever?*"

The gentle tone of his voice only angers her more.

"I have *no* idea about if or when I'll get married," Simran says, throwing her palms in the air. "And I really don't care. That's the furthest thing from my mind right now."

"And you really told Kunal's parents this?" Ranjit asks. "Just like that?"

He asks the question partially because he wants to know and partially because he can't believe it. His daughter had the courage to have that type of conversation?

Simran massages her temples. "I did. I told you I would."

Silence coats the room. Nandini is now picking at her nails. Ranjit noticed this nervous habit back when Nandini was in residency.

He leans back on the couch. "So, now what?"

Simran puts her face in her hands. "Now we move on with life."

"Ah, right," Nandini says. "We just move on."

Simran glares at her. She stands up and takes large, quick steps toward her purse. Nandini and Ranjit watch her walk to the bathroom. Within a few seconds, they hear the slam of the door.

"What are we supposed to do with this mess?" Nandini asks.

Ranjit raises his eyebrows. "Is there anything we *can* do? It seems like everything is already settled."

Nandini mutters something Ranjit can't understand.

He moves to the sofa and squeezes her hand. "I think what's done is done."

"I think so, too," she says, slumping into the cushions. "I just . . . I don't know. . . . I can't really believe it. This. After everything."

"I know. But these things are always unpredictable. Everything is, really. I think we've learned at least that much over the past year." He gives her a knowing look, indicating that he isn't just referring to their daughter.

"Yes . . . but why does she have to do this *now*? She had time to get to know him. Years! And now she does this just a few months before her wedding?"

He nods. "She did have time, yes."

"So then, what was even the point of dating?" she asks. "Do you think something happened? Something she won't tell us?"

"I don't know. One thing is for sure, though."

"What's that?"

"She's capable of more than we give her credit for. Look at what she did for us."

Nandini sighs. "That's true. . . ."

She refuses to say what she's thinking out loud: *I left my family, and they fell apart. If I had stayed back, this wouldn't have happened.*

Ranjit rubs his thumb across her fingers. His hands aren't as rough as usual. The first time they met, when he came to Papa and Mami's home for the meeting, she studied his hands while he sipped chai. They were clean and strong, but not abrasive. She wonders if that was the moment she started feeling something for him beyond an arrangement.

"You should go talk to her," he says. "Alone."

"Not now," Nandini says. "Trust me."

Two minutes later, she sees Simran going into the bedroom.

Nandini walks toward her. She opens the door without knocking. Simran is curled in fetal position on her mattress.

Nandini stands there and soaks in her daughter's long, thick black hair, the back of her blush pink sweat shirt. She might as well be back in middle school, in her bed at home, against the lavender sheets and stuffed animals.

In a strained voice, without turning to face Nandini, Simran asks, "What is it?"

Nandini hesitates for a few seconds and then sits on the edge of the mattress.

She remembers how she felt just before Simran was born, an odd mixture of fear and relief. Ranjit was stuck in a surgical case and had promised her he would be there for the birth. But hours later, it was still only Nandini, the kind but firm Russian nurse, and a young female OB-GYN in the room. She thinks about the never-ending pushing, the forceps that had to be used for Simran's head to finally emerge, the lacerations she endured as a result of her daughter stretching her too far from the very beginning.

For several years, she replayed that night in her head and wished her husband had made it. But over time, she realized that that was how it was supposed to be. The two of them. Her mother had said the same thing: *You can learn from moments long after they've happened.*

Now, Nandini asks, "Are you planning to stay in here until you and Dad go back to New Jersey?"

Simran grips the edge of a plum pillow. "I don't know."

"Okay . . . you have to leave soon to make it back at a good time . . . but if that's what you want to do . . ."

Simran sits up. "If that's what I *want* to do? Is any of this really what you think I want?"

Nandini shakes her head. "How am I supposed to know what you want? It's not as though you told Dad or me about what you were going to do with Kunal."

She thinks Simran is going to yell, but to her surprise, she leans against the back wall and lowers her voice. "I see. You think it's that easy. I'm supposed to just tell you what's going on."

Nandini nods.

Simran scoffs. "You really don't get it."

"What don't I get?"

"For years and years, I'm not encouraged to talk about dating or anything related to it. So, I have to figure that out on my own in high school and college. And then, once I'm engaged, I'm expected to just deal with everything that comes along, because that's what you and all the women in your generation had to do. I wasn't used to talking to you about anything that was confusing or conflicting for me since I never did it before, and now, when all the crap hits the fan, I'm supposed to just *talk* to you? Just so you could have tried to prevent all of it?

"Do you realize something, Mom? There's an entire generation of us, the kids of arranged marriages, who are figuring things out as we go along. I know it isn't what you had to go through, but it's still not easy."

Nandini considers Simran's point. Maybe there were things she could never understand about her. There were plenty of things she felt she could never discuss with her own mom. There still are.

Simran wraps her arms around her knees. "And you want to know the best part? The irony? I realized my relationship wasn't going to work for a lot of reasons, yes . . . but one of them was that I saw how you and Dad were able to work through everything that's happened. I knew Kunal and I didn't have that in us. So, that was *great*. My parents' arranged marriage showed me what my own marriage was going to lack."

She collapses onto the pillows.

"I should have done things differently. Then you wouldn't have been in this position," Nandini says.

"No, you couldn't have done anything about this," Simran says.

"I just don't know . . . what you're planning to do next."

"Mom, seriously? After everything I just said, *that's* how you're going to follow it up?"

"Is that not a fair concern? To want to know what my daughter is doing with her life? You're gallivanting off to India with Nani for God-knows-what and th—"

"You know I'm going there to help her teach."

"Really? That's it?" Nandini asks. "And you really have to be there?"

Simran stares at her lap. "You know how stubborn she is. I feel like I can really be there for her. And I want to be. I *need* to be. You can say whatever you want. But nothing is going to stop me from going."

"So, you're going to help her teach, and then come back . . ."

"Yes . . . and I'm working on some things of my own and will see where they le—"

Nandini cuts her off. "What things? Things that will lead somewhere? Be of help for you?"

Simran peers at Nandini for a few seconds. "God, Mom, what are you so scared of? Is it about what people are going to think and say? Why does that even matter?"

Why *does* that even matter? After all of Nandini's years of constant fear—*what if this isn't good enough, what if that person gets offended, what if I'm seen as bad*—what was the point? Simran makes sense. But maybe the inherent pressure and guilt of the culture had lodged itself deep inside her, to the point where she couldn't even be rational about her own daughter's decisions.

"You're right," Nandini says. "It doesn't matter. You're the one who taught me that. And if I can't do the same for you, if I can't teach you to live for yourself and not for others, then what's the point?"

Simran stares at her, and for a second, Nandini thinks she has the perfect words to say. But then Simran burrows under the comforter and turns away.

Nandini steps out of her bedroom. She takes one last glance at Simran. She isn't crying. She was able to discuss her plans without hesitation. She's different from how she was even two months ago.

Maybe there were things she could never understand about her. But maybe, at the same time, there were plenty of things they understood about each other without even realizing it.

Nandini closes the bedroom door. When she's back in the living room, she sees Ranjit picking up the plastic cups of chai.

"Look at how we've come full circle," he says, glancing around her apartment.

"What do you mean?"

"Being in a small apartment. Drinking out of plastic cups. Barely any furniture. It's like we just moved from India."

"You're right," she says, unsure of why this hadn't occurred to her before. "We really have come full circle. Who would have thought that I'd need to be back in a tiny apartment, alone?"

She pictures herself waking up for work tomorrow morning and feels a vibration of excitement. Everything about her day seems noteworthy: slipping into low black heels and her white coat, seeing patients in Greg's (now her) clinic, going to the hospital for teaching rounds with the residents, coming home and sipping chai while reading the newest *New England Journal of Medicine* issue.

Ranjit laughs. "I don't think anybody could have predicted any of this."

Nandini smiles at him, and then her expression becomes grave. "I think I should come back to New Jersey with you. At least until all of this Simran stuff calms down."

He shakes his head. "There's no need for that. And you have a lot going on here."

"I can take a day or two," she says.

"Really? How many e-mails have you gotten today?"

"I don't know."

"Check," he says as he points to her phone.

Nandini opens her e-mail. There are twelve new ones today and five from yesterday. She's invited to give a grand rounds presentation and a lecture to the GI fellows. There are a few e-mails from residents about how to interpret lab values, upcoming conferences, and an interesting journal article. She is now someone people turn to. Someone people respect. Someone *she* respects.

"Seventeen new e-mails," she says to Ranjit.

"That's what I thought."

Twenty minutes later, the three of them are outside, standing against Ranjit's green BMW.

Simran hugs her before climbing into the passenger seat. "Mom, don't worry about anything."

Nandini nods. Before she can say anything, Simran hugs her again. "I love you."

"I love you too, *beta*," she says, not wanting to let her go.

Nandini walks over to the other side of the car and exchanges a hug and kiss with Ranjit, something they wouldn't have done months ago but feels natural now. Ranjit sits in the driver's seat. An old Dev Anand song plays when he turns on the car.

"Have a safe drive. Call me when you reach," she tells them as they wave at her.

Nandini remembers how she used to cry when she would leave Simran and Ronak to go to the clinic. She was always able to wait until she got into the car, but once the ignition started, the tears followed.

And now, as she watches her husband and daughter drive away, she finds herself holding back tears again.

When she's back in her apartment, she lingers in the living room. The folding chairs are pushed against the wall. The evening sun streams through the blinds. It's quiet without her family.

Too quiet.

She starts tearing up again.

Stop being so emotional.

But maybe it's okay. There is no way to have everything, despite those irritating articles about women "having it all." There would always be conflicting desires, certain parts of herself that had to be dormant so the others could emerge.

And somehow, despite the years of feeling inadequate at work and home, her marriage evolved to allow this for her. New opportunities. Purpose. Growth. She and Ranjit have become different people.

Nandini walks toward her laptop and settles onto the couch. She has work to do.

Twenty

Simran

Your cappuccino," the waiter says as he hands Simran a full mug.

"Thanks." Simran rearranges her frothy drink and avocado toast around the free tabloid she picked up on the way to Le Pain Quotidien. She notices that the woman next to her ordered two chocolate chip cookies but isn't eating them. She's simply taking a picture of them for Instagram and then pushing the plate away. *What a waste of amazing cookies*, Simran thinks. She guesses that's why Manhattan thin can be just as extreme as Los Angeles thin.

"Do you want anything else?"

Simran shakes her head. She's sitting in one of her favorite restaurants, alone, and leaving for India in three days. She shouldn't want anything else.

Simran scrolls through her text messages. She and Kunal haven't spoken in two weeks, since he showed up at her apartment in the middle of the night. She tried to push him away after they started kissing, but they hooked up.

Simran forced him to leave right after.

When she told him not to contact her again, she sounded self-assured and stern, but really, since then, her sleep has been interrupted with dreams about him.

She's managed to delete his number and unfriend him on Facebook. With just one click, someone went from being the biggest part of her life to being a virtual stranger.

Sometimes, Simran misses the worn-out feel and citrus whiff of Kunal's freshly laundered cotton T-shirts. It doesn't help that she sees signs of Kunal everywhere: in one guy with bushy eyebrows on the subway, another hailing a cab in teal scrubs, and more in copies of the Atul Gawande books he always read.

But now, his texts make her more angry than relieved. She hates him for making her break up with him, and she hates him even more for not fighting when it mattered. She hates him for having all her high school and college years, for her history to be woven and stored with him. Eventually, she accepts that maybe a lot of her, even most of her, can hate him, but there are certain pieces that never will.

She tries to focus on her cappuccino and the buzz of people eating and conversing around her. When that doesn't work, she flips through the tabloid and tries not to hate herself for picking it up in the first place.

There's a picture of Jennifer Lopez and Alex Rodriguez drinking at the Soho House, another of John Legend and Chrissy Teigen walking down Fifth Avenue. There was a recent event at the Whitney Museum and a Dalí-themed cocktail night at the MoMA. A list of "50 Things You Must Do in NYC" is after the featured events. Simran should probably try to do something from there before she goes to India.

At the back of the magazine, there's a gossip column about noteworthy New Yorkers.

And that's when she sees Neil's face.

A thumbnail of his head shot is in the lower left corner, under a section titled "The 5 Most Eligible Bachelors in New York. Turn the page for more!"

She listens to the magazine and turns the page.

Neil's wearing his thick black glasses, a navy blue shirt, and a gray blazer. His face is twisted into a smirk, which deepens the wrinkles around his eyes.

Bachelor # 1
Name: Neil Desai
Job title: *New York Times* **op-ed columnist**

How do you respond to rumors stating you are already in a relationship?

I am dating at the moment. Nothing serious, though.

What are you looking for in a significant other?

Sense of adventure, creativity, someone willing to go against convention.

What is hardest part about dating in NYC?

People don't present their true selves until date ten (if even then). That and the exhausting dating apps.

What is your biggest turn-on and turn-off?

Turn-on: someone who is kind to people who can do nothing for her, i.e., Uber drivers, homeless musicians, etc. Turn-off: inability to commit.

What was your biggest heartbreak?

It's hard to choose. I was engaged, but we both realized we wanted different things. And then I met someone who was already engaged, so we obviously wanted different things.

What is the best part about living in NYC?

All of the restaurants, of course!

Any fun upcoming plans?

I'm actually moving to China at the end of this month. I've been there on and off throughout the past year but just accepted a full-time offer in the *Times* office there. I'm looking forward to what's ahead.

Simran grips the edges of the page.

I was engaged, but we both realized we wanted different things. And then I met someone who was already engaged, so we obviously wanted different things.

Her heart rate increases as she opens a document she had started on her phone. It's a letter to Neil, about everything that had happened between them. She tells him she'd never met anyone like him in her entire life and never would again. She tells him he made her realize everything she needed to change in her life. She tells him she's sorry about the way things unfolded, that she needs some time to herself right now, but maybe, after she's back from India next year, they can reconnect, see where things go.

She reads the bottom of the article:

Editor's note: Until recently, Desai was working out of
Hong Kong. He returned to New York City to host a
series of panels on the changing face of journalism at
NYU's Skirball Center for the Arts. Meet him this week!

Below, there are dates and times for the panels. All of them
are preceded by a cocktail reception that anyone can attend for a
"bargain deal" of one hundred dollars.

She fishes out her credit card (this is her last month funded by
her parents). She opens Safari on her iPhone to the NYU Skirball
Center's website and purchases a ticket for tomorrow night.

By the next evening, she's already rehearsed everything she
wants to tell Neil. She takes an extra-long shower, blow-dries and
straightens her hair, and slips into the one-shoulder red dress that
always makes her feel confident.

Simran takes one last glance in her bathroom mirror. An internal tug tries to hold her back and urges her to keep life simple.
But a larger part of her knows that this conversation was always
going to happen.

On the subway ride to the West Village, all she can think
is *Neil will be there, Neil will be there, Neil will be there.* Her heels
are starting to blister by the time she makes it to the audito-
rium. She reaches inside her purse, where she packed her com-
pact, eyeliner, and lipstick for a quick touch-up before anything
begins.

Neil is already standing at the entrance. Simran used to worry
her feelings for him came from the fact that she always viewed
him in comparison to Kunal. But now, seeing him standing next

to a side table, scrolling through something on his phone, she knows that they were a force of their own.

Simran tilts her head down. Neil sees her before she's even opened the glass door.

"Oh, Simran," he says. "Hey."

Her limbs are heavy and numb. "Hey."

"Nice dress."

"Thanks," Simran says, thinking that he *would* notice a nice dress on a woman. "I like your outfit, too."

He's wearing a gray linen suit, but his clean-shaven face and tousled hair make him seem young and vulnerable. Simran wishes they had known each other as kids.

"Are you okay?"

"Yes," Simran says with a laugh, even though there's nothing funny. She's suddenly conscious of how sweaty she must look.

People start to file into the lobby. Some of them make eye contact with Neil. Others rush for the hors d'oeuvres. Soft jazz music blasts through the speakers.

Neil gives her a look that says, *What are you doing here?*, which makes her realize how out of place she must seem.

She steadies her feet. "I, um, wanted to talk to you."

"To *me*?" he asks, pointing to himself. "Here?"

"Yes."

He smiles. "You came all the way here to talk? Why didn't you just text or call?"

Simran chuckles. Why *didn't* she just text or call? "I don't know. I thought I should try to see you in person."

"What's this about?"

Simran looks around them. "Do you think we could talk alone? Just for a little bit?"

Neil looks as though he's going to say no but then says, "Uh, sure."

He motions to a hallway on the other side of the floor. Simran takes deep breaths as they walk together. She has the same contradictory sense of anticipation and relief that she had when they met at Milk Bar.

"So, what's up?" he asks once they're standing in an empty corner.

They smile at a couple who walks off the elevator. A group of journalism students passes them and yells a hi to Neil. She can't give him her entire rehearsed speech. He's too in demand here.

"So, I'm going back to India in a few days, but I couldn't leave without te—"

"Whoa, wait. You're going back to India?"

Simran nods. "I'll explain that later. But first, I just had to talk to you about everything that happened between us. I'm sorry about the way I handled all of it. I really am so sorry. You caught me off guard in a way nobody ever has, and I didn't know what to do, with Kunal, with my whole life, really."

Simran felt more when she first met Neil than she had after years of being with Kunal. Maybe genuine commitment involves always knowing that what you have with that person, in any moment, is better than any potential you could have with someone else.

Simran is interrupted by someone yelling Neil's name.

Laura Martinez.

"Why are you hiding back here?" Laura slips her arms around Neil's waist.

"I'll be back there in a sec," Neil says.

Laura faces Simran. "You look familiar."

Simran manages to squeak, "We briefly met at your signing. I'm Simran."

"Right! Nice to see you again," she says, giving Simran a genuine smile.

"You too," Simran says. "I should let you two get back to the event."

"No, don't let me interrupt," Laura says, and then faces Neil. "I just wanted you to know that all of the bedroom things are packed."

As Laura walks away, her nude Louboutin heels click against the floor.

"You're moving?" Simran asks. "New apartment?"

Neil shuffles closer to her. "I'm starting a full-time position in China."

Simran's pulse diminishes. "That's great."

"And Laura's coming with me."

Simran tries to speak, but nothing comes out. After what feels like a full minute, she stammers, "Oh, I didn't realize, you were in a, that you and her, or you and anyone . . ."

"We've been trying to keep it a secret. Her agent doesn't want her to move. Thinks it'll kill her career."

Simran clutches the sides of her torso. "That's . . . great. I'm glad everything's working out so well."

She catches a glimpse of who Neil was when they met, who Neil has always been. Guys like him give perfect girls their perfect endings.

"Look, I'm happy for you. For both of us." He leans in to give her an acquaintance-worthy half hug and a kiss on the cheek.

"Yes . . . I am, too. And I owe you a lot, Neil. I really do."

Neil shakes his head. "You've done everything on your own. Keep me posted on how things pan out with your writing, okay? And best wishes with your engagement."

He offers his words in a way that's both smooth and insincere. The same tone he probably uses at book signings or with people he secretly hates.

But Simran nods anyway. "Of course. Thank you. It was good to see you."

Before Neil can say anything, Simran hurries down the hallway, never looking back. Once she's at the subway, she whisks past the giant map with New York's veinlike routes and takes an empty seat.

She glances at her phone. It's getting late. Neil's probably on the panel by now. Maybe he and Laura will leave early and have sex in his now-empty apartment.

It doesn't matter. None of it matters. The train starts to chug and lights flash by, making Simran feel as though she's in a giant disco ball. She takes three deep breaths and places her hands on her knees. For the first time in a long time, she feels it: an absence of pressure on her chest.

Maybe this whole time, Simran was trying to establish a self to be proud of when, really, she is many different women at once. In one of her psychology classes, she learned about how people repress parts of themselves that get the least validation, but those parts still exist, waiting to reemerge. Now she can picture all of her selves having a glass of wine at a dimly lit bar.

Simran arrives at her stop twenty minutes later but stays in her seat. The doors close, and she leans back. For the first time in a long time, she can't wait to be home.

Nandini

"Dr. Mehta, does this look right?"

Nandini turns around to face three internal medicine interns. The one who asked the question, Julia, is holding up an iPad screen that has a patient's thyroid labs.

Nandini scans the labs and then shifts her focus back to Julia. "Looks great. Which medication should we treat the patient with?"

Julia's eyes dart to her other co-residents. She runs her fingers over the bell of her stethoscope as she thinks about the right answer. A bead of sweat collects at the top of her forehead. For a second, Nandini regrets putting Julia on the spot. When she was being quizzed by attendings during her own residency, the public part of it was the worst. The fear that she'd humiliate herself in front of her colleagues. The worry that she didn't study enough and everyone would realize she didn't deserve to be there. Her mind often went blank, and sometimes she'd close her eyes, as if the answer would come to her out of nowhere. Thanks to Greg, over the years, she learned how to take a deep breath and trust herself.

"It's okay," Nandini says now. "Take your time. We're not in a rush."

Julia gives her a nervous smile. A few seconds later, she names the correct thyroid medication and starting dose.

"Very good," Nandini says.

The residents follow her down the gray hallways, which are stained with fluorescent lighting. The linoleum floors are shiny. Various smells of sickness and healing permeate the air: vomit, metallic blood, rubbing alcohol, bandages. The hospital has become another home for her now, a place she navigates with ease.

The rest of the morning is taken up with rounds, teaching residents at patients' bedsides, and boring meetings about new hospital procedures. Despite the hectic pace, she's learned to cherish her rituals, even her new morning ones. Spraying lavender oil onto her wrists and neck. Slipping into her low black heels. Taking out her crisp white coat from the crinkled dry-cleaning bag. Applying one coat of dark red lipstick, a gift from Yuwa. Scanning into the front entrance of the hospital with her ID badge. The contours of her new life have become familiar to her now.

She is even getting used to coming home to an empty apartment, to not having to cook or visit people or return phone calls. All throughout her medical career, she would work and then come home to someone asking her what was for dinner or if she could go to the grocery store for peanut butter or when she would have a chance to examine someone's headache. It kept her grounded in a way. Despite her gratitude, she still feels guilty now about being able to use her time solely for herself. Guilt is like that, though. It leaves a residue.

"It really is over," Nandini says to Mami on the phone later that night. "Simran isn't getting married."

"You know it's for the best," Mami says. "You of all people should understand the danger of staying with somebody who is wrong for you."

"This is different," Nandini says. "She dated him."

She listens to Mami lecture her about how it isn't as different as it may seem, and even so, the times have changed.

"Can you believe that the last time I spoke to Simran, she told me she's proud of me? That she understands me more?"

"I do believe that," Mami says. "And you should, too."

"I don't even know if she knows what she's saying anymore. There's just so much that has changed. With my daughter. My own family. My whole *life*," Nandini says.

She doesn't tell Mami about the crying fits she's had multiple times a week. Often, there is a trigger, like remembering something Greg had told her years ago or picturing his frail, limp body during his final days. It isn't fair that he can't be here. The hospital halls seem more subdued without him. And sometimes, she cries even when she isn't thinking about him. It's as though she is filled to the brim with an expansive, painful emptiness.

"I think that despite all our worrying, things have turned out okay," Mami says.

"I hope so," Nandini says, not believing her own words.

She will always worry, no matter what. Anxiety, she's realized, lives in the future. It's about the what-ifs. She's always struggled with this, but for the first time, she feels a sense of freedom and acceptance in this. *It won't ruin me.*

She lets Mami talk about everything else that's on her mind: the latest gossip about Priyanka Chopra, her neighbor's affair, and the accomplishments of the girls at school. She and her mother are closer now through long-distance phone calls than they were in all the years they spent together in India. Maybe in their family, the women come together only when they separated.

She sits on the futon in her cold, sparsely decorated living room, feeling a sense of peace from the darkness and her mother's voice.

Twenty-One

Simran

I s this seat taken?" Sheila points to the chair next to Simran.

Simran shakes her head. "Go ahead."

"I'm glad I got here early. I've been meaning to talk to you."

Simran holds out her palms. They've already had a few conversations about Sheila's fresh engagement, and though they were supposed to be fun and exciting and everything else Simran would have imagined, there was still an underlying turbulence they both refused to acknowledge.

The waiter takes their drinks order: a Blue Moon for Sheila, a glass of champagne for Simran. Once they have their drinks, Sheila takes a large gulp and faces Simran. "I'm sorry I was such a judgmental bitch to you this past year."

"It's only part of your charm," Simran says, and they both laugh. "And I'm sorry, too."

"I think I was mad at you. Really mad," Sheila says. "I felt like I didn't even know you."

"*I* didn't even feel like I knew me, Sheila."

Everyone in Simran's life had a cemented image of her and couldn't handle that changing. *The people who love us can hinder our growth more than anyone.*

"I get that now," Sheila says. "At the time, it was as though all of this shit kept coming out. It all made me look at you in a different way."

Simran dips a piece of bread in olive oil. "Don't you think I looked at *myself* in a different way? You have no idea how lonely this past year has been. God, I cried myself to sleep so many times, and the entire situation was hard enough without you freaking out about it every ten minutes. I've been mad at you, too, you know."

Sheila nods. "You should have been. I know that if I was going through anything like this, you would have been at my place every day, with wine, and listened to me blab for hours. I didn't do that for you."

Sheila touches Simran's arm. "I really am sorry. And I'm proud of you."

"It's fine. *I'm* fine. Really." As the words leave Simran's mouth, she feels their truth. She *is* fine.

Sheila and Simran keep a hushed eye contact. Their words need room to simmer.

"So . . . your e-mail was good. To the point," Sheila says, referring to the e-mail Simran sent to everyone who was invited to the wedding.

Dear Friends and Family,

Due to some unforeseen circumstances, Kunal and I have decided to end our engagement. We appreciate all the love and support you've provided for us throughout the years. Please give us some time and space during this period. Thank you for being there for us.

Best,
Simran and Kunal

"Thanks," Simran says. "I've gotten so many replies asking what happened. I don't think some people understood what I meant by the 'please give us some time and space' part. And whatever, I know that everyone's talking about it, picking it apart, but it's just awkward, having to go through what happened over and over again."

"I bet. But if it's any consolation, you're handling it quite well."

Simran takes a sip of her champagne. "Thanks. I'm just not sure when things completely get better. When do things feel normal again?"

"It depends," Sheila says. "But the shitty, weird feeling does go away. Eventually. It really does. Think back from freaking, I don't know, kindergarten to now. It's all passed in a blink, right? So will this. Are you, uh, going to try to be friends?"

Simran stares into the distance. "No. He left a message last week . . . the same things as before. Wanting to change. Wanting to work it out."

"And? What do you say to that?" Sheila asks.

"Nothing." Simran hesitates for a few seconds and adds, "It's a little too late. But then, I don't know if it would have made a difference if he said it before. People are who they are. It's just that it—we—weren't all bad, you know? I just regret the way I went about so many things. Like, should I have done this earlier? And no matter how much I know it was the right thing to do, plenty of people are reminding me that I shouldn't have gone through with it. Apparently, I'm now at risk of being alone forever."

Sheila squeezes Simran's arm. "Sometimes people need wake-up calls."

Simran shakes her head. "What? You think that's what this is for him?"

"No, I mean you."

"Me?"

Sheila sighs and folds her hands together. Her nails are bitten. "This weekend I realized that you're obsessed with these books about free-spirited women who do whatever the hell they want. It's this dichotomy in you. Most of you is doing what you think you should be doing and is fine with that, while this other part of you admires, and maybe even craves, the idea of being a woman who says 'screw it' to all of that. I don't think Kunal would have let you be that other woman."

"He wouldn't have. I know that," Simran says. "And when I take a step back and look at it all rationally, I'm ready to leave and have a fresh start, my own start. And I really am happy for you. And proud, for sticking with what you wanted even though it wasn't easy."

Maybe friendships aren't that different from other relationships. They're easy to take for granted because they tend to be effortless. But in the end, they require work and forgiveness, a place to move forward from. Sheila has seen Simran through more than any man ever will. They both owed each other more freedom: the freedom to differ in their opinions, the freedom to carry out their own decisions and accept each other's.

"Hey, hey," Vishal says, interrupting them.

He's holding a bouquet of pink tulips wrapped in brown paper. Simran takes the flowers and hugs him before he sits across from her and Sheila.

Simran hands the flowers to Sheila. "These are gorgeous, but you should keep them. I'm about to leave the country, and I'd hate for them to die."

Vishal laughs. "Ah, I should have thought of that."

"Don't worry," Simran says. "It was a really sweet thought."

"So, you're doing much better than I expected," he says.

"Why thank you. I've been hearing that a lot," Simran says, wondering if that itself indicates something about her (ex) engagement. She'll always love Kunal, but that's not enough. It never was.

After Vishal orders a Jack and Coke, he pushes his chair in closer. "I know everything that went down wasn't just because of Neil."

"No, it wasn't, but that doesn't make any part of the Neil situation acceptable."

"Sometimes people get into situations they can't help," he says. "It's okay. You've always spent too much time in that little, inner world of yours. And we've all known that you worry too much about everyone else. It just caught up to you."

He shoots Simran a quick smile, and she knows that's something they have in common. They define themselves by their relationships, by the ones they love.

"I just don't want you to worry anymore, okay? You always get to where you need to be, and there are some things you just can't control. I used to think I should change my personality for someone else, not be such a pushover because it would always screw me over. But now with Ami, I know it's worked out. She needs a guy like me, and I need someone like her who appreciates me."

"So, you think this is it? With her?"

He hesitates at first and then nods. "I do. If it keeps going in this direction, you might be attending *two* weddings next year."

"Oh, Vishal!" Simran says. "That's amazing."

"Will you think that even if I make you an honorary groomsman?" He clinks his glass against hers. "You'll have to wear a kurta and all."

"Of course," Simran says.

Simran always thought that the men who would mean the most to her would be the ones she fell for romantically, but maybe in her story, it's Vishal who has the true staying power.

"How much shit have people been talking about me?" Simran asks, finishing off her champagne. One year ago, she never would have been able to ask the question so nonchalantly.

"Nobody's talking shit," Vishal says at the same time Sheila blurts, "Well, I guess some people think you're a callous bitch for breaking up with your fiancé."

"Ah. How lovely," Simran says.

"Yeah, I uh, ran into Priya from your intro psych class the other day, and she was like, 'Why did Simran leave Kunal when he was so in love with her?' and 'I can't believe she got involved with that Neil Desai guy.' You know, just a bunch of bullshit. I told her she had no idea what she was talking about," Sheila says, and they both smile, knowing Sheila phrased it much more harshly.

"Don't bother. My own extended family members think I'm some walking scandal. And you know what? They can knock themselves out!"

"Damn, well, listen to you," Vishal says, raising his glass.

They finish off the bread and request another basket. More people saunter into the restaurant. Waiters pass out black leather menus and laminated wine lists. A busboy lights candles in the center of each table.

Simran's parents walk in. They settle at the end of the table, and Simran motions to the waiter to tell him their entire party is here. They order dinner quickly, and for the next hour, they discuss Simran's plans and then her friends' upcoming weddings.

"We're going to take a trip to the beach this weekend," Dad says.

"Oh? Why?"

He wraps his arms around Mom's shoulders. "The kids are gone! Away! It's time for us to enjoy. Of course, your mother is working even harder than ever, and whenever I visit her, it's been so rushed. She's going to take some time off so we can have a little road trip. And, fine, so she can also prepare for the AMA conference."

"I know! I can't believe I'm missing your speech," Simran says.

Mom laughs. "I doubt anyone will find it interesting."

"Of course they will," Dad says.

"They will," Simran says, not knowing how to process that her parents seem to be dating.

Mom raises her glass after their tiramisu arrives. "I'd like to propose a toast: to Simran, who goes after what she wants, even when it gives her parents gray hairs."

Mom smiles in that way anyone does when they're making a joke based on the truth. Simran's parents might never respect her choices from this year. But she can handle that now. They'll all get over it.

"To Simran," Ranjit, Vishal, and Sheila echo.

Simran thanks everyone and gives Vishal, Sheila, and Dad a hug. They all walk toward the front of the restaurant, leaving Mom and Simran alone.

"Mom," Simran says.

Her mother is more independent than she ever realized. It's as though over the past year, she's gotten to know another person, a split woman, who is one part her mother and one part someone else altogether.

She wants to grab her mother's hands. She wants her to know she's strong. She wants to tell her she's proud of her and that she's only starting to realize how much she never understood about her.

But before Simran speaks, Mom wraps her arms around her.

Mom's eyes are wet when she pulls away. "Have fun in India, *beta*."

"I will. I promise."

Simran takes a walk around the city. One street blends into the next until New York trickles down her stomach, making her dress stick to her.

After she's back in her apartment, it takes her only thirty minutes to finish packing for India. Everything is in its place. All of her shoes are lined at the door, and any pictures of Kunal are facedown.

She plucks *The Awakening* and tosses it onto the bed and thinks of her mother, who has never been able to truly just be with herself until now. Simran's parents always said they came to America to give her and Ronak the opportunities they never had, but she never thought that those opportunities could manifest in so many ways. She's loved and learned in ways they never could.

Outside her window, she sees it: her former self, rustling through the branches, becoming as vertical as the concrete around it. In front of her building, a woman in a red coat raises one hand into the air and uses the other to clutch her boyfriend's arm. A cab pulls up and whisks both of them away, bleeding into Manhattan.

Simran walks toward the table at her entrance and places her right hand on Ganesha's feet. The brown envelope resting against the statue appears smooth despite how many times she's touched it. She opens it again.

> *Dear Simran,*
>
> *Congratulations on your acceptance into Columbia University's Graduate School of Journalism.*

She scans the letter to make sure, once more, it's real. Her dream, confined to an eight-and-a-half-by-eleven space.

Some things could only come to her after she let go of her old life and embraced uncertainty, who is more like a handsome stranger she'd like to know better.

Slowly, she becomes herself.

Acknowledgments

There are so many people who have worked to bring this book into existence.

Jessica Watterson, you are truly a dream agent. From our first phone call, your enthusiasm drew me in and I knew I had found the best person to work with. Your editorial guidance, support, and encouragement kept me going during moments of intense self-doubt. I'm so proud to be a part of your list. You are a rock star and I'm beyond lucky to be able to work with you.

To Kristine Swartz, you brought this book to life and I am so grateful that you took a chance on this story. Thank you for everything from your top-notch editing skills to perfect Maison Kayser recommendations to your compassion and empathy. I can't tell you how much it means to me that you work to bring diverse stories into the world. You are truly a gem and it's been so fulfilling to explore Nani, Nandini, and Simran under your guidance.

Fareeda Bullert, you made me feel so at home from the first time we met. Thank you for being an amazing marketing director and supporting my love of chocolate chip cookies. Danielle Keir, thank you for being so wonderful to work with and also being a source of comfort at the end of my pregnancy. Rita Frangie and Farjana Yasmin, thank you for giving this novel a breathtaking, vibrant cover that I'm constantly getting messages about. Andrea Monagle, thank you for your incredible attention to detail. Megha Jain, thank you for making *WBIW* look so elegant and put together.

To the rest of the team at Berkley, you all know how to make an author feel valued and excited. I am so proud and grateful to be a Berkley author.

Thank you to Susan Dalsimer, Emily Murdock Baker, and Laura Stine for your help during my first attempts at writing. To Mr. Greg Fleenor, I thank you for all the wisdom you imparted throughout high school English class. Roshani Chokshi and Lydia Kang, I can't tell you how much your words meant to me when I was so close to giving up. Emily Giffin, thank you for your warmth and encouragement from the very first time Samir and I met you.

Jaimini Dave Maniar, thank you for indulging my love for *The Baby-sitters Club* and *Sweet Valley High*. Bansari Modi Shah and Morgan Radford, you read drafts of this book well before I knew what I was doing and encouraged me nonetheless. I am lucky to have you as my sisters.

Mom, your love of books coupled with your genuine curiosity about people led me to become a writer. Every year, I become more aware that you've been through more than I'll ever know. Thank you for finding a way to make every situation fun and teaching me something new every day. Dad, you have always encouraged me to speak up. Your work ethic has inspired me since I was a baby. Your sensitivity, patience, and love have given me the confidence to be myself. I will never fully grasp the full extent of the sacrifices you've made. Thank you for being the best father anyone could have. Maansi, you are the bright light of our family. Thank you for pushing all of us out of our comfort zone and making sure things are never boring. Akshay, you may be the youngest in our family but we all continue to learn from you. Thank you for being the most caring brother. You deserve all of the Jeni's ice cream you want.

Samir, when I first saw you on stage, I knew I had to introduce myself. That mixture of awe and excitement led to the creation of Neil Desai. Thank you for getting to know these characters as your own, reading every draft of the manuscript, and being the best dad-ager anyone could hope for. You're the only person who has been there for every step of this journey and you will always be my inspiration. Somehow, life with you keeps getting better and better.

Baby Sahil, thank you for the gifts of joy, uncertainty, and growth. You've already shown us your stubborn streak and love for Bollywood music. We can't wait to fill your world with more stories.

Lastly, thank you to every person who took the time to read this story.

To anyone who has ever felt different, struggled to find a story that represents them, or been told to put their book down already, I hope this book can provide some solace.

Well-Behaved Indian Women

Saumya Dave

Discussion Questions

1. This book examines the bonds mothers and daughters share. Were there any parts of Mimi and Nandini's or Nandini and Simran's relationships that you identified with?

2. Nandini faces racism and misogyny at work. Discuss the occurrences and how she handles the situations. Would you have reacted the same? Have you ever experienced something similar?

3. Simran and Kunal have many years of history together. Do you think Simran made the right choice in the end? Why or why not? Have you ever been in a situation where you struggled with whether to keep working through it, or to let go?

4. All three women are figuring out how to hold on to their identities while feeling the pressure to be the "Perfect Indian Woman." How does this struggle ultimately impact their decisions?

5. Mimi has a secret that she does not share with her daughter or granddaughter. Do you think she was right to keep it to herself or did she owe her family the truth?

6. Planning a wedding can either bring family together or push them apart. How did planning Simran and Kunal's wedding affect the characters in this story?

7. Communication ends up being the key to fixing the relationships in this story. What secrets do the characters keep from the important people in their lives, and why? How do these secrets ultimately impact their relationships with one another and themselves?

8. Simran, Nandini, and Mimi all redefine their relationship with ambition throughout the novel. How does age impact their choices? Is it ever too late to pursue a goal?

9. Ranjit mentions that Nandini should give him the benefit of the doubt instead of assuming the worst. How did their relationship change?

10. Sheila has known Simran since their childhood, while Yuwa meets Nandini in her fifties; however, both friendships are defined by their chemistry and honesty. How did these friendships affect the decisions Simran and Nandini made?

Saumya Dave is a psychiatrist and mental health advocate. Her essays, articles, and poetry have been featured in the *New York Times*, *ABC News*, Refinery29, and other publications. She is the co-founder of thisisforHER, a nonprofit at the nexus of art and women's mental health, and an adjunct professor at Mount Sinai, where she teaches a Narrative Medicine class. She recently completed her Psychiatry Residency at Mount Sinai Beth Israel, where she was a chief resident and an inductee into the AΩA Medical Honors Society. She currently resides in New York City with her husband and son. This is her first novel.

CONNECT ONLINE

SaumyaDave.com

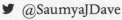 @SaumyaJDave

📷 @SaumyaJDave

Ready to find
your next great read?

Let us help.

Visit prh.com/nextread